**'You've learnt your lessons well, DePiero...in the beds of however many countless lovers you've entertained. Were they the ones to teach you that intoxicating mix of innocence and artless sensuality designed to ensnare a man?'**

Siena looked at Andreas, stunned at his words. He had no idea. He couldn't tell her gauche responses were all too *real*. And she vowed then that he never would know, however she had to do it.

She fought to find some veneer of composure and said, as cynically as she could considering she was shaking inwardly like a leaf, 'What else did you expect? A real *bona fide* virgin heiress? This is the twenty-first century, Xenakis. Surely you know better than most that virgins are as mythical as unicorns?'

D1388746

**Abby Green** got hooked on Mills & Boon® romances while still in her teens, when she stumbled across one belonging to her grandmother in the west of Ireland. After many years of reading them voraciously, she sat down one day and gave it a go herself. Happily, after a few failed attempts, Mills & Boon bought her first manuscript.

Abby works freelance in the film and TV industry, but thankfully the four a.m. starts and the stresses of dealing with recalcitrant actors are becoming more and more infrequent, leaving her more time to write!

She loves to hear from readers, and you can contact her through her website at www.abby-green.com. She lives and works in Dublin.

**Recent titles by the same author:**

EXQUISITE REVENGE
ONE NIGHT WITH THE ENEMY
THE LEGEND OF DE MARCO
THE CALL OF THE DESERT

**Did you know these are also available as eBooks?**
**Visit www.millsandboon.co.uk**

# FORGIVEN BUT NOT FORGOTTEN?

BY

ABBY GREEN

All the characters in this book have no existence outside the imagination of the author, and have no relation whatsoever to anyone bearing the same name or names. They are not even distantly inspired by any individual known or unknown to the author, and all the incidents are pure invention.

All Rights Reserved including the right of reproduction in whole or in part in any form. This edition is published by arrangement with Harlequin Enterprises II BV/S.à.r.l. The text of this publication or any part thereof may not be reproduced or transmitted in any form or by any means, electronic or mechanical, including photocopying, recording, storage in an information retrieval system, or otherwise, without the written permission of the publisher.

This book is sold subject to the condition that it shall not, by way of trade or otherwise, be lent, resold, hired out or otherwise circulated without the prior consent of the publisher in any form of binding or cover other than that in which it is published and without a similar condition including this condition being imposed on the subsequent purchaser.

® and TM are trademarks owned and used by the trademark owner and/or its licensee. Trademarks marked with ® are registered with the United Kingdom Patent Office and/or the Office for Harmonisation in the Internal Market and in other countries.

First published in Great Britain 2013
by Mills & Boon, an imprint of Harlequin (UK) Limited.
Harlequin (UK) Limited, Eton House, 18-24 Paradise Road,
Richmond, Surrey TW9 1SR

© Abby Green 2013

ISBN: 978 0 263 90013 2

Harlequin (UK) policy is to use papers that are natural, renewable and recyclable products and made from wood grown in sustainable forests. The logging and manufacturing process conform to the legal environmental regulations of the country of origin.

Printed and bound in Spain
by Blackprint CPI, Barcelona

# FORGIVEN BUT NOT FORGOTTEN?

This is especially for Crispin Green, Polly Green,
Barney Green and Katie Green.
I'm so proud to be your half-sister
and one of the 'Greens in Cornwall'.

# PROLOGUE

SIENA DEPIERO HELD her older sister's hand tightly as they left their *palazzo.* Even though she was twelve and Serena was fourteen they still instinctively sought each other for support. Their father was in an even more mercurial mood than usual today. Their car was waiting by the kerb, a uniformed driver standing by the open door. Siena knew that her father's bodyguards were nearby.

Just feet away from the car a tall young man with dark hair seemed to spring from nowhere, stopping their father in his tracks. He was gesticulating and calling their father *Papà.* Siena and Serena had come to a halt too, with burly guards standing between them and this confrontation.

Siena looked around the bodyguards. She could instantly see the resemblance of this young man to their father. He had the same shaped face and deep-set eyes. But how could he be related? Suddenly there was a dull crunching sound and the young man was sprawled on the ground, looking up with shock on his face, blood running from his nose. Their father had hit him.

Siena gripped Serena's hand tight in shock at the sudden violence. Their father turned back and gestured angrily for them to follow him. The path was so narrow that they had to step over the young man's legs. Siena was too scared to look at him—he was so wild and feral.

They were ushered into the back of the car and Siena heard their father issue terse instructions to his men. Just then she heard the young man roar, 'I'm Rocco, your son—you bastard!'

When their father got into the car and it pulled away, Siena couldn't stop herself from looking behind them. She saw their father's men dragging the young man out of sight. She felt sick. Serena was looking stonily ahead but her hand gripped Siena's.

Their father caught Siena by the ear painfully and jerked her head round. Siena clamped her mouth shut. She knew better than to make a sound.

He forced her to look at him. 'What do you think you are doing?'

'Nothing, Papà.'

His mouth was a thin line of anger. 'Good, because you know what happens if you anger me.'

Serena's grip on Siena's hand was so tight she nearly cried out. Quickly Siena said, 'Yes, Papà.'

After a long, tense moment their father let her go and faced the front again. Siena knew very well what happened when she angered him. He would punish her sister Serena. It was never her. Always her sister. Because that was what amused him.

Siena didn't look at her sister, but they kept their hands tightly gripped together for the rest of the journey.

# CHAPTER ONE

ANDREAS XENAKIS DIDN'T like the strength of the thrill of triumph that moved through him. It signified that this moment held more importance for him than he'd care to admit. Bitterly, he had to concede that perhaps it did. After all, practically within touching distance now was the woman who had all but cried *rape* for her own amusement, to protect her untarnished image in her father's eyes. She'd merited him a savage beating, losing his job, being blacklisted from every hotel in Europe and having to start over again on the other side of the world. Far away from anyone he'd known or who had known him.

She was still exquisite. More so. Andreas had found himself imagining that she couldn't possibly be as stunning as she'd been since he'd seen her five years ago. But she was. She was a woman now, not a teenager.

Her hair was so blonde it shone almost white under the soft lighting of a hundred chandeliers. It was pulled up into a high bun. She held herself with the same effortlessly regal bearing he'd first noticed in that glittering ballroom in Paris. His mouth compressed. She was a thoroughbred in the midst of lesser beings. He could see how women near her instinctively shut her out, as if sensing competition.

His eyes moved over the curve of her cheek and jaw. The patrician line of her nose more than hinted at the blue-blooded heritage of her Italian ancestry, diluted only in part by her half-

English mother who had been related to royalty. Her skin was still pale and looked soft: as soft as a rose petal. Andreas's belly clenched hard to recall just how soft it *had* felt under his fingers.

He'd touched her reverently, as if she were an ethereal goddess, and he'd felt as if he was marking her, staining her purity with his touch. His hands were fists by his sides now as he thought of how she'd urged him on with breathy, sexy entreaties in his ear: *'Please...I want you to touch me, Andreas.'* Only to turn on him almost in the same breath and accuse him of attacking her…

She turned then, to face towards him, and that low, simmering anger was eclipsed when blood rushed to his head and to his groin, making him simultaneously dizzy and hard.

He couldn't escape the impact of those huge, glittering bright blue eyes ringed with long dark lashes. But it was her mouth which drew his gaze and kept it. Sinfully lush and pink. Just waiting to be kissed…crushed under his. Andreas had to consciously will down the intense desire. He was fast being reduced to the instincts of an animal, and he hated her for having this effect on him. Still. *For ever*, mocked the small voice in his head.

*No.* Andreas rejected it fiercely. Not for ever. Just until he'd had her. Until they'd finished what she'd started when she'd upended his life so cruelly and comprehensively. Because she'd been curious and bored. Because she'd had the power. Because he'd been nothing.

Resolve firmed in Andreas's gut. He was far from nothing any more, and thanks to a cruel twist of circumstances Siena DePiero was reduced to lower than he'd ever been, rendering her exposed and vulnerable—to him.

Her blonde head dipped out of view momentarily and Andreas's insides contracted with something indefinable that went beyond where he wanted to investigate. He didn't like the fact that he was uncomfortably aware of other men's interest, of their gazes after her, covetous and even lascivious. It made him feel possessive and that was not welcome.

She'd had the gall to play with him once. Andreas desired her. That was all. His eyes caught sight of her bright blonde head again and he watched and waited as she drew ever closer to him in the crowd.

Siena DePiero was in the act of navigating through the crowd with a heavy tray, trying not to upend the contents over someone's feet, when a broad chest at her eye level stopped her from moving forward.

She looked up and had the impression of a very tall man, broad all the way through to his shoulders. A pristine tuxedo with a white bow-tie marked him out as slightly different. As Siena's mouth opened to say *excuse me* her gaze reached his face and her heart stopped.

He was no stranger.

*Andreas Xenakis. Here.*

The recognition was instantaneous. The knowledge was cataclysmic. It was as if mere minutes had passed since she'd last seen him, yet it had been five years. He looked bigger, darker, leaner.

She could instantly read the unmistakable light of cold hatred in his eyes and her insides contracted painfully. Of all the people to meet in this situation… No one would get more mileage out of it than Andreas Xenakis. And could she even blame him? a small voice mocked.

'Well, well, well.'

His voice was painfully familiar, immediately twisting her insides into a knot of tension.

'Fancy meeting you here.'

Siena could feel his eyes rake her up and down, taking in her server's uniform of white shirt, black tie and black trousers. The effect he had on her now was as devastating as it had been five years before. It was as if she had been plugged into an electrical socket and the current was running through her blood, making it hum, as disturbing and disconcerting as she remembered—especially in light of what had happened.

Her insides contracted even more painfully.

Dark slashing brows framed his incredible navy blue eyes. High cheekbones drew the eye down to a strong jaw. And his mouth…that beautiful sensuous mouth…was all at once sexy and mocking. He lifted one brow, clearly waiting for a response.

Struggling to retain some sense of composure, when she felt like a tiny boat being lashed on high seas, Siena managed to find her voice and said coolly, 'Mr Xenakis. How nice to see you again.'

His arched brow went higher and he let out a curt laugh. His voice wasn't so heavily accented any more. It had more of a mid-Atlantic twang. 'Even now you can make it sound as if you're greeting me at your own dinner party—not serving drinks to people you once woudn't deign to look in the eye.'

Siena flinched minutely. She didn't have to be psychic to recognise that the man who stood before her now was a much harder and more ruthless creature than the man she'd met in Paris. Xenakis's meteoric rise to become one of the world's most prominent hoteliers at the ridiculously young age of thirty had been well documented in the press.

'I'm flattered you remember me,' he drawled, 'After all we've met only once—as memorable as that meeting was.'

He mocked her. Siena felt like pointing out pedantically that it had actually been twice. After all, she'd seen him again the morning after that catastrophic night. But *that* memory was far too much to handle right now.

'Yes.' She glanced away for a minute, uncomfortable under that dark gaze. 'Of course I remember you.'

Suddenly it was too much. The tray of glasses started to wobble alarmingly in Siena's hands as the full magnitude of seeing him again hit her. Surprising her, Andreas took it competently out of her white-knuckled grasp and put it down on a nearby table before she could object.

Just then they were interrupted by Siena's boss, who was shooting none too subtle daggers at Siena while smiling obsequiously at Andreas.

'Mr Xenakis, is everything all right here? If my staff have been in any way remiss—'

'No.' His voice was abrupt, cold. He truly was Lord of all he surveyed now. Exuding power and confidence and that tangible sexual charisma.

Feeling a little dizzy, Siena tuned back in to Xenakis's voice, being directed to her boss.

'Everything is fine. I am acquainted with Miss—'

Siena cut in urgently before Xenakis could say her hated name, 'Mr Xenakis, like I said, it was nice to see you again. If you'll excuse me, though, I really should get back to work.'

Siena picked up the heavy tray again and, without looking at Andreas Xenakis or her boss, fled on very shaky legs.

Andreas followed the progress of the bright blonde head, inordinately annoyed with this small rotund man for interrupting them. He was saying now, in a toadying voice, 'I'm so sorry about that, Mr Xenakis. Our staff have the strictest instructions not to make conversation with any of the guests, but Miss Mancini is new—'

Andreas bit out coldly, '*I* spoke to *her*, actually.' Then he realised something and looked at the man, 'You say her name is Mancini?'

'Yes,' her boss said absently, and then he smiled even more slimily, saying *sotto voce* to Andreas, 'Of course her looks are a bonus—she could be a model, if you ask me. I don't know what she's doing waitressing, but I can't complain. I've never had so many requests for her phone number.'

Andreas desisted from informing the man that she was waitressing because she was *persona non grata* in polite society across Europe. He pushed aside the fact of her name-change and felt something like rage building inside him. He fixed the manager with a look that would have felled many. 'I presume you do not give out her number, of course?'

The man immediately went puce and blustered, 'Well, I… Well, of course not, Mr Xenakis. I don't know what kind of a service you think I'm running here, but I can assure you—'

'Don't worry,' Andreas sliced in cuttingly. 'I *will* be assured once I've checked out your company thoroughly.'

With that he turned and walked in the direction he'd last seen Siena moving. He had something much more urgent to take his attention now: making sure Siena DePiero didn't disappear into thin air.

A couple of hours later Siena was walking quickly through the moonlit streets around Mayfair. She still hadn't fully processed that she'd seen Andreas Xenakis, here in London, where she'd come to hide and move on with her life. To her everlasting relief she hadn't bumped into him again, but she'd been horribly aware of his tall form and had endeavoured to make sure she stayed on the far side of the room at all times.

Now, as she walked and felt the blisters on her heels, she cursed herself for letting Andreas get to her like that. Yes, they had history. She winced inwardly. It wasn't a pretty history. She didn't want to be reminded of the blazing look of anger and betrayal on his face when she'd stood beside her father five years ago, holding her dress up over her chest, and agreed shakily: *'Yes, he attacked me, Papa. I couldn't stop him…'*

Andreas had cut in angrily, his Greek accent thick. 'That's a downright lie. She was begging me—'

Her father had held up an imperious hand and cut Andreas off. He'd turned to face Siena and she'd looked up at him, terrified of his power to inflict punishment if he chose to believe Andreas.

He'd said quietly, 'He's lying, isn't he? You would *never* let a man like this touch you, would you? Because you know you're infinitely better than him.'

Struggling to hide her disgust and hatred, Siena had given the only answer she could. She'd nodded and felt sick. 'Yes, he's lying. I would never allow someone like him to touch me.'

Thinking of the unpalatable past made Siena feel trembly and light-headed. She didn't want to contemplate the very uncomfortable fact that he still had such a profound effect on her.

Once again, though, she marvelled at how far removed he was from the man who had once presided over servers in a hotel. In all honesty she was surprised he'd recognised her at all from his lofty position. She knew how easy it was to see only the hand that served you, not the person. Siena recalled her father's blistering anger when he'd berated her once for aiding a waiter who'd dropped a tray at one of his legendary parties. He'd hauled her into his offce and gripped her arm painfully.

'Don't you know who we are? You step over people like him. You do *not* stop to help them.'

Siena had bitten back the angry retort on her lips. *Just like you stepped over your own illegitimate son in the street? Our own brother?* That audacious comment alone would have merited her sister a severe beating. That was his preferred twisted form of torture—if Siena provoked him, Serena would be punished.

Siena saw the bus stop in the distance and breathed a sigh of relief. Tomorrow she would have forgotten all about bad memories and running into Andreas Xenakis. Her insides lurched, mocking her assertion. For one second earlier, when she'd first seen Andreas, she'd imagined she was dreaming.

She'd never forgotten what she had done to that man by falsely accusing him. More often than she cared to admit she remembered that night and how, with just a look and a touch, he'd made her lose any sense of rationality and sanity. On some level, when she'd read about his stellar success in the newspapers, she'd been relieved; to see him flourishing far better than she would have ever expected assuaged some tiny part of the guilt she felt.

Resolutely Siena pushed down her incendiary thoughts. Familiar nagging anxiety took their place. She wondered now, as she approached the bus stop, if the two jobs she had would be enough to help her sister. But she knew with a leaden feeling that nothing short of a miracle could do that.

Siena had just arrived under the shelter of the bus stop when she noticed a sleek silver sports car pulling up alongside where she stood. Even before the electric window lowered on the passenger side Siena's heart-rate had increased.

The starkly handsome features of Andreas Xenakis looked out and Siena backed away instinctively. His presence was evidence that he wasn't about to let her off so easily. He wanted to torture her and make the most out of her changed circumstances. In a second he'd jumped out of the car and was lightly holding her elbow.

'Please.' He smiled urbanely, as if stopping to pick up women at bus stops resplendent in a tuxedo was entirely normal for him. 'Let me give you a lift.'

Siena was so tense she felt as if she might crack in two. Very aware of her ill-fitting thin denim jacket in the biting early spring breeze, and the fatigue that made her bones ache, she bit out, 'I'm fine, thank you. The bus will be along shortly.'

Andreas shook his head. He had that same incredulous expression that he'd worn when she'd spoken to him before. 'Are your co-workers aware you could probably have conversed with every foreign guest in that room in their own tongue?'

Hurt at this back-handed compliment, and his all too banal but accurate assessment of her misery Siena pulled her arm free. She acted instinctively, wanting to say something to prick his pride and hopefully push him away. 'I said I'm fine, thank you very much. I'm sure you have better things to do than follow me around like some besotted puppy dog.'

His eyes flashed dangerously at that, and Siena hated herself for those words. They reminded her of the poison that had dropped from her lips that night in Paris. They were the kind of words Andreas would expect her to say. But they weren't having the desired effect at all. She should have realised that he wasn't like other men—she remembered the way he'd stood up to her father with such innate pride. One of the very few people who hadn't cowered.

He merely looked even more dangerous now, and grabbed her arm again. 'Let's go, Signorina DePiero. The bus is coming and I'm blocking the lane.'

Siena looked past Andreas and saw the double-decker bus bearing down. A sharp blast of the horn made her flinch. She could see the others waiting at the bus stop shooting them dirty looks because their journey home was being held up.

Siena looked at Andreas and he said ominously, 'Don't test me, Siena. I'll leave the car there if I have to.'

Another blast of the horn had someone saying with irritation, 'Oh, just take the lift, will you? We want to get home.'

For a second Siena felt nothing but excoriating isolation. And then Andreas had led her to the car and was handing her into the low seat before shutting the door. He slid smoothly into the other side.

'Do up your belt,' he instructed curtly, before adding acidly, 'Or are you used to having even *that* done for you?'

His words cut through the fog of shock clouding her brain

and she fumbled to secure the belt with hands that were all fingers and thumbs.

She retaliated in a sharp voice. 'Don't be ridiculous.'

Andreas expertly negotiated the car into the stream of traffic. It was so smooth it felt as if they were gliding above the ground. It had been long months since Siena had been in such luxurious confines, and the soft leather seat moulded around her body, cupping it in a way that was almost sensual. Her hands curled into fists on her lap against the sensation and her jaw was taut.

She unclenched it. 'Stop the car and let me out, please. I can make my own way home. I got in purely to stop you causing a scene.'

'I've spent six months looking for you, Siena, so I'm not about to let you go that easily.'

Six months ago her father had disappeared, leaving his entire fortune in tatters, and leaving Siena and Serena to stand among the ashes and take the opprobrium that had come their way in their father's cowardly absence. Siena looked at Andreas with horror on her face and something much more ambiguous in her belly. Tonight *hadn't* been an awful coincidence?

Shakily she said, 'You've been looking for me?'

His mouth tightened and he confirmed it. 'Since the news of your father's disappearance and the collapse of your fortune.'

He glanced at her and she held herself tightly, wanting to shiver at the thought of his determination to find her again. To punish her? *Why else?* a small voice crowed.

Softly, lethally, he said, 'We have unfinished business, wouldn't you agree?'

Panic constricted Siena's throat. She wasn't ready for a reckoning with this man. 'No, I wouldn't. Now, why don't you just stop the car and let me out?'

Andreas ignored her entreaty and drawled easily, 'Your address, Siena…or we'll spend the night driving around London.'

Siena's jaw clenched again. She saw the way his long-fingered hand rested on the steering wheel. For all of his nonchalance she suddenly had the impression that he was actually far more intractable than her father had ever been. He'd certainly proved that he had a ruthless nose when it came to business.

Siena had on more than one occasion closeted herself in her father's study to follow Andreas's progress online. She'd read about him shutting down ailing hotels with impunity, his refusing to comment on rumours that he didn't care about putting hundreds out of work just to increase his own growing portfolio. In the same searches she'd seen acres of newsprint devoted to his love-life, which appeared to be hectic and peopled with only the most beautiful women in the world. Siena didn't like to admit how she'd noticed that they were all lustrous brunettes or redheads. Evidently blondes weren't his type any more.

Suspecting now that he would indeed drive around all night if she didn't tell him, Siena finally rapped out her address.

'See? That wasn't so hard, was it?'

Siena scowled and looked right ahead.

There was silence for a few minutes, thickening the tension, and then he said, 'So, where did you get Mancini from?'

Siena looked at him. 'How did you know?' Then she remembered and breathed out shakily. 'My boss must have mentioned it.'

'Well?' he asked, as if he had all the time in the world to wait for an answer.

Tightly, Siena eventually replied, 'It was my maternal grandmother's maiden name. I didn't want to risk anyone recognising me.'

'No,' the man beside her responded dryly, 'I can imagine why not.'

Anger at his insouciance, and the ease with which he'd just turned up to humiliate her, made Siena snap, 'You really shouldn't have followed me, you know.'

He replied all too easily. 'Look on it as a concerned friend merely wishing to see how you're doing.'

Siena snorted scathingly but her heart was thumping, '*Friend?* Somehow I doubt you've ever put yourself in that category where I'm concerned.' It was more likely to be a definite foe.

Andreas Xenakis shot her a look then, and Siena recoiled back in her seat. It was so…so carnal and censorious.

He growled softly, 'You're right. We were closer to lovers. And friends don't, after all, cry rape when it suits them to save face.'

Siena blanched. 'I *never* used that word.'

Andreas's jaw clenched hard. 'As good as. You accused me of attacking you when we both know that only seconds before your father arrived you were begging me to—'

'Stop!' cried Siena, her breathing becoming agitated.

She could remember all too well how it had felt to have Andreas Xenakis pressing her down into the chaise longue, the way she'd strained up towards him, aching for him to put his hands on her *everywhere*. And when he'd moved his hand up between her stockinged legs she'd parted them…tacitly telling him of her intense desire.

'Why?' Andreas drawled. 'You can't handle the truth? I thought you were made of sterner stuff, DePiero. You forget you showed your true colours that night.'

Siena turned her head and looked stonily out of the window. The truth was that she had no excuse for her reprehensible behaviour that night. She *had* begged Andreas to make love to her. She *had* kissed him back ardently. When he'd pulled her dress down to expose one breast she'd sighed with exquisite pleasure and he'd kissed her there.

The car pulled up to a set of traffic lights at that moment, and the urge to escape was sudden and instinctive. Siena went to open her door to jump out, but with lightning-fast accuracy Andreas's arm restrained her with a strength that was awesome. Long fingers wrapped around her slender arm, and the bunched muscle of his arm against her soft belly was a far more effective restraint than if he'd locked the doors. Her skin tightened over her bones, drawing in and becoming sensitised. Her breasts felt heavy and tight, her nipples stiffening against the material of her bra.

The car moved off again and Siena pushed his arm off her with all her strength. That brief touch was enough to hurtle her back in time all over again and she struggled to contain herself. The fact that he was so determined to toy with her like this was utterly humiliating.

He pulled up outside a discreetly elegant period apartment building on a wide quiet street. He'd hopped out of the car and was at her open door, holding out an expectant hand, before she knew what was happening.

Siena shrank back and looked up at him. 'This isn't where I live.' *It's a million miles from where I live,* she thought.

'I'm aware of that. However, it is where *I* live, and as we were passing I thought we'd stop so we can catch up on old times over a coffee.'

Siena held back a snort of derision and crossed her arms, looking straight ahead with a stony expression. 'I am not getting out of this car, Xenakis. Take me home.'

Andreas's voice was merely amused. 'First I couldn't get you into it and now I can't get you out of it. They say women are mercurial…'

Before she knew it Andreas had bent down to her level and reached in to undo her seat belt. Siena flapped at his hands in a panic until he stilled them with his. His face was very close to hers and Siena could feel her hair unravelling. She was breathing harshly. His scent teased her nostrils, exactly as she remembered it. Not changed. Oaky and musky and very male.

A voice came from behind Andreas. 'Mr Xenakis? Do you want me to park the car?'

Without taking his eyes off Siena's, Andreas answered, 'Yes, please, Tom. I'll be taking Ms DePiero home shortly, so keep it nearby.'

'Aye-aye, sir,' came the jaunty response.

Siena struggled for a few seconds against Andreas's superior strength and will. She saw the boy waiting behind him. Innate good manners and the fear of causing a scene that had been drummed into her since babyhood made her bite out with reluctance, 'Fine. One coffee.'

Andreas stood up, and this time Siena had no choice but to put her hand in his and let him help her out of the low-slung vehicle. To her chagrin he kept a tight hold of her hand as he tossed his keys to the boy and led her into the building, where a concierge held the door open in readiness.

Once in the hushed confines of the lift Siena tried to pull her hand back, but Andreas was lifting it to inspect it. He opened out her palm and his touch made some kind of dangerous lethargy roll through her, but she winced when she followed his gaze. Her palm sported red chafed skin, calluses. Proof of her very new working life.

He turned it over and Siena winced even more to see him inspecting her bitten nails—the resurgence of a bad habit she'd had for a short time in her teens, which had been quickly overcome when her father had meted out a suitable punishment on Serena, her sister.

Her hands were a far cry from the soft lily-white manicured specimens they'd used to be. Exerting more effort this time, and knowing that she'd just been cured of her nail-biting habit once again, she finally pulled free of Andreas's grip and said mulishly, 'Don't touch me.'

With a rough quality to his voice that resonated inside her, Andreas asked, 'How did they get like this from waitresssing?'

Siena fought against the pull of something that felt very vulnerable. 'I'm not just waitressing. I'm working as a cleaner in a hotel by day too.'

Andreas tipped up her chin and inspected her face, touched under her eyes where she knew she sported dark shadows. That vulnerability was blooming inside her, and for a second Siena thought she might burst into tears. To counteract it—and the ease with which this man seemed to be able to push her buttons—she said waspishly, 'Feeling sorry for the poor little rich girl, Andreas?'

At that moment the lift bell pinged and the doors opened silently. Siena and Andreas were locked in some kind of silent combat. Andreas's eyes went dark, their blue depths becoming distinctly icy as he took his fingers away from her face and smiled.

'Not for a second, Siena DePiero. You forget that I've seen you in action. A piranha would be more vulnerable than you.'

Siena couldn't believe the dart of hurt that lanced her at his words, and was almost glad when he turned. With his hand on her elbow, he led her out of the lift and into a luxuriously carpeted corridor decked out in smoky grey colours with soft lamps burning on a couple of tables.

The one door indicated that Andreas had no neighbours to disturb him, and Siena guessed this must be the penthouse apartment in the building. The lift doors closed behind them and then Andreas was opening the door and standing aside to allow Siena to precede him into his apartment. Only his assurance to the car park valet that he would be taking her home shortly gave Siena the confidence to go forward.

She rounded on him as he closed the door and blurted out belatedly, 'Don't call me DePiero. My name is Mancini now.'

After a long second Andreas inclined his head and drawled, with a hint of dark humour, 'I'll call you whatever you like...'

Stifling a sound of irritation, Siena backed away and turned around again, facing into the main drawing room. Her eyes widened. She'd grown up in the lap of luxury, but the sheer understated level of elegance in Andreas's apartment took her breath away. She'd been used to seeing nothing but *palazzos* laden down with antiques and heavy paintings, everything gold-plated, carpets so old and musty that dust motes danced in the air when you moved...but this was clean and sleek.

Siena only became aware that she had advanced into the drawing room and was looking around with unabashed curiosity when she saw Andreas standing watching her with his hands in his pockets. The sheer magnificence of the man in his tuxedo shocked her anew and she flushed, wrapping her arms around herself in an unconscious gesture of defence.

Andreas shook his head and smiled wryly before walking towards a sideboard which held several bottles of drink and glasses. He said now, with his back to Siena, 'You really know how to turn it on, don't you?'

Siena tensed. 'Turn what on?'

He turned around, a bottle of something in his hand, eyes gleaming in the soft light. 'It must be automatic after years of acting the part of innocent virginal heiress...'

When Siena was stubbornly silent, because he had no idea how close to the truth he skated, Andreas gestured half impatiently and clarified, 'That air of vulnerability, and looking as though butter wouldn't melt in your mouth.'

Hating herself for being so transparent, and hating him for misjudging her so comprehensively while knowing she couldn't very well blame him for his judgement, Siena schooled her expression. She carefully uncrossed her arms and shrugged one shoulder negligently. 'What can I say? You have me all figured out, Mr Xenakis.'

He poured a dark liquid into two glasses and came over, holding one out. 'I know I offered you a coffee, but try this. It's a very fine port. And you didn't have a problem using my name when we first met. Mr Xenakis is so...*formal.* Please, call me Andreas.'

Siena took the glass he offered, suddenly glad of something to hold onto—anything to will down the memory of how she had used his name before, *'Andreas, please kiss me...'*

He gestured to the comfortable-looking couch and chairs arranged around a low coffee table which held huge books of photographs that looked well thumbed. 'Please, take a seat, Siena. Make yourself comfortable.'

Siena was torn for a moment between wanting to demand he take her home and curling up in the nearest chair so she could sleep for a week.

A little perturbed by how weak she suddenly felt, she went and sat down in the nearest chair. Andreas sat on the couch to her left, his long legs stretched out and disturbingly close to her feet, which she pulled primly close to her chair.

He smiled and it was dangerous.

'Still afraid you might catch some social disease from me, Siena?'

## CHAPTER TWO

'DON'T BE SILLY,' Siena replied quickly, humiliated when she thought of what had happened, of the vile untruths she'd uttered and all to protect her sister.

When she thought of how innocently she'd wanted him that night in Paris and how it had all gone so horribly wrong she felt nauseous. This man hated her. It vibrated on the air between them and Siena had the very futile sense that even if she tried to defend herself and tell him what her reasons had been for acting so cruelly he'd laugh until he cried. He looked so impervious now. Remote.

Andreas sat forward, the small glass cradled between long fingers. 'Tell me, why did you leave Italy?'

Siena welcomed this diversion away from dangerous feelings and looked at him incredulously, wondering how he could even ask that question. She hated the familiar burn of humiliation that rose up inside her when she thought of the odious charges that had been levelled at her father after his business had imploded in on itself, revealing that he'd been juggling massive debts for years and that everything they possessed, including his precious family *palazzo* in Florence, was owned by the banks.

Her mouth twisted. 'As you can imagine, the price on myself and my sister's heads fell dramatically when it became apparent that we'd lost our fortune. I'm sure I don't need to tell you that we became *personae non grata* overnight.'

Andreas's eyes narrowed. 'No. It would be untruthful of me not to admit that I knew your father had been soliciting prostitutes for years, and about the evidence of his involvement in drugs and political corruption. But proof that he'd been trafficking women all over Europe for sex must have been the killer blow for two penniless heiresses. No one wants to be seen to be associating with a scandal of that level.'

The shame Siena felt nearly strangled her. Her father had solicited prostitutes while married to their mother because it had excited him. He'd fathered a son with one of those women. She'd thought she'd hated her father before...but she'd hated him even more when he'd disappeared into thin air to avoid the numerous charges levelled against him. To this day no one knew where he was, and Siena never wanted to see him again.

The thought of all those poor defenceless and vulnerable women being sold into a life of torture and degradation... Even now bile rose in her throat, because it had also been proved that her father had been more than just involved in a peripheral sense. He'd been an active participant.

Andreas must have seen something in her expression and he said quietly. 'Your father's sins are not your sins.'

Siena was taken aback at this assertion. She looked at him, unable to read his face. 'Perhaps not, but people don't want to believe that.'

'Did the press in Italy gave you a hard time?' He answered her disbelieving look with a shrug. 'I was travelling in South America for work when the full extent of your father's scandal hit. By the time I got back to Europe your father had disappeared and a new scandal was unfolding. I missed most of it.'

Siena thought of the relentless days of headlines like: *Heiresses no more. Who will marry the poor little rich girls now?* And: *Serena DePiero caught in flagrante just days after dis-*

*graced father's disappearance!* That had been the moment Siena had known she had to get herself and Serena out of Italy. Her sister had been spiralling dangerously out of control, and she'd been barely clinging onto sanity after everything they'd known had been ripped asunder.

Siena hadn't expected any quarter from the press—she'd seen how they delighted in savaging the once lofty and untouchable of society—and thanks to her father's extreme hubris the DePieros had had it coming. Nevertheless she voiced an understatement in a flat voice. 'Yes, you could say they gave us a hard time.'

Andreas was surprised at the lack of emotion in Siena's voice. The lack of reproach or injury. He could well imagine the field-day the press had had at seeing two blonde and blue-eyed princesses reduced to nothing.

Once again he had to marvel at her sheer natural beauty. She wore not a scrap of make-up but her skin glowed like a pearl. In this world of artifice and excess she really was a rare jewel. Even in the plain shirt and tie, that threadbare denim jacket, he could see the tantalising curves of her body. Fuller now that she was a woman, not a teenager.

Desire was hot and immediate, tightening his body. A fit of pique went through Andreas when he realised that he'd subconsciously avoided blonde women in the last five years, seeking out the complete opposite and telling himself that she'd burned his taste for blondes. But she hadn't. He just hadn't wanted any blonde except *her*.

Women didn't usually reduce him to such immediate carnal reaction, no matter how desirable or beautiful. And yet she had from the very first moment he'd laid eyes on her...

Andreas looked at her now with fresh resolve filling his belly and lifted his glass. 'To whatever the future might bring.'

Siena had a very scary suspicion that the future Andreas was envisaging had something to do with *her*. Very deliberately she ignored his toast and drained her glass, put it down on the nearby table. The alcohol blazed its way down her throat.

Andreas looked merely amused and chided softly, 'A 1977 port should be savoured a little more delicately than that, but each to their own.'

He downed his too. Siena blanched. She could just imagine how much it had cost. Her father had thought of himself as an expert in fine wines so she'd learnt something by proxy.

Thinking of her father made her think of her sister, and that made her stand up jerkily, only vaguely aware of the stunning view of London on the other side of the huge windows. 'I really do need to get home. I have an early start in the morning.'

Andreas rose too, as fluidly as a panther, rippling sinew and muscle very evident despite the severe cut of his suit. As if it barely contained him. Siena would have taken a step back, but the chair was behind her.

She sensed a spiking of electricity in the air and there was a pregnant pause just before he said innocuously, 'Very well.'

He went to a discreet phone on the sideboard and picked it up, saying to someone, 'I'm coming back down. Please have my car brought round. Thank you.'

He extended his arm to allow her to precede him from the room, and to Siena's utter chagrin her overwhelming feeling wasn't one of relief. She was a little confused. She'd expected…*more.* More of a fight? And yet he was happy to let her go so easily. Something bitter pierced her. Perhaps he'd just wanted to amuse himself by seeing the disgraced heiress up close and he was already bored.

So why did she feel so desolate all of a sudden?

Andreas stepped into the lift behind Siena and pressed the button. He might be giving her the illusion of letting her go, but that was not his intention in the slightest. Seeing her again had merely solidified his desire to have her in his bed. Finally.

Acquiescent and *his*. That disdain she did so well would have no place in the relationship they would have. She was in no position to argue or resist him, and the thought of seeing her come undone was heady in the extreme.

His car was waiting by the kerb and a young security guard jumped out, giving the keys to Andreas, who held the passenger door open for Siena to get in.

Siena stood stiffly by the open door and looked at Andreas without meeting his eye. She was still trembling at the way his hand had rested lightly on the small of her back the whole way down in the elevator. And also at the speed with which he now appeared to want to get rid of her.

'If you can point me in the direction of the nearest tube I'll make my own way home.'

Andreas's voice was like steel. 'It's almost eleven-thirty at night. There is no way you're taking the tube alone. Get into the car, Siena, or I will put you in myself. Don't think I won't.'

Siena looked at him properly and saw how stern he seemed. She felt a shiver of something go through her—recognition of how huge and broad he was against the night sky. And yet she wasn't scared of him. Not as she'd been of her father. She somehow knew instinctively that Andreas would never lash out like that. Violence towards women was born of weakness and fear. Andreas didn't have that in him. And it surprised her to admit that she trusted this gut feeling so much.

Knowing that if she walked off now he'd just follow her again, Siena gave in and slid into the car, its luxurious confines once again surrounding her like a cocoon. Until Andreas got in beside her and the atmosphere turned from relaxing to electric.

As they pulled away from the kerb Andreas asked easily, 'Did your sister come to London with you?'

Instantly Siena tensed. She answered carefully, 'No… She went to…to the south of France to stay with friends of hers.'

Andreas glanced at Siena, who was looking stonily ahead.

He had to concede that she'd never taken after her more obvious sister by appearing in the gossip columns. Siena clearly preferred to clean toilets rather than to be seen in polite society again and be exposed to ridicule or censure.

He had to admit to a grudging and surprising respect that Siena was doing the sort of work she would have taken completely for granted her whole life. Perhaps now that their father was gone Siena saw no need to be responsible for the precious family name and was happy to wash her hands of her infamous sister, who had been well known as a party girl.

In truth, Andreas didn't really care about Serena. The sister he was concerned about was sitting right beside him, her legs looking very long as she angled them well away from him. He allowed himself a small predatory smile to think of a time when they would be wrapped around his hips as he finally exorcised this demon from his blood for good.

He hadn't elaborated on the fact that he had been actively looking for her for six months. In fact he'd been thinking about her ever since Paris. However, it had only been six months ago, when he'd finally had the luxury of time after establishing himself, that he'd begun to focus on such a personal pursuit. Siena DePiero had always been in his sights…

To Siena's relief Andreas seemed to be done with questioning her, and they drove in silence through the empty London streets. Rain started to spatter gently on the windscreen. For the first time since she'd left Italy Siena felt a pang of homesickness and it surprised her. She'd left Italy never wanting to see it again.

She'd spent many a night looking out of her window dreaming of another life—one without constrictions and pain and tension and always the unbearable pressure to act a certain way. She'd dreamed of a life full of love and affection. The only affection she'd really known had come from her sister—her poor, damaged sister. Their mother had died when they were both small girls. Siena had only the vaguest memories of a fragrant blonde woman who'd used to come into their room at night dressed in glittering finery.

She realised that they were close to her street already, and she directed Andreas into the labyrinth of smaller streets that led to her home. He pulled to a stop and looked out incredulously at the bleak, lonesome apartment block standing on wasteground.

'You're living *here?*'

Defensively Siena said, 'It's near the tube and the bus.'

Andreas was shaking his head in disbelief. He undid his seat belt and got out. Siena noticed that he'd taken an umbrella from somewhere and was holding it up now, as he came to her door and opened it.

She got out and the wind whipped around her, tugging her hair out of its bun completely. Feeling flustered, she said, 'Look, thanks for the lift…'

She moved to walk around Andreas and go into the flats, but stopped when Andreas kept pace beside her. She looked at him. 'Where do you think you're going?'

He was grim. 'I'm walking you to your apartment. You are *not* going in there alone.'

A new sense of pride stiffened Siena's backbone. 'I've been living here alone for months now and I've been fine. I can assure you that—'

Andreas wasn't listening. He'd taken her elbow in his hand and was guiding her across the litter-strewn ground. Irritation raced up Siena's spine. This was exactly what her father had used to do.

Once inside the main door, which hung haphazardly on broken hinges, and under the unforgiving flourescent lights, Siena pulled free, 'This is fine.'

Andreas was folding down the umbrella, though, and then he spotted a sullen youth lurking in a corner. He called the boy over and handed him a folded note and the umbrella. 'Keep an eye on the car for me?' he said.

The boy looked at the money and went white, then looked back to Andreas and nodded his head vigorously.

He took the umbrella before speeding off to stand guard.

Siena didn't like how the tiny gesture of Andreas giving him the umbrella made her feel soft inside. Churlishly she said, 'It'll be up on blocks by the time you leave.'

'O, ye of little faith,' Andreas murmured, and hit the elevator button.

Siena watched as he grew impatient when the lift didn't materialise straight away, and stood back to point at the stained concrete stairs. 'It's a cliché, I know, but the lift isn't working—and I'm all the way up on the fourteenth floor.' She couldn't quite keep the satisfaction out of her voice.

The light of determination was a definite glint in Andreas's eye as he said, 'Lead the way.'

Siena was huffing and puffing by floor ten, and very aware of Andreas right behind her. When they finally reached the door to her flat she turned to face him. She felt hot, and the hair on the back of her neck felt damp with perspiration. Her heart was hammering.

'Thank you. This is me.'

Andreas barely had a hair out of place, and not so much as a hint of the effort of climbing up fourteen sets of hard concrete stairs. Although somewhere along the way he had tugged his bow-tie loose, and the top button of his shirt was open, revealing the top of his olive-skinned chest and some springy dark hair.

Siena's belly clenched hard. She could remember impatiently undoing his shirt buttons that night in Paris, ripping his tie open…

Andreas was looking around the bare corridor. Someone

was shouting in a nearby flat and then something smashed against a door, making Siena flinch.

Andreas cursed and took the keys out of her numb fingers. 'Let's get you inside.'

He was doing it again. Taking command, all but pushing her through the door into a bare and forlorn-looking space filled with stained carpet. Siena had done her best to get rid of the stains, with little success. She only hoped that they weren't what she thought they were…

Siena put on her one small lamp and regretted it as soon as she did so, because it sent out a far too seductive pink and warm glow. Feeling thoroughly threatened now, she put out her hand for her keys and snapped, 'You've seen me safely in—now, please leave.'

Looking supremely at ease, Andreas just shut the door behind him and said softly, 'This must be hard for you…'

Siena went very still and her hand dropped to her side. He had no idea…how *easy* this had been for her. To leave behind the tainted trappings of suffocating wealth and excess had been a relief. But that was something no one would ever understand. She'd certainly never be explaining it to *this* man, who had grabbed onto success and wealth with both hands and was thoroughly enjoying it. And could she begrudge him that? Even if his methods were dubious? Of course not. She had given up that right five years before.

She put her hand out again for her keys. 'I have to be up early for work.'

Andreas didn't move. He just looked at her, those dark, unreadable eyes roving over her face and over her hair, which was tumbled around her shoulders now, making Siena want to drag it back, tie it up.

Feeling desperate, she said, *'Please.'*

'But what if you didn't have to get up early?'

Siena blinked at Andreas, not understanding him. She

shook her head. 'What do you mean? I start work at six-thirty a.m. It takes me an hour to get there…'

Andreas's face was so starkly beautiful in the dim light that she could feel herself being hypnotised. Much as she had been when she'd stood in front of him in that hotel boutique shop, in that dress. She'd taken it off after that night and thrown it in the bin, unable to look at it and not feel sickened.

He said now in a silky tone, 'What I mean is that you have a choice, Siena… I'd like to offer you an alternative.'

It took a second…but then his words sank in along with the very explicit look in his eyes. Since she'd been in England other men had posed much the same question—like the man who had come back to get something from his hotel room and found her making his bed. Except what he'd been offering had been stated in much cruder terms.

Shame and something much hotter curled through her belly, making self-disgust rise. She took a sidestep back and injected as much icy disdain as she could into her voice. 'If you're suggesting what I think you're suggesting then clearly you refuse to believe that I want you to leave me alone.'

Andreas took a step closer and panic spiked in Siena, making her take another step back. She felt out of her depth and unbelievably vulnerable. All of the familiar surroundings of her old life were gone. The part she'd played had been as good as scripted. Now she was utterly defenceless, and the one man in the world who hated her guts was propositioning her. And she hated that it didn't disgust her the way it should.

He reached out to trail a finger down one cheek, across her jawbone and down to where the pulse beat hectically under her skin at her throat. 'Even now you affect disgust, but your body betrays you. What happened in Paris…you were as involved as I was—as hot and eager as anything I've ever seen. And yet you didn't hesitate to shift the blame to me to keep yourself pure in your father's bigoted eyes. God forbid the untouchable heiress had been rolling around on a chair with a mere hotel employee.'

Siena slapped his hand away and stepped back, hating how breathy she sounded. 'Get out of here now, Xenakis. Rehashing the past is of no use.'

The anger Andreas had been keeping in check spilled over into his voice. 'You can't bring yourself to offer up even the most grudging of apologies, can you? Even now, when you don't have a cent to your name or a reputation to safeguard.'

Shame gripped Siena—and guilt. Ineffectually she said, 'I…am…sorry.'

Derision laced Andreas's voiceas he sneered, 'Spare me the insincere apology when it's all but dragged from you.'

His face was suddenly etched with self-disgust, and he half turned from Siena, raking his hair with a hand. She had a vivid memory of seeing him the following morning, shocked at his black eye and swollen jaw. Evidence of her father's men's dirty work. She'd tried to apologise then, but hadn't been able to speak over his very justified wrath.

Contrition and a stark desire to assure him that she *was* truly sorry made her reach out impulsively to touch his sleeve. She dropped her hand hurriedly when he looked at her suspiciously. She gulped under his almost black gaze and said truthfully, 'I never intended to…to lie about what happened. Or that you should lose your job.'

Andreas smiled, but it was harsh. 'No, possibly you didn't. You would have had your fun with me on the chaise longue of that boutique and then you would have gone on your way, with another notch on your busy bedpost. You forget that I know exactly what you girls were like: avaricous, bored and voracious. But you hadn't counted on Papà finding you *in flagrante delicto,* and you made sure that he would not suspect his precious daughter had such base desires. It was much easier to accuse a poor Greek hotel employee.'

Siena blanched. That was exactly what she had done. But not for *her* survival, for her sister's. That was something she could never imagine explaining to this intractable, vengeful man. Especially not when Serena was still so vulnerable. And not when Siena was still reeling with the effect he had on *her.*

Andreas slashed his hand through the air and said curtly, 'You're right, though. Rehashing the past is of no use.'

Those dark blue eyes narrowed on Siena again, with a renewed gleam of something that looked suspiciously like determination.

'Are you really telling me you're so proud that you relish living like this?' His voice became cajoling. 'Don't you miss sleeping until lunchtime and having nothing to worry about other than what time you've scheduled your beauty appointments or which dress you'll wear that evening?' He continued relentlessly. 'Are you really expecting me to believe that you wouldn't have all that back if you could? That you wouldn't seize the opportunity to walk amongst your peers again?'

Siena felt sick. The thought of allowing this man to get any closer, where he could possibly discover the vulnerability hidden deep inside her, made her break out in a cold sweat. He thought she had the wherewithal to handle him, that it would be second nature, when she didn't have the first clue about handling a man like him.

She pushed aside the fact that her apology had been as futile as she'd believed it would be and tossed her head in her most haughty fashion, eyes flashing. 'I would prefer to clean your toilets rather than do as you're suggesting. Perhaps you think that because I'm desperate I'll say yes to becoming your mistress. Is that it, Xenakis?'

Andreas smiled and bared his teeth. 'I thought I told you to call me Andreas—and, yes, I think you'll agree because you miss your life of luxury. But, more than that, because despite everything you want me…'

Siena went cold. She did want him, but he had no clue who she really was, or why she'd had to betray him so awfully. He had no idea about the tender beating inner heart of her that had very fragile hopes and dreams for a life far from the one she knew. He only saw a spoilt ruined heiress and a way to humiliate her. Because she'd rejected him. He had no idea who she'd had to protect, and that *that* was why she'd let him be accused in the worst way possible. She'd had no choice.

She knew now that, if given a chance, this man would take her and humiliate her for his own pleasure. For revenge.

In her most cutting voice Siena said, 'Contrary to your over-inflated view of your own levels of attraction, I *do not* want you. I may well be in a desperate situation *Mr Xenakis,* but I still have my pride and I wouldn't become your mistress for your sick amusement if you were the last man on this earth.'

Andreas looked at the woman standing just a few feet away from him and felt like clapping. Her clothes were crumpled and stained, her hair was tumbled around her face and shoulders in messy golden abandon, but she could have been a queen berating a lowly subject. And he wanted her with a hunger bordering on the very word she'd used herself: *desperation.*

He growled, 'I'm not in the habit of propositioning women who don't want me, Siena.'

She backed away at that, and reiterated with not a little desperation, 'I *don't* want you.'

'Liar.'

She saw the danger in Andreas's eyes. He advanced on her and she backed away, panic constricting her vocal cords, stopping her from saying anything. Panic at the awful, traitorous way her body was already getting hot, tingling with anticipation. If he kissed her now… Her mind blanked at the thought.

'Once again you're just too proud to admit you want me, Siena DePiero, and I'm going to prove how much you want me right now.'

It was insulting how easily Andreas was able to gather her into his arms and pull her close. From somewhere deep inside Siena dredged up the fight she needed. This man was far too dangerous to her. When he pulled her even closer and his head started to descend Siena acted on a visceral reflex to protect herself. She stiffened in his arms and lifted a hand to try and block his mouth from touching her. He obviously misread her intention and caught her wrist with lightning-fast reflexes. The strength of his grip made her gasp.

'Oh, no, you don't.'

Siena protested, 'But I wasn't—'

'No?' Andreas's mouth was hard.

He didn't believe her. Siena had never hit anyone in her life, and she felt sick at the thought that he could believe her capable of such violence.

'I wouldn't have hit you…' she whispered, willing him to believe her, staring directly into fathomless deep blue eyes.

Andreas's expression was stern. 'And you won't ever get the chance.' The threat in his voice was a very sensual one.

He kept her close with one arm secure around her waist and let her wrist go to bring his other hand up to cup her jaw with surprising gentleness, considering what he'd believed her about to do. And then, before she could make another move, Andreas angled his head down and his mouth closed over hers.

Shock rendered Siena helpless against the sensual attack Andreas administered. His mouth moved over hers with a confidence that was heady, eliciting an immediate response from Siena that she wasn't even aware of giving.

He was the only man who'd kissed her like this and she'd gone up in flames the first time. Nothing had changed. Heat pooled in her lower belly and spread slowly outwards, incinerating everything in its path. Her breasts tightened and felt heavy, achy. His arms around her were like a steel cage, but it was one she was pathetically loath to escape.

Siena was drowning in the scent of musky male, dimly aware of Andreas's hand moving down her jaw, caressing, and his fingers undoing the tie at the throat of her shirt, opening the top buttons.

His tongue teased her lips, making her strain to get closer, to allow him access so that he could stroke his tongue along hers. This was the headiest of illicit pleasures…

Unbeknownst to Siena, her hands had unfurled from the fists they'd been against Andreas's chest and were now spread out wide. She was up on tiptoe, as if to get closer to him. Andreas's hand cupped the back of her head, fingers tangled in long, silky blonde strands of hair. His other hand gripped her hip, kneading the flesh, making Siena move against him.

It was only when she felt air touch the exposed flesh of her neck and throat that Siena came to her senses and pulled back. She looked up, completely dazed, into dark blue eyes. Heavy-lidded and explicitly sexual.

Slowly realisation came over her like a chill wind, making all that heady sensuality wither away. One touch and she'd become a slave to her senses. Unable to rationalise anything.

Siena used her hands to push back violently, almost falling over in the process.

A million and one things were clamouring in her head, but worst of all was that she'd spectacularly—in neon lights and with fireworks—humiliated herself. She winced when she recalled her haughty tones—*'I don't want you.'* And what had she just been doing? Proving herself a liar *again.*

She grasped at her open shirt and couldn't look Andreas in the eye. 'I'd like you to leave now.' Her voice sounded rusty and raw to her ears.

# CHAPTER THREE

ANDREAS LOOKED AT Siena, holding onto her open shirt, looking almost shell-shocked, pale as the moonlight outside. His chest felt tight. This reaction was not something he'd expected. And then he realised: acting was second nature to this woman. It was in her blood—that made *his* blood boil. To have been duped again, even for a nanosecond…

His voice was harsh. 'There's no one here to cry wolf to now, Siena. You have to take responsibility for your actions.'

He started forward and suddenly her head came up. Her blue eyes were once again sparkling like jewels, her chin determined. Andreas stopped, his body still throbbing with heat. But he forced it back. Something hardened inside him. To think that for a second that he'd seen some kind of vulnerability…? Ludicrous.

He forced himself to be civilised when he felt anything but. 'You still want me, Siena, and you can deny it all you want but it's a lie. I am not leaving here without you tonight. You'll pay for what you did: *in my bed.*'

Siena opened her mouth and shut it again, shock pouring into her body. He sounded so utterly determined. As if he was prepared to carry her bodily from this place. Siena's mind skittered away from that all too disturbing scenario to think of his other assertion. How could she deny she wanted him after that little display of complete lack of control? His words terrified her, though—his easy assumption that she would just *go with him.* Just as her father had always expected her to do his bidding.

She'd tasted personal freedom for the first time since their father had disappeared and it terrified her to think of someone dictating her every move again.

Siena dropped her hand from her open top buttons and lifted her chin. 'You seriously think that I'll just walk out of here with you? How unbelievably arrogant *are* you?'

Andreas's eyes darkened ominously. 'I paid a high price for your petulant need to save face with your father that night, Siena. I was sacked and blacklisted from every hotel in Europe overnight, and I had the very unsavoury rumour of my having forced myself on a woman dogging my heels. My fledgling career was ruined. I had to go to America to start again.'

Siena couldn't bear to feel that shame again and she lashed out. 'So—what? I pay you now by becoming your mistress?'

Andreas smiled and it was feral. 'That and more, Siena DePiero. You pay me by admitting to yourself *and me* just how much you want me.'

She looked at this man in the soft light of her grotty flat. He was standing like a maurauding pirate, legs firmly planted wide apart. Chest broad and powerful. Strip away the civilised veneer of the tuxedo and this man was a pure urban animal of the most potent kind.

*He's been looking for you for six months. He's not just going to walk away…* The realisation sent tendrils of panic mixed with something much more humiliatingly exciting through Siena's blood. The confines of the tiny flat seemed to draw in around them even more.

She emitted a curt laugh to hide her trepidation. 'So—what? You'd lock me into your penthouse apartment and take me out like a toy of some kind for your pleasure only?' She'd been aiming to sound scathing but her voice betrayed her, sounding almost as if she was considering this.

Andreas's eyes gleamed in the dim light and he smiled. 'I can't deny that that image does have its appeal, but, no, I'd have no problem being seen with you in public. *I* don't have an issue with public opinion—unlike some people.'

Andreas was looking at her coolly, clearly waiting for her to say something.

'And what then?' she asked, feeling a little hysterical at being in this situation, discussing this with Andreas Xenakis. 'You just drop me back here at the side of the road when you're done?'

Andreas's mouth firmed. 'I take care of all my…lovers.' He shrugged negligently. 'They're usually self-sufficient, but with your range of language skills alone I don't doubt that with a little help you could find a decent job…certainly something better than menial labour.'

Siena laughed. The hysteria was taking over. Controlling herself with an effort, she looked at Andreas. 'This truly is a turn-up for the books, isn't it? *You* offering to help *me* find a job…'

Siena's cutting voice was hiding one of her deepest vulnerabilities: the fact that she had no qualification beyond her exclusive education. Yes, she had numerous languages and could speak them fluently. Yes, she knew how to host a dinner party for fifty people and more. Yes, she knew how to arrange flowers and how to behave in front of royalty and diplomats, how to conduct conversation ranging from world politics to the history of art… But when it came to the real world—real life—she knew nothing. Had no skills or qualifications. She'd been destined for a life of social politics. And Andreas knew that.

She prayed he wouldn't touch her again and moved around him on wobbly legs to open the front door. There were no more disturbing sounds coming from her neighbours. She looked back into the room with relief, to see that Andreas had followed her. But the relief was short-lived when he gently but firmly pushed the door shut again.

Sounding eminently reasonable, Andreas said, 'I'm offering you an opportunity, Siena, a chance to move upwards and make a life for yourself again.'

Siena crossed her arms against this threat. He wasn't moving. She forced herself to look up at him. Her mouth twisted and she spoke her fears. 'We both know it's not an *offer,* Andreas. You haven't spent six months searching for me to just walk away.'

He smiled again and agreed equably, 'No, I haven't. It really wouldn't be such a chore, Siena… I'd see to it that you enjoyed yourself. You'd want for nothing.'

'For as long as your interest lasts?'

His face immediately became more stark and Siena knew she'd hit a nerve. She was intrigued despite herself. 'That's all I'm offering, Siena. A finite amount of time as my lover until we're both ready to move on. I have no desire for anything more permanent—certainly not with you.'

Siena barely registered his insult. She was fighting against his dark pull and she opened the door again—only to have Andreas reach out lazily and shut it. She wanted to stamp her feet and glared at him.

'Look, Xenakis—'

'No!'

His voice stopped the breath in her throat. He looked fierce and magnificent in the gloom. He came closer and her heart thudded painfully.

'*You* look. This is only going to end one way: by you agreeing to come with me now. If you want a further demonstration of how susceptible you are to me then by all means I'm happy to provide it here and now, but—' He cut himself off and looked around the room with clear disgust, then back to Siena. 'I personally would prefer to make love to you for the first time in more…luxurious surroundings.'

The thought and, worse, the knowledge that he could take her here if he so wanted made Siena move further away. She felt as if a noose was tightening around her neck.

Andreas watched as Siena distanced herself and curbed the almost animalistic urge he had to put her over his shoulder and carry her bodily out of this pathetic, stinking place. His blood was boiling with lust and determination. As soon as his mouth had touched hers he'd known with a visceral certainty that he would *not* be leaving her behind in this place. He didn't like to admit that a part of him couldn't bear to think of her in these surroundings. It was like dropping a perfect diamond into the filthiest of stagnant ponds.

Trying to curb the impatience he felt, Andreas pointed out, 'You don't have anyone to turn to, Siena. If you're hoping for some blue-blooded knight to ride up on a white horse and forgive you the sins of your father it's not going to happen. Don't forget—I *know* your sins.'

Siena turned to face Andreas again, hugging her arms even tighter around herself, unaware of how huge her eyes looked in her face.

His words had cut her far deeper than she wanted him to see. He was right. She didn't have anyone to turn to. She and Serena did have an older half-brother, but she had little doubt that after the treatment he'd received at the hands of their father, not to mention the way Siena and her sister had ignored him so blatantly when they'd seen him in the street the day he'd confronted their father, he would not relish her getting in touch out of the blue. He had become a billionaire financier against all the odds and must despise her just as he must despise their father, for humiliating him like a dog in the street.

Her sister was in no position to be of any support and never really had been, despite being the older by two years. And that brought Siena back to the stark realisation that *she* might have no one to turn to, but Serena was expecting to turn to Siena when she needed her. And she needed her now. Dismay filled her. How could she have forgotten even for a moment about Serena?

The hectic pulse of her blood mocked her. The reason was standing just feet away from her. Siena could feel the fight draining from her weary body. A sense of inevitability washed over her. It had been no coincidence that Andreas had met her tonight. He'd *searched* for her. And he would not rest now he knew where she was. She had nowhere else to go. Nowhere to hide. No resources.

As if he sensed the direction her thoughts were taking, Siena could see Andreas's eyes flash triumphantly in the gloom.

Suddenly, as if she'd been injected with a dose of adrenalin, her brain became clear. Thinking of her sister focused her thoughts. *If* she was going to walk out of this apartment with this man she had to make sure that the one person who needed *her* was going to benefit.

The thought of telling Andreas about her sister, appealing to his humanity, was anathema. If anything, this evening had proved just how far Andreas was willing to go to seek his revenge. If she told him about Serena he might very well use her against Siena in some way, exactly as her father had. Siena shivered at the very thought. No way could she ever let that happen again.

She knew, though, that the very audacious plan forming in her head would ensure Andreas's hatred of her for ever.

Andreas's blood hummed with anticipation as he watched the woman who stood just feet away, her chin still lifted defiantly, even though they both knew she was about to give in.

She would be *his*. Her little act of pride had just been an exercise in proving to Andreas that he was still the last man she'd choose on earth, even if there was enough heat between them to melt an iceberg. And even if she *was* desperate.

His mouth tightened into a line. If anything it just proved that he was right: Siena wanted out of her challenging circumstances and back into the world she knew so well.

All *he* cared about was sating this burning desire inside him. Witnessing Siena DePiero swallow her pride and her denial of their mutual attraction would be a delicious revenge, and the very least he deserved after suffering so acutely at her hands.

'Well, Siena? What's it to be?'

Siena hated the smug tone of arrogance in Andreas's voice. She couldn't believe she was even contemplating what she was about to do, but assured herself she could do this. She had to.

In a way it should be easy—she'd merely be reverting to the type she'd played well for as long as she could remember: that of a privileged heiress with nothing more on her mind than the dress she'd wear to the next charity function. No one except for Serena had ever known of her deep hatred of that vacuous world where people routinely stabbed one another in the back to get ahead. Where emotions were so calcified that no reaction was genuine.

Before she could lose her nerve altogether, Siena blurted out, 'I will come with you—right now if you wish.' She saw Andreas's slow smile of triumph curling his mouth and said quickly, before he thought he was about to have everything his way, 'But I have terms for this…if we're to embark on…' Words failed her. She simply could not articulate what he wanted and expected. What she'd agreed to in her head.

He arched a dark brow. 'This affair? Becoming lovers? Companions?'

Siena flushed. The word *companions,* even though he'd

meant it sarcastically, struck her somewhere very deep and secret. They would never be companions.

Feeling agitated, she moved behind her one rickety chair, putting her hands on its back as if it could provide support. She nodded once, jerkily. 'Yes. I have terms.'

Andreas folded his arms across his chest. He looked almost amused, and Siena welcomed this as it made the fire grow in her belly. He only wanted her for one thing, and she was only exploiting him for his desire.

Baldly she declared, 'I want money.' And then she winced inwardly. She'd been brought up to be the ultimate society diplomat, yet here with this man she regressed to someone barely able to string a sentence together. She was too raw around him. She couldn't call up that fake polite veneer if her life depended on it.

As Andreas registered Siena's words something dark solidified in his gut. He should have expected this. A woman like Siena DePiero would never come for free. She would expect him to pay handsomely for the privilege of bedding her. As much as he'd paid for touching her in the first place.

Disgust evident in his voice, he said coolly, 'I've never paid for a woman in my life and I'm not about to start now.'

Siena went as pale as parchment and Andreas had to curb the urge to sneer. *How* could she look so vulnerable when she was effectively standing there asking for payment to be his mistress?

Two spots of colour bloomed then in her cheeks and bizarrely he felt comforted. He could see her struggling with whatever she wanted to say. Finally she got out, 'Those are my terms. I want a sum of money or else I'm not going anywhere—and if you come near me I'll scream the place down.'

His lip curled. 'Just like your neighbours? I didn't see anyone rush to *their* aid.'

Siena flushed more. It made Andreas bite out, 'Just how much money are we talking about?'

He saw Siena swallow and she licked her lips for a second, effortlessly drawing Andreas's eye to those lush pink swells and making that heat in his body intensify. Damn her, but he wanted her—possibly even at a price.

Siena felt sick. But she was too far gone to stop now. She saw the disgust etched in the lines of his starkly handsome face. He would despise her for this, but if he could despise her and still want her that was fine with her.

She named her price. The exact amount of money she would need to ensure Serena's care for a year. If she was going to do this then she had to make it worthwhile. Six months wouldn't be enough to ensure Serena's long-term recovery. A year in therapy and rehabilitation would.

Andreas whistled softly at the amount and Siena saw how his eyes became even icier. He came close again and she fought not to back away, her eyes glued to his. In a bizarre way, now that she'd said it, she found a weight lifting off her shoulders.

'You value yourself very highly.'

Siena burned. Shame came rushing back. Nevertheless, she tossed her head and said defiantly, 'What if I do?'

Andreas looked her up and down and walked around her. Siena could feel his eyes roving over her body.

He said from behind her, 'For that kind of money I think it would be within my rights to sample the goods again before making a decision, don't you? After all, that's just good business sense.'

Siena whirled around indignantly even as heat suffused every particle of her skin, but words got lodged in her throat. She would be the worst kind of hypocrite if she were to lambast him.

She could see that Andreas was livid, with dark colour slashing his cheeks. Before she could stop him he was snaking a hand around her neck and pulling her towards him. She had to go with it or fall off balance completely.

He ground out with disgust, 'I don't pay women for sex. I never have and I never will. It's heinous and disgusting and demoralising. Especially when you want it as much as I do…'

And with that his mouth was on hers and he was obliterating any sense of reality—again. Siena's thoughts were lost in a blaze of heat. Her hands were on Andreas's chest and he'd gathered her closer by curling his arm around her back, arching her into him, where she could feel the burgeoning evidence of his arousal against her belly.

His mouth was forcing hers open, and once that happened she didn't have a chance. His tongue found and tangled with hers, stroking along it, demanding a response. Siena mewled deep in her throat, almost pitifully. Andreas was possessing her with sensual mastery and, far from being disgusted, she found that her arms itched to climb higher, to curl around Andreas's neck, and her tongue was dancing just as hotly as his.

His hand left her waist and travelled up along her ribs. Siena was aware of an intense spiking of anticipation in her blood as her breasts seemed to swell in response, nipples peaking painfully, waiting for his touch.

But Andreas didn't cup her breast as she was suddenly longing for him to do. He stopped just short and pulled his head back. She opened her eyes with an effort, to see his, hot and molten, searing her alive, damning her for her audacity and stubborn denial of their attraction. Her breath was coming in rapid bursts and a million and one things were vying for supremacy in her brain, all of them urging her to pull away—fast. But she couldn't move.

Roughly he said, with disgust lacing his voice again, 'Much as I hate to admit it, I think that perhaps you might just be worth paying an astronomical amount of money to bed.'

He was the one to pull away, leaving Siena feeling adrift and wobbly.

He ran a hand through his hair and looked at her, his mouth taut with condemnation. 'You've learnt your lessons well, De-Piero…in the beds of however many countless lovers you've entertained. Were they the ones to teach you that intoxicating mix of innocence and artless sensuality designed to inflame a man?'

Siena looked at Andreas, stunned at his words. He had no idea. He couldn't tell her gauche responses were all too *real*. And she vowed then that he never would know—however she had to do it.

She fought to find some veneer of composure and said, as cynically as she could, considering she was shaking inwardly like a leaf, 'What else did you expect? A disgraced virgin heiress? This is the twenty-first century—surely you know better than most that virgins are as mythical as the knight on a white horse you just spoke of?'

Andreas stalked away from her, tension emanating from his body in waves. In that moment he hated her, and he hated himself, because he knew he didn't have the strength to just walk away and leave her here. To show her nothing but disdain. If he did he knew she would torment him in dreams for ever. He'd spent five years haunted by her. He had to have her—had to have this closure once and for all. And he despised himself for his weakness.

He looked at Siena and to his chagrin all of his previous thoughts were blasted to smithereens and rendered to dust. Her hair was tousled from his hands, her cheeks were rosy and her lips full and pouting, pink from his kisses. Her chest still rose and fell with uneven breaths and those glorious blue eyes flashed defiantly.

Andreas had the very strong urge to take her right here in this scummy flat—to turn that expression of defiance into something much more acquiescent. And he would if he thought that once would be enough. But he knew with a preternatural prickling of awareness that it wouldn't be enough. He hardened his resolve. She would *not* reduce him to such baseness.

Siena was slowly regaining control of herself. His words rang in her head: *'I don't pay women for sex. I never have and I never will. It's heinous and disgusting and demoralizing.'* The pity of it was she agreed with every word he'd said, and had to admit to respecting him for it.

She finally dragged her almost stupefied gaze from his and walked on very shaky legs back to the door, about to open it—because surely he would be leaving now, for good? Once again Siena didn't like the hollow feeling that thought brought with it.

Before she could open the door, Andreas said ominously, 'What do you think you're doing?'

Siena looked at him, the breath catching in her throat for a moment. 'But you just said you wouldn't pay…'

Andreas's face was like stone, his eyes so dark they looked navy. 'Yes, I did, and I meant it.'

Siena struggled to understand. 'So, what…?'

Andreas crossed his arms. 'There are other means of payment that aren't so…' his lip curled '…obvious.'

Something very betraying kicked in Siena's gut at the thought that he wasn't leaving her. 'What do you mean?'

'Gifts…' He smiled cynically. 'After all, how many women and men have benefited from the largesse of their lovers for aeons? You can do what you like with them when our relationship is over, and if that means converting them into the money you want so badly then you're welcome to do it.'

Suspicious now, and feeling supremely naive because she'd never been in this situation before, she said, 'Gifts…what kind of gifts?'

Andreas's jaw tightened. 'The expensive kind. Jewels. Like the ones you were wearing that night.'

Siena flushed to recall the priceless diamond earrings and necklace her father had presented her with on the evening of that exclusive debutante ball in Paris. They'd belonged to her mother, but had been seized by the authorities along with everything else she had owned.

Siena found herself feeling almost a sense of sick relief that he wouldn't just be handing her a sum of money. The thought of receiving jewellery made what she'd just asked for a little more palatable, despite the fresh shame heaped on top of old shame. Siena comforted herself with the thought that Andreas must have presented plenty of his lovers with tokens of his affection.

'Fine,' she said shakily, barely believing she was agreeing to this. 'I'll accept gifts in lieu of payment.'

Andreas smiled. 'Of course you will.'

Siena had a vision of walking out of here with him and fresh panic galvanised her to ask, a little belatedly, 'What.. what will you expect of me?' She held her breath.

Andreas's smile faded. He suddenly looked harsh, forbidding. Not like a man who wanted her in his bed so badly that he'd sought her out and was prepared to pay her in kind for it.

'Considering the price you've put on yourself…I will expect you to be a very willing, affectionate and inventive lover. I'm a very sexual man, Siena, and I pride myself on satisfying my lovers, so I expect the same in return. Especially from you.'

Siena struggled to hold down a hysterical giggle. *Inventive lover?* He'd be lucky if she managed not to betray her innocence, and she could imagine now with a lancing feeling of pain just how unwelcome *that* knowledge would be. It might even be enough to turn him off altogether. As tempted as Siena was to suddenly blurt out that intimate truth, she thought of her sister and clamped her mouth shut. No going back. Only forward to accept the consequences of her actions, which she'd set in motion five years before.

Not wanting to think of how his assertion that he was 'a very sexual man' had impacted her deep inside, Siena asked rather shakily, 'How long will you want me for?'

Andreas came close to Siena, where she stood near the door, and touched her jaw with his finger, making her shiver with helpless sensation. His eyes travelled up and down her body with dark intent and then rose back to hers.

With almost insulting insouciance he said, 'I think about a week should satisfy my desire for retribution and for you.'

Siena flinched minutely. There was a wealth of insult in his assumption that a week would be enough, and Siena hated that it felt like an insult when it should feel like a reprieve. Anyone could handle anything for a week. Even this.

'A week, then.' Siena assured herself that seven days was a blip in the ocean of her life. She could do it.

Andreas smiled, but it didn't reach those dark eyes. 'I'm already looking forward to this time next week, when the past truly will be in the past. For ever.'

Siena's sense of vulnerability increased. 'The feeling is mutual, believe me.'

After a tense moment Andreas dropped his hand, stepped back and said, 'Get your stuff packed, Siena, and don't leave anything behind.'

'But I'll be coming back here...'

Andreas's mouth thinned as he took in the meagre furnishings with a disdainful glance. 'You won't be returning here. *Ever.*'

Siena opened her mouth to protest and then stopped. Of course he thought she wouldn't be coming back here if she was going to turn his gifts into cash. Andreas didn't know that in a week's time she'd be as broke as she currently was, and she didn't want his razor-sharp brain to pick that up.

Faintly she assured herself that she'd worry about it when the time came and went into the tiny bedroom and pulled out her case. Only a few hours ago she'd had nothing more on her mind than how to get through the evening without keeling over from exhaustion and the constant niggling worry about how she would be able to look after Serena, because they didn't have enough money to continue paying for her psychiatric care.

But now her life had been turned upside down and she had a very unexpected and unwitting benefactor for Serena.

The next week stretched ahead like a term of penal servitude. But, treacherously, Siena felt a shiver of anticipation run through her. Would Andreas expect her to sleep with him tonight? The thought made her heart leap into her throat and her mouth went dry. She wasn't ready—not in a million years.

The thought of all that intense masculinity focused on her was overwhelming when she was so inexperienced. Siena felt numb as she started to pull the paltry collection of clothes from the rail. She didn't even have a wardrobe. She could almost laugh when she thought of the palatial bedroom she'd had all her life, with its medieval four-poster bed. It would have encompassed this entire flat about twice over…

A huge shadow darkened her bedroom door and Andreas rapped out with clear impatience, 'Actually, you can leave everything here. Unless there's something of sentimental value. I'll be supplying you with a new wardrobe.'

Siena just looked at Andreas. She saw an austerely handsome man, eager to get out of this hole of a place and take her with him so that he could mould her into what he wanted. He was so sure of himself now—a Titan of industry, used to having what he wanted when he wanted.

Siena didn't doubt that most of the women in Andreas's life were only too happy to comply with his demands, and she had to quash the dart of something dark at the thought of those women. Dismay gripped her. It wasn't jealousy. It couldn't be jealousy. She hated this man for what he was doing and what he'd become—he was welcome to his hordes of satisfied lovers.

Self-derision that she could allow this to happen to her and the knowledge that she had no choice because this was her only hope to help Serena made Siena's spine straighten. Tersely she bit out, 'Give me five minutes.'

## CHAPTER FOUR

'WHAT WILL HAPPEN to my flat?'

Siena was trying not to notice Andreas's big hands on the steering wheel of his car, the way he handled it with such lazy confidence. Of course his car hadn't been on blocks when they'd gone outside. The young kid had been watching it like a hawk and had stared at Andreas as if he was a god.

Siena didn't know how to drive. Her father hadn't deemed it necessary. Why would she need to drive if she was going to be chauffeur-driven everywhere?

Sounding crisp, Andreas replied, 'I'll have my assistant settle up with your landlord. She can also inform your employers that you won't be coming back.'

Siena's hands tightened in her lap. In a way it was karma. She'd lost him his job and now he was losing her hers. Just like that. With a mere click of his fingers, Andreas was changing her life and ripping her very new independence out from under her feet. If she only had herself to worry about she wouldn't be here now, she assured herself inwardly, and hated the tiny seed of doubt that even then she could have held out against Andreas's will, or the guilt she felt.

She wondered what Andreas would have done if he'd known that she couldn't care less for his fortune? That his money wasn't for her at all? But she was forgetting that this man didn't care. Just as the younger man from five years ago hadn't cared. He'd only wanted her because it had been a coup to seduce one of the untouchable debutantes; their supposed virtue had been more prized and guarded than a priceless heirloom in a museum.

Except that virtue had been a myth. Siena had known all too well just how *touchable* the vast majority of her fellow debs had been. They'd looked innocent and pure, but had been anything but. She could recall with vivid clarity, how one of the girls—a princess from a small but insanely wealthy European principality—had boasted about seducing the porter who had brought her bags up to her room while her mother had slept in a drug-fuelled haze in the next room. She'd threatened the man with losing his job if he told anyone.

Siena's mouth hadn't dropped open—but only because her own sister had told her far more hair-raising stories than that, and had inevitably been a main participant when she'd been a debutante.

That evening she'd managed to escape from her father and had tried to find Andreas, to explain why she'd lied, hating herself for the awful falsehood. She'd explored an area reserved for staff only, and had come to an abrupt halt outside a half-open door when she'd heard a newly familiar voice saying heatedly, 'If I'd known how poisonous she was I'd never have touched her.'

A voice had pointed out coldly, 'You've done it now, Xenakis. You shouldn't have touched her in any case. Do you really think you would ever have had a chance with someone like her? She'll be married within a couple of years to one of those pale-faced pretty boys in that ballroom, or to some old relic of medieval Italian royalty.'

Andreas had said bitterly, 'I only kissed her because she was looking at me as if I was her last supper—'

The other voice came again, harder now. 'Don't be such a fool Xenakis. She seduced you because like every other spoilt brat in there she was bored—and you were game. Do you seriously think she hasn't already got a string of lovers to her name? Those girls are not the innocents they seem. They're hardened and experienced.'

Siena had barely been breathing by then, her back all but flattened to the wall by the door. She'd heard Andreas emit an expletive and then she'd heard footsteps and fled, unable to countenance offering up an apology after that character assassination—after hearing his words, *'I only kissed her because she was looking at me as if I was her last supper.'*

The following morning Siena had woken early and felt stifled in her opulent bedroom. She'd dressed in jeans and a loose sweatshirt and had sneaked out through the lobby at dawn, with a baseball cap on her head in case she saw anyone she knew. She'd craved air and space—time to think about what had happened.

That searing conversation she'd overheard had been reverberating in her head and she had run smack into a stone wall. Except it hadn't been a wall. It had been Andreas, standing beside a motorbike, in the act of putting on a helmet. Siena's baseball cap had fallen off, and she'd felt her long hair tumble around her shoulders, but shock had kept her rigid. In the cold light of day, in a black leather jacket and jeans, he'd looked dark and menacing. But she'd been captivated by his black eye and swollen jaw.

Startled recognition had turned to blistering anger. 'Don't look so shocked, sweetheart. Don't you recognise the work of your father's men? Don't you know they did this to avenge your honour?'

Siena had felt nauseous, and had realised why his voice had sounded so thick the previous evening. She should have known. Hadn't her father done the same thing, and worse, to her half-brother—his own son?

'I—' she'd started, but Andreas had cut her off with a slash of his hand through the air.

'I don't want to hear it. As much as I hate you right now, I hate myself more for being stupid enough to get caught. You know I've lost my job? I'll be lucky to get work cleaning toilets in a camping site after this…'

He'd burnt her up and down with a scathing look.

'I'd love to say that what we shared was worth it, but the only thing that would have made it remotely worth it is if you'd stopped acting the innocent and let me take you up against the wall of that dressing room as I wanted to. *Then* your father might not have caught us in the act.'

The crudeness of his words—the very confirmation that all the time she'd been quivering and shivering with burgeoning need, half scared to death, he'd assumed she was putting on some sort of an act and had wanted to take her standing up against the wall—had frozen Siena inside. Not to mention the excoriating knowledge that he'd merely made the most of an opportunity, and she'd all but thrown herself at him like some kind of sex-crazed groupie.

He'd taken her chin in his fingers, holding her tight enough to hurt, and he'd said, 'As the French say, *au revoir,* Siena DePiero. Because some day our paths will cross again. You can be sure of that.'

He'd let her go, looked at her and uttered an expletive. With that he'd put on his helmet, swung his leg over the powerful bike and with a roar of the throttle had left her standing there, staring after him as if she'd been turned to stone.

The streets of London at night made Siena's memories fade. But the tangible anger she'd felt from Andreas that day would never fade.

'We're here.'

Siena looked to see that they were indeed pulling up outside

Andreas's apartment. Butterflies erupted in her belly. It felt as if aeons had passed since she'd been there already that evening.

The same young man who had parked the car earlier appeared to open her door. Siena was relieved, not wanting to touch Andreas. He was waiting as she emerged from the car with her one case in his hand. She couldn't stop him putting a hand to her back as he guided her into the apartment block. Futile anger burned down low inside her at being so vulnerable to this man…

Andreas was very aware of Siena's pale and tightly drawn features as they stood in the lift. He held her pathetically small case in his hand and had to quash the dart of something that felt ridiculously like pity at the knowledge that this was all she possessed now, when she had been one of the most privileged women in Europe. He reminded himself that this woman was one of the most invulnerable on the planet. She'd contrived every single moment of that evening in Paris, and when it had come to it she'd saved her own pretty neck.

Back in that grotty flat, when she'd asked how long this would last, Andreas had been about to say a month until he'd stopped himself. He'd never spent longer than a week with a lover, finding that he invariably needed his space or grew bored. So to find himself automatically assuming he'd need a *month* was unprecedented. He wanted Siena with a hunger that bordered uncomfortably on the obsessional, but there was no way she was going to turn out to be any different from his other lovers.

But, a snide inner voice pointed out, this was already different, because he was bringing her back to his apartment without even thinking about it. He'd never lived with a lover before. He'd always instinctively avoided that cloying intimacy. It made him feel claustrophobic. Andreas cursed himself now and wondered why he hadn't automatically decided to put Siena in a suite in a hotel, rather than bring her to his place. He didn't want to investigate his adverse gut reaction to that idea, when it was exactly what he *should* be doing.

Andreas hated that she was already making him question his motives and impulses. It made him think of dark, tragic memories and feelings of suffocation.

Before Andreas had left his home town at the age of seventeen he'd had a best friend who had been planning on leaving with Andreas. They were going to make something of themselves—*make a difference.* But that final summer his friend had fallen for a local girl and had become a slave to his emotions, telling Andreas he no longer wanted to travel or achieve anything special. He just wanted to settle down. Andreas had been incapable of changing his mind, and he'd watched his smart, ambitious friend throw away his hopes and dreams.

When his friend had found his girlfriend in bed with someone else he'd been so distraught that he'd killed himself. Andreas had been deeply affected by this awful violence. By the way someone could lose themselves so completely and invest so much in another person. *For love.* When that love hadn't even been reciprocated.

Andreas's own father had achieved a scholarship to a university in Athens—the first in his family to do so. But before he could go he'd met and fallen in love with Andreas's mother. She'd become pregnant and his father had decided to stay and get married, giving up his chance to study medicine.

Andreas had always been aware of his father's missed chance at another life. And after witnessing his friend's descent into horrific tragedy he'd been more determined than ever to leave. He had vowed never to let himself be sidetracked by *feelings.*

And he hadn't... Until he'd had far too close a brush with disaster in Paris, when he'd lost himself for a moment with a blonde seductress who had blown hot and then colder than the Arctic. She'd been a necessary wake-up call. A startling reminder of what was important. Not to get side-tracked.

Andreas reassured himself that this time things were different. When the lift stopped and the doors opened a rush of anticipaton and pleasure seized him, washing aside all his doubts. Siena DePiero was here and that was all he needed to know. Having her anywhere but close to him was not an option.

He'd been waiting for this moment for a long time—ever since that night, when he'd felt a kind of helpless anger and a sense of betrayal that he never wanted to feel again. Ever since that following morning, when she'd emerged from the hotel like a manifestation of his fantasies, her hair tumbled around her shoulders, backlit against the Paris dawn light. He'd wanted her then—fiercely. Even after what she'd done. It had taken all of his strength to get on his motorcycle and leave her behind.

'This is your room.'

Andreas was standing back to let Siena go into a vast bedroom. She'd just been given a tour of the jaw-dropping apartment. Silently she went in, relieved to hear Andreas say: *'your room'*. It was stunning, decked out in sumptuous but understated dark blues and complementary greys. A king-sized bed dominated the room, and Siena could see a glimpse of a white-tiled *en suite* bathroom and an entrance to another room.

Exploring, she found herself walking through a large dressing alcove to a separate lounge area, with a sofa, chairs, desk and a TV. Effectively she had her own suite.

She turned around to see Andreas leaning with his shoulder against the entrance to the dressing room, his hands in his pockets giving him a rakish air.

'This is…lovely,' she said stiffly, knowing that *lovely* was woefully inadequate in the face of this opulence. She was stunned again at Andreas's world now, and stunned anew to see him in his open-shirted tuxedo and realise that only hours before Andreas Xenakis had still been firmly in her shameful guilt-ridden past, not her tumultuous present.

*But he was going to find you sooner or later,* an inner voice reminded her.

'I'll arrange for a stylist and a beautician to come tomorrow, to attend to whatever you need.'

To make her beautiful for *him.*

Siena felt light-headed all of a sudden and swayed ever so slightly.

Immediately Andreas was standing straight, alert. 'What is it? Are you hungry?'

Siena beat back the waves of weakness, determined not to show Andreas any vulnerability. She shook her head. 'No. It's nothing. I'm just tired. I'd like to go to bed now.'

Andreas just looked at her for a long moment and then as if deciding something, he stepped back and said, 'By all means, Siena. You're my guest now and you know where everything is. Help yourself to anything you want.'

He backed away, and just before he got to her bedroom door he said softly, 'You should sleep while you can, Siena. You'll need it.'

Siena fought back a fresh wave of light-headedness at hearing him say that and watched as he walked out of the room, closing the bedroom door behind him. Sudden weariness nearly felled her. Her head hurt after everything that had happened. She couldn't take any more in.

Finding her small suitcase, she extracted what she needed and dressed for bed. She couldn't block out the way her weak body rejoiced to sink into expensive bedclothes, and gratefully slipped into what felt like a coma.

Andreas knew he was in the grip of a dream but he couldn't seem to pull himself out of it. He was back in that glittering ballroom in Paris. He could feel the ambition rising up within him to *own* such a place one day. It would be a remarkable achievement for a boy from a small town outside Athens with only the most basic qualifications to his name.

And then, like a camera zooming in for a close-up, all he could see was *her* face. Pure and beautiful. Haughty and cold. Perfect. The white-gold of her hair was in a complicated chignon. Jewels sparkled brilliantly at her neck and ears. Her profile was as regal as any queen. The only thing marring the picture was the blood-red stain of wine that was blooming outwards from her chest and up over her cleavage.

The dream faded and shifted, and now they were in that boutique, surrounded by mannequins in beautiful dresses and sparkling jewels behind locked displays. She was laughing, girlishly and innocently, huge blue eyes sparkling with mischief as she pointed to one of the mannequins and said imperiously, 'I want *that* one!'

Andreas bowed down in a parody of a manservant and she laughed even more, watching as he clambered into the window display to tussle with the mannequin and take off the dress. She was in fits of giggles now, watching him wrestle the stunning dress off the dummy before finally handing it to her with a flourish of triumph.

She curtseyed and said, with a flicker of those black lashes, 'Why, thank you, kind sir.' And then she vanished into the dressing room, pulling velvet folds of material behind her.

There was a fizzing sensation in his blood. Andreas felt buoyant when only minutes ago, surveying the crowd in the ballroom, he'd felt cynical…

And then she was there, in front of him again, and Andreas was falling into eyes so blue it hurt to look at them. And then the hurt became a real pain, and he looked down stupidly, to see a knife sticking out of his belly and blood everywhere.

He looked up and she was smiling cruelly. 'No, I did not ask you to touch me. I would never let someone like you touch me.'

His friend who had died, Spiro, was behind Siena, laughing at him. 'You thought you could remain immune?'

And then Andreas was falling down and down and down…

Andreas woke with a start, clammy with sweat, his heart pounding. He looked down and put a hand to his belly, fully anticipating seeing a knife and blood. But of course there was none. It was a dream. A nightmare.

He'd had that dream for months after he'd left France but not for a long time. He remembered. *Siena.* She was here, in his apartment. His heart speeded up again and he got out of bed, pulling on a pair of boxers. He assured himself that it was just her presence that had precipitated the dream again.

But it had left its cold hand across the back of his neck. He went into the darkened drawing room and poured himself some whisky, downing it in one. He slowly felt himself come back to centre, but was unable to shake the memory of that evening.

Andreas had been duty manager, overseeing the exclusive annual debutante ball, making sure it went without a hitch. He'd viewed all those beautiful spoilt young women with a very jaundiced eye, having heard all sorts of stories about their debauched ways.

Still, he'd barely believed them. They'd all looked so *innocent.* And none more so than the most beautiful of them all: Siena DePiero. He'd noticed that she was always slightly apart from the others, as if not part of their club. And the way her father kept her close at all times. He'd read her aloofness as haughtiness. And then he'd seen the moment when her dinner partner had accidentally spilled red wine all over her pristine white dress. Andreas had clicked into damage limitation mode and smoothly offered to take her to the boutique for a fresh dress.

Her father had been clearly reluctant to let her out of his sight but had had no choice. He wouldn't let his daughter be presented at the ball in a stained gown. And so Andreas had found himself escorting the cool beauty to the boutique, and had been very surprised when she'd confided huskily, 'Please excuse my father's rudeness. He hates any sort of adverse attention.'

Andreas had looked at her, taken aback by this politeness when he'd expected her to ignore him. Shock had cut through his cynicism because she'd looked nervous and blushed under his regard. To his complete embarrassment he'd found his body reacting to her…this very young woman, even though he'd known she wasn't that young. Her eighteenth birthday was the following day, and her father had already organised a brunch party with some of the other debutantes to celebrate.

He'd said something to put her at ease and she'd smiled. He'd almost tripped over his feet. By the time they'd reached the boutique his body had been an inferno of need. Siena had been chattering—albeit hesitantly and charmingly.

In the empty shop the sexual tension between them had mounted, instantaneous and strong enough to make Andreas reel. He'd had lovers by then—quite a few—and thought he knew women. But he'd never felt like that before. As if a thunderbolt had connected directly with his insides.

Her artless sensuality and apparent shyness had been at such odds with her cool and haughty beauty. With the reputation that had preceded her. That preceded all the debs every year.

She'd grimaced after a few minutes and looked around the shop, before glancing at a dress on a mannequin in the window. It was fussy-looking, but not far removed from what she wore.

'That's the one my father will approve of.'

She'd sounded so resigned and disappointed that Andreas had inexplicably wanted to see her smile again. He'd hammed it up, extricating the dummy from the dress. And he'd made her laugh.

Then she'd disappeared into the dressing room and Andreas had found every muscle in his body locked tight as he thought of her in a state of undress, fantasising about hauling back the curtain, pulling down his trousers, wrapping her legs around his hips and taking her there and then, against the wall…

And then she'd emerged and his blood had left his brain completely. She'd turned around and showed him a bare back, asking with a shy look over her shoulder, 'Can you do me up?'

To this day Andreas wasn't sure how he'd done it without pulling that dress down and off completely. But he hadn't. She'd turned round and some of her hair had been coming loose. He'd reached out and tucked one golden strand behind her ear and she'd blurted out, 'What's your name?'

Andreas had looked at her and said, 'Andreas Xenakis.'

She'd repeated his name and it had sounded impossibly sexy with her slight Italian accent. 'Andreas.'

And then all Andreas could remember was *heat* and *need.* His mouth had been on hers and she'd been clinging to him, moaning softly, sighing into his mouth, her tongue making a shy foray against his, making him so hard…

Andreas's mind snapped back to the present. He was holding his glass so tightly in his hand he had to relax for fear of shattering it. He grimaced at his body's rampant response just at the memory of what had happened and willed himself to cool down.

He looked out at the millionaire's view of London he could afford now. A far cry from his roots and from painful memories of lives wasted. His mouth twisted. *Wasted because of love.* But, strangely, his usual sense of satisfaction deserted him. Because a new desire for satisfaction had superseded it. For a satisfaction that would only come from taking Siena into his bed and sating himself with her.

He'd never forgotten the way she'd changed in an instant that night—from a she-witch, writhing underneath him, begging him to touch her and kiss her all over, to pushing him off as if his touch burnt her. The way she'd sprung up, holding her dress against her, looking at him accusingly. He'd only realised then that there was someone else in the room. Her father. Looking at him with those cold eyes, as if he were a piece of scum.

The dream and the memory made Andreas shiver. Because it reminded him of how duped he'd been that night. How, despite his better instincts, he'd let himself believe that Siena had really been that giggling, shy, artlessly sexy girl. And, worst of all, how she'd made him want to believe that girl existed.

He should have known better. He of all people. As soon as he'd started working in the city of Athens his looks had attracted a certain kind of sexually mature and confident woman. Inevitably wealthy. They'd offered him money, or promotion, and had laughed at his proud refusal to get help via their beds. One had mocked him. 'Oh, Andreas, one day that hubris will get you into trouble. You'll fall for a pretty girl who pretends not to be as cold and hard as the rest of us.'

And he had. He'd fallen hard. In front of Siena and her father that night. In all honesty Andreas hadn't truly become so cynical yet that he'd believed someone as young as Siena could be so malicious and calculating. But he'd watched her transform from shy sex kitten to a cold bitch. Colder than any of those other women he'd known. And just like that he'd grown his cynical outer skin and his heart had hardened in his chest.

Since then he'd surrounded himself with the kind of women who populated the world he now inhabited. The kind who were sexually experienced and worldly-wise. He had no time for women who played games or who pretended they were something they weren't. And he would never, *ever,* believe in the myth of sweet innocence again.

A flare of panic in his gut propelled Andreas out of the drawing room, setting down his glass as he did so. He went to Siena's bedroom door and opened it silently. It took a second for his eyes to adjust to the dimmer light, and when it did and he saw the shape on the bed his heart slowed. Relief made a mockery of all of his assurances that he was in control but he pushed it aside.

For a second he'd thought it part of the dream. That she wasn't really here. That he was still looking for her.

He found himself standing by her bed and looking down. She was on her back, hair spread out around her head, breathing softly, dressed only in a T-shirt. Her breasts were two firm swells that had the blood rushing to Andreas's groin *again*.

Triumph was heady. She was here. She would be his.

Andreas knew that if her father's business hadn't imploded the way it had he would have been equally determined to get to her, but it would have been much harder to get close.

In the dim light he could see dark shadows under her eyes and he frowned. She looked tired and he felt his chest constrict. Just then she moved slightly, making him tense. As she settled she snored softly. Andreas found his mouth tipping up at this most incongruous sound from one so perfect.

Then he remembered the way she'd asked for money and the smile faded. He had to remember who she was, how she had fooled him so easily into thinking she was something she was not. He'd already learnt his lesson and he wasn't about to repeat his mistake.

The following evening Siena was standing at the window of the main living area in Andreas's palatial apartment. She turned her back on the evocative dusky view of London's skyline and sighed. She couldn't be more removed from the hovel of a flat she'd been living in. But as much as she'd hated it, on some perverse level she'd loved it because it had been symbolic of her freedom.

And now once again she was incarcerated in a gilded prison. Andreas had already gone to work when she'd woken up that morning, and she'd been relieved not to have to deal with him when she still felt dizzy with how fast things had moved. He'd left a curt note, informing her that it was his housekeeper's day off but she must help herself to whatever she wanted, and that a stylist and a beautician would be arriving later that morning.

Sure enough, a couple of hours later two scarily efficient-looking women had arrived, and within hours Siena had been waxed, buffed and polished. She now had a dressing room full of clothes, ranging from casual right up to *haute couture.* Not to mention cosmetics, accessories and lingerie so delicate and decadent it made her blush. And shoes—a whole wall of shoes alone.

The sheer extravangance had stunned Siena. Her father had been extremely tight with his money, so while she and Serena had always been decked out in the most exclusive designs it had been to perpetuate an image—nothing more.

Andreas had called a short while before and informed her that there should be some beef in the fridge. He'd instructed her to put it in the oven so they could eat it when he returned to the apartment. Siena had just spent a fruitless half-hour trying to figure out which furturistic-looking steel appliance was the oven, to no avail.

She went back into the kitchen now, to try again, and started to go hot with embarrassment at her pathetic failing when she still couldn't figure it out. Her father had forbidden Siena and her sister ever to go near the kitchen of the *palazzo,* considering it a sign of a lack of class should either of his daughters ever know its ins and outs.

Before Siena had a chance to explore further she heard the

apartment door open and close and distinctive strong footfalls. She tensed and knew Andreas had to be in the doorway, looking at her. She turned around slowly and fought to hide her reaction to seeing him in the flesh again, dressed in a dark suit. His sheer good looks and charisma reached out to grab her by the throat. She could feel her body responding, as if it had been plugged into an energy source coming directly from him to her.

Siena retreated into attack to disguise her discomfiture. She lifted her chin and crossed her arms. 'I didn't put the beef in the oven because I refuse to be your housekeeper.'

Andreas regarded her from the doorway. Siena noticed that his jaw was darkly stubbled in the soft light. He was so intensely masculine and her blood jumped in response.

'Well, then,' he said with deceptive lightness as he came further into the room, his hair gleaming under the lights, 'I hope you had a decent lunch today. Because I refuse to be your chef just because you can't be bothered to take something out of the fridge and put it in the oven.'

At that moment Siena felt an absurd rush of self-pity. She was actually starving, because she'd only had a sandwich earlier, but she clamped her mouth shut because she knew she was acting abominably. And if she had no intention of telling him why then she had no one to blame but herself. She would spend all day tomorrow working out where the blasted oven was and how to work it even if it killed her.

Lying through her teeth, and trying desperately not to look at the succulent lump of meat he was taking out of the fridge, Siena said loftily, 'I'm not hungry anyway. In fact I'm quite tired. It's been a long day. I'm going to go to my room, if you have no objections.'

Andreas looked up from his ministrations and said easily, 'Oh, I object all right. I think you could do with being forced to watch me eat after your pettish spoilt behaviour, but the expression on your face might put me off my food.'

He went on coolly. 'As it happens I have some work to continue here this evening…so feel free to entertain yourself. You don't have to confine yourself to your room Siena, like some kind of martyr.'

She turned and walked out, not liking the way Andreas was dealing with preparing himself dinner so dextrously. It caused something to flutter deep inside her. She didn't like these little signs that Andreas couldn't be boxed away so neatly.

She was about to go towards her room when she found herself seeking out the more informal sitting area that Andreas had shown her the previous evening. She forced herself to relax in front of the TV, even though she really wanted to escape to her room and avoid any more contact with Andreas.

A short time later Andreas gave up any attempt to work. It was impossible when he knew that Siena was somewhere nearby. He shook his head again at her spoilt behaviour. He didn't know why it had surprised him, but it *had*. It was as if some stubborn part of him was still clinging onto the false image of that sweet girl in Paris, before she'd morphed into the spoilt heiress.

He got up and put his cleared dinner plate in the dishwasher in the kitchen, noticing as he did that nothing else had been touched. His mouth flattened into a hard line at this further evidence of Siena's stubborness. She was too proud for her own good. He walked back out and stopped when he heard the faint sound of canned laughter. He followed the sound and found Siena curled up on the couch, fast asleep. Her lashes cast long dark shadows on her cheeks.

Absently Andreas found the remote and switched the TV show off. Siena stirred but didn't wake. He'd been blocking out how it had felt to see her in his kitchen when he'd come home earlier. Dressed in softly worn jeans and a T-shirt. Hair in a ponytail. Bare feet. He wasn't sure what he'd expected but it hadn't been that. He wasn't used to women dressing down, but told himself that she was obviously making a petty point, refusing to make an effort for him.

He knew Siena had seen the beautician, and inevitably his mind wandered to the parts of her body that would be sleek, smooth. He hadn't noticed any discernible physical difference but then, he reminded himself cynically, it was hard to improve on perfection. And even as she was now, asleep on a couch in jeans and a T-shirt, she *was* perfection.

Andreas saw her hands now and bent down. They looked softer already, and he could see that her bitten nails had been cleaned up, but they had been filed very short. He felt that constriction in his chest again at noticing that.

And then suddenly she was awake, looking up at him with those huge startling blue eyes. For a moment something crackled between them, alive and powerful. And then he saw Siena register where she was and with whom. The way she grew tense and her eyes became wary. He straightened up.

Siena struggled to a sitting position, more than discomfited to find Andreas watching her so coolly while she slept. 'What time is it?' Her voice felt scratchy.

He flicked a glance at his watch. 'After midnight.'

Siena stood up and only realised then how close she was to Andreas, and how tall he was when she was in bare feet. 'I should go to bed.'

'Yes,' he observed. 'You seem to be extremely tired. It must have been all that pampering and choosing dresses today.'

Siena was about to protest at the unfairness of his attack, and inform him of just how hard she had been working, but the words died in her throat. He was too close all of a sudden, those dark navy eyes looking at her and reminding her of another time when they'd stood so close and she'd breathed, *'Andreas...'*

She moved back suddenly, but forgot about the couch behind her and felt herself falling back. With the reflexes of a panther Andreas reached out and circled her waist with his hands, hauling her against him.

The breath whooshed out of Siena's mouth. Her hands were on his chest and he felt hot to the touch even through his shirt. 'What...' Her mouth went dry at the thought that he might kiss her. 'What are you doing?'

'What I'm doing, Siena, is...' He stopped and the moment stretched between them.

Siena fancied she could hear both their hearts beating in unison. In that moment she wanted him with a sudden fierce longing deep in her abdomen. She was mesmerised by his mouth. She wanted him to kiss her. And that knowledge burned inside her...

'...letting you go to bed.'

# CHAPTER FIVE

ANDREAS HAD PUT Siena away from him before she'd realised what he was doing and instantly she felt foolish. She blushed and he raised a brow.

'That really is some skill—to be able to blush at will. But you forget that it's wasted on me, Siena. I'm a sure thing. You don't have to pretend with me.'

Siena's betraying flush increased—with anger now. 'That's good to know. I won't waste my energy, then.'

She whirled around to leave but was caught when Andreas reached out to take her hand. Electricity shot up her arm. She looked back warily.

'Actually, I have something for you. Come with me.'

Curious, Siena followed Andreas into his huge dimly lit study. It was a beautiful room, very masculine, with floor-to-ceiling shelves that heaved with books. He had the latest high-spec computers and printers.

He'd gone to a picture in the corner and pulled it out from the wall to reveal that it hid a safe. He entered the combination and pulled out a long velvet box. He came over and opened it, so that Siena could see that it was a stunningly simple yet obviously very expensive diamond bracelet.

Her heart thumped once, hard, and she felt a little sick. Andreas was taking it out and reaching for her wrist so that he could put it on. He said coolly, 'You've been here for one night already. I don't see why I can't reward you.'

Feeling very prickly, and not liking the way the cool platinum and stones sat against her pale wrist, winking brilliantly, Siena said acerbically, 'You don't have to reward me as if I'm a child, Andreas.'

He dropped her wrist and looked at her, his eyes turning dark. 'I know you're not a child, Siena. I'm rewarding you because you asked me to. Tomorrow evening we are going to a charity function in town…tonight will be the last night you sleep alone.'

Trepidation and fear were immediate. The thought of being seen and recognised, having people point and whisper about the disgraced DePieros… But Siena wouldn't let Andreas see how much it terrified her, or let him see how even more terrifying she found the thought that this time tomorrow night she would be in his bed…

Siena backed away. 'I can't wait.'

She'd almost got to the door when Andreas called her name again. She took a deep breath and turned around.

'I've arranged for one of London's top jewellers to come to the apartment tomorrow morning.' His jaw tightened. 'You can choose a selection of jewels to your hard little heart's content.'

Siena said nothing. She suddenly looked starkly pale and whirled around, walking quickly out of the room. Andreas watched her go and had to relax his hands because they'd clenched to fists. Once again he wasn't sure what kind of reaction he'd expected, but it hadn't been that.

He had to take a deep breath, and he wondered why he wasn't following his base instincts and taking her here and now. Either on the couch earlier, or here in his office. Or following her to her bedroom. She was here. She was his. She was making him pay for it. But he wouldn't do it now. Because she made him feel a little wild and out of control.

She reminded him far too easily of the raw, ambitious young man he'd once been. Desperate to be a part of the world she'd so easily inhabited because he'd believed that if he was, then he'd truly be as far away from stagnating in his home town as he could possibly be. But he'd changed since then. Being forced into exile had made him appreciate his home and where he came from. It had given him a more balanced view.

He might not want to be a part of his family's cosy, settled world, but he respected it and their choices. A tiny voice mocked him, reminding him that sometimes when he went back now he found himself feeling a pang when he saw the interaction between his sisters and their husbands and children. It even made him feel slightly threatened—as if, if he stayed too long, everything he'd worked for would disappear and he'd become that young man again, with nothing to his name.

He would not let Siena bring back those memories or reduce him to such baseness. She'd done it once before, before he'd even realised what was happening, and she'd torn his world apart.

No, he would be urbane and civilised—all the things he'd become since he'd stood before her in Paris and been made to feel utterly helpless, at the mercy of the huge emotions seething inside his gut. She didn't have that power over him any more and she never would.

Back in her room, Siena struggled to get the diamond bracelet off but refused to go and ask Andreas for help. She was far too volatile when in close proximity to him. Finally it sprang free and Siena put it down with a kind of fascinated horror. He'd given her a diamond bracelet—just like that. Tomorrow he'd be giving her a lot more. And tomorrow night…

Siena sank back down onto the end of the bed and crossed her arms over her belly.

She wanted to hate Andreas for this…but she had no real

reason to hate him. So he'd used her five years ago, when she'd all but thrown herself at him...? What young red-blooded man wouldn't have done the same? It wasn't his fault it had meant nothing to him. She was the one who had imbued the situation with a silly fantasy that something special had happened between them. Had he deserved to lose his job and be beaten up over it? *No.*

She shivered when she thought of that young beaten man, getting on his bike to ride away that dawn morning, and the man he'd become now. For a second that morning, despite his anger, Siena had had a fantasy of getting on the back of that bike with him and fleeing into the dawning light. If she hadn't had to think of her sister she might well have done it.

Siena knew very well that if Andreas hadn't stopped kissing her the other night in her flat he would have had her there and then, realised that she was woefully inexperienced, and most likely walked away without a backward glance, having satisfied his curiosity and his desire for revenge. Treacherously, that thought didn't fill her with the kind of relief it ought to.

What happened to her when he touched her was scary. It was as if he short-circuited her ability to think rationally. When she'd woken on the couch earlier and found him staring at her she'd reacted viscerally: her blood humming and her body coming alive. There hadn't been a moment's hesitation in that acceptance. And then she'd realised where she was and why and reality had come tumbling back...

Andreas's restraint towards her told her that he was in far more control of this situation than she was. The thought of going out in public...the thought of Andreas making love to her... Siena would have to call on that well-worn icy public persona—the one her father had so approved of because it made her seem untouchable and aloof. Desirable. Unattainable.

She clenched her hands to fists. The only problem was,

she was all too attainable. The minute Andreas touched her *aloof* and *icy* went out of the window to be replaced with heat and insanity.

Much to Siena's relief, when she woke and went exploring in the morning there was no sign of Andreas initially—but her skin prickled with that preternatural awareness that told her he was somewhere in the apartment. She figured he might be in his study, and made sure to avoid going near it.

To her added relief there was an array of breakfast things left out in the kitchen, but she didn't like the way her belly swooped at the thought that he'd done this for her. She poured herself some coffee, which was still hot, and took a croissant with some preserves over to the table and sat down.

'Nice of you to join the land of the living. I was beginning to think I might need a bucket of cold water to wake you.'

Siena looked up and nearly choked on her croissant. She hadn't even heard him coming in, and to see him dressed in jeans and a dark polo shirt moulded to his impressive chest was sending tendrils of sensation through every vein in her body.

She swallowed with difficulty, but before she could say anything Andreas was looking at his watch and saying, with not a little acerbity, 'Well, it *is* ten a.m., I expect this is relatively early for you?'

Siena fought down a wave of hurt as she thought of how hard she'd been working for the last few months. Usually by now she'd have done half a day's work. But of course he was referring to her previous life. In fact she'd always been an early riser, up before anyone else. What she wasn't used to, however, was the current exhaustion she was feeling, thanks to the unaccustomed hard work. And that made her angry at herself for being so weak.

She kept all of this hidden and said to Andreas sweetly,

'Well, I'd hate to disappoint you. Tomorrow I can make it midday, if you like?'

He prowled closer, after helping himself to more coffee, and said, 'I'd like it very much if we were in bed together till one o'clock.'

It took a monumental effort not to react to his provocative statement. He was so *audacious*. He sat down at the table, long legs stretched out, far too close to Siena's. She fought the urge to move her own legs.

'Yes, well, I can't imagine you neglecting your business to that level.' After all, she knew well how her father had consistently relegated his children to the periphery, only to be trotted out for social situations.

She looked away from that far too provocatively close rangy body and concentrated on eating the croissant.

'Don't worry,' Andreas commented drily, 'my business is doing just fine.'

Siena flashed back, 'At the expense of all those poor people who are losing their jobs just because of your insatiable ambition.'

Andreas's eyes narrowed on her and Siena cursed herself. Now she'd exposed herself as having followed his progress.

'So you read the papers? I would have thought that you should know better than to believe everything you read in print. And since when have you been concerned with the *poor people?*'

There was ice in his tone, but also something more ambiguous that sounded like injured pride, and Siena felt momentarily confused. A sliver of doubt pierced her. Weren't those stories true?

Andreas uncoiled his tall length, and stood up, going to the sink, where he washed out his cup—a small domestic gesture that surprised Siena.

He turned and said, 'The jeweller will be here shortly.'

He'd walked out before Siena could respond, and she watched his broad back and tall body disappear, radiating tension. She felt wrong-footed. As if she should apologise!

Siena took her things to the sink, where she washed up perfunctorily and thought churlishly that at least she could figure out the taps. Just as she was turning to leave an older lady walked in, smiling brightly. 'Morning, dear! You must be Ms DePiero. I'm Mrs Bright, the housekeeper.'

Siena smiled awkwardly and said, 'Please call me Siena…'

As accomplished as she was in social situations, Siena was an innately shy person and came forward faltering slightly. The older woman met her halfway and took her hand in a warm handshake, smiling broadly. Siena liked her immediately and smiled back.

Siena wisely took the opportunity to ask Mrs Bright about the kitchen, and liked the woman even more when her eyes rolled up to heaven and she said in a broad Scots accent, 'I thought I'd need a degree in rocket science to figure it all out, but it's actually very simple once you know.'

When Siena explained about the previous evening Mrs Bright said conspiratorially, 'Don't worry, pet. I couldn't work out which one was the oven either at first.'

Unbeknown to the two women, who were now bent down by the oven, Andreas had come back to the doorway. He listened for a moment and then said abruptly, 'The jeweller is here, Siena.'

The two women turned around and he could see the dull flush climbing up Siena's neck. He flashed back to the previous evening, when he'd found her looking so defiant in the kitchen, refusing to put the meat in the oven.

She said thank you to the housekeeper and walked over to him. Andreas caught her arm just as she was about to pass and said, *sotto voce,* 'You didn't know where the oven was. Why didn't you just tell me?'

He could see Siena's throat work, saw that flush climb higher, and felt curiously unsteady on his feet.

Eventually she bit out, avoiding his eye, 'I thought you'd find it funny.'

Andreas didn't find it funny in the least. He said, 'You could have told me, Siena. I'm not an ogre.'

Siena was trembling by the time they got to the drawing room, where Andreas had directed her. Two small men were waiting for them, with lots of cases and boxes around them and an array of jewels laid out on a table before them. Siena noticed a security guard in the corner of the room. She felt sick.

Later that evening Siena was waiting for Andreas. He'd gone to his office that morning after the jewellery show-and-tell, and she'd been left with a small ransom's worth of jewellery. A special safe had been installed in Andreas's office just for her use.

She still felt jittery. Andreas had insisted that to fully appreciate whether or not the jewellery was suitable Siena should get changed into an evening gown. He'd led her, protesting, into her dressing room and picked out a long black strapless dress.

'Put this on.'

Siena had hissed, 'I will not. Don't be so ridiculous. I'll know perfectly well what will suit me and what won't.'

'Well, seeing as I'm paying for the privilege of your company this week, I'd like to see you try out the jewellery in more suitable garb than jeans and a T-shirt—which, by the way, I expect to be in the bin by the end of today.'

'You're just doing this to humiliate me.' Siena had crossed her arms mulishly and glared at Andreas, who had looked back, supremely relaxed.

'Put the dress on, Siena, and put your hair up. Or I'll do it for you. I'll give you five minutes.'

With that chilling command he'd turned and walked out of

the room. Siena had fumed and resolved to do no such thing. But then an image of Andreas, striding back into her room and bodily divesting her of her jeans and T-shirt, had made her go hot. He wouldn't, she'd assured herself. But a small voice had sniggered in her head. *Of course he would.*

Gritting her teeth and repeating her mantra—*one week, one week*—Siena folded her jeans and T-shirt into her small suitcase, with no intention of following his autocratic command to throw them away, and slipped on the dress. It was simple in the way that only the best designer dresses could be, and beautifully made. Gathered under her bust in an Empire line, it flowed in soft silken and chiffon folds to the floor.

The bodice part of it clung to her breasts, making them seem fuller, and was cut in such a way as to enhance her cleavage. Siena had felt naked. Her father would never have allowed her to wear something so revealing…so sensual.

She'd pulled her hair back into a ponytail and returned to the salon barefoot. When the two jewellers had stood up on her return Siena had barely noticed, only aware of the dark blue, heavy-lidded gaze that had travelled down her body with a look so incendiary she'd almost stumbled.

Andreas had taken her hand and pulled her in beside him on a small two-seater couch, his muscular thigh far too close to hers through the flimsy covering of her dress. His arm had moved around her, his fingers grazing the bare skin of her shoulder, drawing small circles, making her breath quicken and awareness pierce her deep inside.

She'd cursed him and tried to move away—only to have him clamp his hand to her waist, pulling her even more firmly against him, so that her breasts had been crushed to his side and she'd been acutely aware of how hard his chest felt. The way his big hand curled possessively around her, fingers grazing her belly.

The jewellery itself had been a blur of glittering golds and diamonds, pearls, sapphires and emeralds. Andreas had picked things out and taken Siena's wrist to slip jewelled bracelets on, before adding them to a growing pile. When he'd put necklaces around her neck his hands had trailed softly across her bare shoulders, his fingers lightly touching her collarbone. Siena's face had flamed. It had felt like such an intimate touch.

She had tried to hold herself as rigidly as possible, aghast at how much it was affecting her to be subjected to what were relatively chaste touches. They'd been under the beady eyes of the jewellers, but Siena had had to remind herself they were being observed.

Losing count of the mounting pile of jewellery, Siena had been ready to scream by the time Andreas had tried a simple platinum and diamond necklace and matching bracelet on her and said, 'Wear this dress and these jewels tonight.'

She had bitten back a retort—a knee-jerk reaction to being dictated to. Her new-found sense of independence had surged forth, but then she'd reminded herself that he'd bought her. Therefore he could have her any which way he wanted. She'd had a very disturbing image of herself, naked, splayed across Andreas's bed, dressed in nothing but all these jewels.

When Andreas had finally declared himself satisfied the other men had started to gather up the remaining jewellery. But Siena had spotted something out of the corner of her eye. A flash of something delicate and golden. Before she could stop herself she'd reached out to touch the necklace, hidden in folds of velvet.

As she'd lifted it out it had become clear that it didn't have the same glittering *wow* factor of the other gems, but it was exquisite: a simple golden chain with a wrought-gold birdcage detail. The tiny filigree door was open and further up the chain was a bird flying, suspended. Siena's belly had clenched. Something about the bird flying out of its cage had resonated deeply within her.

The senior jeweller had cleared his throat uneasily. 'That's actually not meant to be part of the display we brought today. It was included by accident. It's by a Greek jeweler…'

'Angel Parnassus.' Siena had said, half absently. She knew the famous delicately crafted designs of the renowned jeweler and had always admired them.

'Yes…' the man had confirmed.

'We'll take that too,' Siena had heard Andreas say brusquely.

She'd started to protest, hating that Andreas had witnessed her momentary distraction and vulnerability. She'd looked at him and his eyes had been hard.

'It's a fraction of the price of the earrings you'll wear tonight. Have it if you like it so much, Siena.'

Siena hadn't wanted anything for *herself,* but she'd had no chance to speak. Andreas had already been standing up, shaking hands with the two men, seeing them out, leaving her with the necklace clutched in her hand.

Siena heard a noise now and tensed, her attention brought back to the present. Andreas had arrived a short while before, knocking on her door to check that she was nearly ready. When she'd swallowed the frog in her throat and assured him that she was, he'd disappeared—presumably to get ready himself. Siena was waiting in the drawing room, feeling ridiculously nervous at the thought of the evening ahead. This was a situation she'd never experienced before.

She was wearing the black dress, as decreed by Andreas. But when it had come to the jewels Siena had had a moment of rebellion. Instead of the diamond necklace and bracelet he'd wanted her to wear she'd picked out a bold diamond and sapphire necklace, with a matching cuff bracelet.

Somehow the brashness of the necklace felt like some kind of armour. But then Siena heard a familiar footfall behind her and any illusion of armour went out of the window.

* * *

When Siena turned to face Andreas he felt as if someone had just punched him in the belly. For a second he couldn't breathe. He'd dreamed of her so often like this…as he remembered her… Stunningly beautiful, elegantly aloof. Untouchable in a way that made him ache to touch her.

Her hair was drawn back and up into a high bun, effortlessly simple and yet the epitome of classic grace. Her make-up was understated, perfect. Nothing so brash as red lipstick. She didn't need it. The drama came from her cool blonde perfection.

His eyes narrowed on her necklace and a spurt of something hot went through him. 'You have defied me.'

Siena's chin hitched up minutely. 'You may have all but bought me for a week, but that does not mean I can't exercise some free will.'

Andreas inclined his head and tamped down on the hotness inside him. 'Indeed. That necklace is equally…beautiful.'

He had to admit that it set off her rather understated appearance with just the right amount of *élan.* The thick collar piece was studded with tiny diamonds and it curled around her neck and throat in a sinuous line down to where an enormous sapphire pendant hung against the creamy pale skin of her upper chest. The dark blue of the precious stone inevitably made the lighter blue of her eyes pop out.

Andreas pushed down the niggling vague doubts he'd had all day, ever since he'd overheard the conversation between her and Mrs Bright in the kitchen, when he'd learned that Siena had preferred to appear like a spoilt brat rather than reveal she didn't know where the oven was.

And then her reaction to the jewellery hadn't been the unmitigated greed and glee he'd expected to see. Siena had barely looked at the impressive array of jewellery, and the one thing that had caught her eye had been a simple gold pendant. Exquisite, yes, but not in the same league as the other jewels at all.

Andreas put such disturbing thoughts out of his head now. She hadn't shown much interest in the jewellery because she would be converting it all into cold hard cash within days. How could he forget that?

More importantly, by tonight all that cool, untouchable beauty would have come undone. She would be bucking against him and begging for release. She would no longer look so pristine. She would be as naked and sated as he intended to be. Flushed and marked by his passion.

His blood surged. He put out his hand. 'Come. It's time to go.'

A couple of hours later, after a sumptuous sit-down dinner, Siena was standing at Andreas's side and it felt as if her skin was slowly going on fire. Since he'd taken her hand in his in the apartment to lead her out he hadn't stopped touching her. Even if it was just a hand at the small of her back to guide her into the ultra-luxe Grand Wolfe Hotel, where the charity dinner banquet was taking place.

For someone who generally shied away from physical contact, because she'd never really experienced it growing up, Siena was dismayed at how much her body seemed to gravitate towards Andreas's touch. She wished pettily that she could break out in a rash, allergic to his touch.

'Drink?'

She looked at Andreas to see him holding out a glass of champagne. Siena shook her head. After a couple of glasses of wine with dinner, and an aperitif of Prosecco when they'd arrived, her head was feeling woozy enough. Andreas merely shrugged and put the glass back on a passing waiter's tray.

'Uncomfortable?'

Siena looked at Andreas again. For a second she thought

he meant in her dress or shoes, but then she saw the gleam in his eye and thought to herself, *Bastard.* She schooled her expression. 'I'm perfectly comfortable, thank you, considering the level of public interest in seeing who your new mistress is, and the realisation that she is one of the disgraced DePieros.'

Siena knew Andreas had to be aware of the way people had been looking and pointing all evening. The way a hush would fall when she came close, only to spark a flurry of whispers as they passed.

'Don't tell me it's actually *affecting* you? The debutante who so coldly excised a momentary mistake from her life?'

Andreas's voice was mocking and Siena held herself stiffly. She hadn't known just how much it would affect her to be in public again, exposed to people's excoriating judgement, but could she blame them? Even now as she caught someone's eye they looked away hurriedly.

Her voice was cool. 'Why would I deny you your moment of public retribution? No doubt this is highly entertaining for you.'

She turned and looked up into his face properly, making his hand which had been resting on the small of her back fall away. It was a tiny pathetic triumph.

'Perhaps,' she said, 'you should consider taking me to Rome to get the full effect of people's censure? After all, here in London I'm relatively unknown.'

Andreas's eyes flashed and he effortlessly put his arm around her and pulled her tight in against him, making Siena gasp softly. His body was so lean and hard. Like a wall of muscled steel. And against her belly she could feel the potent stirring of his body. Inside she went hot.

'I think it's time we danced.'

Before she could even remember what they'd been talking about Andreas was pulling Siena in his wake onto the dance floor, where other couples were already dancing in the seductively dim light. A very smooth jazz band were playing, but Siena hardly even registered the music as Andreas swung her round and into his arms, holding her close.

Siena tried to pull back in his embrace but it was impossible. His arm was a steel band high across her back and her hand was held high in his, against his chest. Dark blue eyes glittered down into hers and reminded her of the deep blue of the sapphire pendant that swung against her chest, the thought leaving a tart taste in her mouth. But even that couldn't impinge when she was this close to Andreas, breathing his evocative masculine scent deep.

Feeling his body harden even more against hers was rendering her completely defenceless. How could she remain immune to this level of sensual attack? This was his punishment, his revenge, right here on this dance floor. Making her mute with aching need and a burning desire which seemed to writhe within her like a coiled snake. Everything else fell away, and she was suddenly terrified that she wouldn't be able to contain this feeling. It was as if they were enclosed in a bubble, completely separate from everyone around them, even though Siena was dimly aware that Andreas was steering them expertly around the floor.

She'd danced with plenty of men since that debutante ball in Paris, usually propelled into their arms reluctantly by her father, but no dance had ever felt this raw or carnal. Andreas's hand on her back rested against bare skin and she could feel his fingers stroking rhythmically, making her legs weaken and the secret apex between them grow hot and wet.

This went far beyond what she'd felt that evening in Paris, when this same man had aroused her with just a look and a sexy smile. She'd been too young then to truly be able to handle everything he'd aroused within her. Now she knew he'd unleashed a completely alien part of her—a part of her that felt wild and needy, aching for something she'd never known before. She'd always found it so easy to be detached, contained, until she'd met him. And all that was rushing back now.

At that moment Andreas stopped, and Siena realised that the music had also stopped. The air crackled between them and Siena knew with a fatalistic feeling in her belly that this was it.

Eyes locked with hers, Andreas said huskily, 'It's time to go.'

Keeping her hand in his, Andreas swiftly negotiated their way off the dance floor. Siena felt as if she couldn't really breathe. Her skin prickled and felt hot. Her belly was tight. Somehow, magically, someone appeared to hand Siena her wrap, and she took it with both hands, pathetically grateful that Andreas wasn't touching her for just a second.

But then her hand was in his again and he was leading her out into the cool spring air. His car was already waiting by the kerb, its back door held open by a hotel doorman.

Once they were in the car it pulled away smoothly from the glittering hotel.

Andreas said curtly to his driver, 'Tom, some privacy, please.'

Instantly Siena saw the silent glide of the black partition cutting them off from the driver. She looked at Andreas and his eyes glowed in the dim light. He looked feral, wild, and her heart beat wildly in her chest.

'Come here,' he instructed throatily.

## CHAPTER SIX

PANIC GRIPPED SIENA. She wasn't ready for this. Threadily she answered, 'No.'

Andreas arched a brow. His voice was deceptively mild. 'No?'

Siena shook her head, and then words were tumbling out. 'Look, you can't just expect that I'm going to—'

But her words were stopped mid-flow when Andreas reached across almost lazily and took her by the waist. He slid her along the seat until their thighs were touching. His hands felt huge around her and her eyes were locked with his. The air around them felt heavy and dense, thick with something Siena didn't really understand.

But when Andreas raised his hands up her body, brushing against the curves of her breasts, and slanted his mouth across hers Siena understood what it was. It was desire, and suddenly she was alive with it. Humming all over. It thickened her blood, forcing it through veins and arteries, pooling low in her pelvis, between her legs.

Her hands had been up, almost in a gesture of self-defence, but now Siena found herself putting them on Andreas's chest, to balance herself when he tugged her forward so that she half lay across him. She couldn't concentrate, couldn't think beyond the hot slide of his mouth against hers, and her mouth opened of its own volition under his.

Their tongues touched and Siena's hands curled into his shirt, bunching it unconsciously, seeking something to hold onto when she felt as if she were falling down and down.

One of Andreas's hands went down to her back and pulled her into him, making her arch against him. She was dimly aware that his other hand had moved up, was undoing her hair so that it fell around her shoulders, sensitising nerve-ends that were already tingling.

The kiss grew hotter. Andreas's tongue stabbed deep. His hand was tangled in her hair now, and he pulled back gently so that he could claim even more access. Siena couldn't hear anything through the blood roaring in her head and ears. When Andreas's mouth left hers she heard a low moan and only seconds later realized it was coming from her.

By then his mouth was trailing hot kisses across her jaw and he was pulling her head back even more, to press his mouth against her throat and down to where she could feel her pulse beat against his tongue.

Siena had the barest sensation of her dress feeling looser before she realised that Andreas had pulled the zip down at the back. He lifted his head and leant back for a moment. Siena tried to force some air into her lungs, but they seized again when she felt him pull down the bodice of her dress to reveal one naked breast.

They were in a cocoon. Siena wasn't even aware of the city streets and lights as they glided through London. They could have been transported to another planet. She was only aware of herself as some very primal feminine being, and of Andreas as her masculine counterpart.

She saw Andreas's head dip down, felt his hot breath feather over an almost painfully tight nipple before his mouth closed around it. Siena sank back against the seat, every bone in her body melting at the exquisite tugging sensation that seemed to connect directly to where a pulse throbbed between her legs.

As if reading her mind, Andreas moved his hand under her dress and up her legs, pushing them apart. She was helpless to resist as he expertly pulled down the bodice of her dress completely and bared her other breast, to which he administered the same torture.

Everything was coalescing within Siena, building to some elusive crescendo of tension. Her hips were rolling and one of her hands was in Andreas's hair, fingers tangling in silken strands as she held him to her breast. Her other hand was clenched tight, and an ache of gigantic proportions was growing between her thighs.

Andreas's long fingers had found her panties and he was tugging them down over her hips. Siena was mindless, wanting Andreas to alleviate this exquisite tension inside her. Her hips lifted and he slid the black lace down her legs, over her feet in their vertiginous heels and off completely.

And then Andreas's mouth left her breast and he straightened up. It took a second for Siena to register that he was just looking at her. Her breasts were bared and throbbing slightly, wet from his mouth and heaving with her laboured breath. Her dress was hiked up almost to her waist and her legs were parted. She saw her flimsy lace panties dangle from his fingers, and then he put them in the pocket of his jacket.

Siena's tongue felt thick. 'What are you doing?'

It was only then that she realised how pristine Andreas looked in his jacket and tie, barely a hair out of place. Far too belatedly she scrabbled with numb hands to pull her dress up over her breasts and down over her thighs.

'I'm making sure there's no delay once we get inside.'

*Inside.* It was only then that Siena became aware that they were outside his apartment building and the young valet was approaching the door of the car. Siena felt Andreas push her forward slightly, the brush of his fingers against her back as he pulled her zip up. Then he was handing her her wrap and the door was opened.

By the time she was out in the cool air she was incandescent with rage—not only at Andreas, but at herself for being so weak. When Andreas touched her back to guide her into the building she jerked away from him. She all but ran to the door and yanked it open before he could open it for her, making straight for the lift, punching the button with unnecessary force. Andreas was a tall dark presence beside her which she ignored.

When they stepped into the lift Siena moved to one corner and resolutely looked forward. To her absolute horror she could feel heat prickling at the backs of her eyes and her throat tightening. She willed down the emotion which had sprung up with every fibre of her being and swept out of the lift when the doors opened.

When Andreas joined her and opened the apartment door he had barely shut it behind him when she rounded on him, hands curled into fists.

'How *dare* you?'

Andreas looked so cool and composed and Siena was completely undone. Her hair was around her shoulders and she'd never felt more vulnerable.

'How dare I what, Siena? Kiss you?' His mouth twisted. 'How could I *not* have kissed you? Don't you know by now that I have a fatal attraction to your unique brand of remote aloofness?'

Siena could have laughed out loud. She'd never felt less remote or aloof. Right then she hated Andreas with a passion that scared her with its intensity.

She couldn't stop the words tumbling out. 'I hate you.'

'Be careful, Siena,' he mocked, 'Love is just the other side of hate, and we wouldn't want you falling for me, now, would we?'

Siena spluttered. '*Fall* for you? I couldn't think of anything less likely to happen.' Her words fell into a hole inside her and echoed painfully.

Siena lifted her chin, determined to get off that disturbing topic and claw back some control. 'I am not going to be ritually humilated by you, whenever and wherever it takes your fancy.'

Andreas prowled closer and drew Siena's lace panties from his pocket, holding them up. Siena died a small death.

'It takes two to tango, Siena, and you were with me every second of the way back there. To be honest I hadn't expected you to be a back seat of the car kind of woman.'

Siena lifted her hand to grab her underwear but Andreas snatched them back out of her reach and then deposited the lacy scrap of material back into his pocket. Without realising he'd even moved, Siena found herself with her back against the main door of the apartment, her wrist held high in Andreas's hand, above her head. He was pressing against her and she could feel herself responding to that tall muscular length all over again. The heated insanity of what had happened came back in lurid Technicolor.

'Let me go,' Siena gritted out, desperately afraid of how susceptible she was.

He shook his head and his eyes glowed like dark jewels. 'Never. You're mine now, Siena, until I say so.'

And then he bent his head and his mouth found hers, and when she tried to turn her head away he only brought his free hand to her head and held her there, captive, as he kissed and stroked her weak resistance away with his clever tongue.

Siena was so full of turbulent emotions and sensations that it was almost a relief to give in to the sheer physicality of the moment. Here, with Andreas kissing her like this, she couldn't think. And she didn't want to.

When he finally released her hand she found herself, not pushing him away but clutching his shoulders, before finding that her hand was sneaking underneath his jacket, to push it off.

Their mouths were fused together, tongues a tangle of heated lust, and when Andreas removed his hands so that he could shrug off his jacket Siena sought and found his bow-tie, undoing it so that she could open the top button of his shirt.

In some very dim place she told herself that she had a desire to see him as undone as she felt, but in truth she just had a growing need to see him naked.

Siena felt her zip being pulled down again, and it was almost a relief to have her breasts freed. Andreas's mouth and tongue was a potent memory. She wanted to feel him again. Her hands took his head, guiding him away from her mouth and down…

Only minutes after she'd stood in front of him, vowing she hated him, Andreas's mouth was on her breast and Siena was once again reduced to some writhing wanton. But her mind skittered weakly away from that anomaly.

Siena felt feverish. Her legs were weak. But she couldn't move. Andreas had straightened and was opening his shirt, ripping it off, and Siena's eyes grew huge and round as she took in his olive-skinned magnificence. Not an ounce of fat. All lean muscle. Flat brown nipples enticed her to lean forward and touch with her tongue, exploring his salty taste.

Andreas groaned softly and slid his hand into her hair. After a minute of her mouth torturing him with some pseudo-innocent touch she must have learned somewhere Andreas dragged her head back. Her mouth was open, she was panting slightly, and her eyes were wide and slumberous, pupils dilated. His erection thickened and with an impatient hand he undid his belt and zip, pulling down his trousers and his briefs with them. He had to have Siena *now.* He couldn't even move from this spot. He was aware that he was about to take her exactly as he'd fantasised five years ago, standing up, like some kind of feral animal. But he didn't care.

All he could see was that white-blonde hair tumbled over bare shoulders, her full round breasts, flushed and moist from his touch and his mouth. All he could think about was how her nipples had felt against his tongue—tight and puckered—the way she'd moaned when he touched her there.

Feeling ruthless, Andreas kicked away his clothes. He was naked now, and Siena's eyes grew bigger as she looked down his body, making him throb with a need to be inside her, thrusting up into the tight core of her body, seeking his release. Finally.

Cursing softly, having a flash of clarity at the last moment, Andreas reached down and pulled protection from his jacket, fumbling in a way he hadn't in a long time as he ripped it open and stroked the rubber along his length.

The scent of Siena's arousal hit him like a ton of bricks and, unable to stop himself, he fell to his knees before her, pulling her dress down all the way until it pooled at her feet in a tangle of chiffon and lace. Now she wore only her shoes, and Andreas removed them, hearing her husky, hesitant-sounding entreaty.

*'Andreas...'*

He ignored it.

His need was too strong to resist.

She was more than he could have ever imagined in his fantasies. Long slender limbs, pale all over. A triangle of blonde curls between her legs. Andreas knelt there and parted her thighs. He could feel her resistance but said gutturally, 'Let me taste you.'

After a second when her legs trembled so lightly he might have imagined it her resistance faltered and Andreas bared her to him, his mouth and tongue seeking and finding her essence, revelling in her sweetly musky smell and taste.

Her hand was in his hair, gripping tightly enough to be

painful, but it only fired him up even more. He could feel his erection strain against its rubber confinement between his legs and knew he couldn't wait. There would be more time to savour her later. But now he had to have her. He had to be buried so deep inside her that he would forget his own name.

Andreas surged up and just managed to catch Siena before she collapsed. He wrapped his arms around her, feeling her back arch into him, her breasts crushed against his chest.

'Wrap your legs around my waist,' he instructed roughly.

Siena put her arms around his neck, and then her legs were wrapped around his waist. Andreas hitched her up and rested her back against the door, so that it would take some of her weight, even though she felt as light as a feather.

Holding her with one arm, he reached down between them and ran his finger along her cleft. *She was so wet.* It nearly undid him there and then. He spread his legs and positioned himself, taking himself in his hand and guiding the head of his erection to those moist folds of flesh.

Andreas forced himself to curb the desire to thrust so far and so deep he'd find instant release. He was more than that. He wouldn't let her do this to him. He found her mouth and braced himself, before thrusting up and into the giving wet clasp of her body.

He felt her open-mouthed gasp of surprise before he registered that he'd felt an impediment to his movement. Sweat broke out on his brow. He drew away and looked at Siena, every nerve and muscle protesting at this interruption.

'What…?'

Siena was pale, and the unmistakable light of shock shone in her eyes. Stripped bare of that hazy pleasure he'd seen a moment ago. He flexed his buttocks and saw her wince as he moved a bit deeper. Her arms tightened around his neck. Andreas felt something cold prickle at his neck. It couldn't be possible… The information simply wouldn't compute…

He spoke out loud. 'You can't be…'

Siena was biting her lip now, and Andreas saw the sheen of moisture in her eyes. It was as if a two-ton lorry had crashed into his chest. He started to withdraw, but as he did he saw that moisture fade and a light of determination come into those glorious eyes.

She tightened her legs around his waist. 'No.' Her voice sounded raw. 'Don't stop.'

It hurt to breathe, but Andreas managed to get out, 'I'll hurt you…if we move—'

'No.' Siena's legs tightened even more. 'We do this. Here. Now. Just the way you said you wanted to five years ago…'

Andreas's brain felt as if it would explode. He was caught between heaven and hell. Siena's musky scent was all around him, her body clasped him, but not in the way he knew it could. He cried out for release.

And there was something so…*determined* about her. The fact that she was still a virgin was too much to process right now.

Andreas gave in. 'Try to relax your muscles…it'll be easier…'

He could see how she concentrated and he felt her body allowing him to go deeper. He all but groaned out loud at the exquisite sensation. She was so tight around him, almost painfully tight.

Moving her slightly, he bent his head and drew one taut nipple into his mouth, rolling it, sucking it back to life. He could feel what it did to Siena when her body relaxed even more, and with an exploratory move Andreas thrust a little higher. She hitched in a breath but he could sense that it wasn't a breath of pain. It was a breath of awareness.

When he lifted his head to look at her again she was not pale any more. She was flushed, biting her lip again. Slowly he withdrew from her body and then thrust back in, going even deeper this time.

Her hips twitched against his. She was breathing heavily now, saying almost against her will, 'I feel so full…'

'I know…just let me…trust me…it'll ease.'

Andreas was surprised he could string a sentence together. His world was reduced to this moment, this woman, this inexorable slide of his body in and out of hers. His passage was becoming easier and sweeter with every second. Siena's head fell back against the door and he could see her eyes closing.

Andreas put his hand to her chin and tugged it down. 'Look at me…Siena.'

She opened her eyes and they were feverish. With a feeling of triumph Andreas felt the ripples of her body around his as the onset of her orgasm approached. Ruthlessly he held his own desperate need for release at bay and pushed her higher and higher, seeing how her eyes widened, her cheeks flushed deep red. Her lips were engorged with blood. Her breasts were flushed, nipples like tight berries.

Somewhere in his head a voice crowed, *She's undone.* But it barely broke through Andreas's single-minded need to drive her over the edge. And when she fell it was spectacular. Her eyes grew even wider. She stopped breathing. Her whole body grew as taut as a string on a bow and then he saw the moment she fell and felt her body clench so tightly around his in waves of spasms that he was helpless except to allow his own release to finally break free.

He could do nothing but close his eyes and bury his head in her breast. Their laboured breathing sounded harsh in the silence of the foyer. His body pulsed within hers minutely. He felt her grip around his neck grow slack as if she couldn't hold on any more.

Eventually Andreas found some strength from somewhere and straightened. Siena was avoiding his eyes now, and she winced slightly as he pulled free and helped her to stand. Their clothes were strewn around them in chaotic abandon, but she still wore the necklace and bracelet.

Andreas had a sudden visceral need to take the jewellery off Siena. It was a reminder that wasn't welcome now. He undid the clasp of the necklace, letting it fall heavily into his hand, and then the bracelet. They clinked together with a hollow sound.

The sound of the jewellery knocking together seemed to resonate deep within Siena. Avoiding looking at Andreas, she bent down to pick up her dress, holding it against her like a very ineffectual shield. Resounding in her head with crystal clarity was the fact that she'd just lost her virginity to this man while standing up, against the door of his apartment.

She could remember the moment when she'd thought he was about to pull away, perhaps to take her into the bedroom. There'd been a look in his eyes that had threatened to shatter something inside her. And then the memory of that dawn morning in Paris, when Andreas had admitted that he'd wanted to take her up against the wall of the dressing room had rushed back.

Siena had seized on it and fought against the pull to make this easier…to be taken to surroundings more conducive for making love for the first time. Because this was not about romance.

She didn't want to think of the deeply disturbing emotion which had surged the moment he'd joined their bodies. That had made her feel weak and tender.

'*Theos,* Siena…' Andreas rasped. 'You were a virgin. Why didn't you tell me?'

She looked at Andreas and paled when she saw the look on his face, relieved to see that he'd pulled on his trousers. She couldn't handle him naked. Desperate to convince him it meant nothing, so that she could consider what it *did* mean in a private space on her own, she shrugged. 'It's no big deal. I was a virgin and now I'm not.'

Andreas's mouth twisted. 'So your father really was going to offer you up to a crusty blue-blooded relic like some virginal sacrifice?'

Siena's chest tightened. That was exactly what he'd planned. 'Yes,' she whispered, her bravado slipping. 'Something like that.'

Andreas cursed and Siena tried to avoid looking at his bare chest. It reminded her of how it had felt, crushed against her breasts.

'You should have told me, Siena…' he grated. 'If I'd even suspected you were innocent I'd have gone slower…been more gentle.'

'I'm fine,' Siena muttered, picking up her shoes, still avoiding looking at Andreas.

The air around them smelled of something unfamiliar but heady. *Sex.* Siena was too overwhelmed even to acknowledge that after the initial pain it had transcended anything she might have imagined.

She saw Andreas's bare feet come into her line of vision and gulped. As his finger tipped up her chin her eyes moved up and took in the fact that his top button was open, revealing that tantalising line of hair which led down— Her gaze landed on his face.

She felt the urge to strike first and said, 'Don't look so shocked just because I was a virgin, Andreas.'

He was angry, eyes blazing now. 'If I'd known I would never have taken you like that…'

'Why?' she taunted. 'It's exactly how you wanted to take me before—I didn't want to deny you the chance to fulfil your fantasy.'

Siena heard the words but wasn't really sure where on earth

the nerve to say them was coming from. She saw Andreas's face turn expressionless, shuttered. He took his hand away and stepped back, making Siena feel bereft.

'You should have a bath. You're likely to be sore.'

Siena was a lot more intimidated by this cool specimen than the anger Andreas had just displayed. The idea that he might have cared enough about her innocence to make it a more pleasurable experience was…

Before she could say anything else that might betray her, Siena fled.

Andreas watched Siena retreat and cursed silently. He'd expected that after making love to her, *finally,* he would be feeling a whole lot more sated and at peace. It was laughable. He'd never felt less sated and at peace. He wanted her again—*now.* Wanted to taste that lush, mutinous mouth, to make her eyes widen with desire again. Wanted to watch her tumble over the edge and feel her body clamp around his with those spasms of orgasm.

Andreas ran a hand through his hair impatiently and then bent to pick up the rest of his own clothes. Under the stinging hot needles of his shower a few minutes later he cursed again, volubly. He certainly hadn't intended on mauling Siena in the back of his car, but by the time they'd been pulling up outside his apartment and he'd realised what he was doing he'd had her panties in his hand, ready to take her there and then in the back seat.

From some distant area of his brain he'd managed to find something to mutter to make it sound as if he'd fully intended divesting her of her underwear so that they could continue where they left off as soon as as they were in a private space. Outside the car, though, she'd all but spat at him—and could he blame her? He'd never been so unrestrained with a woman.

He should have remembered that evening in Paris. Remembered how she was capable of making him lose all sense of civility. But when they'd danced in that hotel… Andreas had been sorely tempted to drag her into the lobby, demand a suite and take her upstairs right there. It was little wonder he'd been unable to resist touching her in the back of the car… she'd been melting into him like his hottest fantasy and he'd been lost.

Andreas switched off his shower with a curt flick of his wrist. *Siena had been a virgin.* He looked at himself in the mirror and saw how fiercely his eyes glittered.

It was the one thing he had not expected in a million years. A lot of his bitterness about what had happened in Paris had centered around the belief that Siena had knowingly seduced him because she was bored…and experienced. But she'd been a virgin. And what virgin got hot and heavy with a hotel duty manager? He knew damn well that if they hadn't been interrupted he would have discovered her innocence that night.

He recalled her pale face when she'd bumped into him the following morning. The way she'd looked when he'd told her how he should have taken her up against the wall of the dressing room. He'd said that because he'd felt like such a fool. Because he'd felt exposed, betrayed. Because he'd believed she was experienced, like all those other scarily worldly-wise debutantes.

The irony of it was Siena had been the real deal. Probably the only one there. And how in hell had she stayed a virgin till now? Andreas wanted to smash something with his fist.

He heard a faint noise from outside his bathroom and hitched a towel around his waist before going out. Siena was standing in the centre of the room, in a voluminous towelling robe, hair damp, and his body reacted instantaneously.

His recent unwelcome revelations made Andreas say curtly, 'Yes?'

He saw how Siena tensed and it only made him want to snarl more—but not at her. At himself.

'I just want you to know that it didn't mean anything…the

fact that you were my…first. And you're right, I should have told you. But I thought…'

Andreas saw her falter and bite her lip for a second. She looked almost unbelievably vulnerable. Then she went on, 'I thought you wouldn't notice, I didn't realise it would be so… obvious.'

Siena wanted the ground to swallow her whole and she looked down.

For a long moment nothing happened, and then Andreas conceded, 'It might not have been obvious to some men… but I knew.'

Siena flushed. She could imagine the kind of man her father would have wanted her to marry—some old lecher from the Italian Middle Ages—and just how that scenario might have played out.

She stubbed her toe against the luxurious carpet of his bedroom. 'Yes, well, I just wanted to assure you that it doesn't change anything.'

Siena looked up warily, very aware of Andreas's naked chest and long powerful legs. The excuse for a towel that barely covered his intense masculinity. Unbelievably, Siena could feel herself clench inwardly at the thought of how he'd surged up and into her…how it had felt when he'd slid in and out, taking her higher and higher.

Too late she realised her mistake in coming here like this and turned to leave, but quick as a flash Andreas inserted himself between her and the door.

'Where do you think you're going?'

Siena gulped. 'To my room. To bed.'

Andreas smiled and it was wicked. 'There's a perfectly good bed here.'

Siena blanched. As responsive as her body was proving to be, she didn't in all honesty think she could take a repeat so soon. She'd stung when she'd lowered herself into the bath and she ached all over.

Reading her mind, Andreas said, 'Don't worry, I think it's too soon—but there are other ways of achieving the same result.'

He took Siena by the hand and led her unresisting—much to her disgust—to the bed. He sat down and pulled her between his legs. His towel parted and when Siena looked down she could see the dark thatch of hair and his body stirring and hardening.

Andreas was undoing her robe and then pulling it open. Siena felt absurdly shy and tried to stop him, but he was too strong. It was off her shoulders, falling down her arms to the ground, and she was naked.

Andreas's gaze was fixed on her breasts and Siena could feel them grow, the tips hardening, tingling. She wanted to groan. How could she be so affected when he just looked at her?

With his hands clamped around her waist, Andreas brought her even closer and lavished her breasts with attention, licking and suckling until Siena wanted to cry out. The first time round it had all been happening so fast she hadn't had a chance to draw breath, drowning in sensations before she could really register them.

Now Andreas was conducting a slow, sensual torture, and Siena found it almost overwhelming. With a smooth move he caught her just as her legs threatened to buckle and laid her on the bed. He whipped aside his towel so that he was naked.

Siena said brokenly, 'I thought you said—'

He put a finger to her mouth and said, 'Shh, I did.'

Siena felt something scary erupt in her chest, because in that moment she realised that she trusted Andreas. He wouldn't hurt her, or push her further than she could go. But now his mouth was on hers and his hands were moulding and cupping her breasts and Siena gave up any coherent thought.

By the time his hand reached between her legs and sought where she felt so hot and wet Siena's hips were rolling impatiently. She wanted Andreas to take her again, soreness be damned. But he wouldn't.

Almost crying with frustration, she felt him move down her body and replace that hand with his mouth. He'd touched her like this before, but now it felt much more intimate. Siena was aware of how wanton she must look—legs stretched apart, hands clutching at Andreas's head, breathing fast, heart thumping painfully.

Andreas found her sensitised clitoris and flicked it with his tongue, while thrusting two fingers into her clasping body. *This* was what Siena wanted and needed. Her back arched and her hips all but lifted off the bed as she became some primal being, focused solely on Andreas's mouth and fingers as they made that tension within her coil so tight that she shouted out as he finally tipped her over the edge.

Siena seemed to float for a long time on a blissful haze of sated lethargy before she opened her eyes and realised that Andreas was lowering her into her own bed and pulling the covers over her. He'd carried her here, after pleasuring her senseless.

Siena quickly clamped her eyes shut again, not wanting to see the expression on his face and not liking how ambiguous her feelings were about his putting her back in her own bed. Eventually she heard his footfall and the sound of her door clicking shut. Her eyes opened again, seeing nothing for a moment in the darkened gloom.

Her whole body tingled and hummed with pleasure…and yet Andreas hadn't sought his own release. Siena turned over and looked unseeingly into the dark. She had no frame of reference for this kind of a relationship, but she hadn't expected Andreas to be a selfless lover.

Her head felt tangled and jumbled. She'd somehow naïvely expected that a physical relationship with Andreas would be something she could ultimately rise above, remain immune to, even if she fell apart slightly. She felt anything but immune now. She felt as if she'd been turned inside out and reconfigured and—terrifyingly—she wasn't sure if she even knew who she was any more.

## CHAPTER SEVEN

THE FOLLOWING DAY, Siena was in one of Andreas's chauffeur-driven cars, being transported to a private airfield. She'd found a cheerful Mrs Bright in the kitchen that morning, and she had directed Siena's attention to a note left for her by Andreas.

Siena had been inordinately relieved not to have to face him again so soon. She'd read the note.

I have a meeting in Paris tomorrow morning. We will spend tonight there and go to the opera this evening. Pack accordingly and be ready to leave at three p.m. Andreas

Siena could see that they were approaching the airfield now, and felt nervous at the thought of confronting Andreas again after he'd explored her body with such thorough intimacy and then deposited her back in her bed like an unwelcome visitor.

They swept in through wide gates and Siena could see a small Lear jet and a sleek silver sports car nearby. Andreas was taking out a small case and suit bag. Her belly swooped. He looked so tall and handsome. Intimidatingly so. Especially now that she knew the barely leashed power of the body underneath that suit.

The car stopped and Siena saw Andreas register it and straighten up. He looked intense, serious, and her nervous flutters increased. She had no experience of how to handle this situation. She smoothed her hand down her dress, feeling vulnerable now when she thought of how she'd chosen it over more casual clothes, how carefully she'd chosen a dress for the evening, along with the ubiquitous jewelry Andreas would expect her to wear. Because, after all, an inner voice reminded her, she'd demanded it.

Andreas watched Siena emerge from the back of the car and was glad he wore sunglasses which would hide the flare of lust in his eyes. She was wearing a champagne-coloured silk shirt dress, cinched in around her waist with a wide gold belt. The buttons were open, giving just enough of a hint of cleavage, and her hair was tumbled around her shoulders in golden abandon.

Her legs were long and bare, flat gold gladiator-style sandals on her feet. She looked effortlessly *un*-put-together in the way that only women wearing the best clothes could. The knowledge made him reel again: she was here and she was his. More irrevocably his than he'd ever imagined. But even now, much to his chagrin, he couldn't seem to drum up that sense of triumph. It was more of a restless need. As if he'd never get enough of her. It made him very nervous.

Andreas wanted to rip open the buttons of that dress and take her right there, standing against the car. *Like you took her against the door of your apartment last night?* Shame washed through him as he recalled the heated insanity of that coupling. The fact of her innocence. And the fact that while he'd managed to restrain himself from making love to her again before she was ready he'd had to touch her again.

Andreas cursed. This woman had made him useless for the whole day. He'd lost his train of thought in meetings and his assistant Becky had looked at him strangely when he'd left his office. He didn't need her to tell him that his usual cool, organised self had deserted him.

Before he could dwell on the disturbing side-effects of having Siena in his life and in his bed, Andreas strode forward and let an attendant take his things before taking Siena's bag in his hand.

And then, because once he came close to her and her scent hit his nostrils he was unable not to, he wrapped his other hand around her neck and pulled her close, settling a hot, swift kiss to her mouth. When he felt momentary hesitation give way to melting, his body hardened.

He drew back and without saying a word took her hand and led her up into the plane.

By the time they'd landed in Paris and were driving into the city centre Siena was feeling even more on edge. Andreas had largely ignored her for the flight, apart from one brief conversation. She wondered if this was what he did: ignored his lovers once he'd taken them to bed?

She'd been completely unprepared for that swift but incendiary kiss by the plane. It had unsettled her for the entire journey, making her nerve-ends tingle. Andreas had appeared unaffected, though, concentrating on his laptop with a frown between his brows and conducting a lengthy business discussion in Spanish. Siena could understand Spanish, as it had been one of her languages at finishing school, and she'd been surprised to hear him discussing the fate of hotel workers in a small hotel he'd just acquired in Mexico.

He'd said, 'That area is challenged enough as it is. I won't have those people struggling to find new jobs when I'm going to need their experience when the new hotel opens. I want you to offer them retainers, or help find them alternative employment until the work on the new hotel is finished.'

He clearly hadn't liked whatever the person on the other end of the phone had said, and had replied curtly, 'Well, that's why you work for me, Lucas, and not the other way around.'

Andreas had caught her looking at him as he'd terminated the conversation, and had raised a brow. She'd flushed and said, 'I'm the first to admit that I don't know much about business, but surely that isn't exactly good financial sense?'

Andreas had settled back in his seat, a small smile curving that sensual mouth. 'You agree with my field manager? And why not? You're right. It's not good financial sense. But the fact is that this small town in Mexico is where my benefactor and mentor came from. When I moved to New York I worked in a hotel for Ruben Carro. He liked me, saw that I had potential, and essentially groomed me to take over from him.

'He had no family or heirs, and unbeknown to me had an inoperable brain tumour. I think he felt an affinity with me, arriving from Europe, penniless. He'd come from Mexico as an impoverished worker. Both his parents were killed trying to get across the border. When he died he left everything to me with the proviso that I continue his name and that I do something to help improve his home town. He left a substantial part of his fortune to be used to that end. Buying this hotel is just the first step. There are further plans to develop the infrastructure and employment opportunities.'

Siena had felt a little shaky hearing all of this. She'd heard of the legendary billionaire hotelier Carro. 'That's a very ambitious project.'

Andreas had smiled. 'I'm a very ambitious man.'

'That's why your hotel chain is known as Xenakis-Carro? After him?'

An unmistakable look of pride had crossed Andreas's face. He'd nodded. 'I'm proud to be associated with his name. He was a good man and he offered me the opportunity of a lifetime. It's the least I can do to continue his legacy.'

Andreas had turned away then, back to his work, and the knowledge had sat heavily in Siena's belly. Clearly the newspaper reports about his business ethics had been wrong, and yet Andreas hadn't cared enough to defend himself when she'd slung that slur his way.

Siena's focus came back to the present now, as the familiar lines of the Champs-Elysées unfolded before them. Dusk was settling over the iconic city and Siena felt tense. She'd always loved Paris. Until the debutante ball. Until that evening. Since then, coming back here had been fraught with painful reminders of her own naïvety and what she'd done. And never more so than now, when she shared a car with the very man who was at the centre of those memories and emotions.

He was looking out of his window and seemed remote. Was he remembering too? Hating her even more? Siena shivered slightly. They were drawing around to the front of the huge glittering façade of a hotel, and Siena only realised where they were when they came to a smooth halt.

She looked at Andreas, who was regarding her coolly from the other side of the car. 'Is this some kind of a sick joke? Returning to the scene of the crime?'

Andreas's mouth tightened, and then he answered far too equably, 'Not at all, Siena. I don't play games like that. We've come here merely because it's impractical to go to another hotel when I own this one.'

Shock hit Siena and she looked out again at the stunning façade of the world-famous Paris hotel where the debutante ball was still held every year. She was aware of Andreas getting out of his side of the car and then he was opening her door. She looked up at him and suddenly, despite her shock, her breath got stuck in her throat and she saw only him, silhouetted against the dusk. He had never looked more gorgeous, or more dark and threatening with his stern visage. Images of the previous night slammed into her. She felt hot deep down inside her, where secret muscles clenched.

He put out a hand and said imperiously, 'Come.'

Siena fought the childish urge to cross her arms and say

stubbornly *no.* But eventually she put her hand into Andreas's and stepped out. He kept a tight hold of it as they walked into the hotel with much bowing and scraping from the staff.

Siena was surprised to see that the hotel had undergone a very beautiful overhaul since she'd seen it last. Gone was the rather over-fussy atmosphere. It felt lighter, younger, yet still oozed elegance and timeless wealth. This, Siena guessed, must be one of the reasons Andreas had become so successful in such a dizzyingly small amount of time.

Andreas was talking briefly to someone who looked like a manager, and then he was walking forward again without even a glance back to Siena. His hand was still tight around hers. A lift set apart from the others was waiting with open doors.

They stepped in and an attendant greeted them politely before pressing the one button. Siena was beginning to feel claustrophobic in the familiar surroundings, and tried to pull her hand free of Andreas's. He turned to look at her and only gripped hers tighter. This silent battle of wills went on behind the attendant, who was looking resolutely forward, avoiding eye contact.

After what seemed like aeons the lift came to a halt and the doors opened. Andreas said *merci* to the attendant and then they were stepping straight into what could only be described as a shining palace of golds and creams, with acres of soft cream carpet, parquet floors with faded oriental rugs, and floor-to-ceiling French doors and windows. Outside the Place de la Concorde was spectacularly lit up like a golden beacon.

Siena forgot herself for a moment, and only came back into the room when she realised that Andreas had finally let her hand go and was striding into the main drawing room, shucking off his suit jacket and dropping it into a nearby chair.

Everything that had brought her here to this moment—the fact that she had slept with this man and so blithely given him her innocence, his cool demeanour since she'd seen him again today—all combined now to make her feel very prickly and unsure of herself.

He had his back to her, hands on his hips, and she remarked caustically, 'So, you bought the hotel where you were once a lowly assistant manager because this is where you've always had the fantasy of bedding the debutante who got you sacked—is that it?'

Slowly Andreas turned around and Siena steeled herself. His hand came up to his slim silver-grey tie and long fingers undid it. He opened the top buttons of his shirt and just looked at her with a burning intensity before saying quietly, 'You regard yourself very highly if you think I did all that just so I might one day get you into bed seven floors above where you once teased me because you were a spoilt little socialite who got bored between her main course and dessert.'

Siena flushed at his rebuke. She knew what she'd said was grossly unfair, but if Andreas came too close she might shatter completely. Once again the knowledge that he wouldn't welcome the truth of that night washed through her with a sense of futility. Even if he did choose to believe her it would mercilessly expose her and her sister to his far too cynical judgement.

He crossed the space between them and Siena's breath caught in her throat. His eyes were narrowed on her. Instinctively Siena took a step back, panic and something much more treacherously exciting rising from her gut.

'Oh, no.' Andreas shook his head and reached for her with strong hands, wrapping them around her waist. 'We have some time before going to the opera and I know exactly how to spend it.'

Breath was a strangled bird in Siena's throat as Andreas blocked out everything behind him and bent his head, slanting that wicked hot mouth over hers. As predictable as the inclement English weather her body fizzed and simmered. Blood rushed to every nerve-point and to all parts of her body, engorging them, making them tight and sensitive.

It felt as if he was devouring her, sucking her under to some dark wicked place where all she wanted was to feel his mouth on hers. Siena wrapped her arms around Andreas's neck and her whole body strained to get closer to his. His tongue was rough and demanding, making Siena mewl a little when he took his mouth away to trail kisses over her jaw and down further.

Siena's spiteful little barb about his motives for buying the hotel had lodged in Andreas's gut, driving him to seek out physicality rather than think about it. But when he had to lift his head to draw in an unsteady breath and Siena's eyes stared up into his he couldn't escape…

He'd claimed otherwise, but he had to admit that once he'd known this hotel was up for grabs he'd had to have it—with a viscerality that went beyond mere business. But when he'd returned here, conquering owner, it hadn't felt as satisfying as he'd thought it would. It had felt somehow empty, hollow.

Andreas tried to force the unwelcome thoughts out of his head. He saw Siena's slightly swollen lips and flushed cheeks, felt her breasts rise and fall against his chest with her breath. Something caught his eye and he looked down to see that the only piece of jewellery she wore was the simple gold birdcage necklace. For some reason it made him unaccountably nervous. As if there was some hidden message he wasn't getting. He wasn't sure he wanted to get it.

He touched the necklace with a finger. 'I hope you've brought something more substantial than this to wear?'

Siena flushed and avoided his eyes. 'Of course.'

Her voice sounded husky, and just like that it pushed Andreas over the brink of control. With a smooth, effortless move he lifted Siena into his arms and strode to the master bedroom. She gave a little squeal and her arms tightened around him.

'This time—' he was grim '—we'll make it to the bedroom.'

When Siena woke a couple of hours later it was to feel fingers running up and down her bare back, along the indentations of her spine. It was delicious, and yet she felt as if she would never be able to open her eyes again. She frowned and made some incoherent mumble, distantly aware of pleasurable aches and sensations in her body, a faint tingling.

'Come on...we don't have much time to get ready.'

Siena's eyes snapped open when she heard that deep dark voice. Andreas was sitting on the edge of the bed in nothing but a small towel, smelling clean and fresh, his hair damp. He'd just had a shower. Siena was instantly awake.

He stood up, and she couldn't help but watch his sheer leonine grace as he unselfconsciously dropped the towel and went to the wardrobe to look for clothes. Siena averted her eyes. She still felt shellshocked by what had just happened. The way Andreas had stripped her bare, laid her on the bed and proceeded to explore her entire body with a thoroughness that had had her gasping, pleading and begging. Like some wanton stranger.

When he'd finally surged between her legs it had been all she could do not to explode right then, and Andreas had been a master of torture, bringing her close to the brink but never over...until she had been crying genuine tears of frustration. She could still feel them now, slightly sticky on her face. She hated that feeling of being a slave to his touch.

Humiliation washed through her and she cursed her relative innocence, not liking the thought of other, more proficient lovers who undoubtedly drove *him* over the edge.

After all, hadn't he specified that he expected her to be an inventive lover? Except when he touched her any semblance of thought went out of the window and she could only feel.

Realising that she was still lying there, naked and mooning, Siena sat up and took advantage of Andreas disappearing into the bathroom to jump out and pull on her dress again, covering up. She noticed that one or two buttons were missing and blushed when she thought of Andreas's big hands, fumbling until he'd become irritated and yanked it open. A small glow of pleasure infused her. Perhaps he wasn't as insouciant as she thought?

Andreas reappeared, and Siena avoided looking at him buttoning his shirt and scooted into the bathroom, closing the door behind her. She rested with her back against it for a moment, breathing in his provocative scent, then closed her eyes and tried to convince herself that she could get through this week and emerge at the other end unscathed and intact.

Andreas heard the shower running and imagined the water running in rivulets over Siena's breasts and body. Arousal was instant and Andreas cursed, gave up trying to close a cufflink as if that was the problem.

He closed his eyes, but all he saw was how Siena had looked lying face down in the bed moments before, naked, arms stretched out, the curve of her breast visible. That stunning face looked somehow very innocent and young in repose, her mouth a soft moue.

Making love to her this time had had none of the madness of last night, but a different kind of insanity. Sliding into her body had felt disturbing—as if he was touching a part of himself that was buried deep. He'd never lost himself so much while making love to a woman that he literally became some kind of primal animal, able only to obey his body's commands.

He'd expected that after making love to her he'd feel a steady beat of triumph. After all, this was exactly what he'd envisaged. Siena, naked and undone on his bed. Underneath him, begging for release.

She'd cried just now, when they'd made love. Sobbed for him to let her go, to stop torturing her. And he didn't like how her tears had affected him, making him feel guilty.

He'd been punishing her as much as himself, and when she'd finally tipped over the edge the strength of her orgasm had almost been too much for him to handle. He'd worn protection, but Andreas wouldn't have been surprised if the strength of his release had rendered it impotent.

In truth he hadn't expected sex to be this good with Siena. He'd expected her to be cool, distanced. Too concerned with how she looked to let herself be really sensual. Slightly uptight. And yet she was blowing his mind.

He heard the shower stop and suddenly felt a very uncustomary spurt of panic. He couldn't guarantee that if she walked out of that bathroom right now he wouldn't be able *not* to take her again and to hell with the opera.

Only one woman had ever entranced him so much that he'd deviated from his plans. And the fact that he'd willingly invited her back into his life was not a welcome reminder of his weakness.

Fear of keeping her father waiting had instilled within Siena an ability to get ready in record time, so she wasn't surprised when she saw Andreas's look of shock when she walked into the main salon a short time later.

The way his eyes widened sent a shaft of something hot to her belly. The dress was, after all, exquisite. It was one-shouldered, a swathe of dusky pink layers of chiffon, shot through with gold. It hugged her chest and waist and then fell to the floor. She'd pulled her hair up and wore a pair of large teardrop pink diamond earrings.

Feeling absurdly nervous, Siena asked, 'Will I do?'

Andreas smiled, but it looked harsh in the soft lighting of the palatial room. 'You know you'll do, Siena. I'm sure you don't need compliments from me.'

Siena flushed. She hadn't been searching for a compliment. Andreas looked more than stunning in a black tuxedo with a classic black bow-tie. His hair gleamed, still slightly damp, and his eyes looked like dark jewels.

He flicked a glance at his watch and then moved towards her.

'We should go or we'll miss the first half.'

Those nerves assailed her again when Andreas took her elbow in his hand, and Siena asked, 'Which opera is it?'

Andreas was opening the main door and he glanced at her. 'It's *La Bohème*.'

Siena couldn't stop the spontaneous rush of pleasure. 'That's my favourite opera.'

Dryly Andreas remarked as they got into the private lift, 'Mine too. Perhaps we have something in common after all.'

The rush of pleasure died. No doubt Andreas was alluding to the disparity in their upbringings. She didn't know much about his early life, but she knew it had been relatively humble.

Curious in a way she hadn't been before, Siena found herself asking when they were in the back of his car, 'Do you come from a big family?'

Andreas looked at her, but his face was in shadow. She could sense him tense at the question and wondered why.

Eventually he answered, 'I have five younger sisters and my parents.'

Siena felt her curiosity increase on hearing this. 'I didn't realise you came from such a big family. Are you close?'

She could make out his jaw tightening. More reluctance. Clearly he didn't want to talk about it. Siena confided nervously, 'It was just me and Serena. I always wondered what it would be like—' She broke off because she'd been about to say: *to have an older brother.* But of course she did have an older brother.

Andreas, as if seizing the opportunity to deflect attention, asked, 'What *what* would be like?'

Siena swallowed. 'Just…what it would have been like to have other siblings.'

Andreas arched a brow. 'More sisters for your father to parade like ice princesses?' Before Siena could react to that Andreas was saying curtly, 'My family is not up for discussion. We come from worlds apart, Siena, that's all you need to know.'

It was like a slap in the face. Siena sat back into the shadows and looked out of the window. That tiny glimpse into Andreas's life had intrigued her, but she berated herself now for showing an interest, and hated that her imagination was seizing on what it would have been like to grow up in a large family. How being an only son might have impacted Andreas, fed his ambition to succeed.

She didn't care, she told herself ruthlessly, as they pulled up outside the opera. A long line of beautifully dressed people were walking in ahead of them. Andreas came around to her door and held out his hand imperiously. Siena longed to be able to defy him but she thought of her only family: Serena, in a psychiatric unit in England, depending on her. She put her hand into Andreas's.

Three nights later Siena was standing in Andreas's London apartment, waiting for him to emerge from his room where he'd gone to get changed. She was already dressed and ready as Andreas had been delayed with work.

Since that evening in Paris things had cooled noticeably between them. Not, she had to admit, that they'd ever really been *warm.* Andreas had barely said another two words to her that night, and when they'd returned from the opera he'd told her he had to do some work and had disappeared into an office in the suite.

When she'd woken the next morning the bed beside her had been untouched, so Andreas must have slept somewhere else. Siena hadn't liked the feeling of insecurity that had gripped her as she'd waited for Andreas to finish his meetings that morning so they could return to London.

However, when they'd returned to London that evening Andreas had led her straight to his bed and made love to her with such intensity that she hadn't been able to move a muscle. Siena didn't like to think of how willingly she'd gone into his arms, or the sense of relief she'd felt. Was she so weak and pathetic after a lifetime of bullying by her father that she welcomed this treatment? She seized on the fact that soon she would be independent again, and that she'd gone into this arrangement very willingly for an end which justified the means.

The following day Andreas had exhibited the same cool, emotional distance, confirming for Siena that this was how it would be unless they were in bed. On one level she'd welcomed it. She didn't need Andreas to charm her, to pretend to something their relationship would never be.

On both evenings they'd gone out to functions. Last night had been a huge benefit for a charity that provided money for children injured in war-torn countries to be brought to Europe or the USA for medical treatment. It covered all their costs, including rehabilitation.

Siena had had tears in her eyes when a beautiful young Afghan woman had stood up to tell her story. She'd been shot because she'd spoken out about education as a teenager and this charity had transported her to America, where she'd received pioneering surgery and not only survived but thrived. She now worked for the UN.

It was only when the head of the charity had introduced the charity's patron and invited him up to speak that Siena had realised it was Andreas. She'd sat there, stunned, listening to him speak passionately about not letting the children of conflict suffer. She'd felt absurdly hurt that he hadn't told her of his involvement.

When he'd come back to the table, Siena had pushed down the hurt. 'What made you want to get involved in something like this?'

His stern expression had reminded Siena that she was straying off the path of being his mute and supplicant mistress, and in that moment she'd wanted to stand up and walk out. Only thinking of Serena had kept her where she was.

Eventually he'd said, 'A child in Mexico was caught in the crossfire between drug gangs. Ruben arranged for him to be brought to New York for treatment…unfortunately the child died, despite the doctors' best efforts. I have eight nieces and nephews and they take their safety and security completely for granted—which is their right. This child from Mexico… It opened my eyes. After he died I knew I wanted to do more…'

Siena had realised then that she could not cling onto any prejudice she'd had about the kind of man Andreas was now she'd met him again. He was not power-hungry and greedy. Or amoral.

Ignoring his silent instruction not to pursue this topic, Siena had asked, 'Do you want children?'

Andreas had looked at her and smiled mockingly, making Siena instantly regret her reckless question. She'd realised then that she'd asked it in a bid to pierce that cool control, because the last time they'd shared any meaningful dialogue it had been about his family.

'Why, Siena? Are you offering to be the mother of my children? So that you can bring them up to follow in your footsteps and tease men before letting them fall to the ground so hard that their whole world shatters? Maybe if we had a daughter we could call her Estella, after that great Dickensian heroine who beguiled and bewitched poor hapless Pip with her beauty only to crush him like a fly…'

She had been so shocked at this softly delivered attack that she'd put down her napkin and stood up, saying quietly, 'You're no Pip, Andreas, and you don't remember correctly. Estella was the victim.'

Siena had walked blindly to the bathroom and shut herself inside. She hadn't been able to stop the hot prickle of tears from overflowing. She'd been stunned at how hurt she felt, and at the mixture of guilt and shame that churned in her gut along with the awful image Andreas had just put in her head.

He could never know how cruel his words were. Her deepest, most fervent dream was some day to be part of the kind of family unit she'd never known.

She'd used to look out of her bedroom window in Florence to a park on the other side of the tiny *piazza* outside their *palazzo.* There she would see mothers and fathers and children. She'd seen love and affection and laughter and she'd ached with a physical pain to know what that would be like. To love and be loved. To have children and give them all the security and affection she'd never known… She'd never even realised until Andreas had uttered those words how badly she still wanted it.

When she'd felt composed enough to return Andreas had been waiting impatiently and they'd left. He'd looked at her in the dark shadows of the back of his car and Siena had instinctively recoiled, unable to bear the thought of him touching her when she felt so raw.

He'd said roughly, 'You say Estella was the victim? From where I'm sitting she looks remarkably robust.'

He'd reached for her then, and Siena had resisted with all the strength in her body, hating him with every fibre of her being. But with remorseless skill Andreas had slowly ground down her defences and her anger until desire burned hotter than anything else…

By the time they'd made it to the apartment she'd forgotten all about her hurt and had been thinking only about Andreas providing her with the release he could give her, like someone pathetically addicted to an illegal substance.

'We should go or we'll be late.'

Andrea's terse voice made Siena jump slightly. She'd been caught up in the memory. She turned around and wondered if she'd ever get used to the little shock of awe when she saw him in a tuxedo. Thinking of the previous evening and what had happened made Siena look down, hiding her gaze. She picked up her wrap and bag and for the first time could appreciate the armour of her shimmering black designer dress. The heavy weight of a diamond necklace at her throat, the earrings in her ears and the bracelet on her wrist would keep her anchored tonight. She couldn't afford to lose herself for a second. Or let him goad her.

If Andreas had a hint of her vulnerability he'd annihilate her.

# CHAPTER EIGHT

ANDREAS WAS DRIVING them to the function in his sports car. It served the purpose of occupying his hands and his mind, so that he wasn't in danger of ravishing Siena in the confined space of the back of his chauffeur-driven car. He would not debase himself again by proving that he could not last a few minutes without touching her. He didn't want to think of the amount of times he'd almost made love to her in the back of that car.

It made him think of the other night and how he'd still had to touch her even when she'd detonated a small internal bomb with her question about whether or not he wanted children. He didn't want to remember how she'd looked when he'd likened her to Estella from *Great Expectations* not once, but twice. It had worked, though. He'd welcomed the anger sparking in her eyes. Far easier to deal with that than the look in her eyes when she'd asked her question so inoccuously.

Lovers had asked Andreas before if he wanted children, and in every case Andreas had looked at them coolly and mentally ended the affair with little or no regret. Siena had asked and he had felt a primal surge of something very proprietorial. Something very disturbing that *wasn't* an immediate and categoric rejection of what should be anathema to him. In that moment he'd felt exposed and reminded of his humiliation in Paris. Had Siena seen something he'd been unaware of?

Something that had told her it was okay to ask that question because one week would not be enough for him? Because inevitably he couldn't help but want more?

Andreas had felt like Pip then, from that great book. Chasing after an ever unattainable beauty. Forever destined to fall short. And so he'd lashed out. Had watched her pale and told himself she was acting.

He needed to maintain the distance he'd instigated in Paris. Too much had made him uneasy there and since: Siena's insight into why he'd bought that hotel, the hunger for her which only seemed to be growing stronger, not weaker, and the way she'd asked him about his family…making him remember what he'd worked so hard to avoid.

So much of Andreas's youthful rejection of his family had been brought into sharp focus after his humiliating rejection at her hands. He'd gone abroad with little or no warning, and he knew it had confused and upset his parents. They'd never really understood his hunger to succeed, how he'd had an irrational fear of not making it out of that small town—especially after Spiro had died.

Andreas reminded himself that this wasn't a relationship like any other. With other lovers Andreas made an effort, small-talked, was witty and charming. With Siena it was about settling a score, sating the fever in his blood, exorcising the demons. He conveniently blocked out the fact that he appeared to be no closer to his goal than he had been a few days ago…

A couple of hours later Siena was feeling pain in the balls of her feet from the high heels. She wondered what Andreas would say if he knew that, contrary to his opinion of her, she'd give her right arm never to go to one of these functions again. Just then a tall, very good-looking man with dark hair approached Andreas and the two men greeted each other warmly. Siena found herself transfixed by Andreas's wide smile. She'd seen it so rarely since they'd met again, and never directed at *her*.

He was introducing the stranger. 'This is Rafaele Falcone, of Falcone Industries. He's recently moved to London to extend his domination of the motor industry.'

Siena recognised the name of the iconic Italian car company and put her hand out. She smiled at the other man, who matched Andreas in height and build. He truly was sinfully gorgeous, with astonishing green eyes, and Siena had a fleeting moment of wishing he would have some effect on her which might prove that Andreas didn't dominate her every sense. But when their hands touched there was nothing—despite the fact that Rafaele held her hand for a split second longer than was necessary, with a smile that made Siena feel like apologising because its effect was wasted on her.

'If you find things getting dull with Xenakis, do give me a call.'

He was handing her a card, flirting outrageously, and Siena found herself smiling at his chutzpah with genuine amusement. She was reaching for the card out of politeness when it disappeared into Andreas's fingers. His arm had come around her waist and brought her to his side in a way that had her looking at him, bemused. He'd never claimed her like this in public before.

Rafaele Falcone was putting up his hands in a gesture of mock defeat and backing away. 'We'll talk soon, Xenakis, I'll be interested to hear how that deal goes, and I have a new car being launched next month that I think you'll like…'

His gaze encompassed Siena and she flushed, suddenly not liking the way he was all but telling her of his interest if she were not with Andreas. She wasn't really used to this kind of casual interplay. Her father had always been so protective.

When he'd turned and walked away Andreas let Siena go and turned to her. He was livid, and Siena took a step back.

'Don't even *think* about it.'

Siena was genuinely confused. 'Think about what?'

Andreas jerked his head in the direction of his departing friend. 'Falcone is off-limits.'

Rage filled Siena, and she knew it was coming from a dangerous place—more from Andreas's dogged coolness in the past few days than what he'd just said. His possessiveness made her feel something altogether much more disturbing.

'How dare you? When we're done I can do what I like, and I intend to. If I think that includes having a rampant affair with Rafaele Falcone then I'll be sure to give him a call.'

For a second Andreas looked so feral that Siena felt fear snake down her spine. He looked capable of violence.

'You're mine, Siena,' he growled. 'No one else's.'

She lashed back. 'One week, Xenakis. I'm yours for one week. You're the one who put a time limit on it.' Realisation hit her then, along with something very hollow. 'And that one week is up in two days—or have you come to enjoy my company so much that you'd forgotten? Perhaps you want more?'

Siena wasn't sure what was goading her when she said waspishly, 'If you're so concerned with keeping me out of other men's beds it's going to cost you a lot more than a few baubles.'

'So this is how you're funding yourself after our father's spectacular crash and burn? I shouldn't be surprised.'

It took long seconds before Siena realised that it wasn't Andreas who had spoken in his deep voice. It was another voice—one that rang the faintest of bells. She tore her eyes from Andreas and looked to her left. She felt the blood drain from her face.

*Rocco DeMarco. Her brother.*

Siena barely heard Andreas acknowledge him tersely, 'DeMarco.'

Her brother's dark brown eyes left Siena momentarily to

flick to Andreas, and he inclined his head slightly. 'Xenakis. I see that my little half-sister Siena has found a benefactor to keep her in the style to which she's accustomed.'

His resemblance to their father stunned her anew, as it had all those years before, and Siena wanted to weep with the ill-timing of this meeting. It was effortlessly confirming his worst opinion of her.

Faintly she said, 'You recognise me.' It wasn't a question.

Those dark eyes went back to her. His mouth curled. 'I followed the demise of our father in the press with great interest. You and your sister were featured prominently, but it would appear you've landed on your feet.'

Feeling weak, Siena said, 'This…it's not what it seems.'

Disgust was evident in Rocco's expression, ice in his eyes, and Siena felt an ache in her heart. He was her flesh and blood.

'Did you really think I would ever forget you? After you and Serena stepped over me like a piece of trash in the street? And as for our father… Tell me—have you heard from him?'

Siena shook her head, feeling sick. How could she explain here and now to this man that she hated her father as much as he did?

Just then a petite and very pretty red-haired woman joined Rocco, slipping her hand into his arm. The change in her brother was instantaneous as he drew her close and looked down at her, warmth and love shining from his eyes. When he looked back at Siena the ice returned and she shivered.

'This is my wife—Gracie. Gracie, I'd like you to meet Siena. My youngest half-sister.'

Siena watched the woman tense and a wary expression came into her kind hazel eyes. Clearly she understood the significance of this meeting. She held out a hand, though, and Siena forced herself to shake it, feeling sick. She only noticed then the other woman's very pregnant belly, and something sharp and poignant lanced her at the realisation that she might have a nephew or niece already.

Rocco looked at Andreas and said with deceptive lightness, 'I presume from your expression that Siena hasn't told you about our familial connection? Or about when I confronted our father and he knocked me to the ground as if I was nothing more than a dog in the street?'

'Rocco…'

Siena heard his wife speak reprovingly, but his face remained ice-cold.

Siena found herself appealing to the other woman instinctively, saying, 'I was only twelve. Things really weren't as they seemed.'

The compassion in his wife's eyes was too much for Siena. She pulled free of Andreas, whose expression she did not want to see, and all but ran from the room. The emotion blooming inside her was too much. Here was incontrovertible proof that she and Serena were on their own. She'd known very well that she couldn't go to their brother, but it was another thing to see it for certain, no matter how kind his wife looked.

She'd always harboured a secret fantasy that one day she might go to Rocco and explain about their lives. That truly they weren't all that different in the end…they had a common nemesis: *their father.*

Her throat burned as she tried to suppress the emotion, expecting Andreas's presence at any moment. He wouldn't stand for her running out like that. Not when she had a duty to fulfil by his side. Perhaps he'd be so disgusted by what he'd just learned that he'd be happy to see the back of her?

She heard his voice, cold behind her in the quiet part of the lobby she'd escaped to.

'Why didn't you tell me Rocco DeMarco was your half-brother?'

Siena didn't turn around, struggling to compose herself. 'It wasn't relevant.'

Andreas snorted indelicately. 'Not relevant? He's one of the most powerful financiers in the world.'

Siena turned then and looked up at Andreas, steeling herself for his expression. It was exactly as she'd feared: a mixture of disgust and confusion. Siena retreated into attack to hide her raw emotions. She shrugged minutely. 'As you can see he hates my guts, and my sister's. Why should I bother myself with my father's bastard son—born to a common prostitute?'

Siena's insides were lacerated at her words. It was the opposite of what she believed. After that day when he'd confronted their father Siena had used to dream of him returning in the dead of night to take her and Serena away with him. But there was no way she would reveal that to Andreas.

'Why, indeed?' Andreas said now, and looked at her strangely. And then he started walking away, towards the entrance.

Siena faltered for a moment and went after him, having to hurry to keep up. When it was clear he was asking for his car, she asked a little breathlessly, 'Don't you want to go back inside?'

Andreas glanced at her and said curtly, 'Rocco DeMarco and his wife are friends of mine. I won't have them feeling the need to leave just because you're with me. I told them we'd leave.'

Pain, sharp and intense, gripped Siena as the car pulled up beside them and the valet jumped out, handing Andreas the keys. Solicitous as ever, even when he despised her, he saw Siena into the car and walked around the bonnet. Siena had the bleakest sense of foreboding that this was it. And after a silent journey back to the apartment Andreas confirmed it.

Barely looking at her, he was in the act of removing his jacket and taking off his cufflinks when he said, 'I'll arrange for a security guard to take you to the jewellers in the morning. There you'll be able to get your money.'

Siena stood stock-still. The stark finality of his words seemed to drop somewhere between them and shatter on the floor.

Faintly, pathetically, she said, 'But…there's two days left.'

Andreas speared her with a cold look. 'Five days is enough for me.' His mouth twisted. 'Don't worry. I won't dock you any *payment*.'

His words seem to bounce off her. She was numb. Just like that he'd lifted her up and now he was dropping her from a height. And yet…what else had she expected?

Siena felt sick when she had to admit that on some very deep and secret level she'd imagined that Andreas might not despise her so utterly—but when had they ever had a chance to go beyond that?

He'd stonewalled any attempts she'd made to talk about personal things, or even non-personal things, and yet this evening she could remember a betraying flare of hope at seeing him so possessive when another man flirted with her.

But that had been purely male posturing. No doubt he'd be quite happy to see her in anyone else's arms when *he* was done with her. Which was now, Siena realised a little dazedly.

She hated herself for not feeling more relieved, and she felt humiliated. Because she had to acknowledge that, despite telling herself she was with Andreas for this week purely to help her sister, she knew it was a lie. She would have wanted Andreas no matter what. For herself. Because he'd always been her dark fantasy. He would only ever have wanted her in revenge, so she'd had to have him like this or not at all.

Using Serena had been a buffer—a device for fooling herself that she was somehow in control…

Siena felt cold inside. The only good thing that could come out of this now was the help she could give her sister. She would take this man's largesse and damn herself in his eyes for ever. She'd do it with a willing heart because she had no right ever to have imagined anything else.

Siena forced herself to move, to say something. 'Goodnight, then.' It couldn't be more apparent that Andreas would not touch her now if his life depended on it.

She was walking away when she heard him say, 'It's goodbye, Siena. I'll be gone in the morning. I leave for New York to work.'

Siena turned and a wave of emotion surged upwards. She couldn't stop the words tumbling out in spite of her best intentions to stay cool. 'I *am* sorry, Andreas. Really sorry for what happened…it wasn't my intention…'

And then, before she could say anything more, she fled.

Andreas looked at the empty space Siena had left behind, along with the most fragile scent, and wanted to storm after her, to whirl her around and demand to know what she'd meant by *'it wasn't my intention'*. He wanted to put her over his shoulder and take her to his bed one more time.

But it would not be enough, he realised. It would never be enough. His body burned with need. Even after that distasteful scene with her half-brother and the knowledge of what he'd been through.

Andreas had had no idea of their connection. But as Rocco had spoken he'd felt the man's pain and had all too well been able to imagine the scenario—the two precious blue-eyed heiresses stepping over their prone brother.

It had brought back all of his own anger and rage, far too easily forgotten in the heat of passion or when Siena looked at him with those huge blue eyes. He too had suffered at those hands.

Until she'd reminded him that a week was almost up he had forgotten. And that had sent shockwaves through his system—along with a knee-jerk impulse to negate it, to tell her he'd let her go when he was ready.

But he'd caught himself in time. He'd forgotten and she'd remembered, because *she* was counting each day and evaluating how much she'd take from him.

*She'd made him jealous.* He thought of the red haze of rage that had settled over his vision on seeing his friend Rafaele Falcone flirt with Siena. And how she'd smiled at him so guilelessly, as she'd once smiled at him… That was when the scales had finally fallen from Andreas's eyes, and he'd realised how in danger he was of becoming a slave to his desire for this woman—how, far from being exorcised, she was gaining a stronger hold over him.

Andreas castigated himself. He should never have looked for her. It had been a huge mistake. Tomorrow she would be gone and he *would* move on.

*A month later, London.*

Andreas stepped into his apartment, bone-weary. He'd extended his trip to New York, not liking to investigate why he'd wanted to avoid coming back to London too soon. Silence descended around him, telling him he was alone. He ignored the hollow sensation and put down his bag.

He walked into the main salon and a vision hit him right between the eyes of Siena as she'd turned to face him that last evening in her black dress. So perfect. So beautiful. Andreas cursed and quickly walked out again.

He went to the kitchen, but that only brought him back to the moment when he'd heard Mrs Bright clucking and explaining to Siena about the oven. Or how Siena had looked sitting in jeans and a T-shirt, eating a croissant with her fingers.

Telling himself he was being ridiculous, he went to her room and opened the door, almost steeling himself for her scent. It lingered only faintly, but it was enough to have heat building low in his pelvis. He cursed her ghostly presence again. He was about to walk out when he spotted something out of the corner of his eye and walked towards the dressing area.

He couldn't be certain, but it looked as if every single piece of clothing he'd bought her was still there, neatly hung up or folded away. The long pink chiffon gown. The black dress she'd worn that first night, which had ended up on the floor of the foyer as he'd taken her up against the front door with all the finesse of a rutting bull… Andreas flushed.

The clothes would have been worth a fortune, if she had felt inclined to sell them, but they were here. Something very alien gripped Andreas and he strode out and into his study. Already he could see the safe door open and all of the jewellery gone.

He didn't like his momentary suspicion that perhaps she'd left the jewellery too. Some last second attack of conscience, because… *Why?* he mocked himself. *Because she'd come to feel something for you?*

Andreas pushed aside the rogue thought, not liking how it made him break out in a cold sweat. He sat down and picked up his phone. He had to know for sure.

'Yes, Mr Xenakis. She came that morning, as you'd arranged, and handed back every item of jewellery. We exchanged it all for a very fair price. She was a pleasant young lady.'

Andreas did not want to get into a conversation about how Siena DePiero could turn on the charm when it suited her, and he was about to put the phone down when the man on the other end said, 'Actually…there was one item she wanted to keep. Ah… Let me see…'

He was clearly looking at some list, and Andreas bit down on his impatience. He really didn't want to hear about which emerald bracelet Siena had—

'Ah, yes. Here it is.'

The man interrupted his train of thought.

'She wanted to keep the gold birdcage necklace by Angel Parnassus, and she was very insistent that she pay for it out of her own money. Everything else was cashed.'

Andreas muttered his thanks and put the phone down. As soon as Siena had singled out that understated necklace it had made him nervous, and he didn't like to be reminded of that now—of that elusive sensation that he'd missed something.

With a curse, Andreas stood up and went to his room to change for the reception of a wedding that he was invited to that evening in one of his London hotels.

His brief interlude with Siena DePiero was over, and he didn't really care why she had wanted to hang onto some relatively inexpensive piece of gold. Nor did he want to dwell on the fact that she was out there, somewhere in the city, living off his money and undoubtedly seducing the next billionaire stupid enough to fall under her spell.

A sudden vivid image of her with Rafaele Falcone made Andreas feel as if something had just punched him in the gut, and he had to breathe deeply to ease the sensation.

*Curse her to hell.* He was done with her for good, and soon the bad taste left in his mouth would fade. If she was with Rafaele Falcone he was welcome to her.

Siena turned away from another group of wedding guests who had barely looked at her as they'd helped themselves to some of the *hors d'oeuvres* she was offering from a silver tray. She welcomed the anonymity. She'd had this job for two weeks now, and she knew how lucky she was to have found another job so easily.

Every penny that had come from the sale of the jewellery from Andreas had gone straight to cover Serena's fees. She'd spent an emotional afternoon with her sister, assuring her that she would be okay, and in that moment Siena had had no regrets about what she had done.

It was when she lay in bed at night, in a similarly dingy apartment to her last one, or took the bone-rattling bus journey to work every day that she felt acute regret for deceiving Andreas all over again. She'd never forget the way he'd looked at her that last evening, or the painful reunion with her brother. Something she hadn't yet divulged to Serena.

Siena was making a beeline towards another group of guests in their finery when one of the men turned slightly to speak to a man at his side. Siena stopped in her tracks just feet away. Her belly plummeted. It couldn't be. The universe couldn't be so cruel.

But apparently the universe *could* be that cruel. Andreas Xenakis glanced momentarily in her direction and Siena saw the shock of recognition cross his features.

She immediately turned on the spot and walked quickly away, assuring herself a little hysterically that he wouldn't have recognised her. He would thhink he was mistaken because he would have assumed she'd be on a yacht, sunning herself in the Mediterranean, spending the money she'd received.

But even as she thought that she knew it was too good to be true. A heavy hand fell on her shoulder and she was whirled around so fast that the tray flew out of her hands, landing upside down on the plush and very expensive carpet nearby.

Siena immediately jerked free and bent down to pick up the tray and limit the damage, terrified her stern boss might have seen. Andreas bent down too, and Siena hissed at him, hating the way her heart was threatening to jump free of her chest, 'Please just leave me alone. I can't afford to lose this job.'

'And why,' he asked with deceptive mildness, 'would that be, when only weeks ago you cashed in a small fortune? No one could have run through it that quickly.'

Siena finished putting the last of the ruined canapés on the tray and lifted it up again. She looked at Andreas and hated how shaky she felt. 'Just pretend you haven't seen me. *Please.* If I'd had any idea you'd be a guest here...'

'Mr Xenakis, is everything all right?'

'No, it's not all right,' Andreas snapped at Siena's boss, who blanched.

Siena went hot with embarrassment. People were looking at them now, interested in whatever it was that had taken Andreas Xenakis's attention. The sense of déjà-vu as Siena remembered how she'd first seen him again was not welcome.

Andreas took the tray out of Siena's hand and before she knew what was happening handed it to her boss, taking her hand. 'I'm sorry, but you'll have to do without her. She's resigning from her job.'

Siena gasped, 'No, I'm not! How dare you?' But her words were lost as Andreas all but dragged her through the throng of merry wedding guests. She tried to free herself but Andreas's grip was too tight.

He stopped suddenly and she almost careened into his back—only to hear him say to the tall dashing groom and his stunning bride, 'So sorry...something has come up. I wish you all the best.'

And then he was moving again.

Her face puce with mortification, Siena was forced to follow. When they were finally in the clear, in a relatively empty corridor, Siena broke free and stopped in her tracks. She was shaking with adrenalin and shock.

'How *dare* you just lose me my job like that?'

Andreas rounded on her, eyes blazing. Siena couldn't fail to react to his sheer masculine magnificence. His jaw was slightly stubbled and an insidious image slipped into her mind of him waking in bed with some new lover who had distracted him enough to persuade him back into bed. Something she'd never done. She'd never woken in his arms.

'Lose you your job?' he practically shouted. 'Why the hell are you working as a waitress again when you walked away with a small fortune in your pocket just a month ago?'

Siena opened her mouth and shut it again. What could she say? That she liked back-breaking work and being on her feet for eight hours solid at a stretch? Of course she didn't.

She just needed Andreas gone so that she could get on with trying to forget about him and all the tangled emotions he was responsible for. She folded her arms. 'It's none of your business.'

Andreas folded his arms too, as immovable as a large, intimidating statue. Siena knew with a flicker of trepidation that she'd never make him budge.

'You owe me an explanation, Siena.'

Siena shook her head, panic surging. 'No, I don't owe you anything.'

Andreas looked stern. 'Oh, yes, you do—and especially after this stunt.'

He reached for her hand again and started leading her down the corridor, away from the high society wedding. A sense of inevitability washed through Siena. She knew she hadn't a hope of resisting Andreas when he was like this.

To her dismay she realised that they were in one of his hotels when he went to the reception desk and she heard him demand the key for the Presidential Suite. Then they were in the lift and ascending to the top floor. He still had hold of her hand, and Siena didn't like the way her body was already reacting to his touch—her blood pooling hotly in her belly and fizzing through her veins.

When Andreas opened the door to an opulent-looking suite he led her in and only let her go when they were safely inside. Siena walked into the reception room. The lights of the Houses of Parliament shone from across the river in the gathering dusk.

She felt self-conscious in her uniform, which consisted of a black knee-length skirt, a white shirt and black bow-tie. Her hair was pulled back into a ponytail, face scrubbed free of make-up, and the only jewellery she wore was the gold bird-cage necklace she'd kept. It seemed to burn into her skin like a brand now, even though she'd actually used the last of her own money to pay for it.

She heard the sound of Andreas pouring himself a drink and turned around to find him handing her a small tumbler of Baileys. She was surprised that he'd remembered her favourite drink and took it in both hands, avoiding his eye.

'Sit down, Siena, before you fall down.' His tone was admonitory.

Siena looked around and saw a chair sitting at right angles to the couch. She sat down and took a tiny fortifying sip of her drink, feeling the smooth, creamy liquid slide down her throat.

Andreas went and stood with his back to her at the window and Siena regarded that broad back warily, her eyes dropping to his buttocks. Instantly she had a flashback to how it had felt to have him between her legs, thrusting so deep—

He turned around abruptly and she flushed.

'So, is it that you have some masochistic penchant for menial labour after a life of excess? Or perhaps you've acted completely out of character, had a fit of conscience and handed all the money over to a worthy charity? I want to know what you've done with my money, Siena. After all, it's not an inconsiderable sum…'

Siena saw the narrow-eyed gaze focused on her and sensed his insouciance was a very thin veneer hiding simmering anger. Futility threatened to overwhelm her. She could try to lie—*again*—make up some excuse. But she did owe this man an explanation. A lot more than an explanation. She owed him his money back.

Carefully she put down her drink. Her mind was whirling

with what she was contemplating. Could she just…*tell* him? Appeal to his sense of compassion? After all, hadn't she seen it in action?

Knowing that her sister was finally safe and would be looked after for the forseeable future, and telling herself that she didn't have to divulge *everything,* Siena tried to glean some encouragement from Andreas's expressionless face.

She looked down at her hands in her lap for a long moment, and just before the silence stretched to breaking point said quietly, 'The money was for my sister, not me.'

Silence met her words, and she looked up to see Andreas was genuinely confused. 'You said she was in the South of France with friends…'

Siena could see when understanding dawned, but it was the wrong kind of understanding, and she winced when he spoke.

'*She* needed the money? To fund her debauched lifestyle? *That's* why you were willing to prostitute yourself?'

His crude words drove Siena up out of the chair. She realised somewhat belatedly that she would never have got away with such a flimsy explanation. Her whole body was taut, quivering.

'No. It's not like that.' Siena bit her lip and took a terrifying leap of faith. 'Serena was never in the South of France. She's here. In England. She came with me when we left Italy. I lied.'

Andreas's mouth twisted, 'I know your proficiency for lies, Siena. Tell me something I don't know.'

Siena winced again, but she knew she deserved it. Unable to bear being under Andreas's scrutiny like this, she moved jerkily over to the other window and crossed her arms, staring out at the view as if it would magically transport her out of this room.

'My sister…is ill. She's had mental health issues for years. They probably started not long after our mother died, I was three and Serena was five. She had always been a difficult child…I remember tantrums and our father locking her in her room. Her illness manifested itself as bouts of severe depression in her early teens, along with more manic periods when she would go out and go crazy. It got so bad that she had psychotic episodes and hallucinations. She tried to take her own life during one of those times…not to mention developing a drink and drug addiction.'

Siena heard nothing from Andreas, and was too scared to look at him, so she continued, 'Our father was disgusted at this frailty and refused to deal with it. It was only after her suicide attempt that she was diagnosed with severe bipolar disorder. Our father wouldn't allow her to take medication for fear that it would leak to the press…' Siena's voice grew bitter. 'Despite her party girl reputation she was still a valuable heiress—albeit slightly less valuable than me.'

Siena closed her eyes briefly, praying for strength in the face of Andreas's scorn, and turned to face him. His face was still expressionless.

'Go on,' he said coolly.

'When our father disappeared Serena went through a manic phase. It was impossible to control her. Physically she's stronger than me, and her drinking was out of control. All I could do was wait until the inevitable fall and then persuade her to come to England. She knew she needed help. She wanted help. I found a good psychiatric clinic and she was accepted. I had some money left over from our mother's inheritance that hadn't been seized by the authorities and that paid for our move, and for Serena for the first few months of her treatment. It's complicated, because she has to be treated for her addictions first.'

Siena looked away, embarrassed by her own miscalculation. 'I thought that with my wages I could continue to pay for her upkeep, but I hadn't really factored in the weekly cost. When I met you…again…there was only enough money left for a few weeks. She's at a delicate stage in her treatment. If she'd had to leave now because we couldn't afford it, the doctors warned me that it could be catastrophic.'

Siena braced herself for Andreas's reaction, remembering all too well their father's archaic views on mental illness.

Desperate to try and defend her sister, Siena looked back, eyes blazing. 'She's not just some vacuous socialite. It *is* a disease. If you could have seen her…the pain and anguish… and there was nothing I could do…'

To Siena's chagrin, hot tears prickled and she quickly blinked them back. 'She's my sister, and I'll do anything to try and help her. She's all I have left in the world.'

'What about your half-brother?' Andreas asked quietly.

Siena still couldn't make out his expression and her heart constricted when she thought of Rocco.

'I knew I could never go to him. You saw yourself what his reaction was. I expected it. I remember that day he spoke of. It's etched into my memory.' Quietly she said, 'I didn't mean what I said about him…afterwards. I was angry and felt vulnerable. The day we saw him confront our father, if Serena or I had so much as looked in his direction we would have been punished mercilessly. You have no idea what our father was capable of.'

'Why don't you tell me?'

Siena felt as if she was in some kind of a dreamlike state. Andreas was asking these innocuous questions that cut to the very heart of her, making her talk about things that she'd talked about with no one. *Ever.* Not even Serena.

Her legs suddenly felt weak and she went back to the couch and sat down. She looked up at Andreas and said starkly, 'He was a sadist. He took pleasure from other people's pain. But especially Serena, because she had always been so wilful and difficult to control. She became his punching bag because he knew that I was the one he could depend on to perform, to be good.'

Siena took a shaky breath and glanced at her pale hands. 'I learnt what would happen from an early age if I wasn't good. He caught me painting over one of the *palazzo* murals one day…a painter had left some paints behind. He told me to follow him and sent for Serena. He brought us into his study and told Serena to hold out her hand. He took a bamboo stick out of his cupboard and whipped her until she was bleeding. Then he told me that if I ever misbehaved again this was what would happen: Serena would be punished.'

Siena looked at Andreas. She felt cold inside. 'Serena didn't blame me. Not then. *Never*. It was as if in spite of her own turmoil she knew that what he was doing was just as damaging to me.'

Andreas's voice was impossibly grim, sending a shiver down Siena's spine. 'How old were you when this happened?'

'Five.'

For long seconds there was silence. Siena fancied she could see something in Andreas's eyes. His jaw twitched, and then he said, 'I want you to tell me what happened in Paris that night.'

Siena had known it would come to this. She owed Andreas this much. An explanation. Finally. Not that it could change the past or absolve her of her sins.

She fought to remain impassive, not to appear as if this was shredding her insides to bits. 'That evening in Paris… when my father caught us…I panicked. I had not premeditated what happened. I was overwhelmed at the strength of the attraction between us. I'd noticed you all evening. I'd never felt anything like it before…'

Siena looked back at her hands. 'I know you might not believe that…especially after I tried to make you believe I was more experienced than I was…' She was afraid of what she'd see if she looked at him so she kept her gaze down. 'When my father appeared I knew instantly what I had done—how bad it was. Serena was going through a rough patch. She was at home in Florence, being supervised by a doctor, but only because I had begged our father not to leave her alone…I was terrified of what he would do if he thought that what we'd been doing had been…mutual.'

Siena felt movement and then Andreas was sitting down beside her. His fingers were on her chin and he was forcing her to look at him. Her belly somersaulted at the look in his eyes. It was burning.

'You're telling me that you *didn't* set out to seduce me? That it *wasn't* just boredom? And that you only denounced me out of fear of what your father would do?'

Siena swallowed. Shame filled her belly. She whispered, 'Yes. I was a coward. I chose to protect my own sister over you… But I had no idea how far my father would go.'

Andreas let her chin go and stood up, his whole body vibrating with tension—or anger. Siena couldn't make out which.

And then he exploded, '*Theos,* Siena. You wilfully ruined my life just because you were too scared to stand up to your *father?*'

Siena stood up. It was as if a lead weight was making her belly plummet. She should have expected this, but still her head swam and her stomach churned. 'I'm sorry, Andreas… so sorry. I went looking for you that night to try and explain…'

Suddenly Siena's powers of speech failed her. All she could see was Andreas's eyes, burning into her, scorching her. With a soft cry she felt the world fall away, and only heard the faintest of guttural curses before everything went black.

# CHAPTER NINE

ANDREAS STOOD WATCHING Siena's sleeping form on the bed. He'd only just managed to catch her before she crumpled to the floor, and he cursed himself for lashing out. Emotions had roiled in his gut. He'd been so angry—incandescent—to learn the truth of what had happened. *If it was the truth.*

A small part of him wanted to insist that she was lying—making it up, thinking on her feet—but he'd seen the ashy pallor of her face. The way her eyes had looked inward, not even seeing him. No one could have faked that.

The magnitude of what this meant, how it changed things, was impossible to take in. *If it was the truth.*

Andreas threw off his jacket and dropped it to a nearby chair, where he sat down and pulled at his bow-tie. He'd taken off Siena's shoes and covered her with a blanket. From here he could see that perfect profile, the shape of her body, and he felt the inevitable beat of desire. It had surged into his blood as soon as he'd seen her again, as if it had merely lain dormant.

His fists clenched. The thing was, could he believe her? Andreas's mind went back to that cataclysmic evening, and when he thought about it now, without the haze of anger and rage, he could remember that Siena had been icy, yes, but there had been something else in her eyes. Terror?

Her father had had a tight grip on her arm. Too tight. He'd

forgotten that detail. And her father had fed her the words: *'You would never kiss someone like him, would you?'*

Andreas felt disgust. She'd been a day away from eighteen. Innocent. Naïve. Terrified of her father. And not for herself, for her vulnerable sister.

Questions piled on top of questions.

Andreas frowned as another wisp of a memory returned. He'd been called to his boss's office after DePiero's henchmen had laid into him, and had had to explain what had happened.

Andreas had been so angry at his own pathetic naïvety when he should have known better that he'd lashed out. Tried to make it seem, at least to himself, as if he might have had some control over the situation. At one point they'd heard a noise outside and Andreas had gone to the door, which had been ajar. He'd looked out and thought he was seeing things when a flash of ballgown disappeared around a corner.

Had that been Siena? Looking for him? Andreas frowned deeper, trying to remember what he'd said, and it came back in all its brutal clarity: *'I'd never have touched her if I'd known she was so poisonous...'*

He could laugh now. As if he'd had a choice! As if he'd have been able to stop himself from touching her! She'd enthralled him then and she enthralled him today. He was incapable of not touching her if she was within feet of him.

Uneasiness prickled over Andreas's skin. Without the anger and rage he'd clung onto for so long he felt stripped bare and made raw by all these revelations. And yet one thing was immutable: now that Siena was back in his life he was not about to let her go again easily.

When Siena woke she was completely disorientated. She had no idea who or where she was. And then details started emerging. She was in a huge bed and what looked like a misty dawn light was coming through the open curtains. She could see only sky.

She looked around and saw a palatial room, rococo design. She frowned. How did she know it was rococo? She was covered in a soft blanket and her head felt sore. Siena raised it and winced when her hair tugged. She pulled it free of the band, loosening it.

She pulled back the blanket and saw she was in a white shirt and black skirt. It all came rushing back. The reception. *Seeing Andreas.* Him pulling her out, bringing her here. All her words tumbling out. She'd told him…*everything.* He'd been angry. And she'd fainted. Siena was disgusted with herself.

Siena put a hand over her eyes, as if that could stop the painful recollections. Slowly she sat up and pushed the blanket aside, stumbled on jelly legs to the bathroom. When she saw herself in the mirror she made a face. She looked wan and washed out, her hair all over the place. She felt sticky in her uniform. She saw the shower and longed to feel clean again, so she stripped off and turned on the powerful spray, stepped under the teeming water.

*Andreas.* She shivered. After washing herself thoroughly Siena stepped out and dried herself off. It was time to face Andreas in the cold light of day.

When Siena emerged into the main reception room of the sumptuous suite she still wasn't prepared to see Andreas sitting at a table, drinking coffee and eating some breakfast. She'd dressed in her shirt and skirt, leaving off the bow-tie and shoes. She was barefoot and felt self-conscious now—which was ridiculous when this man knew every inch of her body in intimate detail.

Andreas lowered his paper and stood up. A chivalrous gesture that caught at Siena somewhere vulnerable. She moved forward, her heart thumping against her breastbone. 'I'm sorry.' Her voice was husky. 'I don't know what came over me… Thank you for letting me sleep.'

Andreas pulled out a chair at right angles to his and said coolly, 'Sit down and have something to eat. You've lost weight.'

Siena came forward and avoided his eye. She *had* lost weight. She'd hadn't had much money for food. Sensing his gaze, Siena looked at Andreas and it was intense.

Tightly he said, 'I'm sorry for lashing out at you like that last night… It was just…a lot to take in.'

Siena's heart contracted. 'I know. I'm sorry.'

'I checked out what you told me about Serena.' He sounded defensive. 'I would have been a fool not to after everything…'

The brief warmth that had invaded Siena cooled. 'Of course.'

Siena felt fear trickle down her spine even as hurt lanced her. He hadn't trusted her. 'What are you going to do?'

Andreas's mouth tightened. 'Nothing. Your sister deserves all the care she can get after a lifetime of being subjected to that kind of treatment.'

Siena felt momentarily dizzy. 'Thank you,' she said, and then she blurted out, 'I'll pay you back…the money. If you could let me set up a payment plan…?'

Andreas looked at her incredulously. 'On the kind of wages you've been earning? You'd be paying me out of your pension.'

Siena flushed and straightened her back, clinging to the small amount of pride she had left. 'I'll find another job. There are grants for people on minimum wage, training schemes…'

Andreas was grim. He poured her some coffee and pushed a plate of bread towards her. 'You don't need to pay me back. If you'd told me in the first place what you needed the money for I would have helped you.'

Now Siena was the one to look at him incredulously, and she remarked bitterly, 'Forgive me if I don't believe you. You hate my guts. You wanted revenge. If I had told you that my feckless sister was in a clinic to sort out her addictions and mental health issues you would have sneered in my face.' Siena looked down. 'I was afraid you might try to use her to get back at me—after all, that's what my father always did.'

Siena missed the way Andreas winced slightly.

He said heavily, 'My best friend committed suicide years ago, and I witnessed the devastation it wrought. I don't underestimate mental health illness for a second. I might not have been initially inclined to help, but if you had explained to me—'

Siena looked up, unsettled by this nugget from his past. 'What? Explained the tawdry reality of our lives? The sadistic bullying of our father?'

Andreas's eyes narrowed on her. 'Why did Serena not leave once she could?'

Siena swallowed, 'She didn't leave because of me. She wouldn't leave me behind. And then…once I got older…she was too dependent on our father's money to fuel her drink and drugs addiction. When she *could* have left she didn't want to. As perverse as that sounds.'

Andreas was grim. 'And so as long as she stayed you were stuck too?'

Siena nodded.

Andreas put down his napkin. 'Now that I know…everything…I will take care of Serena's bills. You don't have to pay me back.'

Siena's heart lurched. 'But I do. You don't owe me—*us*—anything.' The line of her mouth was bitter. 'I owe you so much. More than I can ever repay. If it wasn't for me you would never have been sacked or had to leave Europe.'

To Siena's dismay she could feel tears threaten, but she forced herself to look at Andreas. 'You don't know how much I wanted to go back in time, to undo what happened.'

Andreas's eyes grew darker and he leaned forward. 'That's wishful thinking. If we had that moment over again nothing could have kept us from touching each other. It was inevitable.'

Siena's heart beat faster. Her belly swooped. 'What are you saying?'

'What I'm saying is that the chemistry between us was too powerful to ignore. Then and now.'

Stupidly Siena repeated, *'Now?'*

Andreas nodded and stood up. He came around the table and took Siena's hands, pulling her up out of her chair. He was suddenly very close, very tall. Siena could feel his heat reach out and envelop her, and a wave of intense longing came over her, setting her whole body alight. She'd not even admitted to herself how much she'd missed him in the past month, how she'd ached for him at night.

'We're not done, Siena.'

Andreas put his hand to the back of her neck, fingers tangling in her hair, and urged her closer. And then his mouth was on hers, hot and urgent. She could feel him hardening against her belly and she groaned. She couldn't deny this either—not when every cell in her body was rejoicing.

She lifted her arms and fisted her hands in Andreas's hair, bolder than she'd been before, arching herself into him. The knowledge resounded in her head. He knew everything but he still wanted her. She'd believed his desire had died a death the night he'd let her go. A fierce exultation made her blood surge, and her heart soared when he pulled back and looked at her for an incendiary moment. She felt him picking her up and quickly covering the distance back to the bedroom.

As he was lying her on the bed Andreas was already opening the buttons of her shirt, and Siena's hands were mirroring his. She almost wept when her fingers were too clumsy. Andreas took her hands away and ripped it open, buttons popping everywhere.

An urgency that Siena hadn't experienced before infused the air around them. Her shirt was open and Andreas pulled the cups of her bra down so that her breasts spilled free. He bent his head to pay homage to the puckered peaks, making Siena cry out at the exquisite sensation.

Siena barely noticed that Andreas was arching her into him so that he could undo her skirt at the back, but then his mouth was gone and he was lying her down again so that he could pull her skirt over her hips and thighs and off.

It was hard to breathe. Especially when she saw his hands go to his belt and he made quick work of taking off his trousers and boxers. And then he was naked. And aroused. Siena's heart-rate increased when she saw the telltale moisture bead at the tip of his erection, and a gush of heat made her even wetter between her legs.

Andreas came down on the bed beside her, the rising sun outside making his body gleam. With deft hands her shirt and bra followed her clothes and his to the floor and soon they were both naked.

A surge of something scarily tender gripped Siena. She raised a hand and touched Andreas's jaw, relishing the stubble prickling against her palm.

He took her hand and brought it down, curling her fingers around him. Her eyes widened when she felt the solid strength of him, how he twitched and seemed to swell even more. Her hand moved up and down in an instinctive rhythm and Siena watched Andreas's cheeks flush with blood, his eyes grow even darker.

Stretching up, she pressed her mouth to his, open, her tongue seeking and finding his, sucking it deep. Her breasts were full and tight, and Andreas's hand moved down her body until he pushed between her legs, making them fall apart. His fingers found the moist evidence of her arousal and stroked with a rhythm that made her curve into him, pull her mouth from his so she could suck in oxygen.

And then his fingers thrust into her, and Siena's body spasmed with pre-orgasmic pleasure.

Andreas's voice was guttural, rough. 'You're so ready for me. I want you *now.* I've missed you.'

*'I've missed you.'* Siena's heart stopped for a long second and she searched Andreas's face. He looked as if he was in a fever. She slammed down on the momentary joy his words had provoked. He was talking in the heat of the moment, that was all.

Her whole body seemed to be poised on the brink. She felt Andreas take her hand from him and heard the ripping of foil, and then he was back, the blunt head of his erection pressing against her body, teasing.

Siena opened her legs wider, bit her lip and arched upwards, forcing Andreas to impale her. The pleasure was like nothing she'd experienced yet with this man. It was more intense than anything before.

Andreas slid deep into her body before pulling out again, and then moved back in. Siena's head went back and she looked up at him, her chest feeling so full that she could only gasp when he slid so deep that it felt as if he touched her heart…and in that moment the knowledge burst into Siena's consciousness.

She loved this man. She loved him as she'd never loved another being—not even her sister.

But she couldn't fully absorb it. Andreas was wresting away her ability to think as his powerful body surged, robbing her of breath and speech.

The intense dance between their bodies became all she could focus on. She was willing herself not to tip over the edge too soon, revelling in Andreas's power and control. But then it became too much. She couldn't hang on. Not when she wrapped her legs around Andreas's hips and their chests were crushed together. And not when he bent his head and found one taut peak, sucked it deep.

Siena cried out as emotion soared and realisation struck her: she'd thought she'd never experience this again.

Her body tightened on that delicious plateau just a second before she fell and fell, her body clenching tight around Andreas's shaft, urging him on until he too fell and their bodies were just a sweaty tangle of limbs on the tousled covers of the bed.

When Siena woke again she was disorientated once more, but this time because Andreas was in bed with her, his head resting on one hand as he looked at her. She blushed, and he smiled, and her heart palpitated. So much had happened in the space of twenty-four hours.

His smile faded. 'I want you to come home with me.'

Those words caused a lurch in Siena's chest. 'Home? To your apartment?'

Andreas nodded, and then said with familiar intractability, 'I'm not going to take no for an answer. You're coming with me, Siena.'

She looked at him for a long moment. His jaw was more stubbled now. He had that look she recognized. Slightly stern. Determined.

Feeling claustrophobic under his dark blue gaze, Siena looked away and saw the bathroom robe at the end of the bed, where she'd thrown it earlier. Moving before she could lose her nerve, she sat up and reached for it, pulling it around her and awkwardly feeding her arms into the sleeves. She got out of the bed to stand apart from him, belting the robe tightly and trying not to think of how dishevelled she felt. *How deliciously sated.*

'Andreas…' she began, not really knowing what to say.

He lay back against the pillows, arms behind his head, broad chest swelling with the movement, and Siena was hopelessly distracted for a moment.

With an effort she tore her avid gaze away and looked back to his eyes, narrowed on her. She started again. 'Andreas.'

He arched a brow.

'Things are...different now. I owe you a huge sum of money.' Siena blushed. 'I didn't feel comfortable taking the jewellery, or cashing it in, but I felt as if taking care of Serena was more important than my guilty conscience.'

She steeled herself, but it was hard when Andreas was like a lounging pasha in the bed.

'But now I won't feel comfortable unless you let me come to some agreement. I can't. It's not right. Not with everything else that has happened. I'd prefer to let you have your money back and try to take care of Serena myself than let you pay.'

Andreas sat up. 'That is not an option. Not now that I know what her situation is. You *will* let me pay, Siena.'

Siena wrung her hands and all but wailed. 'But can't you see? I'll be beholden to you for ever. I can't have that. My father was a tyrant...he owned us.' She saw a dangerous look on Andreas's face but rushed on. 'I'm not saying you're the same...but I couldn't bear to go back into that kind of...obligation.'

Andreas rested his arms on his knees, still managing to look intimidating despite his being naked under the sheets.

'You weren't so conflicted when you walked away with a fortune in jewellery.'

Siena's face grew hotter. 'I didn't think I'd ever see you again. I only took it because I thought I was making the best choice—that the end justified the means.' She hitched her chin. 'You were only too happy to let me walk away. And it's not as if you got nothing in return.'

His eyes flashed, but he said silkily, 'That's true. After all

I got the precious DePiero innocence. But now I want you to come back to me.'

*'Come back to me.'* Siena felt weak. Questions reverberated in her head: *For how long? Why? Is it just about the sex?*

A voice answered her. *Of course it was just about the sex.*

'I—' Siena began, but Andreas cut in harshly.

'We both know I can have you flat on your back moaning with need in seconds—don't think I won't prove to you that you can't just walk away from this.'

Andreas didn't like the feeling of panic that gripped him when her eyes grew wide. He had nothing to hold Siena now. Not really. Only a complete lowlife would make her pay him back for her sister's treatment.

So quietly that he almost didn't hear her, Siena said, 'If I come back to you I want things to be different.'

Andreas went still, not liking the way his blood surged. She looked serious, and heart-stoppingly beautiful with her hair feathered over her shoulders.

'I want to find a job—a better job if I can—and start paying you back.' Andreas opened his mouth but Siena held up a hand, stopping him. 'That's non-negotiable. I have some skills…I can type and file. I used to act as my father's secretary when his PA was off or on leave, and I worked sometimes at a local school, helping the special needs assistants. I'm hoping that will count for something.'

'Also, I don't want any more jewellery.' She shuddered slightly. 'I don't want to see another piece of jewellery as long as I live.'

'Anything else?' Andreas prompted, seeing her biting her lip and feeling the rush of need make him harden again.

'As soon as this…chemistry…whatever it is…is over it ends. Because it won't last for ever, will it? It can't…'

There was a tinge of desperation to her voice that resonated in Andreas and he held out a hand. 'It's not over yet… Come here, Siena.'

She stood stubbornly apart. 'Do you agree? To what I've said?'

'Yes,' Andreas growled, his need making his voice sound harsh. 'Now come here.'

*Six weeks later.*

''Night, Siena. See you on Monday. Have a good weekend.'

Siena smiled. ''Night, Lucy. I hope your little girl feels better soon.'

The other woman left and the door swung shut behind her. Siena looked around and stretched. She was the only one left in the typing pool. She was due to receive her very first pay-check next week, and it was almost embarrassing how excited she was about it.

Sometimes she couldn't fathom how lucky she was: Serena was safe and secure, and receiving the best treatment, and Siena was fulfilling a lifelong ambition to be independent. Well, she qualified, as independent as she could be with a dominant alpha male lover who resented everything that took her away from him. Even though, as she'd pointed out heatedly, he didn't count *his* work in that equation…

She got up and went to the rack to get her coat. She looked out of the window. A spurt of desire heated her insides when she saw a familiar silver sports car and Andreas standing beside it, phone to his ear.

She hadn't seen him in two days as he'd been in New York on business.

She'd been working here for almost a month now, but he insisted on picking her up every day, or having his driver do it.

He'd grumbled in bed the other morning at dawn, 'I want

you to come with me. *Why* do you insist on working when you don't have to?'

Siena had rolled her eyes. It was a familiar argument, but she stuck to her guns, not wanting to lay out in bald language that one day, when Andreas stopped desiring her, she'd be on her own again.

He was the one who had patiently helped her put together a CV which flagrantly glossed over the fact that she had no *bona fide* qualifications. He'd pulled her close on his lap and they'd sat in his study in front of his computer. 'Anyway, it doesn't matter," he'd said. "You'll walk into the office and they'll all be drooling too hard to even notice what's on your CV…'

Siena had punched him playfully, hating the see-saw emotions that still gripped her in his presence. It was different this time. *He* was different. Not more open, exactly—he always kept a piece of himself back—but she was seeing a side to him now that made her fall for him a little more each day. He was lighter, made her laugh.

It reminded her painfully of what it had been like the evening they'd met in Paris, before the world had crashed down around them. She resolutely pushed aside the painful knowledge that for him it had just been an opportunity…

When she'd got the job, after two rounds of interviews, Andreas had surprised her by cooking a traditional Greek dinner and producing a bottle of champagne with a flourish.

Siena could see him now, looking at the door of her building with barely disguised impatience, and hurriedly put on her coat and got her bag. As she went downstairs she reflected that Andreas still hadn't ever really opened up to her about his personal life. After mentioning his family the last time, and the way he'd shut down, she didn't like to bring it up.

After all, she thought a little bleakly, what was the point? It wasn't as if she was ever likely to become a more permanent fixture in Andreas's life.

When she got outside the breath stuck in her throat at the narrow-eyed, heavy-lidded look he gave her. She wasn't unaware of the interest of women passing by, and a fierce surge of possessiveness gripped her. A primal reaction of a woman to her mate.

He put his phone in his pocket and caught her to him, slanting his mouth across hers in a kiss that was not designed for public consumption. Siena didn't care, though. Two days felt like two months, and she arched her body into his and fisted her hands in his hair.

When he pulled away he chuckled and said, 'Miss me, then?'

Siena blushed. She was so *raw* around him. She affected an airy look and said, 'Not at all. How long were you gone anyway?'

The ease that had built up between them in the past few weeks made Siena feel dizzy sometimes. It was so different from how it had been before.

Andreas scowled. 'You'll pay for that. *Later*.'

He stepped back and opened the car door, letting Siena get in. She took a deep breath, watching him walk around the car with that powerful, leonine grace, and her belly somersaulted.

When he got in she felt unaccountably shy. 'My boss came and told me today that I might be getting a promotion—moving up to work with someone as a personal secretary within another month.'

Andreas looked at her and put a large hand on her leg, under her skirt, inched it up. 'I can offer you a promotion if you want—to my bed.'

Siena rolled her eyes and stopped Andreas's hand with her own—mostly because she was embarrassed by how turned on she already was.

'I'm already in your bed. You know I'm not going to give up my job…'

Andreas rolled his eyes and put his hand back on the wheel. 'At least they won't be demanding your attention over the weekend. You're mine for the next forty-eight hours, DePiero.'

Siena noticed then that they weren't taking the turn for where he lived in Mayfair and asked idly, 'Where are we going?'

Andreas glanced at her and looked a little sheepish.

Instantly Siena's eyes narrowed. 'Andreas Xenakis, what are you up to?'

He sighed. 'We're going to Athens for the weekend.' As if he could see her start to protest he held up a hand and said, 'I promise you'll be back at your desk by nine on Monday morning.'

'But I don't have anything with me—do you have to go to a function?'

Andreas nodded. 'It's a charity ball. I instructed my secretary to go to the apartment and pack some clothes, get your passport.'

At times like this it still stunned Siena how much power Andreas had.

They hadn't been to many functions in the last few weeks, but then Andreas said, with an edge to his voice, 'My youngest sister has just had a new baby. I promised my parents we'd call for lunch on Sunday before going home.'

Siena tamped down the flutters in her belly when he said *'we'*. 'Oh?' she said, in a carefully neutral voice. 'That sounds nice.'

She avoided Andreas's eyes, not wanting him to remember how he'd reacted when she'd asked him about his family before. Not wanting to remind him of *before* at all.

The following evening, in the ballroom of the hotel where they were staying, Andreas looked at Siena weaving through the crowd as she came back from the ladies' room. The ache that seemed to have set up residence in his gut intensified. She was wearing the black dress she'd worn on their first night out—except this time her face wasn't a mask of faint hauteur and she wore only the gold birdcage necklace.

It was so obvious now that she'd put on a monumental act when she'd been with him for that week. Uncomfortably he had to concede the many signs had given her away, if he'd cared to investigate them at the time. Her antipathy for the jewellery, her visible reluctance at being on the social scene, which he'd put down to embarrassment but which he now knew went deeper. *Her innocence.* Both physically and actually.

When Andreas thought of her father, he wanted to throttle the man.

And even though her brother was a billionaire she hadn't attempted to go to him for a hand-out.

Siena's make-up was as subtle as ever, and yet she outshone every woman in the room. She *glowed.* She saw him in the crowd and she smiled—a small, private smile. Andreas wanted to smile back—he could feel the warmth rising up within him, something deeper than mere lust and desire—but something held him back. That ache inside him was unyielding.

He saw Siena's smile falter slightly and fade. Her eyes dropped and Andreas felt inexplicably as if he was losing something. Someone waving caught his eye and he looked over to see a familiar face with relief. He welcomed the distraction from thinking too much about the way Siena made him feel.

When she arrived by his side, however, he couldn't stop himself from snaking an arm around her, relishing her proximity. *His.* It beat like a tattoo in his blood.

Belying his turbulent emotions, he said, 'How would you like to meet the designer of your necklace? She's the wife of a friend of mine and they're just across the room.'

Siena's hand flew to the gold chain and she looked up, eyes

wide and bright. 'Really? Angel Parnassus is here? I'd *love* to meet her!'

As Andreas led Siena by the hand through the crowd he pushed down the way her simple joy at meeting a mere jewellery designer made something inside him weaken. Things might have changed but the essentials were the same. Siena was with him only until he could let her go…and that day would come. *Soon.*

# CHAPTER TEN

ANDREAS HAD ORGANISED a helicopter to take them from Athens on Sunday to a small landing pad near his parents' town. Siena couldn't stop the flutters of apprehension in her belly, and wasn't unaware of Andreas's almost tangible tension.

A four-wheel drive vehicle was waiting for them at the landing pad and soon they were driving out and ascending what looked like a mountain.

Curiously, Siena asked, 'How often do you come home?'

Andreas's profile was remote. 'Not often enough for my mother.'

Siena smiled but Andreas didn't. She couldn't understand his reluctance to come home. If she'd come from a family like his she didn't think she'd ever have left…

She could see a town now, colourful and perched precariously on a hill above them. 'Is that it?'

'Yes,' Andreas answered.

When they drove in Siena looked around with interest. It looked modestly prosperous—wide clean streets, people walking around browsing market stalls and colourful shops. They looked friendly and happy. Siena could see a lot of construction work going on and had an instinct that Andreas was involved, for all his apparent reluctance to come home.

They drove up through winding streets until they emerged

into a beautifully picturesque square with a medieval church and very old trees.

Andreas came to a stop and Siena opened her seat belt, saying, 'This is beautiful.'

'You can see all the way to Athens on a clear day.'

'I can believe that,' Siena breathed, taking in the stunning view.

Andreas got out and she followed suit, and suddenly from around the corner came a screaming gaggle of children. They swarmed all over Andreas, and Siena's heart twisted at seeing him lift a little one high in the air with a huge smile on his face.

She intuited that he might not like coming home, for whatever reason, but he loved his family.

He put the child down and the other children disappeared as quickly as they'd arrived. He held out his hand for her and smiled wryly. 'Some of my nieces and nephews. They'll have heard the helicopter.'

Siena took his hand. She'd followed his lead, dressing down in smart jeans and a soft dusky pink silk top with a light grey cardigan. Flat shoes made her feel even smaller next to Andreas, fragile, and it wasn't altogether welcome.

As they approached a very modest-looking stone house, with trailing flowers around the windows and door, there were shouts and laughter coming from inside and a baby's wail. Siena unconsciously gripped Andreas's hand, making him look at her.

'Okay?'

She smiled and gulped. 'Yes. Fine.' But she wasn't. Because she'd suddenly realised that if Andreas's family were as idyllic as she feared they might be it would break her open.

But it was too late to turn back. A small, rotund grey-haired woman had come bustling out and was drawing Andreas down to kiss him loudly on the cheeks. When he straightened she had tears in her eyes and was saying, 'My boy…my boy…'

Then Andreas drew Siena forward and introduced her in Greek, of which Siena could only understand a little. His mother looked her up and down and then took her by the arms in a surprisingly strong grip. She nodded once, as if Siena had passed some test, and drew her into her huge soft bosom, kissing her soundly.

Siena felt inexplicably shy and blushed profusely, not used to this amount of touching from a stranger. But Andreas's mother had her hand in hers and was leading her into a lovely bright house, very simple.

There seemed to be a bewildering amount of people and Siena tried to remember all of Andreas's sisters' names: Arachne, who had the new baby, which slept peacefully in a corner; Martha, Eleni, Phebe and Ianthe. They were all dark and very pretty, with flashing eyes and big smiles.

Andreas brought Siena over to meet his father, whom she could see was quite bowed with arthritis, but it was easy to see where Andreas's tall good looks had come from. The man was innately proud, his face marked with the strong lines of his forebears.

Lunch was a somewhat chaotic affair, with children running in and out and everyone talking over everyone else. But the love and affection was palpable. Andreas had one of his nephews curled up trustingly in his lap, and Siena's womb clenched as she saw how at ease he was with the children.

And then Siena recalled his cruel words when she had asked him if he wanted children.

When Arachne, his youngest sister, approached Siena after lunch with the new baby Siena froze with panic. Being faced with this brought up all her deepest longings and fears. For how could she ever be a mother when she had no idea what it felt like to *have* a mother?

But Arachne wouldn't take no for an answer and she handed the baby into Siena's arms, showing her how to hold her.

Andreas had seen Siena's look of horror when Arachne approached her with the baby and had got up, incensed at the thought that she was rejecting his family, but his mother stopped him.

'Wait. Let her be,' she said.

It was only then that Andreas watched and saw Siena's look of horror replaced by one of intense awe and wonder. He realised it hadn't been horror. It had been panic. He could remember his own panic when he'd held a baby for the first time. He realised that Siena had never held a baby before.

Before he could stop himself he was walking over to sit beside her.

She glanced at him and smiled tremulously. 'She's so perfect and tiny. I'm afraid I'll hurt her.'

'You won't,' Andreas said through the tightness in his throat. To see the baby at Siena's breast, Siena's hair falling down over her cheek, her little finger clutched in a tiny chubby hand… Andreas dreaded the inevitable rise of claustrophobia but it didn't come. Something else came in its place—a welling of emotion that he couldn't understand and which wasn't the habitual grief for his dead best friend that he usually felt in this place. This felt new. Far more fragile. Tender. *Dangerous.*

When the baby mewled Siena tensed and whispered, 'What did I do?'

Weakly, Andreas used it as an excuse to break up that disturbing image, gently taking his niece and putting her over his shoulder, patting her back like a professional. Siena's worried face made emotion swell.

'Nothing,' he said gruffly. 'She's probably just hungry again.'

His sister came and took the baby out of Andreas's hands. Andreas watched as Siena stared after Arachne and the baby with an almost wistful look on her face. That galvanised him into moving up onto his feet and he caught her by the hand. She looked at him.

'We should leave if we're to get back to Athens and make our flight slot this evening.'

Just then Andreas's mother came up. She was saying something but she was speaking too fast for Siena to understand. When she was finished Siena asked, 'What did she say?'

Andreas looked at Siena with an unreadable expression. 'She asked if we'd stay for the night...'

Siena couldn't help the silly fluttering of something, but then Andreas reminded her, 'You have to be back for work in the morning.'

Siena's stomach fell. *Work*. 'Oh, yes...'

Andreas's eyes glinted. 'You don't want to miss that, do you?'

Siena looked at him and saw the challenge. He would stay if she relented over her work. She met it head-on and took her hand out of his. 'No, I don't.' Even though she found herself wishing that they *could* stay here longer. Not that she would admit it to Andreas.

Andreas's family bade them a friendly farewell, with Andreas suffering under copious kisses and hugs from his sisters and nieces and nephews. And then his mother came and pulled Siena close again, hugging her tight. When she put her away from her his mother tucked some wayward hair behind her ear in an effortless yet profoundly simple maternal gesture.

She looked at Siena with the kindest dark eyes, and Siena felt as if she could see all the way through to her deepest heart's desires and pain. A ball of emotion was spreading inside Siena and for a panicky second she wanted to burst into tears and bury her head in this woman's chest, to seek a kind of comfort she'd only dreamt existed.

But then Andreas was there and the moment was defused. And soon they were back in the Jeep, and in the helicopter, and by the time they'd got to the plane Siena felt as if she was under control again.

'What did you think?'

Siena turned to look at Andreas, where he was sprawled across the other side of the aisle on the small private jet. She'd been avoiding looking at him because she still felt a little raw. How could she begin to explain to this man that seeing his family had been like a dream of hers manifested? All that love and affection in one place…

'I liked them very much.'

'Still,' Andreas said, with something Siena couldn't decipher in his voice, 'it's not really your scene is it? The rustic nature of a backwater like that and a big, sprawling messy family?'

Siena felt nothing for a second, as if protecting herself, and then hurt bloomed—sharp and wounding. After everything he now knew about her Siena couldn't believe that he still had her very much placed in a box.

It seemed as if not much had really changed at all, in spite of the last few weeks. She wanted to berate him, ask him what his issues over going home were, but she was feeling too fragile. Clearly she still had to play a part.

Feeling very brittle, Siena forced a short sharp laugh. 'As you said yourself, we're from worlds apart.'

And she turned her head and looked out of the window, blinking back the hot prickle of tears, feeling like a fool.

Andreas pushed down the uncomfortable awareness that Siena was upset. Bringing her to see his family had been a mistake. He should have gone on his own. Maybe then he wouldn't have seen them in another light, and not in the usual suffocating way he usually did. Maybe then he wouldn't have noticed his father with one of his nieces on his knee, telling her a story. Wouldn't have had to wonder for the first time in his life what the anatomy of his family would have looked like if his father hadn't stayed to support his wife and children.

There were plenty of marriages in that town that were fragmented because the men had had to go to Athens to work, leaving their family behind. But his father had chosen to stay, and as a result they'd all had a very secure and stable upbringing.

Andreas didn't like to acknowledge that seeing Siena in that milieu hadn't been as alien as he'd thought it would be. She'd charmed them all with that effortless grace, and he could recognise now her genuine warmth.

Andreas glanced at Siena but her face was turned away, her hair spilling over her shoulders and touching the curve of her breast. She was not the woman he'd believed her to be. Not in the slightest.

Andreas looked out of the window beside him blindly, as if she might turn her head and see something he struggled to contain. He thought of how quickly she'd dismissed meeting his family and clung to that like a drowning man to a raft. Of course she'd *liked* his family, but she would never be a part of that world in an indelible way.

Andreas assured himself that the very ambiguous emotions she'd evoked when he'd seen her cradle his baby niece had merely been a natural response to his realisation that one day he too would have to settle down and produce an heir. For the first time it wasn't an image that sent a wave of rejection through his body.

But it wouldn't be with Siena DePiero. Never her.

In bed that night, Siena and Andreas came together in a way that Siena could only lament at. This heat was inevitable between them, and it was good at hiding the fact that there was little else. She wished she could be stronger, but she felt as if time was running out and so she seized Andreas between her legs with a fierce grip, urging him on so that when the explosion came it was more intense than it had ever been.

When he was spooning her afterwards, and she was in a half-asleep haze, Siena opened her eyes. What she'd said earlier about Andreas's family hadn't been truthful, and she was sick of lying to him.

She turned so that she was on her back, looking into Andreas's face. He opened slumberous eyes and that heat sizzled between them again. *Already.* Siena ignored it valiantly and put her hand on Andreas's when it started exploring up across her belly.

'No… I wanted to say something to you…'

Siena felt the tension come into Andreas's big body. He removed his hand from her.

She took a deep breath. 'Earlier, when you said that your home town and meeting your family probably wasn't really my scene, I agreed with you… Well, I shouldn't have. Because it's not true. It's more my scene than you could ever know, Andreas. That's the problem. I dreamed my whole life of a family like yours. I longed to know what it would be like to grow up surrounded with love and affection…'

Siena couldn't read Andreas's expression in the dim light but she could imagine she wouldn't like it.

'When your mother hugged me earlier…she really hugged me. I've never felt that before, and it was amazing. I'm glad you took me. It was a privilege to meet them.'

There was a long moment of silence and then Andreas said in a tight voice, 'You should sleep. You have to be up early.'

When Siena's breaths had evened out and he knew she was alseep Andreas carefully took his arms from around her, noting as he did so that not one night since she'd come back had they slept apart. He got out of bed and pulled on a pair of loose sweats and walked out of the bedroom.

He went into the drawing room and spent a long time looking out of the window. Until he could see the faintest smudge of dawn light in the sky. The knowledge resounded inside him that he couldn't keep fighting it.

Then he went into his study and opened his safe and took out a small box. He sat down and opened it and looked at it for a long time. For the first time since he'd met Siena again the dull ache of need and the emotions she caused within him seemed to dissipate.

Eventually he pulled out a drawer and put the box in it, a sense of resolve filling his belly. It was the same sense he'd felt when he'd laid eyes on Siena for the first time in five years, except this time the resolve came with a lot of fear, and not a sense of incipient triumph.

He had to acknowledge, ruefully, that he'd felt many things in the last tumultuous couple of months, and triumph had figured only fleetingly.

*A week later*

It was Friday evening and Siena was leaving work. Andreas's driver was waiting for her outside the office and she got into the back of the car. Andreas had called earlier to say he'd been held up in Paris, asking if she would come to meet him if he arranged transport. Siena had said yes.

So now she was being taken to his private plane, which would take her to Paris. Trepidation filled her. She wasn't sure what it would be like to be in Paris with Andreas now... He'd been in a strange mood all week. Monosyllabic and yet staring at her intensely if she caught him looking. It made her nervous, and Siena had a very poisonous suspicion that perhaps Andreas wasn't quite done with torturing her. Perhaps he was going to call time on their relationship in Paris, where it had all started?

And yet the other night he'd surprised her by asking her abruptly why she loved the birdcage necklace so much. She'd answered huskily that to her it symbolised freedom. She'd felt silly, and Andreas hadn't mentioned it again.

At night, when they'd made love, it had felt as if there was some added urgency. Siena had felt even more shattered after each time. Last night she'd been aghast to realise she'd been moved to tears, and had quickly got up to go to the bathroom, terrified Andreas would notice…

Siena knew she wouldn't be able to take it for much longer. Being with Andreas was tearing her apart. Perhaps Paris was the place where *she* should end it once and for all if he didn't?

When she got to Paris her heart was heavy and the weather matched her mood: grey and stormy. The hotel was busy, and with a lurch Siena recognised that it must be the weekend of the debutante ball as she saw harassed-looking mothers with spoilt-looking teenagers.

Surely, she thought to herself wildly, Andreas wouldn't be so cruel…

But then he was there, striding towards her, and everything in Siena's world shrank to him. She was in so much trouble. He kissed her, but it was perfunctory, and with a grimace he cast a glance to the young debs and their entourages of stylists and hair and make-up people.

'I'd forgotten the ball was this weekend…'

Relief flooded Siena and she felt a little weak.

Andreas was saying now, 'I've booked dinner. We'll leave in an hour. I just have some things to finish and I'll meet you in the room.'

Siena went up and tried to calm her fractured nerves after seeing the debs and being back here again. *Still* Andreas's mistress. She forced herself to have a relaxing bath, weary after her week in the office but still exultant to be working.

When Andreas arrived he was in a smart black suit, open shirt, and she had dressed in a gold brocade shift dress.

Solicitously Andreas took her arm and led her out to the lift, down to the lobby, and then into his car. He was so silent that Siena asked nervously, 'Penny for them?'

He turned to look at her blankly for a second, a million miles away, and then focused. He smiled tightly. 'Nothing important.'

He looked away again. Siena's sense of foreboding increased.

They were taken to a new restaurant on the top floor of a famous art gallery with grand views over Paris. The Eiffel Tower was so close Siena felt as if they could touch it. They were finishing their meal before Siena realised that they'd had the most innocuous of conversations. Touching on lots, but nothing really. As if they hardly knew each other.

The bill arrived and suddenly Siena felt as if something was slipping out of her grasp. A panicky sensation gripped her, but now Andreas was standing and they were leaving… She took his hand and thought guiltily that if he didn't say anything neither would she.

Andreas didn't make conversation in the car on the way back—again—and Siena was quiet too, not knowing what to say in this weird, heavy silence. When they got back to the hotel one of the duty managers rushed up to Andreas with a worried look.

After a brief, terse conversation Andreas turned to Siena, 'One of the guests at the ball has had a heart attack. I need to make sure everything is being attended to.'

Siena put a hand on his arm. 'I'll come with you if you like?'

Andreas looked at her and his eyes seemed to blaze with something undefinable. But then he said, 'No, you should go to bed. I'll see you in the morning.'

Siena watched him stride away, so tall and proud, master of the domain from where once *she'd* had him cast out. She felt a sense of futility. It would always be between them. Insurmountable.

After Siena had got into bed she tried to stay awake for a long time, in case she heard Andreas return, but sleep claimed her. When she did wake she was groggy, and it felt as if it was still dark outside.

Andreas was saying, 'Siena… I need you to get up… I've laid out some clothes for you.'

Siena sat up woozily and saw Andreas straighten.

'I'll wait for you outside.'

He was dressed in jeans and a light sweater. She saw a pile of clothes on the end of the bed—jeans and a similar sweater for her, and a jacket. He was walking out of the room.

Feeling dazed and confused, wondering if she was dreaming, Siena got up and quickly dressed. She looked outside for a second and saw that it was close to dawn. Where had Andreas been all night?

Pulling her hair back into a knot, she emerged and saw Andreas standing with his back to her in the salon. He turned when she walked in and even now, half-asleep, he took her breath away. His jaw was stubbled.

'Where were you?' she asked huskily.

'Nowhere important. Caught up with the guests. I want to take you somewhere…'

He came and took her by the hand. There was such an intensity to his expression that Siena couldn't decipher it, so she just said, 'Okay.'

When they were in the lift on the way down Andreas looked ahead and didn't say anything. Siena tried to stop her mind from leaping to all sorts of scenarios. She was waking up now, and as they walked through the hushed and quiet lobby she had a painful sense of *déjà-vu.* She thought of another dawn morning, five years ago. Of the turmoil in her heart and head as she'd walked out, unseeing, straight into Andreas's chest.

They walked around the corner of the hotel, intensifying Siena's sense of *déjà-vu,* and then she saw the huge gleaming motorbike. Siena blinked. Maybe she *was* dreaming.

Andreas was letting her hand go and taking out a helmet. When he drew her close to put it on her head Siena knew this was no dream. She couldn't decipher the expression on Andreas's face. It was forbidding. Then he was putting on his own helmet and lifting one leg over to straddle the bike.

He showed her where to put her foot, and with her hand on his shoulder to balance Siena swung her leg over the bike, sliding down into the seat behind Andreas, her front snug against his back.

He lifted up and pushed down and the bike roared to life, shattering the peace of the morning. Andreas reached back and pulled one of Siena's arms around his waist, and then the other one, showing her where to hold him. Her heart was thumping and she knew she was definitely awake as the bike straightened and they took off.

Unbelievably, it was Siena's first time on a motorbike, and she instinctively tightened her arms around Andreas's waist. It was exhilarating—the wind whipping past them, feeling the bike dip dangerously as Andreas took the corners.

When they stopped at a red light he turned his head and said above the noise, 'Okay?'

Siena nodded and then shouted, 'Yes!' when she realised he couldn't see her. And then they were off again.

Siena felt as if they were the only two people in the world as the faintest of pink streaks lined the dawn sky. Only a handful of cars passed them by.

Siena looked at the closed-up shops and bars that only hours before would have been teeming with people. The Eiffel Tower appeared in the distance, grey and stoic in the dawning light, bare of its glittering night-time façade. Siena preferred it like that.

They wound their way through the streets and Siena noticed that they were starting to go uphill. And then she saw the huge white shape of the Sacré Coeur in the distance. Through a series of winding, increasingly narrow streets they got closer and closer, until Andreas brought the bike to a stop under some trees.

He got off and removed his helmet, still with that enigmatic look on his face.

Siena pulled her helmet off and asked, 'Why are we here?'

Andreas took her helmet and said, 'Not yet. Another couple of minutes.'

He put the helmets away and pocketed the keys. He held out his hand. Siena put her hand in his and let him lead her up a path and through a small wooded area until the iconic church loomed above them, stately and awe-inspiring.

They were already quite high up, and Andreas led the way onward until they reached the steps outside the main doors. Siena turned around and saw the whole of Paris laid out in front of them, jaw-dropping in its beauty. She'd seen this view before but never like this, at dawn, without hordes of tourists, and with a dusky mist making everything seem hazy and dreamlike.

There was just one other couple. The woman was wearing what had to be her boyfriend's dinner jacket over a long dress and they were arm in arm, leaning over the balustrade that looked out over the ascent from the hill. They were too engrossed to notice Siena and Andreas.

'Let's sit.'

Siena looked to see Andreas indicate the steps. They sat down. He muttered something that Siena couldn't make out and then said, 'It's too cold.'

The stone *was* cold, but Siena wouldn't have swapped it for the world. 'No, it's fine… Andreas, why are we here?'

For the first time Siena noticed that Andreas was avoiding her eye and then she looked more closely. Her heart lurched. She might almost say that he looked nervous… He seemed to take a deep breath, and then he turned to look at her. The tortured expression on his face nearly took her breath away. Then he took her hands in his and she didn't say anything.

He looked down for a moment, and then back up. Siena had never seen him hesitant like this, and her heart beat fast.

'That morning…the morning after…when you came out of the hotel and I got on my bike and left…this is where I came. I came to this exact spot and sat on these steps and I looked out over this view and I cursed you.' Andreas gripped her hands tight, as if to reassure her, and then he continued.

'But mostly I cursed myself for being so stupid… You see, I thought *I* was the fool, to have been seduced by you. I thought you were like those other debutantes. Worldly-wise and experienced. Spoilt and bored.'

Siena tried to speak, familiar pain gripping her. 'Andreas—'

He shook his head. 'No. Let me speak, okay?'

Siena's heart lurched and she nodded. Andreas looked impossibly young at that moment.

'From the moment I saw you in that room I wanted you. When the opportunity came to be alone with you I jumped at it. And you were nothing like I'd expected. You were sweet and funny, so sexy and innocent.'

His mouth twisted. 'And yet those were all the very things I thought you'd fabricated when you stood at your father's side and denounced me. When his men took me outside I felt I deserved a beating for having been so duped… When I was called into my boss's office I lashed out at you—you received the full brunt of my pain. You see, I was arrogant enough to believe that no woman could enthral me. I wasn't going to have my head turned so easily. I'd vowed to get out of my small town and make something of myself. I wasn't going to get caught up in suffocating domesticity like my father had and waste my life…and I wasn't going to fall in love with some girl only to find out she didn't love me, as my friend Spiro did to his tragic cost. Yet within minutes of setting eyes on you you'd turned me inside out and I didn't even know it.'

Siena wasn't sure if she was breathing. His eyes burned like two dark sapphires.

'After what happened I put you down as a rich, cold-hearted bitch. But I couldn't stop thinking about you. I wanted out of my world and into your world so badly. I wanted to be able to stand in front of you some day and show you that I wasn't nothing. Prove that you had wanted me. You heard that conversation with my boss, didn't you?'

Siena's eyes were locked on Andreas. Slowly she nodded, and whispered, 'I went looking for you. I wanted to apologise, to explain.'

Andreas's mouth thinned. 'I probably wouldn't have believed you—just like I never gave you the chance to speak the next morning.'

Siena's hands tightened in his. Her voice was pained. 'You had to *leave* Europe. *I* did that to you.'

Andreas extricated one hand and lifted it to tuck some wayward hair behind Siena's ear. He smiled. 'Yes, and it was probably the best thing that could have happened to me. I got to America fired up with ambition and anger and energy. I caught Ruben's eye…and the rest is history. If that night hadn't happened and I'd stayed here I might be lucky enough to be managing that hotel now. I certainly wouldn't *own* it… I don't think I even knew my own potential until I went abroad.'

Siena said fiercely, 'You would have succeeded, no matter what.'

Andreas's hand cupped her jaw and he said seriously,

'Would it even mattter to you if I was just the manager of some middle-of-the-road hotel?'

Siena's heart stopped for a second and then galloped on. She shook her head and said honestly, 'No, not in the slightest.'

Andreas's fingers dropped from her chin and he took her hand again. He looked pained. 'There's something I should have said to you long before now…when you asked me if I wanted children…'

Siena remembered what he'd said that night and started to speak, not wanting to be reminded, but Andreas squeezed her hand.

'No. It was unforgivable and cruel, what I said. You touched a nerve and I lashed out. And I'm sorry. You didn't deserve it. You are not a cold-hearted tease. Any child would be lucky to have you as its mother, Siena.'

Siena felt tears prickle and blinked rapidly. His apology was profound, and she couldn't speak, so she just nodded in acknowledgement. Andreas drew in a shaky breath and reached into the pocket of his jeans to take something out. And then he got down on one knee before her, with the whole of Paris bathed in dawn light behind him.

Her eyes grew huge as she saw that he held a small black velvet box. His hands were shaking.

He looked at her and admitted, 'I can't believe I'm doing this… I always associated this with the death of ambition and success. I had a horror of somehow ending up back in my home town, having nothing. I thought my father had sacrificed too much by not taking up a college scholarship, by getting my mother pregnant and then marrying her having baby after baby. Staying stuck.'

'But your parents…' Siena said softly, still moved by his apology, trying not to let her heart jump out of her chest as she thought about that box. 'They created something wonderful. And if you hadn't had that secure foundation you might never have believed you *could* escape.'

Andreas smiled wryly. 'I know…*now.*' His smile faded slightly. 'When you admitted to me how you felt about meeting my family…my mother…I knew I had to stop fighting it. That I had to stop trying to box you into a place that made it easier for me to deal with you… I tried to make you admit you hated it, but that was only to bolster my own pathetic determination to avoid looking at how it made me feel. The fact is, going home with you…it made all those demons run away. I saw only love and affection. The security. And I felt for the first time as if I could be part of it and not be consumed by it.'

Siena looked from the box to Andreas. He was still on his knees. 'Andreas…?'

He opened the box and Siena looked down to see a beautiful vintage ring nestled in silk folds. It had one large round diamond at its centre, in an Art Deco setting, and was surrounded by small sapphires on either side. It was ornate, but simple, and Siena guessed very old.

Andreas sounded husky. 'I know you said you never wanted another piece of jewelry, but this was my grandmother's engagement ring. My mother gave it to me for my future wife when I was eighteen and heading off to Athens to work for the first time. I resented the implication that I would have to get married. I hated it and everything it symbolised and I vowed that it would be a cold day in hell before I gave it to anyone. Consequently it's languished at the back of many safes over the years—until this week. When I took it out and got it cleaned. Because I'd finally met the one person I could contemplate giving it to.'

Siena felt slightly numbed. Andreas held the ring up now, out of the box, and took her hand. She could feel him trembling—or maybe it was her trembling.

'Siena DePiero…will you do me the honour of becoming

my wife? Because you're in my head and my heart and my soul, and you have been for five years—ever since I first saw you. First you were a fascination, then you became an obsession, and now…I love you. The thought of you being in this world but not with me is more terrifying than anything I've ever known. So, please…will you marry me?'

Siena opened her mouth but all that came out was a sob. Her heart felt as if it was cracking open. Tears blurred her vision. She tried to speak through the vast ball of emotion making her chest full.

'I…' She couldn't do it. She put her hand to her mouth, trying to contain what she felt.

She saw the look on Andreas's face—stark sudden pain as it leached of colour. He thought she was saying *no.* Siena put her trembling hands around Andreas's face and looked at him, fought to contain her emotion just for a moment.

'Yes…Andreas Xenakis…I will marry you.' She drew in a great shuddering breath. 'I love you so much I don't ever want to live without you.'

That was all she could manage before she put her arms around his neck and noisy sobs erupted. His hand was on her back, soothing until the sobs stopped and she could draw back. Siena didn't care how she looked. Andreas was smiling at her as he'd smiled a long time ago, with no shadows of the past between them. Just love.

He took her hand and slid the ring onto her finger. It fitted perfectly and she looked at it in shock, still slightly disbelieving. She looked into his eyes. Her breath hitched. 'That morning…when you left on your bike…I wanted to go with you.'

Andreas smiled and ran his finger down her cheek. 'I wanted to take you with me, even as I cursed you.'

'I wish you had,' Siena whispered, emotional as she thought of the wasted years.

'Your sister,' Andreas reminded her ruefully.

Siena smiled too, a little sadly. 'Yes…my sister.'

Andreas moved back onto the steps beside her and held her face in his hands. 'Serena is being looked after and she will be okay, I promise you. Here and now is for *us*. This is where we start…and go on.'

Siena looked at him, her smile growing, joy replacing the feeling of regret. 'Yes, my love.'

And then, after kissing her soundly, he drew her between his legs, wrapped his arms around her and together they watched the most beautiful city in the world emerge from the dawn light into a new day.

# EPILOGUE

TWO AND A HALF years later Siena stood under the shade of a tree on the corner of the square near Andreas's parents' house. It was a fiesta day: long trestle tables were laid out, heaving with food and drink, and Andreas's extended family were milling around, children running between people's legs, causing mayhem and laughter. Flowers bloomed from every possible place.

Siena could see the bright blonde head of her sister Serena, where she sat at one of the tables. Just then Andreas's mother came past and bent to kiss her head affectionately.

When Serena had been discharged from the clinic they had brought her here and she had moved in with Andreas's parents. Receiving the unconditional maternal love that Andreas's mother lavished on everyone had done more for Serena than any amount of drugs and therapy.

They'd just bought her an apartment in Athens and she was starting a job. Every day she got stronger and better, surrounded by people who loved her.

Once Serena had been strong enough Andreas had set up a meeting between them and their brother Rocco. It had been very emotional. Rocco had regretted his harshness on meeting Siena for the first time. But now they had a half-brother, a niece and a nephew, and Siena had a best friend in Gracie, his wife. The only reason they weren't here today was because Gracie's brother was getting married in London.

Siena's eyes didn't have to search far to find the centre of her universe. Her husband and her eighteen-month-old son, Spiro, their two dark heads close together.

She could see Andreas start to look around, searching for her. She recognized that possessive look of impatience so well, and it sent thrills deep into her abdomen, where she harboured the secret of a new life unfolding.

She put her hand there for a moment, relishing the moment she would tell him later, and Andreas's head turned as he found her. Siena smiled and swallowed her emotion, and walked forward into the loving embrace of her family.

* * * * *

**Meeting Leon Valente had been so bittersweet.**

Eliza had known all along their fling couldn't go anywhere, but she had lived each day as if it could and would. She had been swept up in the romantic notion of it, pretending to herself that it wasn't doing anyone any harm if she had a few precious weeks of pretending she was free. She had not intended to fall in love with him, but she had seriously underestimated Leon Valente. He wasn't just charming, but ruthlessly, stubbornly and irresistibly determined with it.

'I have another proposal for you,' he said now.

Eliza swallowed tightly and hoped he hadn't seen it. 'Not marriage, I hope?'

He laughed, but it wasn't a nice sound. 'Not marriage, no,' he said. 'A business proposal—a very lucrative one.'

Eliza tried to read his expression. There was something in his dark brown eyes that was slightly menacing. Her heart beat a little bit faster as fear climbed up her spine with icy-cold fingers. 'What are you offering?'

'Five hundred thousand pounds. On the condition that you spend the next month with me in Italy.'

From as soon as **Melanie Milburne** could pick up a pen she knew she wanted to write. It was when she picked up her first Mills and Boon® at seventeen that she realised she wanted to write romance. After being distracted for a few years by meeting and marrying her own handsome hero, surgeon husband Steve, and having two boys, plus completing a Masters of Education and becoming a nationally ranked athlete (masters swimming), she decided to write. Five submissions later she sold her first book and is now a multi-published, bestselling and award-winning *USA TODAY* author. In 2008 she won the Australian Readers' Association most popular category/series romance, and in 2011 she won the prestigious Romance Writers of Australia R*BY award.

Melanie loves to hear from her readers via her website, www.melaniemilburne.com.au or on Facebook: www.facebook.com/pages/Melanie-Milburne/351594482609.

**Recent titles by the same author:**

UNCOVERING THE SILVERI SECRET
SURRENDERING ALL BUT HER HEART
ENEMIES AT THE ALTAR
*(The Outrageous Sisters)*
DESERVING OF HIS DIAMONDS?
*(The Outrageous Sisters)*

**Did you know these are also available as eBooks?**
**Visit www.millsandboon.co.uk**

# HIS FINAL BARGAIN

BY
MELANIE MILBURNE

All the characters in this book have no existence outside the imagination of the author, and have no relation whatsoever to anyone bearing the same name or names. They are not even distantly inspired by any individual known or unknown to the author, and all the incidents are pure invention.

All Rights Reserved including the right of reproduction in whole or in part in any form. This edition is published by arrangement with Harlequin Enterprises II BV/S.à.r.l. The text of this publication or any part thereof may not be reproduced or transmitted in any form or by any means, electronic or mechanical, including photocopying, recording, storage in an information retrieval system, or otherwise, without the written permission of the publisher.

This book is sold subject to the condition that it shall not, by way of trade or otherwise, be lent, resold, hired out or otherwise circulated without the prior consent of the publisher in any form of binding or cover other than that in which it is published and without a similar condition including this condition being imposed on the subsequent purchaser.

® and TM are trademarks owned and used by the trademark owner and/or its licensee. Trademarks marked with ® are registered with the United Kingdom Patent Office and/or the Office for Harmonisation in the Internal Market and in other countries.

First published in Great Britain 2013
by Mills & Boon, an imprint of Harlequin (UK) Limited.
Harlequin (UK) Limited, Eton House, 18-24 Paradise Road,
Richmond, Surrey TW9 1SR

© Melanie Milburne 2013

ISBN: 978 0 263 90014 9

Harlequin (UK) policy is to use papers that are natural, renewable and recyclable products and made from wood grown in sustainable forests. The logging and manufacturing process conform to the legal environmental regulations of the country of origin.

Printed and bound in Spain
by Blackprint CPI, Barcelona

# HIS FINAL BARGAIN

With special thanks to
Rose at The Royal Guide Dogs of Tasmania
for her time in helping me research this novel.
Also special thanks to Josie Caporetto and Serena Tatti
for their help with Italian phrases.
Thanks to you all!

# CHAPTER ONE

IT WAS THE meeting Eliza had been anticipating with agonising dread for weeks. She took her place with the four other teachers in the staffroom and prepared herself for the announcement from the headmistress.

'We're closing.'

The words fell into the room like the drop of a guillotine. The silence that followed echoed with a collective sense of disappointment, despair and panic. Eliza thought of her little primary school pupils with their sad and neglected backgrounds so similar to her own. She had worked so hard to get them to where they were now. What would happen to them if their small community-based school was shut down? They already had so much going against them, coming from such underprivileged backgrounds. They would never survive in the overcrowded mainstream school system. They would slip between the cracks, just like their parents and grandparents had done.

*Like she had almost done.*

The heartbreaking cycle of poverty and neglect would continue. Their lives—those little lives that had so much potential—would be stymied, ruined, and possibly even destroyed by delinquency and crime.

'Is there nothing we can do to keep things going for

a little while at least?' Georgie Brant, the Year Three teacher asked. 'What about another bake sale or a fair?'

The headmistress, Marcia Gordon, shook her head sadly. 'I'm afraid no amount of cakes and cookies are going to keep us afloat at this stage. We need a large injection of funds and we need it before the end of term.'

'But that's only a week away!' Eliza said.

Marcia sighed. 'I know. I'm sorry but that's just the way it is. We've always tried to keep our overheads low, but with the economy the way it is just now it's made it so much harder. We have no other choice but to close before we amass any more debt.'

'What if some of us take a pay cut or even work without pay?' Eliza suggested. 'I could go without pay for a month or two.' Any longer than that and things would get pretty dire. But she couldn't bear to stand back and do nothing. Surely there was something they could do? Surely there was someone they could appeal to for help…a charity or a government grant.

Something—*anything.*

Before Eliza could form the words Georgie had leaned forward in her chair and spoke them for her. 'What if we appeal for public support? Remember all the attention we got when Lizzie was given that teaching award last year? Maybe we could do another press article showing what we offer here for disadvantaged kids. Maybe some filthy-rich philanthropist will step out of the woodwork and offer to keep us going.' She rolled her eyes and slumped back in her seat dejectedly. 'Of course, it would help if one of us actually knew someone filthy-rich.'

Eliza sat very still in her seat. The hairs on the back of her neck each stood up one by one and began tingling at the roots. A fine shiver moved over her skin like the rush of a cool breeze. Every time she thought of Leo Valente her body reacted as if he was in the room with her. Her heart picked up its pace as she brought those darkly handsome features to mind…

'Do *you* know anyone, Lizzie?' Georgie asked, turning towards her.

'Um…no,' Eliza said. 'I don't mix in those sorts of circles.' *Any more.*

Marcia clicked her pen on and off a couple of times, her expression thoughtful. 'I suppose it wouldn't hurt to try. I'll make a brief statement to the press. Even if we could stay open until Christmas it would be something.' She stood up and gathered her papers off the table. 'I'm sending the letter to the parents in tomorrow's post.' She sighed again. 'For those of you who believe in miracles, now is a good time to pray for one.'

Eliza saw the car as soon as she turned the corner into her street. It was prowling slowly like a black panther on the hunt, its halogen headlights beaming like searching eyes. It was too dark inside the car to see the driver in any detail, but she immediately sensed it was a man and that it was her he was looking for. A telltale shiver passed over her like the hand of a ghost as the driver expertly guided the showroom-perfect Mercedes into the only available car space outside her flat.

Her breath stalled in her throat as a tall, dark-haired, well dressed figure got out from behind the wheel. Her heart jolted against her ribcage and her pulse quickened. Seeing Leo Valente face to face for the first time in four years created a shockwave through her body that left her feeling disoriented and dizzy. Even her legs felt shaky as if the ground beneath her had suddenly turned to jelly.

*Why was he here? What did he want? How had he found her?*

She strove for a steady composure as he came to stand in front of her on the pavement, but inside her stomach was fluttering like a moth trapped in a jam jar. 'Leo,' she said, surprised her voice came out at all with her throat so tightly constricted with emotion.

He inclined his darkly handsome head in a formal greeting. 'Eliza.'

She quickly disguised a swallow. His voice, with its sexy Italian accent, had always made her go weak at the knees. His looks were just as lethally attractive—tall and lean and arrestingly handsome, with eyes so dark a brown they looked almost black. The landscape of his face hinted at a man who was used to getting his own way. It was there in the chiselled line of his jaw and the uncompromising set to his mouth. He looked a little older than when she had last seen him. His jet-black hair had a trace of silver at the temples, and there were fine lines grooved either side of his mouth and around his eyes, which somehow she didn't think smiling or laughter had caused.

'Hi…' she said and then wished she had gone for something a little more formal. It wasn't as if they had parted as friends—far from it.

'I would like to speak to you in private.' He nodded towards her ground-floor flat, the look in his eyes determined, intractable and diamond-hard. 'Shall we go inside?'

She took an uneven breath that rattled against her throat. 'Um…I'm kind of busy right now…'

His eyes hardened even further as if he knew it for the lie it was. 'I won't take any more than five or ten minutes of your time.'

Eliza endured the silent tug-of-war between his gaze and hers for as long as she could, but in the end she was the first to look away. 'All right.' She blew out a little gust of a breath. 'Five minutes.'

She was aware of him walking behind her up the cracked and uneven pathway to her front door. She tried not to fumble with her keys but the way they rattled and jingled in her fingers betrayed her nervousness lamentably. Finally she got the door open and stepped through, inwardly cringing when she thought of how humble her little flat was compared to his villa in Positano. She could only imagine what he was thinking: *How could she have settled for this instead of what I offered her?*

Eliza turned to face him as he came in. He had to stoop to enter, his broad shoulders almost spanning the narrow hallway. He glanced around with a critical eye. Was he wondering if the ceiling was going to come tumbling down on him? She watched as his top lip developed a slight curl as he turned back to face her. 'How long have you lived here?'

Pride brought her chin up half an inch. 'Four years.'

'You're renting?'

Eliza silently ground her teeth. Was he doing it deliberately? Reminding her of all she had thrown away by rejecting his proposal of marriage? He must know she could never afford to buy in this part of London. She couldn't afford to buy in *any* part of London. And now with her job hanging in the balance she might not even be able to afford to pay her rent. 'I'm saving up for a place of my own,' she said as she placed her bag on the little hall table.

'I might be able to help you with that.'

She searched his expression but it was hard to know what was going on behind the dark screen of his eyes.

She quickly moistened her lips, trying to act nonchalant in spite of that little butterfly in her stomach, which had suddenly developed razor blades for wings. 'I'm not sure what you're suggesting,' she said. 'But just for the record—thanks but no thanks.'

His eyes tussled with hers again. 'Is there somewhere we can talk other than out here in the hall?'

Eliza hesitated as she did a quick mental survey of her tiny sitting room. She had been sorting through a stack of magazines one of the local newsagents had given her for craftwork with her primary school class yesterday. Had she closed that gossip magazine she had been reading? Leo had been photographed at some charity function in Rome. The magazine was a couple of weeks old but it was the only time she had seen anything of him in the press. He had always fiercely guarded his private life. Seeing his photo so soon after the staff meeting had unsettled her deeply. She had stared and stared at his image, wondering if it was just a coincidence that he had appeared like that, seemingly from out of nowhere. 'Um…sure,' she said. 'Come this way.'

If Leo had made the hallway seem small, he made the sitting room look like something out of a Lilliputian house. She grimaced as his head bumped the cheap lantern light fitting. 'You'd better sit down,' she said, surreptitiously closing the magazine and putting it beneath the others in the stack. 'You have the sofa.'

'Where are you going to sit?' he asked with a crook of one dark brow.

'Um…I'll get a chair from the kitchen…'

'I'll get it,' he said. 'You take the sofa.'

Eliza would have argued over it except for the fact that her legs weren't feeling too stable right at that moment. She sat on the sofa and placed her hands flat on her thighs to stop them from trembling. He placed the chair in what little space was left in front of the sofa and sat down in a classically dominant pose with his hands resting casually on his widely set apart strongly muscled thighs.

She waited for him to speak. The silence seemed endless as he sat there quietly surveying her with that dark inscrutable gaze.

'You're not wearing a wedding ring,' he said.

'No…' She clasped her hands together in her lap, her cheeks feeling as if she had been sitting too close to a fire.

'But you're still engaged.'

Eliza sought the awkward bump of the solitaire diamond with her fingers. 'Yes…yes, I am…'

His eyes burned as they held hers, with resentment, with hatred. 'Rather a long betrothal, is it not?' he said. 'I'm surprised your fiancé is so patient.'

She thought of poor broken Ewan, strapped in that chair with his vacant stare, day after day, year after year, dependent on others for everything. Yes, patient was exactly what Ewan was now. 'He seems content with the arrangement as it stands,' she said.

A tiny muscle flickered beneath his skin in the lower quadrant of his jaw. 'And what about you?' he asked with a pointed look that seemed to burn right through to her backbone. 'Are *you* content?'

Eliza forced herself to hold his penetrating gaze. Would he be able to see how lonely and miserable she was? How *trapped* she was? 'I'm perfectly happy,' she said, keeping her expression under rigidly tight control.

'Does he live here with you?'

'No, he has his own place.'

'Then why don't you share it with him?'

Eliza shifted her gaze to look down at her clasped hands. She noticed she had blue poster paint under one of her fingernails and a smear of yellow on the back of one knuckle. She absently rubbed at the smear with the pad of her thumb. 'It's a bit far for me to travel each day to school,' she said. 'We spend the weekends together whenever we can.'

The silence was long and brooding—*angry*.

She looked up when she heard the rustle of his clothes as he got to his feet. He prowled about the room like a tiger shark in a goldfish bowl. His hands were tightly clenched, but every now and again he would open them and loosen his fingers before fisting them again.

He suddenly stopped pacing and nailed her with his hard, embittered gaze. 'Why?'

Eliza affected a coolly composed stance. 'Why… what?'

His eyes blazed with hatred. 'Why did you choose him over me?'

'I met him first and he loves me.' She had often wondered how different her life would have been if she hadn't met Ewan. Would it have been better or worse? It was hard to say. There had been so many good times before the accident.

His brows slammed together. 'You think I didn't?'

Eliza let out a little breath of scorn. 'You didn't love me, Leo. You were in love with the idea of settling down because you'd just lost your father. I was the first one who came along who fitted your checklist—young, biddable and beddable.'

'I could've given you anything money can buy,' he said through tight lips. 'And yet you choose to live like a pauper while tied to a man who doesn't even have the desire to live with you full-time. How do you know he's not cheating on you while you're here?'

'I can assure you he's not cheating on me,' Eliza said with sad irony. She knew exactly where Ewan was and who he was with twenty-four hours a day, seven days a week.

'Do you cheat on him?' he asked with a cynical look.

She pressed her lips together without answering.

His expression was dark with anger. 'Why didn't you tell me right from the start? You should have told me you were engaged the first time we met. Why wait until I proposed to you to tell me you were promised to another man?'

Eliza thought back to those three blissful weeks in Italy four years ago. It had been her first holiday since Ewan's accident eighteen months before. His mother Samantha had insisted she get away for a break.

Eliza had gone without her engagement ring; one of the claws had needed repairing so she had left it with the jeweller while she was away. For those few short weeks she had tried to be just like any other single girl, knowing that when she got back the prison doors would close on her for good.

Meeting Leo Valente had been so bittersweet. She had known all along their fling couldn't go anywhere, but she had lived each day as if it could and would. She had been swept up in the romantic excitement of it, pretending to herself that it wasn't doing anyone any harm if she had those few precious weeks pretending she was free. She had not intended to fall in love with him. But she had seriously underestimated Leo Valente. He wasn't just charming, but ruthlessly, stubbornly and irresistibly determined with it. She had found herself enraptured by his intellectually stimulating company and by his intensely passionate lovemaking.

As each day passed she had fallen more and more in love with him. The clock had been ticking on their time together but she hadn't been able to stop herself from seeing him. She had been like a starving person encountering their first feast. She had gobbled up every moment she could with him and to hell with the consequences.

'In hindsight I agree with you,' Eliza said. 'I probably should've said something. But I thought it was just a holiday fling. I didn't expect to ever see you again. I certainly didn't expect you to propose to me. We'd only known each other less than a month.'

His expression pulsed again with bitterness. 'Did you have a good laugh about it with your friends when you came home? Is that why you let me make a fool of myself, just so you could dine out on it ever since?'

Eliza got to her feet and wrapped her arms around her body as if she were cold, even though the flat was stuffy from being closed up all day. She went over to the window and looked at the solitary rose bush in the front garden. It had a single bloom on it but the rain and the wind had assaulted its velvet petals until only three were left clinging precariously to the craggy, thorny stem. 'I didn't tell anyone about it,' she said. 'When I came back home it felt like it had all been a dream.'

'Did you tell your fiancé about us?'

'No.'

'Why not?'

She grasped her elbows a bit tighter and turned to face him. 'He wouldn't have understood.'

'I bet he wouldn't.' He gave a little sound of disdain. 'His fiancée opens her legs for the first man she meets in a bar while on holiday. Yes, I would imagine he would find that rather hard to understand.'

Eliza gave him a glacial look. 'I think it might be time for you to leave. Your five minutes is up.'

He closed the distance between them in one stride. He towered over her, making her breath stall again in her chest. She saw his nostrils flare as if he was taking in her scent. She could smell his: a complex mix of wood and citrus and spice that tantalised her senses and stirred up a host of memories she had tried for so long to suppress. She felt her blood start to thunder through the network of her veins. She felt her skin tighten and tingle with awareness. She felt her insides coil and flex with a powerful stirring of lust. Her body recognised the intimate chemistry of his. It was as if she was finely tuned to his radar. No other man made her so aware of her body, so acutely aware of her primal reaction to him.

'I have another proposal for you,' he said.

Eliza swallowed tightly and hoped he hadn't seen it. 'Not marriage, I hope.'

He laughed but it wasn't a nice sound. 'Not marriage, no,' he said. 'A business proposal—a very lucrative one.'

Eliza tried to read his expression. There was something in his dark brown eyes that was slightly menacing. Her heart beat a little bit faster as fear climbed up her spine with icy-cold fingers. 'I don't want or need your money,' she said with a flash of stubborn pride.

His top lip gave a sardonic curl. 'Perhaps not, but your cash-strapped community school does.'

She desperately tried to conceal her shock. How on earth did he know? The press article hadn't even gone to press. The journalist and photographer had only just left the school a couple of hours ago. How had he found out about it so quickly? Had he done his *own* research? What else had he uncovered about her? She gave him a wary look. 'What are you offering?'

'Five hundred thousand pounds.'

Her eyes widened. 'On what condition?'

His eyes glinted dangerously. 'On the condition you spend the next month with me in Italy.'

Eliza felt her heart drop like an anchor. She moistened her lips, struggling to maintain her outwardly calm composure when everything inside her was in a frenzied turmoil. 'In…in what capacity?'

'I need a nanny.'

A pain sliced through the middle of her heart like the slash of a scimitar. 'You're…*married?*'

His eyes remained cold and hard, his mouth a grim flat line. 'Widowed,' he said. 'I have a daughter. She's three.'

Eliza mentally did the sums. He must have met his wife not long after she left Italy. For some reason that hurt much more than if his marriage had been a more recent thing. He had moved on with his life so quickly. No long, lonely months of pining for her, of not eating and not sleeping. No. He had forgotten all about her, while she had never forgotten him, not even for a day. But there had been nothing in the press about him marrying or even about his wife dying. Who was she? What had happened to her? Should she ask?

Eliza glanced at his left hand. 'You're not wearing a wedding ring.'

'No.'

'What…um—happened?'

His eyes continued to brutalise hers with their dark brooding intensity. 'To my wife?'

Eliza nodded. She felt sick with anguish hearing him

say those words. *My wife.* Those words had been meant for *her*, not someone else. She couldn't bear to think of him with someone else, making love with someone else, *loving* someone else. She had taught herself *not* to think about it. It was too painful to imagine the life she might have had with him if things had been different.

*If she had been free...*

'Giulia killed herself.' He said the words without any trace of emotion. He might have been reading the evening news, so indifferent was his tone. And yet something about his expression—that flicker of pain that came and went in his eyes—hinted that his wife's death had been a shattering blow to him.

'I'm very sorry,' Eliza said. 'How devastating that must have been...must still be...'

'It has been very difficult for my daughter,' he said. 'She doesn't understand why her mother is no longer around.'

Eliza understood all too well the utter despair little children felt when a parent died or deserted them. She had been just seven years old when her mother had left her with distant relatives to go on a drugs and drinking binge that had ended in her death. But it had been months and months before her great-aunt had told her that her mother wasn't coming back to collect her. She hadn't even been taken to the graveside to say a proper goodbye. 'Have you explained to your daughter that her mother has passed away?' she asked.

'Alessandra is only three years old.'

'That doesn't mean she won't be able to understand what's happened,' she said. 'It's important to be truthful with her, not harshly or insensitively, but compassionately. Little children understand much more than we give them credit for.'

He moved to the other side of the room, standing with his back to her as he looked at the street outside. It seemed a long time before he spoke. 'Alessandra is not like other little children.'

Eliza moistened her parchment-dry lips. 'Look—I'm not sure if I'm the right person to help you. I work full-time as a primary school teacher. I have commitments and responsibilities to see to. I can't just up and leave the country for four weeks.'

He turned back around and pinned her with his gaze. 'Without my help you won't even have a job. Your school is about to be shut down.'

She frowned at him. 'How do you know that? How can you possibly know that? There's been nothing in the press so far.'

'I have my contacts.'

He had definitely done his research, Eliza thought. Who had he been talking to? She knew he was a powerful man, but it made her uneasy to think he had found out so much about her situation. What else had he found out?

'The summer holidays begin this weekend,' he said. 'You have six weeks to do what you like.'

'I've made other plans for the holidays. I don't want to change them at the last minute.'

He hooked one dark brow upwards. 'Not even for half a million pounds?'

Eliza pictured the money, great big piles of it. More money than she had ever seen. Money that would give her little primary school children the educational boost they so desperately needed to get out of the cycle of poverty they had been born into. But a month was a long time to spend with a man who was little more than a stranger to her now. What did he want from her? What would he want her to do? Was this some sort of pay-back or revenge attempt? How could she know what was behind his offer? He said he wanted a nanny, but what if he wanted more?

What if he wanted *her*?

'Why me?'

His inscrutable eyes gave nothing away. 'You have the qualifications I require for the post.'

It was Eliza's turn to arch an eyebrow. 'I just bet I do. Young and female with a pulse, correct?'

A glint of something dark and mocking entered his gaze as it held hers. 'You misunderstand me, Eliza. I am not offering you a rerun at being my mistress. You will be employed as my daughter's nanny. That is all that will be required of you.'

Why was she feeling as if he had just insulted her? What right did she have to bristle at his words? He needed a nanny. He didn't want her in any other capacity.

*He didn't want her.*

The realisation pained Eliza much more than she wanted it to. What foolish part of her had clung to the idea that even after all this time he would come back for her because he had never found anyone who filled the gaping hole she had left in his life? 'I can assure you that if you were offering me anything else I wouldn't accept it,' she said with a little hitch of her chin.

His gaze held hers in an assessing manner. It was unnerving to be subjected to such an intensely probing look, especially as she wasn't entirely confident she was keeping her reaction to him concealed. 'I wonder if that is strictly true,' he mused. 'Clearly your fiancé isn't satisfying you. You still have that hungry look about you.'

'You're mistaken,' she said with prickly defensiveness. 'You're seeing what you want to see, not what is.' *You're seeing what I'm trying so hard to hide!*

His dark brown eyes continued to impale hers. 'Will you accept the post?'

Eliza caught at her lower lip for a brief moment. She had at her fingertips the way to keep the school open. All of her children could continue with their education. The parenting and counselling programme for single mums she had dreamt of offering could very well become a reality if there were more funds available—a programme that might have saved her mother if it had been available at the time.

'Will another five hundred thousand pounds in cash help you come to a decision a little sooner?'

Eliza gaped at him. Was he really offering her a million pounds in cash? Did people *do* that? Were there really people out there who *could* do that?

She had grown up with next to nothing, shunted from place to place while her mother continued on a wretched cycle of drug and alcohol abuse that was her way of self-medicating far deeper emotional issues that had their origin in childhood. Eliza wasn't used to having enough money for the necessities, let alone the luxuries. As a child she had dreamt of having enough money to get her mother the help she so desperately needed, but there hadn't been enough for food and rent at times, let alone therapy.

She knew she came from a very different background from Leo, but he had never flaunted his wealth in the past. She had thought him surprisingly modest about it considering he was a self-made man. Thirty years ago his father had lost everything in a business deal gone sour. Leo had worked long and hard to rebuild the family engineering company from scratch. And he had done it and done it well. The Valente Engineering Company was responsible for some of the biggest projects across the globe. She had admired him for turning things around. So many people would have given up or adopted a victim mentality but he had not.

But for all the wealth Leo Valente had, it certainly hadn't bought him happiness. Eliza could see the lines of strain on his face and the shadows in his eyes that hadn't been there four years ago. She sent her tongue out over her lips again. 'Cash?'

He gave a businesslike nod. 'Cash. But only if you sign up right here and now.'

She frowned. 'You want me to sign something?'

He took out a folded sheet of paper from the inside of his jacket without once breaking his gaze lock with hers. 'A confidentiality agreement. No press interviews before, during or once your appointment is over.'

Eliza took the document and glanced over it. It was reasonably straightforward. She was forbidden to speak to the press, otherwise she would have to repay the amount he was giving her with twenty per cent interest. She looked up at him again. 'You certainly put a very high price on your privacy.'

'I have seen lives and reputations destroyed by idle speculation in the press,' he said. 'I will not tolerate any scurrilous rumour mongering. If you don't think you can abide by the rules set out in that document, then I will leave now and let you get on with your life. There will be no need for any further contact between us.'

Eliza couldn't help wondering why he wanted contact with her now. Why her? He could afford to employ the most highly qualified nanny in the world.

They hadn't parted on the best of terms. Every time she thought of that final scene between them she felt sick to her stomach. He had been livid to find out she was already engaged to another man. His anger had been palpable. She had felt bruised by it even though he had only touched her with his gaze. Oh, those hard, bitter eyes! How they had stabbed and burned her with their hatred and loathing. He hadn't even given her time to explain. He had stormed out of the restaurant and out of her life. He had cut all contact with her.

She could so easily have defended herself back then and in the weeks and months and years since. At any one point she could have called him and told him. She could have explained it all, but guilt had kept her silent.

*It still kept her silent.*

Dare she go with him? For a million pounds how could she not? Strictly speaking, the money wasn't for her. That made it more palatable, or at least slightly. She would be doing it for the children and their poor disadvantaged mothers. It was only for a month. That wasn't a long time by anyone's standards. It would be over in a flash. Besides, England's summer was turning out to be a non-event. A month's break looking after a little girl in sun-drenched Positano would be a piece of cake.

How hard could it be?

Eliza straightened her spine and looked him in the eye as she held out her hand. 'Do you have a pen?'

## CHAPTER TWO

LEO WATCHED AS Eliza scratched her signature across the paper. She had a neat hand, loopy and very feminine. He had loved those soft little hands on his body. His flesh had sung with delight every time she had touched him…

He jerked his thoughts back like a rider tugging the reins on a bolting horse. He would *not* allow himself to think of her that way. He needed a nanny. This was strictly a business arrangement. There was nothing else he wanted from her.

Four years on he was still furious with her for what she had done. He was even more furious with himself for falling for her when she had only been using him. How had he been so beguiled by her? She had reeled him in like a dumb fish on a line. She had dangled the bait and he had gobbled it up without thinking of what he was doing. He had acted like a lovesick swain by proposing to her so quickly. He had offered her the world—his world, the one he had worked such back-breaking hours to make up from scratch.

She had captivated him from the moment she had taken the seat beside him in the bar where he had been sitting brooding into his drink on the night of his father's funeral. There was a restless sort of energy about her that he had recognised and responded to instantly.

He had felt his body start to sizzle as soon as her arm brushed against his. She had been upfront and brazen with him, but in an edgy, exhilarating way. Their first night together had been monumentally explosive. He had never felt such a maelstrom of lust. He had been totally consumed by it. He had taken what he could with her, how he could, relishing that she seemed to want to do the same. He had loved that about her, that her need for him was as lusty and racy as his for her.

Their one-night stand had morphed into a passionate three-week affair that had him issuing a romantic proposal because he couldn't bear the thought of never seeing her again. But all that time she had been harbouring a secret—she was already engaged to a man back home in England.

Leo looked at her left hand. Her engagement ring glinted at him, taunting him like an evil eye.

Anger was like a red mist in front of him. He had been nothing more to her than a holiday fling, a diversion—a shallow little hook-up to laugh about with her friends once she got home.

He *hated* her for it.

He hated her for how his life had turned out since.

The life he'd planned for himself had been derailed by her betrayal. It had had a domino effect on every part of his life since. If it hadn't been for her perfidy he would not have met poor, sad, lonely Giulia. The guilt he felt about Giulia's death was like a clamp around his heart. He had been the wrong person for her. She had been the wrong person for him. But in their mutual despair over being let down by the ones they had loved, they had formed a wretched sort of alliance that was always going to end in tragedy. From the first moment Giulia had set eyes on their dark-haired baby girl she had rejected her. She had seemed repulsed by her own child. The doctors talked about post-natal depression and other failure to bond issues, given that the baby had been premature and had special needs, but deep inside Leo already knew what the problem had been.

Giulia hadn't wanted *his* child; she had wanted her ex's.

He had been a very poor substitute husband for her, but he was determined to be the best possible father he could be to his little daughter.

Bringing Eliza back into his life to help with Alessandra would be a way of putting things in order once and for all. Revenge was an ugly word. He didn't want to think along those lines. This was more of a way of drawing a line under that part of his life.

This time *he* would be in the driving seat. Once the month was up she could pack her bags and leave. It was a business arrangement, just like any other.

*No feelings were involved.*

Eliza handed him back his pen. 'I can't start until school finishes at the end of the week.'

Leo pocketed the pen, trying to ignore the warmth it had taken from her fingers. Trying to ignore the hot wave of lust that rumbled beneath his skin like a wild beast waking up after a long hibernation.

He *had* to ignore it.

He *would* ignore it.

'I understand that,' he said. 'I will send a car to take you to the airport on Friday. The flight has already been booked.'

Her blue-green eyes widened in surprise or affront, he couldn't be quite sure which. 'You're very certain of yourself, aren't you?'

'I'm used to getting what I want. I don't allow minor obstacles to get in my way.'

Her chin came up a notch and her eyes took on a glittering, challenging sheen. 'I don't think I've ever been described as a "minor obstacle" before. What if I turn out to be a much bigger challenge than you bargained for?'

Leo had already factored in the danger element. It was dangerous to have her back in his life. He knew that. But in a perverse sort of way he *wanted* that. He was sick of his pallid life. She represented all that he had lost—the colour, the vibrancy and the passion.

*The energy.*

He could feel it now, zinging along his veins like an electric pulse. *She* did that to him. She made him feel alive again. She had done that to him four years ago. He was aware of her in a way he had never felt with any other woman. She spoke to him on a visceral level. He felt the communication in his flesh, in *every* pore of his skin. He could feel it now, how his body stood to attention when she was near: the blood pulsing through his veins, the urgent need already thickening beneath his clothes.

Did she feel the same need too?

She was acting all cool and composed on the surface, but now and again he caught her tugging at her lower lip with her teeth and her gaze would fall away from his. Was she remembering how wanton she had been in his arms? How he had made her scream and thrash about as she came time and time again? His flesh tingled at the memory of her hot little body clutching at him so tightly. He had felt every rippling contraction of her orgasms. Was that how she responded to her fiancé? His gut roiled at the thought of her with that nameless, faceless man she had chosen over him. 'I think it's pretty safe to say I can handle whatever you dish up,' he said. 'I'm used to women like you. I know the games you like to play.'

The defiant gleam in her eyes made them seem more green than blue. 'If you find my company so distasteful then why are you employing me to look after your daughter?'

'You have a good reputation with handling small children,' Leo said. 'I was sitting in an airport gate lounge about a year ago when I happened to read an article in one of the papers about the work you do with unprivileged children. You were given an award for teaching excellence. I recognised your name. I thought there couldn't be two Eliza Lincolns working as primary school teachers in London. I assumed—quite rightly as it turns out—that it was you.'

Her look was more guarded now than defiant. 'I still don't understand why you want me to work for you, especially considering how things ended between us.'

'Alessandra's usual nanny has a family emergency to attend to,' he said. 'It's left me in a bit of a fix. I only need someone for the summer break. Kathleen will return at the end of August. You'll be back well in time for the resumption of school.'

'That still doesn't answer my question as to why me.'

Leo had only recently come to realise he was never going to be satisfied until he had drawn a line under his relationship with her. She'd had all the power the last time. This time he would take control and he would not relinquish it until he was satisfied that he could live the rest of his life without flinching whenever he thought of her. He didn't want another disastrous relationship—like the one he'd had with Giulia—because of the baggage he was carrying around. He wanted his life in order and the only way to do that was to deal with the past and put it to rest—*permanently.* 'At least I know what I'm getting with you,' he said. 'There will be no nasty surprises, *sì*?'

She arched a neatly groomed eyebrow. 'The devil you know?'

'Indeed.'

She hugged her arms around her body once more, her eyes moving out of the range of his. 'What are the arrangements as to my accommodation?'

'You will stay with us at my villa in Positano. I have a couple of developments I'm working on which may involve a trip abroad, either back here to London or Paris.'

Her gaze flicked back to his. 'Where is your daughter now? Is she here in London with you?'

Leo shook his head. 'No, she's with a fill-in girl from an agency. I'm keen to get back to make sure she's all right. She gets anxious around people she doesn't know.' He handed her his business card. 'Here are my contact details. I'll send a driver to collect you from the airport in Naples. I'll send half of the cash with an armoured guard in the next twenty-four hours. The rest I will deposit in your bank account if you give me your details.'

A little frown puckered her forehead. 'I don't think it's a good idea to bring that amount of money here. I'd rather you gave it straight to the school's bursar to deposit safely. I'll give you his contact details.'

'As you wish.' He pushed his sleeve back to check his watch. 'I have to go. I have one last meeting in the city before I fly back tonight. I'll see you when you get to my villa on Friday.'

She followed him to the door. 'What's your daughter's favourite colour?'

Leo's hand froze on the doorknob. He slowly turned and looked at her with a frown pulling at his brow. 'Why do you ask?'

'I thought I'd make her a toy. I knit them for the kids at school. They appreciate it being made for them specially. I make them in their favourite colour. Would she like a puppy or a teddy or a rabbit, do you think?'

Leo thought of his little daughter in her nursery at home, surrounded by hundreds of toys of every shape and size and colour. 'You choose.' He blew out a breath he hadn't realised he'd been holding. 'She's not fussy.'

Eliza watched as he strode back down the pathway to his car. He didn't look back at her before he drove off. It was as if he had dismissed her as soon as he walked out of her flat.

She looked at his business card in her hand. He had changed it since she had been with him four years ago. It was smoother, harder, more sophisticated.

*Just like the man himself.*

Why did he want her back in his life, even for a short time? It seemed a strange sort of request to ask an ex-lover to play nanny to his child by another woman. Was he doing it as an act of revenge? He couldn't possibly know how deeply painful she would find it.

She hadn't told him she loved him in the past. She had told him very little about herself. Their passionate time together had left little room for heart to heart outpourings. She had preferred it that way. The physicality of their relationship had been so different from anything else she had experienced before. Not that her experience was all that extensive given that she had been with Ewan since she was sixteen. She hadn't known any different until Leo had opened up a sensual paradise to her. He had made her body hum and tingle for hours. He had been able to do it just by looking at her.

*He could still do it.*

She took an unsteady breath as she thought about that dark gaze holding hers so forcefully. Had he seen how much he still affected her? He hadn't touched her. She had carefully avoided his fingers when he had handed her the paper and the pen and his card. But she had felt the warmth of where his fingers had been and her body had remembered every pulse-racing touch, as if he had flicked a switch to replay each and every erotic encounter in her brain. He had been a demanding lover, right from the word go, but then, so had she.

She had met him the evening of the day he had buried his father. He had been sitting in the bar of her hotel in Rome, taking an extraordinarily long time to drink a couple of fingers of whisky. She had been sitting in one of the leather chairs further back in the room, taking much less time working her way through a frightfully expensive cocktail she had ordered on impulse. She had felt in a reckless mood. It was her first night of freedom in so long. She was in a foreign country where no one knew who she was. That glimpse of freedom had been as heady and intoxicating as the drink she had bought. She had never in her life approached a man in a bar.

But that night was different.

Eliza had felt inexplicably drawn to him, like an iron filing being pulled into a powerful magnet's range. He fascinated her. Why was he sitting alone? Why was he taking forever to have one drink? He didn't look the type to be sitting by himself. He was far too good-looking for that. He was too well dressed. She wasn't one for being able to pick designer-wear off pat, but she was pretty sure his dark suit hadn't come off any department store rack in a marked down sale.

Eliza had walked over to him and slipped onto the bar stool right next to him. The skin of her bare arm had brushed against the fine cotton of his designer shirt. She could still remember the way her body had jolted as if she had touched a live source of power.

He had turned his head and locked gazes with her. It had sent another jolt through her body as that dark gaze meshed with hers. She had brazenly looked at his mouth, noting the sculptured definition of his top lip and the fuller, sinfully sensual contour of his lower one. He'd had a day's worth of stubble on his jaw. It had given him an aggressively masculine look that had made her blood simmer in her veins. She had looked down at his hand resting on the bar next to hers. His was so tanned and sprinkled with coarse masculine hair, the span of his fingers broad—man's hands, capable hands—clever hands. Her hand was so light and creamy, and her fingers so slim and feminine and small in comparison.

To this day she couldn't remember whose hand had touched whose first…

Thinking about that night in his hotel room still gave her shivers of delight. Her body had responded to his like bone-dry tinder did to a naked flame. She had erupted in his arms time and time again. It had been the most exciting, thrilling night of her life. She hadn't wanted it to end. She had thought that would be it—her first and only one-night stand. It would be something she would file away and occasionally revisit in her mind once she got back to her ordinary life. She had thought she would never see him again but she hadn't factored in his charm and determination. One night had turned into a three-week affair that had left her senses spinning and reeling. She knew it had been wrong not to tell him her tragic circumstances, but as each day passed it became harder and harder to say anything. She hadn't wanted to risk what little time she had left with him. So she had pushed it from her mind. Her life back in England was someone else's life. Another girl was engaged to poor broken Ewan—it wasn't her.

The day before she was meant to leave, Leo had taken her to a fabulous restaurant they had eaten in previously. He had booked a private room and had dozens of red roses delivered. Candles lit the room from every corner. Champagne was waiting in a beribboned silver ice bucket. A romantic ballad was playing in the background…

Eliza hastily backtracked out of her time travel. She hated thinking about that night; how she had foolishly deluded herself into thinking he'd been simply giving her a grand send-off to remember him by. Of course he had been doing no such thing. Halfway through the delicious meal he had presented her with a priceless-looking diamond. She had sat there staring at it for a long speechless moment.

*And then she had looked into his eyes and said no.*

'Have you heard the exciting news?' Georgie said as soon as Eliza got to school the following day. 'We're not closing. A rich benefactor has been found at the last minute. Can you believe it?'

Eliza put her bag in the drawer of her desk in the staffroom. 'That's wonderful.'

'You don't sound very surprised.'

'I am,' Eliza said, painting on a smile. 'I'm delighted. It's a miracle. It truly is.'

Georgie perched on the edge of the desk and swung her legs back and forth as if she was one of the seven-year-olds she taught. 'Marcia can't or won't say who it is. She said the donation was made anonymously. But who on earth hands over a million pounds like loose change?'

'Someone who has a lot of money, obviously.'

'Or an agenda.' Georgie tapped against her lips with a fingertip. 'I wonder who he is. It's got to be a he, hasn't it?'

'There are female billionaires in the world, you know.'

Georgie stopped swinging her legs and gave Eliza a pointed look. 'Do *you* know who it is?'

Eliza had spent most of her childhood masking her feelings. It was a skill she was rather grateful for now. 'How could I if the donation was made anonymously?'

'I guess you're right.' Georgie slipped off the desk as the bell rang. 'Are you heading down to Suffolk for the summer break?'

'Um…not this time. I've made other plans.'

Georgie's brows lifted. 'Where are you going?'

'Abroad.'

'Can you narrow that down a bit?'

'Italy.'

'Alone?'

'Yes and no,' Eliza said. 'It's kind of a busman's holiday. I'm filling in for a nanny who needs to take some leave.'

'It'll be good for you,' Georgie said. 'And it's not as if Ewan will mind either way, is it?'

'No…' Eliza let out a heavy sigh. 'He won't mind at all.'

# CHAPTER THREE

WHEN ELIZA LANDED in Naples on Friday it wasn't a uniformed driver waiting to collect her but Leo himself. He greeted her formally as if she were indeed a newly hired nanny and not the woman he had once planned to spend the rest of his life with.

'How was your flight?' he asked as he picked up her suitcase.

'Fine, thank you.' She glanced around him. 'Is your daughter not with you?'

His expression became even more shuttered. 'She doesn't enjoy car travel. I thought it best to leave her with the agency girl. She'll be in bed by the time we get home. You can meet her properly tomorrow.'

Eliza followed him to where his car was parked. The warm air outside was like being enveloped in a thick, hot blanket. It had been dismally cold and rainy in London when she left, which had made her feel a little better about leaving, but not much.

She had phoned Ewan's mother about her change of plans. Samantha had been bitterly disappointed at first. She always looked forward to Eliza's visits. Eliza was aware of how Samantha looked upon her as a surrogate child now that Ewan was no longer able to fulfil her dreams as her son. But then, their relationship had always been friendly and companionable. She had found in Samantha Brockman the model of the mother she had always dreamed of having—someone who loved unconditionally, who wanted only the best for her child no matter how much it cost her, emotionally, physically or financially.

That was what had made it so terribly hard when she had decided to end things with Ewan. She knew it would be the end of any further contact with Samantha. She could hardly expect a mother to choose friendship over blood.

*But then fate had made the choice for both of them.*

Samantha still didn't know Eliza had broken her engagement to her son the night of his accident. How could she tell her that it was *her* fault Ewan had left her flat in such a state? The police said it was 'driver distraction' that caused the accident. The guilt Eliza felt was an ever-present weight inside her chest. Every time she thought of Ewan's shattered body and mind she felt her lungs constrict, as if the space for them was slowly but surely being minimised. Every time she saw Samantha she felt like a traitor, a fraud, a Judas.

*She* was responsible for the devastation of Ewan's life.

Eliza twirled the ring on her hand. It was too loose for her now. It had been Samantha's engagement ring, given to her by Ewan's father, Geoff, who had died when Ewan was only five. Samantha had devoted her life to bringing up their son. She had never remarried; she had never even dated anyone else. She had once told Eliza that her few short happy years with Geoff were worth spending the rest of her life alone for. Eliza admired her loyalty and devotion. Few people experienced a love so strong it carried them throughout their entire life.

The traffic was congested getting out of Naples. It seemed as if no one knew the rules, or if they did they were blatantly ignoring them to get where they wanted to go. Tourist buses, taxis, cyclists and people on whining scooters all jostled for position with the occasional death-defying pedestrian thrown into the mix.

Eliza gasped as a scooter cut in on a taxi right in front of them. 'That was ridiculously close!'

Leo gave an indifferent shrug and neatly manoeuvred the car into another lane. 'You get used to it after a while. The tourist season is a little crazy. It's a lot quieter in the off season.'

A long silence ticked past.

'Is your mother still alive?' Eliza asked.

'Yes.'

'Do you ever see her?'

'Not often.'

'So you're not close to her?'

'No.'

There was a wealth of information in that one clipped word, Eliza thought. But then he wasn't the sort of man who got close to anyone. Even when she had met him four years ago he hadn't revealed much about himself. He had told her his parents had divorced when he was a young child and that his mother lived in the US. She hadn't been able to draw him out on the dynamics of his relationship with either parent. He had seemed to her to be a very self-sufficient man who didn't need or want anyone's approval. She had been drawn to that facet of his personality. She had craved acceptance and approval all of her life.

Eliza knew the parent-child relationship was not always rosy. She wasn't exactly the poster girl for happy familial relations. She had made the mistake of tracking down her father a few years ago. Her search had led her to a maximum-security prison. Ron Grady—thank God her mother had never married him—had not been at all interested in her as a daughter, or even as a person. What he had been interested in was turning her into a drug courier. She had walked out and never gone back. 'I'm sorry,' she said. 'It's very painful when you can't relate to a parent.'

'I have no interest in relating to her. She left me when I was barely more than a toddler to run off with her new lover. What sort of mother does that to a little child?'

*Troubled mothers, wounded mothers, abused mothers, drug-addicted mothers, under-mothered mothers*, Eliza thought sadly. Her own mother had been one of them. She had met them all at one time or the other. She taught their children. She loved their children because they weren't always capable of loving them themselves. 'I don't think it's ever easy being a mother. I think it's harder for some women than others.'

'What about you?' He flicked a quick glance her way. 'Do you plan to have children with your fiancé?'

Eliza looked down at her hands. The diamond of her engagement ring glinted at her in silent conspiracy. 'Ewan is unable to have children.'

The silence hummed for a long moment. She felt it pushing against her ears like two hard hands.

'That must be very hard for someone like you,' he said. 'You obviously love children.'

'I do, but it's not meant to be.'

'What about IVF?'

'It's not an option.'

'Why are you still tied to him if he can't give you what you want?'

'There's such a thing as commitment.' She clenched her hands so hard the diamond of her ring bit into the flesh of her finger. 'I can't just walk away because things aren't going according to plan. Life doesn't always go according to plan. You have to learn to make the best of things—to cope.'

He glanced at her again. 'It seems to me you're not coping as well as you'd like.'

'What makes you say that? You don't know me. We're practically strangers.'

'I know you're not in love.'

Eliza threw him a defensive look. 'Were you in love with your wife?'

A knot of tension pulsed near the corner of his mouth and she couldn't help noticing his hands had tightened slightly on the steering wheel. 'No. But then, she wasn't in love with me, either.'

'Then why did you get married?'

'Giulia got pregnant.'

'That was very noble of you,' Eliza said. 'Not many men show up at the altar because of an unplanned pregnancy these days.'

His knuckles whitened and then darkened as if he was forcing himself to relax his grip on the steering wheel. 'I've always used protection but it failed on the one occasion we slept together. I assumed it was an accident but later she told me she'd done it deliberately. I did the right thing by her and gave her and our daughter my name.'

'It must have made for a tricky relationship.'

He gave her a brief hard glance. 'I love my daughter.

I'm not happy that I was tricked into fatherhood but that doesn't make me love her any less.'

'I wasn't suggesting—'

'I had decided to marry Giulia even if Alessandra wasn't mine.'

'But why?' she asked. 'You said you weren't in love with her.'

'We were both at a crossroads. The man she had expected to marry had jilted her.' His lip curled without humour. 'You could say we had significant common ground.'

Eliza frowned at his little dig at her. 'So it was a pity pick-up for both of you?'

His eyes met hers in a flinty little lock before he returned to concentrating on the traffic. 'Marriage can work just as well, if not better, when love isn't part of the arrangement. And it might have worked for us except Giulia struggled with her mood once Alessandra was born. It was a difficult delivery. She didn't bond with the baby.'

Eliza had met a number of mothers who had struggled with bonding with their babies. The pressure on young mothers to be automatically brilliant at mothering was particularly distressing for those who didn't feel that surge of maternal warmth right at the start. 'I'm very sorry… It must have been very difficult for you, trying to support her through that.'

Lines of bitterness were etched around his mouth. 'Yes. It was.'

He didn't speak much after that. Eliza sat back and looked at the spectacular scenery as they drove along the Amalfi coast towards Positano. But her mind kept going back to his loveless marriage, the reasons for it, the difficulties during it and the tragic way it had ended.

He was left with a small child to rear on his own. Would he look for another wife to help him raise his little girl? Would it be another loveless arrangement or would he seek a more fulfilling relationship this time? She wondered what sort of woman he would settle for. With the sort of wealth he had he could have anyone he wanted. But somehow she couldn't see him settling for looks alone. He would want someone on the same wavelength as him, someone who understood him on a much deeper and meaningful level. He was a complex man who had a lot more going on under the surface than he let on. She had caught a glimpse of that brooding complexity in that bar in Rome four years ago. That dark shuttered gaze, the proud and aloof bearing, and the mantle of loneliness that he took great pains to keep hidden.

Was that why she had connected with him so instantly? They were both lonely souls disappointed by experiences in childhood, doing their best to conceal their innermost pain, reluctant to show any sign of vulnerability in case someone exploited them.

Eliza hadn't realised she had drifted off to sleep until the car came to a stop. She blinked her eyes open and sat up straighter in her seat. The car was in the forecourt of a huge, brightly lit villa that was perched on the edge of a precipitous cliff that overlooked the ocean. 'This isn't the same place you had before,' she said. 'It's much bigger. It must be three times the size.'

Leo opened her door for her. 'I felt like I needed a change.'

She wondered if there had been too many memories of their time together in his old place. They had made love in just about every room and even in the swimming pool. Had he found it impossible to live there once she had left? She had often thought of his quaint little sun-drenched villa tucked into the hillside, how secluded it had been, how they had been mostly left alone, apart from a housekeeper who had come in once a week.

A place this size would need an army of servants to keep it running smoothly. As they walked to the front door Eliza caught a glimpse of a huge swimming pool surrounded by lush gardens out the back. Scarlet bougainvillea clung to the stone wall that created a secluded corner from the sea breeze and the scent of lemon blossom and sun-warmed rosemary was sharp in the air. Tubs of colourful flowers dotted the cobblestone courtyard and a wrought iron trellis of wisteria created a scented canopy that led to a massive marble fountain.

A housekeeper opened the front door even before they got there and greeted them in Italian. 'Signor Valente, *signorina*, *benvenuto*—'

'English please, Marella,' Leo said. 'Miss Lincoln doesn't speak Italian.'

'Actually, I know a little,' Eliza said. 'I had a little boy in my class a couple of years ago who was Italian. I got to know his mother quite well and we gave each other language lessons.'

'I would prefer you to speak English with my daughter,' he said. 'It will help her become more fluent. Marella will show you to your room. I will see you later at dinner.'

Eliza frowned as he strode across the foyer to the grand staircase that swept up in two arms to the floors above. He had dismissed her again as if she was an encumbrance that had been thrust upon him.

'He is under a lot of strain,' Marella said, shaking her head in a despairing manner. 'Working too hard, worrying about the *bambina*; he never stops. His wife…'

She threw her hands in the air. 'Don't get me started about that one. I should not speak ill of the dead, no?'

'It must have been a very difficult time,' Eliza said.

'That child needs a mother,' Marella said. 'But Signor Valente will never marry again, not after the last time.'

'I'm sure if he finds the right person he would be—'

Marella shook her head again. 'What is that saying? Once bitten, twice shy? And who would take on his little girl? Too much trouble for most women.'

'I'm sure Alessandra is a delightful child who just needs some time to adjust to the loss of her mother,' Eliza said. 'It's a huge blow for a young child, but I'm sure with careful handling she'll come through it.'

'Poor little *bambina*.' Marella's eyes watered and she lifted a corner of her apron to wipe at them. 'Come, I will show you to your room. Giuseppe will bring up your bag.'

As Eliza followed the housekeeper upstairs she noticed all the priceless works of art on the walls and in the main gallery on the second level. The amount of wealth it took to have such masters in one's collection was astonishing. And not just paintings—there were marble statues and other objets d'art placed on each landing of the four-storey villa. Plush Persian rugs lay over the polished marble floors and sunlight streamed in long columns from the windows on every landing. It was a rich man's paradise and yet it didn't feel anything like a home.

'Your suite is this one,' Marella said. 'Would you like me to unpack for you?'

'No, thank you, I'll be fine.'

'I'll leave you to settle in,' Marella said. 'Dinner will be at eight-thirty.'

'Where does Alessandra sleep?' Eliza asked.

Marella pointed down the corridor. 'In the nursery; it's the second door from the bathroom on this level. She will be asleep now, otherwise I would take you to her. The agency girl will be on duty until tomorrow so you can relax until then.'

'Wouldn't it be better for me to move into the room closest to the nursery once the agency girl leaves?' Eliza asked.

'Signor Valente told me to put you in this room,' Marella said. 'But I will go and ask him, *sì*?'

'No, don't worry about it right now. I'll talk to him later. I suppose I can't move in while the other girl is there anyway.'

'*Sì, signorina.*'

Eliza stepped inside the beautifully appointed room once the housekeeper had left, the thick rug almost swallowing her feet as she moved across the floor. Crystal chandeliers dangled from the impossibly high ceiling and there were matching sconces on the walls. The suite was painted in a delicate shade of duck egg blue with a gold trim. The furniture was antique; some pieces looked as if they were older than the villa itself. The huge bed with its rich velvet bedhead was made up in snowy white linen with a collection of blue and gold cushions against the pillows in the same shade as the walls. Dark blue velvet curtains were draped either side of the large windows, which overlooked the gardens and the lemon and olive groves in the distance.

Once Eliza had showered and changed she still had half an hour to spare before dinner. She made her way along the wide corridor to the nursery Marella had pointed out. She thought it was probably polite to at least meet the girl from the agency so she could become familiar with Alessandra's routine. But when she got to the door of the nursery it was ajar, although she could hear a shower running in the main bathroom on the other side of the corridor. She considered waiting for the girl to return but curiosity got the better of her. She found herself drawn towards the cot that was against the wall in the nursery.

Eliza looked down at the sleeping child, a dark-haired angel with alabaster skin, her tiny starfish hands splayed either side of her head as she slept. Sooty-black eyelashes fanned her little cheeks, her rosebud mouth slightly open as her breath came in and then out. She looked small for her age, petite, almost fragile. Eliza reached over the side of the cot and gently brushed a dark curl back off the tiny forehead, a tight fist of maternal longing clutching at her insides.

*This could have been our child.*

The thought of never having a child of her own was something that grieved and haunted her. All of her life she had craved a family of her own. Becoming engaged to Ewan when she was only nineteen had been part of her plan to create a solid family base. She hadn't wanted to wait until she was older. She had planned to get married and have children while she was young, to build the secure base she had missed out on.

But life had a habit of messing with one's carefully laid out plans.

There was a part cry, part murmur from the cot. '*Mamma?*'

Eliza felt a hand grasp at her heart at that plaintive sound. 'It's all right, Alessandra,' she said as she stroked the little girl's silky head again. 'Shh, now, go back to sleep.'

The child's little hand found hers and she curled her

fingers around two of hers although she didn't appear to be fully awake. Her eyes were still closed, those thick lashes resting against her pale cheeks like miniature fans. After a while her breathing evened out and her little body relaxed on a sigh that tugged again at Eliza's heartstrings.

She looked at the tiny fingers that were clinging to hers. How tragic that one so young had lost her mother. Who would she turn to as she grew through her childhood into her teens and then as a young woman—nannies and carers and a host of lovers that came and went in Leo's life? What sort of upbringing would that be? Eliza knew what it was like to be handed back and forth like a parcel nobody wanted. All her life she had tried to heal the wound the death of her mother had left. Of feeling that it was *her* fault her mother had died. Would it be the same for little Alessandra? Feeling guilty that she was somehow the cause of her mother giving up on life? Of constantly seeking to fill the aching void in her soul?

There was a sound from the door and Eliza turned and saw Leo standing there watching her with an unreadable expression on his face. 'Where's Laura, the agency girl?' he asked.

'I think she's having a shower. I was just going past and I—'

'You're not on duty until the morning.'

Eliza didn't care for being reprimanded for doing something that came as naturally to her as breathing. Sleeping children needed checking on. Distressed children needed comforting. She raised her chin at him. 'Your daughter seemed restless. She called out to her mother. I comforted her back to sleep.'

Something moved through his eyes, a rapid flash of

pain that was painful to witness. 'Marella is waiting to dish up dinner.' He held open the door for her in a pointed fashion. 'I'll see you downstairs.'

'She looks like you.' The words were out before Eliza could stop them.

It was a moment or two before he spoke. 'Yes…' His expression remained inscrutable but she sensed an inner tension that he seemed at great pains to keep hidden.

She swallowed against the tide of regret that rose in her throat. If things had been different they would both be leaning over that cot as the proud, devoted parents of that gorgeous little girl. They might have even had another baby on the way by now. The family she had longed for, the family she had dreamed about for most of her life could have been hers but for that one fateful night that had changed the entire course of her life.

'*Mamma*?'

Eliza swung her gaze to the cot where Alessandra had now pulled herself upright, her little dimpled hands clinging to the rail. She rubbed at one of her eyes with a little fisted hand. 'I want *Mamma*,' she whimpered as her chin started to wobble.

Eliza went over to the cot and picked up the little toddler and cuddled her close. 'I'm not your mummy but I've come to take care of you for a little while,' she said as she stroked the child's back in a soothing and rhythmic manner.

Alessandra tried to wriggle away. 'I want Kathleen.'

'Kathleen had to go and see her family,' Eliza said, rocking her gently from side to side. 'She'll be back before you know it.'

'Where's *Papà*?' Alessandra asked.

'I'm here, *mia piccolo*.' Leo's voice was gentle as he placed his hand on his daughter's raven-black head.

The base of Eliza's spine quivered at his closeness. She could smell his citrus-based aftershave; she could even smell the fabric softener that clung to the fibres of his shirt. Her senses were instantly on high alert. Her left shoulder was within touching distance of his chest. She could feel the solid wall of him just behind her. She was so tempted to lean against the shelter of his body. It had been so long since she had felt someone put their arms around her and hold her close.

'I wetted the bed,' Alessandra said sheepishly.

Eliza could feel the dampness against her arm where the little tot's bottom was resting. She glanced up at Leo, who gave her a don't-blame-me look. 'She refuses to wear a nappy to bed,' he said.

'I'm too big for nappies,' Alessandra announced with a cute little pout of her rosebud mouth, although her deep-set eyes were still half closed. 'I'm a big girl now.'

'I'm sure you are,' Eliza said. 'But even big girls need a bit of help now and again, especially at night. Maybe you could wear pull-ups for a while. They're much more grown-up. I've seen some really cool ones with little pink kittens on them. I can get some for you if you like.'

Alessandra plugged a thumb in her mouth by way of answer. It seemed this was one little Munchkin who was rather practised in getting her own way.

'Let's get you changed, shall we?' Eliza said as she carried the little girl to the changing table in the corner of the nursery. 'Do you want the pink pyjamas or the blue ones?'

'I don't know my colours,' Alessandra said from around her thumb.

'Well, maybe I can teach you while I'm here,' Eliza said.

'You'd be wasting your time,' Leo said.

Eliza glanced at him with a reproving frown. Little children should not be exposed to negative messages about their capacity to learn. It could set up a lifelong pattern of failure. 'Pardon?' she said.

'My daughter will never learn her colours.'

'That's ridiculous,' she said. 'Why ever not?'

He gave her a grim look. 'Because she is blind.'

# CHAPTER FOUR

ELIZA BLINKED AT him in shock.

*Blind?*

Her heart clanged against her ribcage like a pendulum struck by a sledgehammer.

*Alessandra was blind?*

Her emotions went into a downward spiral. How cruel! How impossibly cruel that this little child was not only motherless but blind as well. It was so tragic, so unbearable to think that Leo's little girl couldn't see the world around her, not even the faces of the people she loved.

How devastating for him as a father. How gut-wrenching to think of all the obstacles that little mite would face over her lifetime. All the things she would miss out on or not be able to enjoy as others enjoyed them. The beauty of the world she would never see. It was so sad, so tragic it made Eliza's heart ache for Leo. It made her ache for the little toddler who lived in a world of blackness. 'I'm sorry…I didn't realise…'

'Will you tell me a story?' Alessandra piped up from the changing table.

'Of course,' Eliza said. 'But after that you have to go back to sleep.' Oh, dear God, how did the little babe even know it was night? Anguish squeezed the breath out of her chest. She felt as if she was being suffocated by it. How had Leo coped with such a tragic blow? Was that why his wife had ended her life? Had it been too much for her to cope with a child who was blind?

The agency girl, Laura, came in at that point. 'Oh, sorry,' she said. 'Is she awake? I thought she'd settled for the night.'

'My daughter's bed needs changing,' Leo said curtly.

'I'll see to it,' Laura said and rushed over to the cot.

Eliza had finished the business end of things with Alessandra and gathered her up in her arms again. 'I have just the story for you,' she said and carried her back to the freshly made up cot. 'Do you like dogs?'

'Yes, but Papà won't let me have a puppy,' Alessandra said in a baleful tone. 'He said I have to wait until I'm older. I don't want to wait until I'm older. I want one now.'

'I'm sure he knows what's best for you,' Eliza said. 'Now, let's get you settled in bed before I start my story.'

'Where's Kathleen?' Alessandra asked. 'Why isn't she here? I want Kathleen. I want her now!' Those little heels began to drum against the mattress of the cot.

'I told you she had a family emergency to see to,' Leo said.

'But I want her here with me!' Alessandra said, starting to wail again.

Eliza could see that Alessandra was a very bright child who was used to pushing against the boundaries. It was common after the death of a parent for the remaining parent or other carers to overcompensate for their loss. It was just as common for a child with a disability to be treated the same way. The little girl was used to being the centre of attention and used every opportunity she could to grasp at power.

'Kathleen is going to be away for the next month,' she said. 'But I think it might be nice if Papà gets her to call you on the phone while she's away.'

'Does she miss me?'

'I'm sure she does,' Eliza said. 'Now, let's get those feet of yours still and relaxed, otherwise my story won't come out to play.'

'How long are you staying?' Alessandra asked.

Eliza glanced at Leo but his expression was as blank as a mask. 'Let's not worry about that just now,' she said. 'The important thing is that you get back to sleep. Now, let's see how this goes. Once upon a time there was a little dog who loved to chase…'

'Asleep?' Leo asked as Eliza joined him downstairs a few minutes later.

'Yes.' She came over to where he was standing and looked up at him with a frown. 'Why on earth didn't you tell me?'

'I did tell you.'

'I meant right from the start.'

'Touché and all that.' He gave an indifferent shrug of one broad shoulder before he took a sip from the drink he was holding.

Eliza gave him a cross look. 'You should've told me at the beginning.'

'Would it have influenced your decision in taking up the post?'

'No, but I would've liked to know what I'm dealing with. I could've prepared myself better.' *I could have got all this confusing emotion out of the way so I could think straight.*

'Yes, well, life doesn't always give one the chance to prepare for what it has in store.'

*Tell me about it*, Eliza thought. 'She's a lovely child but clearly a little headstrong.'

His look was brittle. 'Are you saying I'm a bad parent?'

'Of course not,' she said. 'It's very clear you love her as any good parent should. It's just that it seems she's in control of everyone who has anything to do with her. That's very stressful for young children. She needs to know who is in charge. It's especially important for a child with special needs. How long has she—?'

'She's been blind from birth.'

Eliza felt her heart tighten all over again. It was a cramped ache deep in her chest. 'That must have been a huge blow to you and your wife.' How she hated having to say those words—*your wife*.

'It was. Giulia never quite got her head around it. She blamed herself.'

'It seems to me every mother blames herself no matter what the circumstances.'

'Perhaps, but in Giulia's case it was particularly difficult. She thought she was being punished for setting me up.'

'Did *you* blame her?' Eliza asked.

His brows came together over his dark eyes. 'Of course not. It was no one's fault. Alessandra was premature. She has retrolental hyperplasia. It was previously thought to be caused by an excess of oxygen in perinatal care but there's divided opinion between specialists on that now. It's also called ROP. Retinopathy of Prematurity.'

'Can nothing be done?' Eliza asked. 'There are advances happening in medicine all the time. Surely there's something that can be done for her?'

'There is nothing anyone can do. Alessandra can

only distinguish light from dark. She is legally and permanently blind.'

Eliza could hear the pain in his voice but it was even more notable in his expression. No wonder those grey hairs had formed at his temples, and no wonder his eyes and mouth were etched with those lines. What parent could receive such news about their child without it tearing them apart both physically and emotionally?

'I'm so very sorry. I can't imagine how tough this has been for you and will no doubt continue to be.'

'I want the best for my daughter.' His expression was taut with determination. 'There is nothing I won't do to make sure she has a happy and fulfilled life.'

Eliza wasn't quite sure what role she was meant to play in order to give Alessandra the best possible chance in life. The child had suffered enough disruption already without a fly-in, fly-out nanny to confuse her further. What Alessandra needed was a predictable and secure routine. She needed stability and a nurturing environment.

*She needed her mother.*

The aching sadness of it struck Eliza anew. How devastating for a little toddler to have lost the most important person in her life. How terrifying it must be for little Alessandra when she woke during the night and wanted the comfort of her mother's arms, only to find a series of paid nannies to see to her needs. No wonder she was difficult. Even a sighted child would be hard to manage after suffering the loss of her mother.

'What do you hope to gain for her from my period as her nanny?' she asked.

'You're an excellent teacher. You understand small children.'

'I've never worked with a vision impaired child before, only a profoundly deaf one,' Eliza said.

'I'm sure you'll find a way to make the most of your time with her,' he said. 'After all, I'm paying you top dollar.'

She frowned. 'It's not about the money.'

A dark brow arched over his left eye. 'No?'

'Of course not.' She pulled at her lip momentarily with her teeth. 'Don't get me wrong—I'm happy about your donation to the school, but I'm not in this for what I can get for myself. I'm not that sort of person.'

'Is your fiancé rich?'

Eliza felt the searing penetration of his cynical gaze. The insurance payout from the accident, along with the modest trust fund his late father had bequeathed Ewan had provided a reasonably secure income for the rest of his life. Without it, he and his mother, who was his chief carer, would have really struggled. 'He has enough to provide for his…I mean our future.'

'What does he do for a living?' Leo asked.

She looked at him numbly. What could she say? Should she tell him about Ewan's accident? Would it make a difference to how he thought of her? Explaining the accident would mean revealing her part in it. She could still see Ewan's face, the shock in his eyes and the pain of rejection in every plane and contour of his face. He had looked as if she had dealt him a physical blow. Even his colour had faded to a chalk-white pallor. For so long since she had wondered if she could have prepared him better for her decision to end things. It must have come as such a dreadful shock to him for her to announce it so seemingly out of the blue. She had been struggling with their relationship for months but hadn't said anything. But over that time she had found it harder and harder to envisage a future with him. Her love for him had been more like one would have for a friend rather than a life partner. Sex had become a bit of a chore for her. But she had felt so torn because he and his mother were the only family she had known after a lifetime of foster home placements.

*And he had loved her.*

That had always been the hardest thing to get her head around when it came to her final decision to end things. Ewan had loved her from the first moment he had helped her pick up the books she had dropped on her first day of term in sixth form after she had been placed with yet another foster family. She'd been the new kid in town and he had taken her under his wing and helped her to fit in. Being loved by someone had been a new experience for her. Up until that point she had always felt out of place, a burden that people put up with because it was the right thing to do for a kid in need. Being loved by Ewan had made her feel better about herself, more worthy, beautiful even.

*But she hadn't loved him the same way he loved her.*

'He has his own business,' she finally said, which was in a way not quite a lie. 'Investments, shares, that sort of thing.'

Marella came in just then, which shifted the conversation in another direction once they had taken their places at the table.

Eliza didn't feel much like eating. Her stomach was knotted and her temples were throbbing, signalling a tension headache was well on its way. She looked across at Leo and he didn't seem to be too hungry either. He had barely touched his entrée and took only a token couple of sips of the delicious wine he had poured for them both. His brow was furrowed and his posture tense. She sensed a brooding anger in him that he was trying to control for the sake of politeness or maybe because he was concerned Marella would come in on them with the rest of their meal.

'You blame me, don't you?' Eliza said into the cavernous silence.

His eyes were like diamonds, hard and impenetrable. 'What makes you say that?'

She drew in a sharp breath as she put her napkin aside. 'Look—I understand your frustration and despair over your daughter's condition but I hardly see that I'm in any way to blame.'

He pushed back from his chair so quickly the glasses on the table rattled. 'You lied to me,' he said through tight lips. 'You lied to me from the moment we met.'

Eliza rose to her feet rather than have him tower over her so menacingly. 'You lied to yourself, Leo. You wanted a wife and you chose the first woman to fit your checklist.'

'Why did you come on to me in that bar that night?

She found it hard to hold his burning gaze. 'I was at a loose end. I was jet-lagged and lonely. I have no other excuse. I would never do something like that normally. I can't really explain it even now.'

'Let me tell you why you did it.' His top lip curled in disdain. 'You were feeling horny. Your fiancé was thousands of miles away. You needed a stand-in stud to scratch your itch.'

'Stop it!' Eliza clamped her hands over her ears. 'Stop saying such horrible things.'

He pulled her hands down from her face, his fingers like handcuffs around her wrists. The blood sizzled in her veins at the contact. She felt every pore of her skin flare to take more of him in. Her inner core contracted as her body remembered how it had felt to have him thrusting inside her. His first possession four years ago had been rough, almost animalistic and yet she had relished every heart-stopping, pulse-racing second of it.

'You still want it, don't you?'

'No,' she said but her body was already betraying her. It moved towards him, searching for him, hungering for him, *aching* for him.

'Liar.' He brought her chin up, his eyes blazing with fiery intent.

'Don't do this,' she said but she wasn't sure if she was pleading with him or herself.

'You still want me. I saw it that first day when I came to your flat.'

'You're wrong.' She tried to deny it even as her pelvis brushed against his in feverish need.

He grasped her by the bottom and pushed her hard into his arousal. 'That's what you want, isn't it? You're desperate for it, just like you were four years ago.'

Eliza tried to push him away but it was like a stick insect trying to shift a skyscraper from its foundations. 'Stop it,' she begged. 'Please stop saying that.' A bubble of emotion rose in her throat. She tried to swallow it back down but it refused to go away. She didn't want to break down in front of him. She hated that weakness in her, the one where she became overwhelmed and crumbled emotionally. It was the abandoned little seven-year-old girl in her who did that.

She wasn't that little girl any more.

She was strong and independent.

She *had* to be strong.

*She had to survive.*

She had to withstand the temptation of losing herself in the sensual world of Leo Valente, the one man who could dismantle her carefully constructed emotional armour. Her armour had been just fine until he had come along. It had always stood her in good stead. But now it was peeling off her like a sloughed skin, leaving her exposed and raw and vulnerable.

'I'm sorry…' She squeezed her eyes tightly closed for a moment. 'I just need a little minute…'

He dropped his hold as if she had suddenly burned him. 'Save your tears.' He scraped a hand through his hair. 'It's not your pity I'm after.'

Eliza forced her eyes back to his hardened cynical gaze. 'Right now I'm having a little trouble figuring out what it is you actually want from me.'

'I told you. I want you to fill in for Kathleen. That's all I want.'

She watched as he strode to the other side of the room, his movements like his words: clipped and tense. Was it true? Was that *all* he wanted from her? What if he wanted more? Wasn't it too late? An unbridgeable chasm separated them. He'd had a child with another woman. She was still tied to another man. Even if they wanted to be together, how could she desert Ewan when it was her fault he was sitting drooling in that chair?

Maybe this *was* about revenge. It pained her to think Leo would stoop to that. Was he so bitter that he had to make her suffer? What good would it do to either of them to spend a month at war over what had happened four years ago? It wouldn't change anything. Their history would still be the same. Their future would still be hopelessly unattainable.

'You should go to bed.' Leo turned to look at her again. 'Alessandra is not an easy child to manage. You'll need all your reserves to handle her.'

'I'm used to dealing with difficult children,' Eliza said. 'I've made a career out of it.'

'Indeed you have.' He gave her a brief on-off movement of his lips that was a paltry imitation of a smile. 'Goodnight, Eliza.'

She felt as if she was being dismissed again. It didn't sit comfortably with her. She wanted to spend more time with him, getting to know the man he was now. Understanding the agony he was going through in handling a blind, motherless child. He seemed lonely and isolated. She could see it now that she knew what had put that guarded look in his eyes and that tension in the way he held his body. Who was helping him deal with his little girl's disability? Was anyone supporting him? She had met parents of special needs kids before. They carried a huge weight of responsibility on their shoulders. They had told her how shocking and devastating it had been to find they were now members of a club they had never intended to join: the autism club, the hearing impaired club, the learning disabled club—the not quite perfect club. And in most cases it wasn't a temporary membership.

*It was for life.*

'Leo…' She took a step towards him but then stopped when she saw the dark glitter of his gaze. 'I think it's important for Alessandra if she senses that we are friends rather than enemies.'

'How do you propose we do that?'

Eliza felt the mesmerising pull of his gaze. He was so close she could see the dark pepper of his stubble and her fingers twitched to reach up and feel its sexy rasp against her fingertips. She looked at his mouth, her stomach clenching as she remembered how passionately those lips could kiss and conquer hers. Her insides coiled as she thought of how he had explored every inch of her body with his lips and tongue. Was he remembering it too? Was he replaying every erotic scene in his head and feeling the reaction reverberate through his body? 'I…I think it's important we be civil to each other…'

'Civil?' Those fathomless dark eyes burned and seared as they held hers.

'Yes…civil…polite…that sort of thing.' She swallowed a tight little restriction in her throat. 'There's no need for us to be trading insults. We're both mature adults and I think it's best if we try and act as if we… um, like each other…a bit…at least while we're in the presence of Alessandra.'

'And what about when we are alone?' One of his brows lifted in a sardonic arc. 'Are we to continue to pretend to like each other—*a bit*?'

Something about his tone sent a shiver to the base of Eliza's spine. Being alone with him was something she was going to have to avoid as much as possible. The temptation of being in his arms had always been her downfall. Hadn't his rough embrace just proved it? He had only to touch her and her body burst into hungry flames of need. He said he didn't want her, but she saw the glitter of lust in his eyes. He could deny it all he liked but she could feel it like a third presence in the room. It hovered there between them, a silent but ever-present reminder of every erotic interlude they had shared.

His body *knew* hers intimately.

He knew how responsive she was to his touch. He knew how to make her flesh hum and sing. His touch on her body was like a delicate, priceless instrument being played by a maestro. No one could make her body respond the way he did. He was doing it now just by looking at her with that dark assessing gaze. It stroked her as it moved over her body. She felt the fizz and tingle of her lips as his gaze lingered there as if he was recalling how they had felt against his own. She felt a prickly stirring in her breasts when his gaze moved over them. Was he remembering how her tight nipples had felt against his teeth and tongue? Was he remembering how she had whimpered in pleasure as his teeth had sexily grazed her sensitive flesh? She felt the heat of arousal between her thighs even without him lowering his gaze that far. Was he remembering how it had felt to plunge his body into hers until they had both careened into mindless oblivion?

'I'm not here to spend time alone with you.' She gave him an arch look. 'I'm here to look after your daughter. That's what I'm being paid to do, isn't it?'

His gaze was inscrutable but she could see a tiny muscle clenching on and off in his jaw. 'Indeed it is.' He moved to the door. 'I'm going out for a short while. I don't know what time I'll be back.'

'Where are you going?' She mentally grimaced. She hadn't meant to sound like a waspish wife checking up on him.

He gave her a satirical look. 'Where do you think I might be going?'

Eliza felt her stomach plummet in despair. *He had a mistress*. No wonder he had pulled away from her. He already had someone else who saw to those needs. Who was she? Was it someone local? Had he set her up in a villa close by? Please don't let it be their villa—the villa where she had spent those blissful three weeks with him.

She set her mouth in a contemptuous line. 'Nice to

see you haven't let the minor inconvenience of widowhood and single parenthood get in the way of your sex life.'

His dark eyes glinted warningly. 'You are not being paid to comment on any aspect of my private life.'

'Did you get her to sign a confidentiality agreement too?' She threw him an icy glare. 'Did you pay her heaps and heaps of money to keep her mouth shut and her legs open?'

The silence was so tense it rang like the high-pitched whistle of a cheap kettle.

Eliza felt his anger. It was billowing in the air between them like invisible smoke. It sucked all the oxygen out of the room until she found it hard to breathe. She had overstepped the mark. She had let her emotions gallop out of control. She had revealed her vulnerability to him.

'Isn't jealousy a little inconsistent of you, given you're wearing another man's ring?' he asked in a deceptively calm tone.

She forced herself to hold his gaze. 'Relationships are not meant to be business contracts. You can't do that to people. It's not right.'

His lip curled mockingly. 'Let me get this straight—*you're* telling me what's right and wrong?'

She drew in a sharp breath to try to harness her spiralling emotions. 'I'm sorry. I shouldn't have said anything. It's none of my business who you see or what arrangements you make in order to see them.'

'You're damn right it's none of your business.'

Eliza bit down on her lip as he strode out of the room, flinching when he clipped the door shut behind him. The sound of his car roaring to life outside was like a glancing blow to her heart. She listened to him drive out of the villa grounds, her imagination already torturing her with where he was going and what he would be doing when he got there.

# CHAPTER FIVE

LEO UNMOORED HIS motor launch and motored out to a favourite spot where he could look back at the twinkling lights fringing the Amalfi coast. He dropped anchor and sat on the deck, listening to the gentle slap of the water against the hull and the musical clanging of the rigging against the mast of a distant yacht as the onshore breeze passed through. A gibbous moon cast a silver glow across the crinkled surface of the ocean. It was the closest he got to peace these days, out here on the water.

It was laughably ironic that Eliza thought he was off bedding a mistress. He hadn't been with anyone since Giulia had died ten months ago. Not that his relationship with her had been fulfilling in that department. He had tried to make it work a couple of times in the early days, but he had always known she was lying there wishing he were someone else.

Hadn't he done the same?

He hadn't wanted to hurt her by treating her as a substitute, so in the end they had agreed on a sexless arrangement. He could have had affairs; Giulia had told him to do whatever he had to do and she would turn a blind eye, but he hadn't pursued it. He had the normal urges of any other man his age, but he had ignored them to focus on his responsibilities as a parent and his ever-demanding career.

But his physical reaction to Eliza was a pretty potent reminder that he couldn't go on ignoring the needs of his body. He had wanted her so badly it had taken every ounce of self-control not to back her up against the nearest wall and do what they both did so well together. His groin was still tingling with the sensation of her body jammed tightly against his. He had felt the soft press of her beautiful breasts against his chest. He had desperately wanted to cover her mouth with his, to rediscover those sensual contours, to taste the hot sweetness of her.

He had intended to keep his distance during her short stay. He had been so confident he would be able to keep things on a business level between them. But, reflecting on it now, he could see how that call from Kathleen when he was in London for his meeting had completely thrown him. He was used to having his life carefully controlled. His domestic arrangements ran like clockwork. He had come to rely heavily on his staff, almost forgetting they had lives and families and issues of their own. When Kathleen had begged him for some time off he'd had to think on his feet and the first person he had thought of was Eliza. He'd told himself it was because she was a talented teacher and used to handling difficult and needy children. But what if the subconscious part of him had made the decision for a completely different reason?

*He still wanted her.*

Who was he kidding? Of course he still wanted her. But would a month be enough to end this torment that plagued him? Those three weeks he'd had with her had never left his memory. He could recall almost every passionate moment they had spent together. The memory of her body lived in his flesh. When he looked at her he felt his blood stir. He felt his heart rate rise. He felt his skin tingle in anticipation of her silky touch. The need to possess her was a persistent ache. Seeing her again had brought it all back. The blistering passion she evoked in him. The heat and fire of her response that made him feel as if she was his perfect mate—that there was no one else out there who could make him feel the way she did. It was going to be impossible to ignore the desire he had for her when every time he came within touching distance of her his body reacted so powerfully.

But wouldn't an affair with her create more problems, which he could do without right now?

On the other hand, he was used to compartmentalising his life. He could file his relationship with her into the temporary basket. Wasn't that what she would want? It wasn't as if she was going to end her engagement for him. She'd had four years to do so and yet she hadn't.

He didn't understand how she could sell herself so short. What was she getting out of her relationship with her fiancé that she couldn't get with *him*? He had offered her riches beyond measure, a lifetime of love and commitment, and yet she had thrown it back in his face. Why? What tied her to a man who *still* hadn't married her? He didn't even *live* with her. What hold did he have over her? Or was Eliza keeping a 'fiancé' up her sleeve so she could flit in and out of any shallow little hook-up that took her fancy? The ring she wore didn't look like a modern design. What if she just wore it for show? What if it was her get-out prop? '*Sorry, but I'm already taken*' was a very good way of getting out of a relationship that had run its course. She might have picked the ring up at a pawn shop for all he knew. If there was an actual fiancé Leo was almost certain she wasn't in love with him. How could she be when she looked at him with such raw longing? He was sure he wasn't imagining it. From the first moment he had laid eyes on her he had felt an electric connection that was beyond anything he had felt before or since.

But this time he wouldn't be offering her anything but an affair. He gave a twisted smile. A shallow hook-up was what he would offer. He would set the rules. He would set the boundaries and he would enforce them if he had to. He would not think about the morality of it. If she was willing to betray her fiancé—if there was one—then it was nothing to do with him.

*She could always say no.*

By two a.m. Eliza had given up on the notion of sleeping. It wasn't the jetlag or the strange bed. It was the restlessness of her body that was keeping her from slumber. A milky drink usually did the trick but could she risk running into Leo by going downstairs to get one? She hadn't heard him return, but then, why would he need to? He had plenty of staff to keep his household running while he indulged in an off-site affair with his latest mistress.

Eliza slipped on a wrap and went downstairs. There was enough moonlight coming in through the windows to light her way. Just as she was taking the last step down, the front door opened. She gave a little startled gasp and put her hand up to the throat where her heart seemed to have jumped. 'Leo?'

He gave her a wry look. 'Who else were you expecting?'

Eliza pursed her lips. 'I wasn't expecting anyone. And I wasn't waiting up for you, either.'

A mocking glint shone in his dark eyes. 'Of course not.'

She jutted her chin at him. 'I was on my way to the kitchen to get a hot drink.'

'Don't let me stop you.'

Eliza looked at his tousled hair. *Bed hair. Just had wild sex hair.* It maddened her to think he could just waltz in and parade his sexual conquests like a badge of honour. 'How was your evening? Did it live up to your expectations?'

Even in the muted light she could see the way his mouth was slanted with a cat-that-got-the-canary smile. 'It was very pleasurable.'

Jealousy was like an arrow to her belly. How could he stand there and be so…so *blatant* about it?

'I just bet it was.'

'You would know.'

Her brows shot together. 'What's that supposed to mean?'

His smile had tilted even further to give him a devilish look. 'You've had first-hand experience at spending many a pleasurable evening with me, have you not?'

Eliza tightened her mouth. She didn't want to be reminded of the nights she had spent rolling and screaming with pleasure in his bed. She had spent the last four years *trying* to forget. She threw him a dismissive look. 'Sorry to burst the bubble on your ego, but you haven't left that much of an impression on me. I can barely recall anything about our affair other than I was relieved when it was over.'

'You're lying.'

Eliza gave him a flinty glare. 'That's what really irks you, isn't it, Leo? It still rankles even after all this time. I was the first woman to ever say no to you. You could have anyone you wanted but you couldn't have me.'

'I could have you.' His eyes burned with primal intent. 'I could have you right now and we both know it.'

She gave a scornful laugh that belied the shockingly shaky ground she was desperately trying to stand on. 'I'd like to see you try.'

His eyes scorched hers as he closed the distance between them in a lazy stroll that sent an anticipatory shiver dancing down the length of her spine. She knew *that* look. It made her blood race through the circuitry of her veins like high-octane fuel. It made her heart thud with excitement and her legs tremble like a tripod on an uneven floor. It made her core clench with an ache that had no cure other than the driving force of his body.

He took her by the upper arms, his fingers digging into her flesh with almost brutal strength. 'You should know me well enough by now to know how foolish it is to throw a gauntlet down like that before me.'

Eliza suppressed another little shiver as she flashed him a defiant look. 'I'm not scared of you.'

His fingers tightened even further as he jerked her hard against him. 'Then perhaps you should be.' And then his mouth swooped down and slammed against hers.

It was a bruising kiss but Eliza was beyond caring. The crush of his mouth on hers brought all of her suppressed longings to the surface of her body like lava out of a volcano. She felt the raw need on her lips where his were pressed so forcefully. She felt it in her breasts as they were pushed up against his chest. She felt it unfurling deep in her core, that twisting, twirling, torturous ache that was moving throughout her body at breakneck speed.

How had she gone for so long without feeling this feverish rush of passion? It was like waking up after a decade of sleep. Every pore of her skin was alive and sensitised. Every muscle and sinew was crying out for the stroke and glide of his touch.

His tongue stroked hers until she was whimpering at the back of her throat. His hands were still hard on her upper arms, his fingertips gripping her with bruising force, but she relished in the feel of his commanding hold. His proudly aroused body was pressed intimately against her. She felt the hard ridge of him against the femininity of her body. The barrier of their clothes was torture. She wanted him naked and inside her, filling her, stretching her—making her feel alive in a way no one else could. She moved against him, speaking in a silent and primal feminine language that was universal.

But, instead of answering the call to mate, he dropped his hold and pulled back from her. He wiped the back of his hand across his mouth as if to remove the taste of her. It was a deliberately insulting gesture and she wanted to slap him for it. But she would rather die than show him how much he had hurt her.

'You've certainly got the Neanderthal routine down pat,' she said, pushing back her hair with a flick of her hand. 'I'm surprised you didn't haul me upstairs by the hair to your lair.'

His dark eyes mocked her. 'Surprised or disappointed?'

She held his look with a sassy one of her own. 'I wouldn't have done it, you know. I wouldn't have slept with you.'

The corner of his mouth kicked up cynically. 'No?'

'I was playing with you.' She straightened her wrap over her shoulders with fastidious attention to detail. 'Seeing how far you'd go.'

When she finally brought her gaze back to his another involuntary shiver trickled down her spine at the sexy, *knowing* glint shining there.

'You know where to find me if you feel like playing some more. My room is three doors down from yours. You don't have to knock. Just come right in. I'll be waiting for you.'

Eliza gave him a crushing look. 'Your confidence is seriously misplaced.'

His mouth tilted sardonically as he turned to make his way up the stairs. 'So is yours.'

Eliza was up early the following morning. Not that she had slept much during the night. The needs Leo had awakened made her feel restless and twitchy. All night long her mind had raced with a flood of memories of their past affair—racy little scenes where she had pleasured him or he had pleasured her. Erotic little flashbacks of her lying pinned beneath his rocking body, or her riding him on top until she gasped out loud. They all came back to haunt her—to torture her with the gnawing ache of want that refused to be suppressed. Was that why he had stepped back when he did? He wanted to make her *own* her need of him. He was playing with her like a cat did with a hapless mouse.

She wasn't going to let him break her. She knew he wanted her pride as a trophy. He wanted to have all the power, to be able to control what happened between them this time around. She understood his motivations. She had hurt him. She *regretted* that.

But on the battleground between them was a small defenceless child.

It wasn't fair to let Alessandra get hurt by the crossfire. Any arguments they had would have to be conducted in private. Any resentment would have to be shelved until they were alone.

As she was dressing after her shower Eliza noticed her upper arms bore the faint but unmistakable imprint of his fingers where he had gripped her the night before. It made her belly quiver to think he had branded her with his touch. She slipped on a three quarter length cardigan to cover the marks. She didn't want to have to explain to Marella or to Laura, the agency girl, how they had got there.

Laura was all packed up ready to leave when Eliza went to the nursery suite. 'Alessandra's still asleep,' she said, nodding towards the little girl's room. 'That's the best she's slept since I've been here. She's been a little terror the whole time. I don't think she's slept two hours straight before. You must have a magic touch.'

'I don't know about that,' Eliza said with a self-deprecating smile.

Laura lugged her backpack over one shoulder. 'I'd better get going. I have a ride waiting for me downstairs.' She offered her hand. 'Good luck with it all. I don't envy you having to answer to Leo Valente. He's quite intimidating, isn't he?'

'He's just being a protective father.'

Laura grunted. 'Yeah, well, I wouldn't want to get on the wrong side of him. Did you know him before or something? I don't mean to pry, it's just that last night I kind of got the impression you two knew each other.'

'I met him briefly a few years ago.' Eliza knew she had to be careful what she said. The confidentiality agreement Leo had made her sign made her think twice before she revealed anything about her previous connection with him. She couldn't risk being quoted out of context. She had no reason to believe he wouldn't be true to his word over the consequences of speaking out of turn. There was a streak of ruthlessness in him now that hadn't been there before. Didn't last night prove it?

'You dated him?' Laura probed.

'Not for long. It wasn't serious.'

Laura gave her a streetwise smile. 'Maybe you could have another crack at it. He's got loads and loads of money. He'd be quite a catch if you could put up with the foul temper.'

'I'm already engaged.'

Laura glanced at her left hand. 'Oh, I didn't realise. Sorry. When's the big day?'

'Yes, when is the big day?' Leo's deep voice spoke from behind them.

Eliza felt her face flood with colour as his gaze hit hers. She wondered how long he had been there. Long enough if that brooding look was anything to go by. 'Laura is just leaving, aren't you, Laura?'

'Yes,' Laura said and made a move for the door. 'I'll see myself out. Bye.'

A prickly silence filled the room once the young woman had left.

'I'd prefer you to refrain from gossiping with the hired help,' Leo said in a clipped tone. 'It's in your contract.'

'I wasn't gossiping. I was simply answering her questions. It would've been rude not to.'

'You're not here to answer questions. You're here to look after my daughter.'

Eliza returned his hardened glare. 'Is that *really* why I'm here? Or it is because you have an axe to grind? Revenge is a dirty word, Leo. It's a dirty deed that could turn out hurting you much more than it hurts me.'

His cleanly shaven jaw locked with tension. 'I'd have

to care about you for you to be able to hurt me. I care nothing for you. I only want your body and you want mine. Last night proved it.'

Anger pulsed in her veins at his arrogant dismissal of her as a person. 'Do you really think I would allow myself to be used like that? To be pawed over like some cheap two-bit hooker you hired off a dark alley?'

There was a condescending glitter in his eyes as they warred with hers. 'I'd hardly call a million pounds cheap. But you can forget about bargaining for more. I'm not paying it. You're not worth it.'

'Oh, I'm worth it, all right.' She put on her best sultry come-to-bed-with-me look. 'I'm worth every penny and more.'

He grasped her so suddenly the breath was knocked right out of her lungs. She felt the imprint of his fingers on the bruises he had left the day before but her pride would not allow her to wince or flinch. 'You want me just as much as I want you. I know the game you're playing. You want to drive up the price. I've sorted out your school, but it's *your* bank account you want sorted out now, isn't it?'

Eliza couldn't stop herself from looking at his mouth. It was flat-lined and bitter now, but she remembered all too well how soft and sensual it could be when it came into contact with hers. Desire flooded her being. She felt the on-off contraction of it deep in her core. He was the only man who could reduce her to this—to this primal need that would settle for nothing less than the explosive possession of his body. Could she withstand this temptation? Could she work for him without giving in to this desperate longing?

'I don't need your money.'

He gave one of his harsh laughs. 'But you'd like it all the same. You're starting to realise what you've thrown away, aren't you?'

'I always knew what I was throwing away.'

His top lip curled. 'Are you saying you have regrets?'

She arched her brow pointedly. 'Don't we all?'

He held her gaze in a stare-down that made the base of her spine fizz like sherbet. 'My only regret is I didn't see you for what you were at the outset. You're a classic chameleon. You can change in the blink of an eye. I had you pegged as an old-fashioned girl who wanted the same things I wanted. But you were not that girl, were you? You were never that girl. You were a harlot on the hunt for sensory adventure and you didn't care where you got it.'

'Why is it such a crime for a woman to want sensory satisfaction?' Eliza asked. 'Why does that make *me* a harlot? What does that make *you?* Why are there no equally derogatory names for men who want to be satisfied physically? Why do women have to feel so bad about their own perfectly natural needs that you men seem to take for granted?'

'What's wrong with your fiancé that he can't give you the satisfaction you want or need?'

The question was like a punch to her chest. 'I'm not prepared to answer that.'

'Does he even exist?'

Eliza looked at him numbly. '*What?*'

'Is he a real person or just someone you made up to use as a get-out-of-jail-free card?' His eyes were hard as they drilled into hers. 'It's a handy device to have a fiancé in the background when you want to get out of an affair that's not going according to plan.'

She swallowed against the lump in her throat. Ewan did exist, but not as he used to be. And it was *her* fault. His life was as good as over. He would never feel the things he used to feel. He could never say the words he used to say. He couldn't even think the thoughts he used to think. He existed…but he didn't. He was caught between the conscious world and the unconscious.

'You're so fiercely loyal to him. But is he as loyal to you?'

Eliza lowered her gaze as she fought her emotions back down. 'He's very loyal. He's a good person. He's always been a good person.'

'You love him.'

She didn't need more than a second to think about it. 'Yes…'

The silence hummed with his bitterness.

How was she going to survive a month of this? What good was going to come out of his attempt to right the wrongs of the past? Nothing could be gained from this encounter. He was intent on revenge but they would both end up even more damaged than they already were. She couldn't fix Ewan and she couldn't fix Leo. She had ruined two lives, three if she counted Samantha.

And what about *her* life—the plans she had made were nothing but pipe dreams now. She wouldn't be able to have the family she wanted. She wouldn't be able to have the love she craved.

*She was trapped, just like Ewan was trapped.*

Eliza turned to the nursery, desperate to get away from the hatred she could feel pouring out of Leo towards her. 'I'm going to check on Alessandra. She should be awake by now.'

'My daughter's orientation and mobility teacher will

be here at ten,' he said. 'Tatiana works with her until lunchtime twice a week. You can either have that time to yourself or observe some of the things she is helping Alessandra with. I don't expect you to be on duty twenty-four hours a day.'

Eliza looked at him again. 'Aren't you worried that she's going to be upset by my being here for such a short time? It sounds like a lot of people are coming and going in her life. It's no wonder she gets upset and agitated. She doesn't know who is going to walk in the door next.'

'My daughter is used to being managed by carers,' he said. 'It's a fact of life that she will always need to have support around her.'

She held his gaze for a beat that drummed with tension. 'I meant what I said last night. I think you should get Kathleen to call her each day. It will give her something to look forward to and it might make the time go a little quicker for her.'

His jaw seemed to lock for a moment but then he released a harsh-sounding breath. 'I'm not sure if Kathleen will be back. I got an email from her this morning. Her family want her to move back to Ireland. She's still thinking about it. She's going to tell me what she's decided in a couple of weeks' time.'

Eliza swallowed. 'Does that mean you'll want me to stay longer?'

His gaze became steely as it nailed hers. 'Your contract is for one month and one month only. It's not up for negotiation.'

'But what if your daughter wants me to stay?'

'One month.' The words came out clipped through lips pulled tight with tension, those bitter eyes hardening even further. 'That's all I'm prepared to give you.'

'Would you really put your plans for revenge before the interests of your daughter?'

'This is not about revenge.'

She made a sceptical sound in her throat. 'Then what *is* it about?'

His eyes roved her body in a searing sweep that made her skin prickle with heat and longing. The memory of his bruising kiss was still beating beneath the surface of her lips. The need he had awakened was secretly pulsing in the depths of her body—an intense ache that refused to go away. She felt it travel from her core to her breasts as his gaze travelled the length and breadth of her body. 'I think you know what this is about.'

*Lust.*

It wasn't a word Eliza particularly liked, but how else could she describe how he made her feel? From the very first moment she had met him he had triggered this earthy response in her. She knew he was experienced—*very* experienced. She had come to the relationship with much less experience, but what she had lacked in that department she had more than made up for in passion. Her response to him had shocked her then and it still shocked her now. Didn't that kiss last night prove how dangerous it was to get too close to him? He would dismantle her emotional armour within a heartbeat. Making love with him would unpick every stitch of her carefully constructed resolve. She could not afford to let that happen. Going back to her bleak and lonely life in England would be so much harder to bear if she experienced the mind-blowing pleasure Leo offered. How would she settle for the bitter plate of what fate had dished up to her if she got a taste of such sweet paradise again?

Eliza threw him a contemptuous look born out of the fear that he would somehow see how terrifyingly vulnerable she was to him. 'And just because you want something, you just go out and get it, do you? Well, I've got news for you. I'm not on the market.'

He came up close with that slow, leisurely stroll he had perfected. She refused to back away but instead gave him the full wattage of her heated glare as she steeled herself for the firm grasp of his hands on her arms.

But he didn't.

Instead he gently brushed the back of his bent knuckles down the curve of her cheek in a barely touching caress that totally ambushed her defences. She felt her composure crack as her throat closed over. Tears formed and stung at the back of her eyes. Her chest felt like an oversized balloon was inflating inside it, taking up all the space so her lungs could no longer expand enough to breathe.

'Why are you doing this?' Her voice was not much more than a thread of sound. 'Why now? Why couldn't you have let things be?'

His expression had lost its steely edge and was now almost wistful. 'I wanted to make sure.'

'Sure of…of what?'

'That I didn't make the worst mistake of my life the night you told me you were engaged.'

Eliza swallowed a walnut-sized knot of emotion. 'You…you had a right to be upset…' She couldn't look at him. She lowered her gaze again and stared at her engagement ring instead.

There was the sound of Alessandra waking in the nursery—the rustle of bedclothes and a plaintive wail.

'I'll go to her.' Leo moved past and Eliza listened as he greeted his little daughter. He spoke in Italian but she could hear the love in his voice that was as clear as any translation. '*Buongiorno, tesorina, come ti senti*?'

Was it wrong to wish he could look upon *her* as his treasure too?

# CHAPTER SIX

WHEN ELIZA CAME into the nursery Leo had Alessandra in his arms. 'I'll carry her downstairs for you but I won't be able to join you for breakfast,' he said. 'I have an online meeting in a few minutes.'

'Good morning, Alessandra,' Eliza said, reaching out to touch the child's hand that was gripping her father's shirt. 'It looks like we've got a date for breakfast.'

The little girl huddled closer to her father's chest. 'I want to have breakfast with *Papà*.'

Eliza exchanged a brief glance with Leo before addressing the child again. 'I'm afraid that's not possible today. But I'm sure *Papà* will make a special effort to have breakfast with you when he can.'

Alessandra's thin shoulders slumped as she let out a sigh. 'All wight.'

Once Leo had placed his daughter in her high chair in the breakfast room he kissed her on the top of the head and, with a brief unreadable glance at Eliza, he left.

Marella, the housekeeper, came bustling in, cooing to the child in Italian. '*Buongiorno, angioletta mia, tutto bene?*' She turned to Eliza. 'You have to feed her.' She nodded at the food in front of the child. 'She can't do it herself.'

'But surely she's old enough to do some of it on her own?'

'You'll have to discuss that with Signor Valente,' Marella said. 'Kathleen always feeds her. Tatiana, the O and M teacher, is trying to get Alessandra to do more for herself but it's a slow process.'

Eliza settled for a compromise by guiding Alessandra's hands to reach for things on her plate such as pieces of fruit or toast. The little girl was reluctant to drink from anything but her sippy cup so Eliza decided to leave that battle for another day. She knew how important it was to encourage Alessandra to live as normal a life as possible, but pushing her too fast, too soon could be detrimental to her confidence.

Tatiana, the orientation and mobility teacher arrived just as Marella was clearing away the breakfast things. After introducing herself, Tatiana filled Eliza in on the sorts of things she was doing with Alessandra while Marella momentarily distracted Alessandra.

'We're working on her coordination and spatial awareness. A sighted child learns by watching others and trying things for themselves, but a vision-impaired or blind child has no reference point. We have to help them explore the world around them in other ways, by touching and feeling, and by listening and using their sense of smell. We also have to teach what is appropriate behaviour in public, as they don't have the concept of being seen by others.'

'It all sounds rather painstaking,' Eliza said.

'It is,' Tatiana said. 'Alessandra is a bright child but don't let that strong will fool you. When it comes to her exercises she's not well motivated. That is rather typical of a vision-impaired child. They can become rather passive. Our job is to increase her independence little by little.'

'She seems small for her age.'

'Yes, she's on the lower percentile in terms of height and weight, but with more structured exercise she should catch up.'

'Is there anything I can do to help while I have her on my own?'

'Yes, of course,' Tatiana said. 'I'll write out a list of games and activities. You might even think of some of your own. Signor Valente told me you are a teacher, yes?'

'Yes. I teach a primary school class in a community school in London.'

'Then you're perfect for the job,' Tatiana said. 'What a shame you can't be here permanently. Kathleen is a sweetheart but she gives in to Alessandra too easily.'

'The post is only for a month,' Eliza said, automatically fingering the diamond on her left hand. 'I have to get back, in any case.'

'Don't get me wrong,' Tatiana said. 'Leo Valente is a loving father, but like a lot of parents of children with special needs, he is very protective—almost too protective at times. I guess it's hard for him, being a single parent.'

'Did you meet Alessandra's mother before she died?' Eliza asked.

Tatiana's expression said far more than her words. 'Yes and I still can't work out how those two ended up married to each other. I got the impression from Giulia it was a rebound relationship on his part.' She blew out a breath as her gaze went to where Alessandra was sitting in her high chair. 'I bet that's a one-night stand he's regretted ever since.'

Eliza could feel a wave of heat move through her cheeks. *I'm sure it's not the only one,* she thought with a searing pain near her heart. 'Leo loves his daughter. There can be no doubt of that.'

'Yes, of course he does,' Tatiana said. 'But it's probably not the life he envisaged for himself, is it? But then, lots of parents feel the same when they have a child with a disability. It's hard to get specialised nannies. Children with special needs can be very demanding. But to see them reach their potential is very rewarding.'

'Yes, I can imagine it is.'

'At least Signor Valente has the money to get the best help available,' Tatiana said. 'But it's true what people say, isn't it? You can't buy happiness.'

Eliza thought of Leo's brooding personality and the flashes of pain she had glimpsed in his eyes. 'No…you certainly can't…'

The morning passed swiftly as Tatiana worked with Alessandra in structured play with Eliza as active observer. There were shape puzzles for Alessandra to do as well as walking exercises to strengthen her muscles and improve her coordination. The little toddler wasn't good at walking on her own, even while holding someone's hand. Her coordination and muscle strength was significantly poorer compared to children her age. And, of course, what was difficult to the little tot was then wilfully avoided.

Eliza could see how a tired and overburdened parent would give in and do things for their child that they should really be encouraging them to do for themselves. It was draining and exhausting just watching the little girl work through her exercises and, even though Tatiana tried to make the session as playful as possible, Alessandra became very tired towards the end. There was barely time for a few mouthfuls of lunch before she was ready for her nap.

Eliza sat in the anteroom and read a book she had brought with her, keeping an ear out for any sign of the little girl becoming restless. An hour passed and then half of another but the child slept on. She could feel her own eyelids drooping when Marella came to the door with a steaming cup of tea and a freshly baked cup cake on a pretty flowered plate.

'You don't have to stay here like a prison guard.' Marella placed the tea and cake on the little table by Eliza's chair. 'There's a portable monitor. Its range is wide enough to reach the gardens and the pool. Didn't Signor Valente show you?'

'No…I expect he had too many other things on his mind.'

Marella shook her head sadly. 'Poor man. He has too much work to do and too little time to do it. He is always torn. He wants to be a good father but he has a big company to run. He'll drive himself to an early grave just like his father did if he's not careful.'

Eliza lowered her gaze to the cup of tea she was cradling in her hands. She thought of Leo getting through each day, feeling overly burdened and guilty about the competing demands of his life. Who did he turn to when things got a little overwhelming? One of his mistresses? How could someone he was just having sex with help him deal with his responsibilities? *Did* he turn to anyone or did he shoulder it all alone? No wonder he seemed angry and bitter a lot of the time. Maybe it wasn't just *her* that brought out that in him. Maybe he was just trying to cope with what life had thrown at him—just like she was trying to do, with limited success.

'I can imagine it must be very difficult for him, juggling it all.'

'After you've had your tea, why don't you take a

stroll out in the garden?' Marella said. 'I'll listen out for the little one. I'll take the monitor with me. I'll be on this floor in any case. I have to remake the bed the agency girl was using.'

Eliza could think of nothing better than a bit of sunshine. It seemed a long time since she had been in the fresh air. The villa was becoming oppressive, with its forbiddingly long corridors and large gloomy rooms. She put her cup down on the table. 'Are you sure?'

'But of course.' Marella shooed her away. 'It will do you good.'

The sun was deliciously warm as Eliza strolled about the gardens, the scent of roses thick and heady in the air. Was it her knowledge of Alessandra's blindness that made the colours of the roses seem so spectacular all of a sudden? Deep blood reds, soft and bright pinks and crimson, variegated ones, yellow and orange and the snowy perfection of white ones. Even the numerous shades of green in the foliage of the other plants and shrubs stood out to her as she wandered past. She went past the fountain and down a crushed limestone pathway to a grotto that was protected by the shade of a weeping birch. It was a magical sort of setting, secluded and private—the perfect place for quiet reflection. She slipped off her cardigan and sat on the wrought iron bench, wondering how many couples through the centuries had conducted their trysts under the umbrella-like shade of the lush and pendulous branches.

The sound of a footfall on the stones of the pathway made Eliza's heart give a little kick behind her ribcage. She stood up from the seat just as Leo came into view. He looked just as surprised to see her. She saw the camera-shutter flinch of his features in that nanosecond before he got control and assumed one of his inscrutable expressions.

'Eliza.'

'Marella told me to take a break. She's listening out for Alessandra. She's got the monitor. I didn't know you had one; otherwise—' she knew she was babbling but couldn't seem to stop '—she told me it would be all right and—'

'You're not under lock and key.'

Eliza tried to read his expression but it was like trying to read one of the marble statues she had walked past earlier in the long wide gallery in the villa. She wondered if he had come down here to be alone. Perhaps it was his private place for handling the difficulties of his life. No wonder he resented her presence. She was intruding on his only chance at solitude.

'I'd better head back.' She turned to pick up her cardigan that she'd left on the seat.

'What have you done to your arms?'

'Um—nothing.' She bunched the cardigan against her chest. It was too late to put it back on.

His frown brought his brows to a deep V above his eyes. 'Did I…?' He seemed momentarily lost for words. 'Did I do that to you?'

'It's nothing…really.' She began to turn away but he anchored her with a gentle band of his broad fingers around her wrist.

His touch was like a circle of flame. She felt the shockwave of it right to the secret heart of her. Her skin danced with jittery sensations. Her heart fluttered like a hummingbird and her breath halted in her throat like a horse refusing a jump.

'I'm sorry.' His voice was a deep bass—deeper than organ pipes. It made her spine loosen and quiver. It spoke to the primal woman in her, especially when he ever so gently ran one of his fingers over the marks he had made on her flesh. 'Do they hurt?'

'No, of course not.' She was struggling to deal with her spiralling emotions. Why did he have to stand so close to her? How could she resist him when he was close enough for her to sense his arrantly male reaction to her? If she moved so much as an inch she would feel him.

*Oh, how she wanted to feel him!*

Could he see how much she ached for him? How desperate she was to have it taken out of her control, to be swept away to a world where nothing mattered but the senses he awakened and satisfied.

'I'd forgotten how very sensitive your skin is.' His fingers danced over her left forearm, leaving every pore screaming for more of his tantalising touch.

Eliza swallowed convulsively. This was going to get out of hand rather rapidly if he kept on with this softly-softly assault on her senses. She could fend him off when he was angry and bitter. She could withstand him—only just—when he was brooding and resentful.

But in this mood he was far more dangerous.

*Her need of him was dangerous.*

She pulled back from his loose hold but it tightened a mere fraction, keeping her tethered to him—to temptation. 'I…I have to go…' Her words sounded desperate, her breathing even more so. She fought to control herself. She didn't want him to see how close to being undone she was. 'Please…let me go…'

'That was my mistake four years ago.' He brought her even closer, his hands going to the small of her back, pressing her to his need. 'I should never have let you go.'

'It wasn't a mistake.' She tried to push against his chest but he wouldn't budge. 'I had to go. I didn't belong with you. I *don't* belong with you.'

His hands gripped her wrists, gently but firmly. 'You keep fighting me but you want this as much as I do. I know you do. I *know* you want me. I feel it every time you look at me.'

'It's wrong.' Eliza was close to breaking. She couldn't allow herself to fold emotionally. She had to be strong. She had to think of poor Ewan. It was her fault he had been robbed of everything. He would never feel love again. He would never feel passion or desire.

Why should *she* feel it when he no longer could?

'Tell your fiancé you want a break.'

'I can't do that.'

'Why not?'

'He wouldn't understand.'

'Make him understand. Tell him you want a month to have a think about things. Is that so much to ask? For God's sake, you're giving him the rest of your life. What is one measly month in the scheme of things?'

Eliza tried to control her trembling bottom lip. 'Relationships can't be turned on and off like that. I've made a commitment. I can't opt out of it.'

His dark eyes glittered. 'Are saying you can't or you won't?'

She forced herself to hold his challenging look. 'I won't be used by you, Leo.'

One of his hands burned like a brand in the small of her back as he drew her closer. 'What's all this talk of me using you?' His voice was still low and deep, making her resolve fall over like a precariously assembled house of cards. 'You want the same thing I want. There doesn't have to be a winner or a loser in this. We can both have what we want.'

Eliza could feel the slow melt of her bones. She could feel that sharp dart of longing deep inside her body, the need that longed to be assuaged. Was it wrong to want to feel his passionate possession one more time? To explore the intense heat that continued to flare between them? But would one month be enough? How could it *ever* be enough? Experiencing that earth-shattering pleasure again would only leave her frustrated and miserable for the rest of her life. She would always be thinking of him, aching for him, *missing* him. It had been hard enough four years ago. He had lived in her body for all this time, making her even more restless and unhappy with her lot in life.

But it *was* her lot in life.

There was no escaping the fact that Ewan's life had been destroyed and that she had been the one to do it. How could she carry on with her life as if it didn't matter?

Of course it mattered.

*It would always matter.*

With a strength Eliza had no idea she possessed, she pushed back from him. 'I'm sorry…' She moved away from him until she was almost standing in the shrubbery. 'You're asking too much. It's all been too much. Finding out about your daughter's blindness… seeing how hard it is for her and for you. I can't think straight…I'm confused and upset…'

'You need more time.'

She squeezed her eyes closed for a moment as if that would make all of this go away. But when she opened them again he was still standing there, looking at her with his unwavering gaze.

'It's not about time…' She bit down on her lower lip. 'It's just not our time…' *It was never our time.*

He tucked a loose strand of her hair behind her ear. Her skin shivered at his tender touch, the nerves pirouetting beneath the surface until she was almost dizzy with longing. 'I've handled this appallingly, haven't I?' he asked, resting that same hand on the nape of her neck.

Eliza wasn't sure how to answer so remained silent. His hand was strong and yet gentle—protective. She longed to be held by him and never let go. But the past—their past—was a yawning canyon that was too wide and deep to cross.

He let out a rough-sounding sigh and, stepping away from her to look out over the rear garden, that same hand that had moments ago caressed her was now rubbing at the back of his neck as if trying to ease giant knots of tension buried there. 'I'm still not sure why I came to you that day in London. I needed a nanny in a hurry and for some reason the first person I thought of was you.' His hand dropped to his side as he turned and looked at her again. 'But maybe it was because I wanted you to see what my life had become.' His expression was tortured with anguish and frustration. 'I've got more money than I know what to do with and yet I can't fix my child. I can't *make* her see.'

Eliza felt his frustration. It was imbedded in every word he had spoken. It was in every nuance of his expression. He was in pain for his daughter—physical and emotional pain. 'You're a wonderful father, Leo. Your role is to love and provide for her. You're doing all that and more.'

'She needs more than I can give her.' He dragged a hand over his face. It pulled at his features, distorting them, making him seem older than his years. 'She needs her mother. But that's another thing I can't fix. I can't bring her mother back.'

'That's not your fault. You mustn't blame yourself.'

He gave her a weary look. 'Giulia was already broken when I met her. But I probably made it a thousand times worse.'

'How did you meet her?'

'In a bar.'

Eliza felt her face colour up. 'Not a great place to find lasting love…'

He gave her a look she couldn't quite decipher. 'No, but then people at a crossroads in their lives often hang out in bars. I was no different than Giulia. We'd both been disappointed in love. She'd been let down by a long-term lover. In hindsight, I would have been much better served—and her, for that matter—if I'd just listened to what had been going on in her life. She needed a friend, not a new lover to replace the one she'd lost.'

'What happened?'

His gaze dropped to the gravel at his feet as he kicked absently at a loose pebble. 'We had a one-night stand.' His eyes met hers again. 'I know you might find this hard to believe, but I don't make a habit of them. I regretted it as soon as it was over. We had no real chemistry. In some ways I think she only went through with it because she wanted to prove something to herself—that she could sleep with another man after being with her lover for so long.' He took a breath and slowly released it. 'She called me a month later and told me she was pregnant.'

'You must have been furious.'

He shrugged one shoulder. 'I wasn't feeling anything much at that stage. I guess that's why I offered to marry her. I truly didn't care either way. As far as I was concerned, the only woman I wanted wasn't available. What did it matter who I married?'

Eliza ignored the flash of pain his words evoked and frowned at him. 'Why was marriage so important to you? Most men your age are quite content with having affairs. They wouldn't dream of settling down with one person for the rest of their life, even when there is a child involved, especially one that wasn't planned.'

'My father loved my mother,' he said. 'It ended badly, but he always instilled in me that it was worth committing to one person. He didn't believe in half measures. His philosophy was you were either in or you were out. I admired that in him.

'I tried my best with Giulia. I gave her what I could but it wasn't enough. At the end of the day we didn't love each other. No amount of commitment on my part could compensate for her guilt over Alessandra's blindness. She just couldn't handle it. She rejected her right from the start. In her mind, it was as if someone had handed her the wrong baby in the hospital. She couldn't seem to accept that this was what life was going to be like from now on.'

'I'm sure there are a lot of parents who feel that way,' Eliza said.

He scored a pathway through his hair, as if even thinking about that time in his life made his head ache. 'The thing was, Giulia didn't want to have *my* baby. She wanted her ex's child.'

Eliza's frown showed her confusion as it pulled at

her forehead. 'But you said she deliberately set out to get pregnant, that she set you up.'

He gave her another weary look. 'It's true. But the thing is, I could have been anyone that night. She wanted to hit out at the man who'd let her down so badly. She wasn't thinking straight. On another night she might not have done it, but of course once it was done it was too late to undo it. She wasn't the type to have an abortion and, to be honest, I didn't want her to. We were both responsible for what happened. I could have walked away from her that night. But, in a way, I think I was trying to prove something too.'

Eliza sank her teeth into her lip, thinking about how devastating all this had been for him. His life had changed so swiftly and so permanently. And *she* had been part of that devastation when she had rejected his proposal. Was she always destined to ruin other people's lives? To make them desperately unhappy and destroy the life they had envisaged for themselves?

'I'm sorry…I can see now why you feel I'm partly to blame for how things have turned out. But who's to say we would've had a great relationship if I had been free to marry you?'

His dark eyes meshed with hers. 'Do you seriously doubt that we couldn't have had a satisfying relationship after what we shared during those three weeks?'

She turned away from his penetratingly hot gaze and folded her arms across her middle, cupping her elbows with her crossed over hands. 'There's much more to a relationship than sex. There's companionship and emotional honesty and closeness. The best sex in the world doesn't make up for those things.'

'Is that what you have with your fiancé? Emotional closeness?'

'I should get back…' Eliza glanced towards the villa. 'Alessandra will be well and truly awake by now. Marella will be wondering what's happened to me.'

She started back along the pathway but she didn't hear Leo following her. She glanced back when she got to the fountain but he had disappeared from sight. She gave an uneven sigh and, with a little slump of her shoulders, made her way inside the villa.

# CHAPTER SEVEN

ALESSANDRA HAD ONLY just woken when Eliza came back to the nursery. 'I've got a special surprise in store,' she said as she lifted her out of the cot.

'What is it?' Alessandra asked, rubbing at one of her eyes.

Tatiana had explained to Eliza that eye-rubbing was something a lot of vision-impaired children did. But while it gave temporary comfort similar to sucking a thumb, as the child got older it was less socially acceptable. Tatiana had advised that distracting the child from the habit was the best way to manage it, so Eliza gently pulled her hand away and circled her tiny palm with the finger play, *Ring a Ring o' Roses.*

Alessandra giggled delightedly. 'Do it again.'

'Give me your other hand.'

The little girl held out her hand and Eliza repeated the rhyme, her heart squeezing as she saw the unadulterated joy on the toddler's face. 'Again! Again!'

'Maybe later,' Eliza said. 'I have other plans for you, young lady. We're going for a walk.'

'I don't want to walk. Carry me.'

'No carrying today, little Munchkin,' Eliza said. 'You've got two lovely little legs. You need to learn to use them a bit more.'

She took the little tot's hand and led her out to the landing and then down the stairs. She got Alessandra to feel the balustrade as she went down and to plant her feet carefully on each step before taking another. It was a slow process but well worth it as by the time they got down to the ground floor she could tell Alessandra was a little more confident.

'Now we're going to go outside to the garden,' Eliza said. 'Have you been out there much?'

'Kathleen used to take me sometimes but then she got stinged by a bee. I cried because I thought it was going to sting me too.'

'Don't worry; I won't let you get stung.' Eliza gave the little child's hand a gentle squeeze of reassurance. 'There's a lot of lovely things to smell and feel out there. Flowers are some of the most beautiful things in nature but the really cool thing is you don't have to see them to appreciate them. Lots of them have really lovely perfumes, particularly roses. I bet after a while you'll be able to tell them apart, just from smelling them.'

Once they were out in the garden, Eliza led Alessandra down to one of the rose gardens. She picked some blooms and held them to the child's little nose, smiling as Alessandra sniffed and smiled in turn. 'Beyoo-tiful!' she said.

'That's a deep red one,' Eliza said. 'It's got a really rich scent. Here's a bright pink one. Its scent is a little less intense. What do you think?'

Alessandra pushed her nose against the velvet bloom. 'Nice.'

'Feel the petals,' Eliza said. 'There aren't any thorns on this one. I checked.'

The little girl fingered the soft petals, discovering each fold, her face full of concentration as if she was trying to picture what she was feeling. 'Can I smell some more?'

'Of course.' Eliza picked a yellow one this time. 'This one reminds me of the sunshine. It's bright and cheerful with a light, fresh fragrance.'

'Mmm.' Alessandra breathed in the fragrance. 'But I like the first one best.'

'That was the red one.' Eliza put them in a row on the ground and got Alessandra to sit on the grass beside her. 'Let's play a game. I'm going to hand you a rose and you have to tell me which colour it is by the smell. Do you think you can do that?'

'Will I know my colours after this?'

Eliza looked at the tiny tot's engaging little face and felt her heart contract. 'I think you're going to be an absolute star at this game. Now, here goes. Which one is this?'

Leo was coming back from speaking to one of the gardeners working on a retaining wall at the back of the garden when he saw Eliza and his little daughter sitting in a patch of sunshine on the lawn near the main rose garden. Eliza's attention was focused solely on Alessandra. She was smiling and tickling his daughter's nose with a rose. Alessandra was giggling in delight. The tinkling bell sound of his little girl's laughter sounded out across the garden. It was the most wonderful sound he had ever heard. It made something that had been stiff and locked inside his chest for years loosen.

He watched as Eliza rained a handful of rose petals from above Alessandra's head. Alessandra reached up and caught some of them, crushing them to her face and giggling anew.

He could have stood there and watched them for hours.

But then, as if Eliza had suddenly sensed his presence, she turned her head and the remaining petals in her hand dropped to the lawn like confetti.

He closed the distance in a few strides and his little daughter also turned her head in his direction as she heard him approach. '*Papà*?'

'You look like you are having a lot of fun, *mia piccola*.'

'I know my colours!' she said excitedly. 'Eliza's been teaching me.'

Leo quirked one of his brows at Eliza. 'You look like you're enjoying yourself too.'

'Alessandra is a very clever little girl,' she said. 'She's a joy to teach. Now, Alessandra, I'm going to pick some more roses. Let's show *Papà* how clever you are at distinguishing which one is which.'

Leo watched as she picked a handful of roses and came back to sit on the lawn next to his daughter. Alessandra's expression was a picture to behold. She held up her face for the brush of each velvet rose against her little nose. She breathed deeply and, after thinking about it for a moment, proudly announced, 'That's the pink one!'

'Very good,' Eliza said. 'Now, how about this one?'

'It's the red one!'

Leo looked on in amazement. How had she done it? It was like a miracle. His little daughter was able to tell each rose from the others on the basis of its smell but somehow Eliza had got her to associate the colour as well. Even though, strictly speaking, Alessandra hadn't learned her colours at all, it was a way to make her distinguish them by another route. It was nothing less than a stroke of genius. He felt incredibly touched that Eliza had taken the trouble to work her way through a task that had seemed insurmountable so that his little girl could feel more normal.

'OK, now, how about this one?' Eliza held up a white one and Alessandra sniffed and sniffed, her little face screwing up in confusion.

'It's not the yellow one, is it? It smells different.'

'You clever, clever girl!' Eliza said. 'It's a white one. I tried to trick you, but you're too clever by half. Well done.'

Alessandra was grinning from ear to ear. 'I like this game.'

Leo looked down at Eliza's warm smile. It made that stiff part of his chest loosen another notch. He imagined her with her own child—how natural she would be, how loving and nurturing. It wasn't just the trained teacher in her, either. He was starting to realise it was an essential part of her nature. She genuinely loved children and wanted to bring out the best in them. No wonder she had been recognised as a teacher of excellence. She cared about their learning and achievement. He could see the joy and satisfaction on her face as she worked with Alessandra. Sure, he was paying her big money to do it, but he suspected it wasn't the money that motivated her at all.

Why couldn't *she* have been Alessandra's mother?

'You're scarily good at this game,' Eliza said. 'I'll have to be on my toes to think of new ones to challenge you.' She got to her feet and took one of Alessandra's hands in hers. 'We'd better get you inside, out of this hot sun. I don't want you to get sunburnt.'

Leo moved forward to scoop his daughter up to carry her back to the villa but she seemed content to walk, albeit gingerly, by Eliza's side. He watched as she toddled alongside Eliza, her little hand entwined with hers, her footsteps awkward and cautious, but, with Eliza's gentle encouragement, she gradually gained a little more confidence.

'Four steps, Alessandra,' Eliza said as they got to the flagstone steps leading to the back entrance of the villa. 'Do you want to count them as we go?'

'One…two…three…four!'

Eliza ruffled her hair with an affectionate hand. 'What did I tell you? You're an absolute star. You'll soon be racing about the place without any help at all.'

Marella appeared from the kitchen as they came in. 'I've been baking your favourite cookies, Alessandra. Why don't we let Papà and Eliza have a moment while we have a snack?'

'*Grazie*, Marella,' Leo said. 'There are a few things I'd like to talk to Eliza about. Give us ten minutes.'

'*Sì, signor*.'

Leo met Eliza's gaze once the housekeeper had left with his daughter. 'It seems I was right in selecting you as a suitable stand-in for Kathleen. You've achieved much more in a day with Alessandra than she has in months.'

'I'm sure Kathleen is totally competent as a nanny.'

'That is true, but you seem to have a natural affinity with Alessandra.'

'She's a lovely child.'

'Most of the people who deal with her find her difficult.'

'She has a disability,' she said. 'It's easy to focus on what she can't do, but in my experience in teaching difficult children it is wiser to focus on what they *can* do. She can do a lot more than you probably realise.'

A frown pulled at his brow. 'Are you saying I'm holding her back in some way?'

'No, of course not,' she said. 'You're doing all the right things. It's just that it's sometimes hard to see what she needs from a parent's perspective. You want to protect her but in protecting her you may end up limiting her. She has to experience life. She has to experience the dangers and the disappointments; otherwise she will always live in a protective bubble that has no relation to the real world. She needs to live in the real world. She's blind but that doesn't mean she can't live a fulfilled and satisfying life.'

He moved to the other side of the room, his hand going to his neck, where a golf ball of tension was gnawing at him. 'What do you suggest I do that I'm not already doing?'

'You could spend more time with her, one on one. She needs quality time with you but also quantity time.'

Guilt prodded at him. He knew he wasn't as hands on as he could be. No one had played with him as a child. His mother had been too busy pursuing her own interests while his father had worked long hours to try and keep his company from going under. Leo wanted to be a better parent than his had been, but Alessandra's blindness made him feel so wretchedly inadequate. It had paralysed him as a parent. What if he did or said the wrong thing? What if he upset her or made her feel guilty for having special needs? Giulia, in her distress, had said unforgivable things in the hearing of Alessandra. He had tried to make up for it, but there were times when he wondered if it was already too late.

'I'll try to free up some time,' he said. 'It's hard when I'm trying to juggle a global business. I can't always be here. I have to rely on others to take care of her.'

'You could take her with you occasionally,' she said. 'It would be good for her.'

'What would be the point?' He threw her a frustrated glance. 'She can't *see* anything.'

'No, but she can feel, and she would be with you more than she is now. You are all she has now. The bond she has with you is what will build her confidence and sustain her through life. Stop feeling guilty. It's not your fault she's blind. It wasn't Giulia's fault. It's just what happened. Those were the cards you were dealt. You have to accept that.'

'You're not a parent. You know nothing of the guilt a parent feels.'

Her eyes flinched as if he had struck her. 'I know much more about guilt than you realise. I live with it every day. I *agonise* over it. But does it change anything? No. That's life. You have to find a way to deal with it.' Her gaze fell away from his as she pushed back a strand of her hair off her face.

Leo frowned as he narrowed his gaze to her left hand. 'Where's your ring?'

She glanced down at her hand and her face blanched. 'I don't know…' She looked up at him in panic, her eyes wide with alarm. 'It was there earlier. I have to find it. It's not mine.'

'What do you mean, it's not yours?'

She shifted her gaze again, her demeanour agitated. 'It's my fiancé's mother's. It's a family heirloom. I have to find it. It must have slipped off somewhere. It's a bit loose. I should've had it adjusted, but I—'

'It's probably in the garden where you were playing with Alessandra,' he said. 'I'll go and have a look.'

'I'll come with you,' she said, almost pushing him out of the way in her haste to get out of the door. 'I have to find it.'

'One of the gardeners will pick it up if it's out there,'

Leo said. 'Stop panicking. It didn't look all that valuable.'

She met his gaze with her distressed one. 'It's not about the monetary value. Why does everything have to be about money to you? It's got enormous sentimental value. I can't lose it. I just can't. I have to find it.'

'I trust my staff to hand it in if they find it. You don't have to worry. No one is going to rush it off to the nearest pawn shop.'

Her brow was a fine map of worried lines. 'You don't understand. I have to find it. I don't feel right without it on my finger.'

He grasped her flailing hand and held it firm. 'Why? Because you need it there as a reminder, don't you? Your fiancé is thousands of miles away but without that ring there to prod your conscience you could so easily forget all about him, couldn't you?'

She pulled out of his hold and dashed out of the room. Leo heard the slapping of her flat shoes along the marbled floor.

He followed at a much slower pace.

He would be perfectly happy if the blasted ring was *never* found.

Eliza looked everywhere but there was no sign of her ring. She went over every patch of the lawn. She went over the rose beds and the pathways but there was no trace of it anywhere. Her rising panic beat a sickening tattoo in her chest. How would she explain it to Samantha? It was so careless of her to have neglected to get it tightened. How would she ever make it up to her? It wasn't just any old ring. It was a symbol of Samantha's lifelong love for her husband Geoff and now *she* had lost it.

Leo had come out and spoken to the gardener before he joined her. 'Any sign?'

Eliza shook her head, her stomach still churning in anguish. 'Samantha will be devastated.'

'Samantha?'

'My fiancé's mother.' She wrung her hands, her eyes scanning the lawn in the vain hope that the sunlight would pick up the glitter of the ring. 'I don't know how I'll ever tell her. I have to find it. I *have* to.'

'The gardener will keep on looking. You should come indoors. You look like you're beginning to catch the sun.'

Eliza glanced at her bare arms. They were indeed a little pink in spite of the sunscreen she had put on earlier. She suddenly felt utterly exhausted. Losing the ring was the last straw on top of everything else. That telltale ache had started deep inside her chest. The tears were not far away. She could feel them burning like peroxide behind her eyes. She put her hand up and pinched the bridge of her nose to try and stop them from spilling.

'*Cara.*' Leo put a gentle hand on her shoulder. 'You're getting yourself in such a state. It's just a ring. It can be replaced.'

She shrugged off his hold and glared up at him with burning resentment. 'That's just *so* typical of you, isn't it? If you lose something you just walk out and get a new one. That's what you did when you lost me, wasn't it? You just went right on out and picked up someone else to replace me as soon as you could.'

The garden seemed to go into a stunned silence after her outburst. Even the light breeze that had been teasing the leaves on the trees had suddenly stilled, as if in shock at the bitterness of her words.

Eliza bit her lip as she lowered her gaze. 'I'm sorry…

That was wrong of me. You had a perfect right to move on with your life…'

There was another tense beat of silence.

'I hope you find your ring.' He gave her a curt nod and turned and strode across the lawn, back past the fountain until finally he disappeared out of sight.

# CHAPTER EIGHT

WHEN ELIZA CAME downstairs after putting Alessandra to bed there was an envelope with her name on it propped up on the kitchen counter.

'That's your ring,' Marella said as she came out of the pantry. 'Signor Valente found it in the grotto. He was out there for ages looking for it.'

'That was…kind of him…' Eliza fingered the ring through the paper of the envelope. 'I think I'd better get it tightened before I wear it again.'

Marella cocked her head at her as she picked up a cleaning cloth. 'How long have you been engaged to this fiancé of yours?'

'Um…since I was nineteen…eight years.'

'It's a long time.'

She shifted her gaze from the penetrating black ink of the housekeeper's. 'Yes…yes, it is…'

'You're not in love with him, *sì*?'

'I *love* him.' Had she answered *too* quickly? Had she sounded *too* defensive? 'I've always loved him.'

'That's not the same thing as being in love,' Marella said. 'I see how you are with Signor Valente and him with you. He stirs something in you. Something you've tried for a long time to suppress, *sì*?'

Eliza felt a wave of colour wash over her cheeks. 'I'm just the replacement nanny. I'll be gone in four weeks.'

Marella gave the counter top a slow wipe as she mused, 'I wonder if he will let you go.'

'I'm absolutely certain Signor Valente will be enormously pleased to see the back of me,' Eliza said with feeling.

Marella stopped wiping and gave her a level look. 'I wasn't talking about Signor Valente.'

A telling silence slipped past.

'Excuse me...' Eliza forced a polite smile that felt more like a grimace. 'I have to check on Alessandra.'

When Eliza came downstairs an hour later Marella was just leaving to attend a family function.

'There is a meal all set up on gas flamed warmers in the dining room,' she said as she tied a nylon scarf around her neck. 'I think Signor Valente is in the study. Will you be all right to handle dishing up? Don't worry about clearing up afterwards. I can do that in the morning.'

'I wouldn't dream of leaving a mess for you to face in the morning,' Eliza said. 'I'm perfectly capable of dishing up and clearing away. Have a good evening.'

'*Grazie*.'

Eliza glanced towards the study once the housekeeper had left. Should she wait until Leo came out for dinner to thank him for finding her ring or should she seek him out now? She was still deciding when the door suddenly opened.

He saw her hovering there and arched a brow. 'Did you want me?'

*I want you. I want you. I want you.* It was like a chant inside her head but it was reverberating throughout her body as well. She could feel that on-off pulse deep in her core intensifying the longer his dark, mesmerising gaze held hers.

'Um…I wanted to thank you for finding my ring,' she said, knowing her cheeks were burning fiery red. 'It was very thoughtful of you to take the time to keep looking.'

'It was behind the seat in the grotto. You must've lost it when you picked up your cardigan.' His dark gaze glinted satirically. 'I'm surprised you didn't notice it missing earlier.'

Eliza set her mouth. 'Yes, well, I'm going to get it tightened so it doesn't happen again.'

He reached for her hand before she could step away. She sucked in a breath as those long, strong, tanned fingers imprisoned hers. Her heart started a madcap rhythm behind her breastbone and her skin tingled and tightened all over. 'W…what are you doing?' Was that her voice, that tiny mouse-like squeak of sound?

His gaze went to her mouth, lingering there. She felt her lips soften and part slightly, her response to him as automatic as breathing. His fingers were warm and dry around hers. She imagined them on other parts of her body, how it had felt to have them caress her intimately, her breasts, her inner thighs, the feminine heart of her that had swelled and flowered under his spine-tingling touch. Her insides clenched with longing as she thought of the stroke of his tongue against her—that most intimate of all kisses. How he had seemed to know from their first time together what she needed to reach fulfilment.

She could see the memory of it in his gaze as it came back to mesh with hers. It made her spine shiver to see that silent message pass between them…the universal language of making love.

Passionate, primal—primitive.

‘*Ho voglia di te—ti voglio adesso.*’ His words were like a verbal caress, all the more powerfully, intoxicatingly stimulating as they were delivered in his mother tongue.

Eliza swallowed as her heart raced with excitement. ‘I don’t understand what you just said…’ *But I’ve got a pretty fair idea!*

Those dark eyes glittered with carnal intent as he grasped her by the hips and, with a little jerk forwards, he locked her against his erection. She felt it against her belly, the thunder of his blood mimicking the sensual cyclone that was happening within her own body. Her breasts ached for his touch. She could feel them swelling against the lace constraints of her bra. Her mouth tingled in anticipation of his covering it, plundering it. She sent the tip of her tongue out to moisten the surface of her lips. Her need of him was consuming her common sense like galloping, greedy flames did to a little pile of tinder-dry toothpicks.

‘I want you—I want you now.’ He said it this time in English and it had exactly the same devastatingly sensual impact.

‘I want you too.’ It was part confession, part plea.

He splayed a hand through her hair, gripping her almost roughly as his mouth came down on hers. It was a kiss that spoke of desperate longing, of needs that had for too long gone unmet, of a man wanting a woman so badly he could barely control his primitive response to her. It thrilled Eliza to feel that level of desire in him because it so completely and so utterly matched her own.

The stroke and glide of his tongue against hers set

her senses aflame. She undulated her hips against him, whimpering in delight as he in turn growled deep in his throat and responded by pressing even harder against her.

His hands moved over her body, skating over her breasts, leaving them tingling and twitching in their wake. She wanted more. When had she not wanted more from him? She wanted to feel his hands on her, flesh-to-flesh, to feel their skin in warm and sensual contact.

Her hands went to the front of his shirt, pulling at it as if it was nothing but a sheet of paper covering him. Buttons popped and a seam tore but she didn't hold back. Her mouth went to every bit of hard muscled flesh she uncovered. From the dish at the base of his neck just below his Adam's apple, down his sternum, taking a sideways detour to his flat dark male nipples, rolling the tip of her tongue over them in turn, before going lower in search of his belly button and beyond.

'Wait.' The one word command was rough and low. 'Ladies first.'

A shiver ran over her. She knew what he was going to do. The anticipation of it, the memory of it made her legs tremble like leaves in a wind tunnel.

He picked her up in his arms, carrying her effortlessly to the sofa inside his study. She felt the soft press of the cushions as he laid her down, those dark eyes holding hers with the unmistakable message of their sensual purpose, thrilling her from her tingling scalp to her curling toes.

He came back over her, but only to shove her dress above her hips. One of his hands peeled off her knickers, the slow but deliberate trail of lace as he pulled them down over her thigh to her ankles, another masterstroke of seduction in his considerable arsenal. She kicked off the lace along with her shoes, snatching in a quick breath as he bent his head to the swollen heart of her.

The intimacy of it should have appalled her given the current context of their relationship, but somehow it didn't. It felt completely natural for him to be touching her like this. To be touching and stroking her body as if it were the most fascinating and delicately fragrant flower he had ever seen.

'You are *so* beautiful.'

Oh, those words were like a symphony written only for her! She didn't feel beautiful with anyone else. No one else could make her body sing with such perfect harmony the way he did.

He took his time, ramping up her arousal to the point where she was sure she was going to scream if he didn't give her that final stroke that would send her careening into oblivion.

'Please...*oh, please...*' The words came out part groan, part gasp.

'Say you want me.'

'I want you. I want you.' She was panting as if she had just run up a steep incline. 'I want you.'

'Tell me you want me like no other man.'

She dug her fingers like claws into the cushioned sofa, her hips bucking as he continued his sensual torture. 'I want you more than anyone else... Oh, God. *Oh, God...*' Her orgasm splintered her senses into a starburst of feeling. It rattled and shook her body like a ragdoll in a madman's hands. It went on and on until she finally came out the other side, limbless and spent and breathless.

Leo moved up her body and set to work on removing her dress and bra. Eliza lifted her arms up like a child as he uncovered her flesh. She sighed with bone-deep pleasure as he took her breasts in his hands.

How had she gone so long without this exquisite worship of her body? Her flesh was alive with intense feeling. Shivers were still cascading down her spine like a waterfall of champagne bubbles. The very hairs on her head were still dancing on tiptoe. Her inner core was still pulsating with the aftershocks of the cataclysmic eruption of ecstasy that had rippled through it.

His hands gripped her hips once more as his body reared over hers. Somehow he'd had the foresight to apply a condom. She vaguely recalled him retrieving one from his wallet in his back pocket before he had shucked his trousers off.

He kissed her again, his mouth hard and yet soft in turn. It was a devastatingly seductive technique, yet another one he had mastered to perfection. She felt his erection poised for entry against her. She opened her legs for him, welcoming him with one of her hands pressed to the taut and carved curve of his buttocks, the other behind his head, pulling his mouth back down to hers as her ankles hooked around his legs.

He surged into her with a groan that came from deep at the back of his throat. It bordered on a rougher than normal entry but she welcomed it with a groan of pleasure. He seemed to check himself and then started to move a little more slowly, but she pushed him to increase his pace with little encouraging gasps and whimpers and further pressure from her hands pressing down on his buttocks.

She felt the rocking motion of his body within hers. She heard the intervals of his breathing gradually increase. She felt the tension in his muscles as they bunched up under the caress of her hands. The friction of his body within hers sent off her senses into another tailspin of anticipatory delight.

But still he wasn't intent on his own pleasure.

He was still focused on bringing about another delicious wave of hers and brought his fingers down to touch her. The way he seemed to know how much pressure and friction she needed to maximise her pleasure was the final undoing of her. The continued thrusting of his body and the delicate but magical ministration of his fingers were an earth-shattering combination. She was catapulted into another crazily spinning vortex of feeling that robbed her of all sense of time and place.

It was all feeling—feeling that was centred solely in her body.

But as she was coming down from the heights of human pleasure her mind resumed enough focus to register his powerful release. It sent another shockwave of pleasure through her body. She had felt every moment of that powerful pumping surge as he lost himself. There was something about that total loss of control that moved her deeply. It had always been this way between them. A mind-blowing combustion of lust and longing, and yet something else that was less easily definable...

As she moved her hands to the front of his body she noticed the pale circle on her bare left ring finger. It was a stark reminder of her commitment elsewhere.

Her stomach sank in despair.

She wasn't free.

*She wasn't free.*

She pushed against his chest without meeting his gaze. 'I want to get up.'

He held her down with a gentle but firm press of his hand on her left shoulder. 'Not so fast, *cara*. What's wrong?'

Eliza couldn't look at him. *Wouldn't* look at him. She stared at the peppery stubble on the bulge of his Adam's apple instead. 'This should never have happened.'

He took her chin between his finger and thumb and forced her to meet his gaze. 'Why is that?'

Her eyes smarted with the tears she resolved she *would not* shed in front of him. 'How can you *ask* that?'

His gaze quietly assessed hers. 'You still feel guilty about the natural impulses you have always felt around me?'

She lowered her lashes, chewing at her lip until she tasted the metallic sourness of blood. 'They might be natural but they're not appropriate.'

'Because you're still intent on tying yourself to a man who can't give you what you want or need?'

She continued to valiantly squeeze back the tears, still not looking at him. 'Please, let's not go over this again. I'm here with you now. I'm doing what you asked and paid me to do. Please don't ask me to do any more than that.'

He released a gusty sigh and got up, dressing again with an economy of movement Eliza privately envied. She felt exposed, not just physically—even though she had somehow managed to drag her discarded dress over her nakedness—but emotionally, and that was far more terrifying.

'Contrary to what you might think, I didn't pay you to sleep with me.' His voice was deep and rough, the words sounding as if they had been dragged along a gravel pathway. 'That is entirely separate from your position here as nanny to my daughter.'

She gave him a pointed look. 'Both are temporary appointments, are they not?'

His eyes were deep and dark and unfathomable. 'That depends.'

'Is Kathleen coming back?'

'She hasn't yet decided.'

'I thought you said my month-long contract was not up for negotiation,' Eliza said with a little frown. 'If she decides not to return, does that mean you'll offer me the post?'

'That also depends.'

She arched her brow. 'On what?'

'On whether you want to stay longer.'

Eliza chewed at her lip. If things had been different, of course she would stay. She would live with him as his lover, as his mistress, his daughter's nanny—whatever he wanted, she would do it because she wanted him so much.

But things *weren't* different.

They were exactly the same as they had been four years ago. It didn't matter what she wanted. It was the shackles of her guilt that would always make her forfeit what she wanted. How could she stay here with Leo and leave her other life behind? It was a fanciful dream she had to erase from her mind, just as she'd had to do in the past.

Eliza thought of little Alessandra, of how attached the child had become to her in such a short time. It wasn't just that the little girl was looking for a mother substitute. Eliza had latched onto her with equal measure. She looked forward to their time together. She felt excited about the ways in which Alessandra was growing and developing in confidence and independence. It wasn't just the teacher in her that was being validated, either. It was the deep-seated maternal instinct in her that longed to be expressed. Alessandra was responding to that strong instinct in her to love and protect and nurture.

If things were different, *she* would have been Alessandra's mother.

There was still a fiendish pain inside her chest at the thought of another woman sharing that deeply bonding experience with Leo. She so desperately wanted to be a mother. Each birthday that passed was a painful, gut-twisting reminder of her dream slipping even further out of her grasp.

Eliza brought her gaze back to his once she was sure she had her emotions hidden behind a mask of composure. 'Staying longer isn't an option…'

'Driving up the price, are we, Eliza?' A ripple of tension appeared along his jaw, his dark eyes flashing at her with disgust. 'That's what you're doing, isn't it? You want me to pay you a little extra to stay on as my mistress. How much do you want? Have you got a figure in mind?'

She took a steadying breath against the blast of his anger and turned away. 'There's no point talking to you in this mood.'

A hard hand came down on her forearm and turned her back to face him. His eyes blazed with heated purpose. She felt it ignite a fire in her blood where his fingers were wrapped around her wrist like a convict iron.

The tension in the air crackled like sheet lightning over a wide open plain.

'Don't turn away from me when I'm speaking to you,' he rasped.

Her chin went up and her eyes shot him their own fiery glare. 'Don't order me about like a child.'

His dark eyes glinted menacingly as they warred with hers. 'I'm paying you to obey my orders, damn it.'

Eliza felt a trail of molten heat roll down her spine but still her chin went even higher. 'You're not paying me enough to bow and scrape to you like a simpering servant.'

Those fingers burned her flesh like a brand. That hard-muscled body tempted her like an irresistible lure. Those dark eyes wrestled with hers until every nerve in her body was jangling and tingling with sensual hunger.

Heat exploded between her legs.

She could almost feel him there, that pounding surge of his body that triggered something raw and earthy and deeply primitive inside her.

'How much?' His eyes smouldered darkly. 'How much to have you in my bed for the rest of the month? How much to have you bowing and scraping and simpering to my every need?'

A reckless demon made her goad him. 'You can't afford me.'

'Try me. I have my limit. If you go over it I'll soon tell you.'

Eliza thought of the small house where Ewan and his mother lived in Suffolk. She thought of how much the bathroom needed renovating to make showering him easier for Samantha. She thought of the heating that needed improving because Ewan, as a quadriplegic, had no way of controlling his own body temperature. And then there were the lifting and toileting and feeding aids that always seemed to need an upgrade.

It all cost an astonishing amount of money.

*Money Leo Valente was willing to pay her to be his mistress for the rest of the month.*

Her heart tapped out an erratic tattoo. Maybe if she took the money it would make her feel less guilty about sleeping with him while she was engaged to Ewan. It would make it impossible to treat their relationship as anything but a business deal.

Well, perhaps not impossible…but unlikely.

*He would have her body but she wouldn't sell him her heart.*

Eliza met his hardened gaze with her outwardly composed one even as her stomach nosedived at the extraordinary step she was taking. 'I want two hundred and fifty thousand pounds.'

His brows lifted a fraction but, apart from that, his expression gave nothing away. 'I'll see that you get it within the next hour or two.'

'So—' she hastily disguised a tight little swallow '—it's not…too much?'

He brought her up against the trajectory of his arousal, the shock of the contact sending a wave of heat like a furnace blast right through her body. 'I'll let you know,' he said and sealed her mouth with the blistering heat of his.

# CHAPTER NINE

WHEN ELIZA WOKE the following morning her body tingled from head to foot. She turned her head but the only sign of Leo having shared the bed with her was the indentation on his pillow beside her.

And his smell…

She breathed in the musk and citrusy scent of him that clung to the sheets as well as her skin. His love-making last night had been as spine-tingling as ever, maybe even more so. For some reason the fact that he was paying her to sleep with him had made her stretch her boundaries with him. It had been heart-stopping and exciting, edgy and wonderfully, mind-blowingly satisfying.

The door of the bedroom opened and he came in carrying a cup of tea and toast on a tray. He was naked except for a pair of track pants that were slung low on his lean hips. 'I've already checked on Alessandra. Marella's giving her breakfast downstairs.'

'I'm sorry…' Eliza frowned as she pulled the sheet up to cover her naked breasts. 'I overslept…I didn't hear her on the monitor.'

'It didn't go off.' He put the tray down on her side of the bed. 'I took it with me. She woke up while I was down making the tea.'

She pushed a matted tangle of hair off her face with a sweep of her hand. This cosy little domestic scene was not what she was expecting from him. It caught her off guard. It made her feel as if she was acting in a play but she had been given the wrong script. She didn't know what was expected of her. 'You seem to be having some problems with your human resources department,' she commented dryly.

His dark glinting eyes met hers as he sat on the edge of the bed beside her. 'How so?'

She gave him an ironic look. 'Your housekeeper is acting as the nanny and your nanny is acting like the lady of the manor—or should I say lady of the villa?'

He trailed the tip of his index finger down the length of her bare arm in a lazy, barely touching stroke that set off a shower of sparks beneath her skin. 'Marella enjoys helping with Alessandra. And I quite enjoy having you playing lady of the villa.'

Eliza shivered as that bottomless dark gaze smouldered as it held hers. 'Wouldn't lady of the night be more appropriate?' she asked with a pert hitch of her chin.

A line of steel travelled from his mouth and lodged itself in his eyes. 'What do you want the money for?'

She gave a careless shrug and shifted her gaze to the left of his. 'The usual things—clothes, jewellery, shoes, salon treatments, a holiday or two.'

He captured her chin and made her look at him. 'You do realise I would have paid you much more?'

Her stomach quivered as his thumb grazed the fullness of her bottom lip. 'Yes…I know.'

He measured her gaze with his for endless, heart-chugging seconds. 'But you didn't ask for it.'

'No.'

'Why not?'

She gave another careless little shrug. 'Maybe I don't think I'm worth it.'

His thumb caressed her cheek as he cupped her face in his hand, his gaze still rock-steady on hers. 'Why would you think that?'

Eliza felt the danger of getting too close to him, of allowing him to see behind the paper-thin armour she had pinned around herself. She had to stay streetwise and smart-mouthed. She couldn't allow him to see any other version of herself.

*The real version.*

'You get what you pay for in life, wouldn't you agree?' She didn't pause for him to answer. 'Say my price was a million pounds. I figure this way you only got a quarter of me.'

His gaze continued to hold hers unwaveringly. 'What if I wanted all of you?'

Eliza felt a momentary flare of alarm in her chest. She had experienced his ruthless intent before. It was dangerous to be inciting it into action again. What he wanted he got. He wouldn't let anything or anyone stand in his way. Hadn't he already achieved what he'd set out to achieve? She was back in his bed, wasn't she? And it didn't look as if he was going to let her out of it any time soon. She held his look with a steady determination she wasn't even close to feeling. 'The rest of me is not for sale.'

His thumb moved back and forth over her cheek, slowly, mesmerizingly, that all-seeing, all-knowing gaze stripping away the layers of her defences like pages being torn from a cheap notepad. 'So which part have I bought?' he asked.

'The part you wanted.'

'How do you know which part I wanted?'

'It's obvious, isn't it?' She brazenly stroked a hand down his naked chest to the elastic waistband of his track pants, giving him her best sultry look. 'It's the same part I want of you.'

She heard him suck in a breath as her hand dipped below the fabric. She felt his abdomen tense. She felt the satin of his skin, the hot, hard heat of him scorching her fingers as they wrapped around him. Her body primed itself for his possession and she didn't care how sweet or savage it was going to be.

She yanked his track pants down further and bent her head to him, teasing him mercilessly with her tongue. He groaned and dug his fingers into her scalp but he didn't pull away, or, at least, not at first. She drew on him, tasting the essence of him, swirling her tongue over and around him, making little flicking movements and little cat-like licks until finally he could stand no more.

'Wait,' he gasped, trying to pull back. 'I'm going to—' He let out a short, sharp expletive as she went for broke. She had him by the hips and dug her fingers in hard. Her mouth sucked harder and harder, wanting his final capitulation the same way he went for hers—ruthlessly.

He came explosively but she didn't shy away from receiving him. He shuddered and quaked, finally sagging over her like a puppet whose strings had been suddenly severed.

Eliza caressed her hands over his back and shoulders, a slow exploratory massage of each of his carved and toned muscles. He had loved her massaging him in the past. And she had loved doing it. He had carried a lot of tension in his body even back then. There was something almost worshipful about touching him this way, with long and smooth strokes of her palms and fingers, rediscovering him like a precious memory she thought she had lost for ever. 'You've got knots in your shoulders. You need to relax more.'

'Can't get more relaxed than this right now.'

'I'm just saying…'

He lifted himself up on his elbows and locked gazes with her. 'We're doing this the wrong way around. It's not the way I usually do things.'

She tiptoed her fingers over his pectoral muscles. 'You're paying me to pleasure you. That changes the dynamic, surely?'

He pulled her hand away from his chest and sat upright, his expression contorted with a brooding frown, his gaze dark and disapproving. 'I know what you're doing.'

'What am I doing?'

'You're playing the hooker card.'

She gave a little up and down movement of one shoulder. 'If the shoe fits I usually wear it. I find it's more comfortable that way.'

'Is that really how you want to play things?'

Her brow arched haughtily. 'Do I have a choice?'

He held her gaze for a long pause before he let out a breath and got to his feet. He scraped a hand through his hair before he dropped it back down by his side. 'The money is in your account. I deposited it an hour ago.'

'Thank you.' She gave him a look. 'Sir.'

There was another tight pause before he spoke. 'I have to go to Paris on business. Marella has agreed to be here to help you with Alessandra. I don't expect you to be on duty twenty-four hours a day.'

'How long will you be away?'

'A day or two.'

'Why don't you take us with you?' she asked. 'It's a shortish trip. It shouldn't be too hard to organise. It would be a little adventure for Alessandra. It will build her confidence to travel and mix with other people other than just you and Marella and me.'

His jaw tightened like a clamp. 'Maybe some other time.'

Eliza suspected his 'maybe some other time' meant *no* other time. What did he think was going to happen to Alessandra if she stepped outside the villa for once? How was his little girl supposed to live a normal life if he kept her away from everything that was normal? 'You can't keep her hidden away for ever, you know.'

'Is that what you think I'm doing?'

'No one even knows you have a child, much less that she's blind.'

'I don't want my daughter to be ridiculed or pitied in the press.' His gaze nailed hers. 'Can you imagine how terrifying it would be for her to be hounded by paparazzi? She's too young to cope with all of that. I won't allow her to be treated like a freak show every time she goes out in public.'

'I understand how you feel, but she needs to—'

He stabbed a finger in the air towards her, his eyes blazing with vitriolic anger. 'You do *not* understand. You don't have any idea of what it's like to have a child with a disability. She can't *see*. Do you hear me? She can't see and there's not a damn thing I can do about it.'

Eliza swallowed unevenly, her heart contracting at the raw emotion he was displaying. He was angry and bitter but beneath all that was a loving father who was truly heartbroken that he could do nothing to help his little daughter. Tears burned in the back of her throat for what he was going through. No wonder he was always so tense and on edge. 'I'm sorry…'

He drew in a tight breath and released it in a slow, uneven stream. 'I'm sorry for shouting at you.'

'You don't have to apologise…'

He came back to where she was still sitting amongst the pillows, a rueful look on his face as he brushed a flyaway strand of her hair off her face. 'I know you're only trying to help but this is a lot for me to handle right now.'

She lowered her gaze again and bit at her lip. 'I shouldn't have said anything…'

He stroked the pad of his thumb over her savaged lip. 'Of course you should. You're an expert on handling children. I appreciate your opinion although I might not always agree with it.'

'I just thought it would be good for Alessandra to stretch her wings a bit.' She met his gaze again. 'But the press thing is difficult. I can see why you want to protect her from all of that. But sooner or later she'll have to deal with it. She can't stay here at the villa for the rest of her life. She needs to mix with other children, to make friends and do normal kid stuff like go to birthday parties and on picnics and play dates.'

He studied her features for a measured pause. 'I might have to go back to London some time next week. If you think Alessandra would cope with it then maybe we could make a little holiday out of it. Maybe take her to Kew Gardens or something. Smell a few roses. That sort of thing.'

Eliza gave him a soft smile and touched his hand where it was resting on the bed beside her. 'She's a very lucky little girl to have such a wonderful father like you. There are a lot of little girls out there who would give anything to be loved by their fathers the way you love her.'

His fingers ensnared hers, holding them in the warmth of his hand. 'You've never told me anything about your father. I remember you told me when we first met that your mother died when you were young. Is he still alive?'

She shifted her gaze to their joined hands. 'Yes, but I've only met him the once.'

'You don't get on?'

'We haven't got anything in common.' She traced a fingertip over the backs of his knuckles rather than meet his gaze. 'We live in different worlds, so to speak.'

He brought her hand up to his mouth and kissed her bent fingers, his eyes holding hers in a sensual tether that sent a wave of longing through her body. 'Your tea and toast are cold. Do you want me to get you some more?'

'You don't have to. I'm not used to being served breakfast in bed.'

He took her currently bare ring finger between his thumb and index finger, his eyes still meshed with hers. 'Doesn't your fiancé treat you like a princess?'

Eliza couldn't hold his gaze. 'Not any more.'

A silence dragged on for several moments.

'Why do you stay with him?'

'I'd rather not talk about it.'

He pushed up her chin to lock her gaze with his. 'Has he got some sort of hold over you? Are you frightened of him?'

'No, I'm not frightened of him. He's not that sort of person.'

'What sort of person is he?'

She flashed him an irritated look. 'Can we just drop

this conversation? I'm not comfortable about talking about him while I'm being paid to be in your bed.'

'Then maybe I should make sure I get my money's worth while you're here, *sì*?' He pinned her wrists either side of her head, his eyes hot and smouldering as his hard aroused body pressed her down on the mattress.

Even if her hands were free, Eliza knew she wouldn't have had the strength of will to push him away. Her lower body was on fire, aching with the need to feel him inside her. He released one of her hands so he could rip away the sheet that was covering her, his hungry gaze moving over her like a burning flame.

His mouth swooped down and covered hers in a searing kiss, his tongue driving through to meet hers in a crazy, lustful, frenzied dance. Her breasts swelled beneath the solid press of his chest, her nipples going to hard little peaks as they rubbed against him.

He reached across her to find a condom in the bedside cabinet drawer but he didn't take his mouth off hers to do it. He kissed her relentlessly, passionately, drawing from her the sort of shamelessly wanton response she'd only ever experienced with him. She used her teeth like a female tiger in heat, biting and nipping and tugging at his lower lip, teasing him with little flicks of her tongue against his, shivering in delight when he did the same back to her.

Once the condom was on he entered her with a thick, surging thrust that made her gasp out loud. There was nothing slow and languid about his lovemaking. It was a breathtakingly fast and furious ride to the summit of pleasure. She felt the pressure building so quickly it was like a pressure cooker about to explode. Her body needed only the slightest bit of extra encouragement from his fingers to send her over the edge into a tumultuous release that made her head spin along with her senses.

But he wasn't stopping things there.

Before she had even caught her breath he flipped her over on her stomach, straddling her from behind, those strong hands of his on her hips as he thrust deep and hard, again and again until she was shivering with pleasure both inside and out.

There was something so wickedly primal and earthy about this dominant position. She felt as if he was taming her, subduing her even as he pleasured her. She heard his breathing rate increase as he fought for control, the grip on her hips almost painful as he thrust above her.

She raised her bottom just a fraction and the change of friction set off an explosion of feeling that shuddered through her like an earthquake: tremor after tremor, aftershock after aftershock, until finally she came out the other side, totally spent and limbless.

His hands tightened on her hips to hold her steady as he came. She felt every spasm of his body. She heard those harsh, utterly male groans of ecstasy that delighted her so much.

Did he experience the same rush of pleasure with the other women he slept with? Was it foolish of her to think she was somehow special? That what he experienced with her was completely different than with anyone else? That the sensational heat of their physical connection was the real reason he had brought her back into his life, not just as a fill-in nanny for his daughter?

Leo turned her back over and looked at her for a long moment. It wasn't easy to read his expression. Was he, like her, trying to disguise how deeply affected he was by what they had both shared? 'I want you to promise me something.'

Eliza moistened her kiss-swollen lips. 'What?'

'If we go to London next week, there is to be no physical contact with your fiancé.'

His sudden change in mood was jarring to say the least. But then, what had she been expecting him to say?

'What are you going to do?' she asked. 'Keep me under lock and key?'

A flinty element entered his gaze as it held hers. 'I am not having you go from my bed to his and back again. Do I make myself clear?'

She resented him thinking she would do such a thing, even though she knew it was perverse of her to blame him given she hadn't told him the truth about her situation. She wondered if she should just tell him. Maybe he would understand her painful dilemma much more than she gave him credit for. Sure, she'd left it a bit late, but she might be able to make him understand how terribly conflicted she felt.

'Leo…there's something you need to know about Ewan—'

'I don't even want you to speak his name in my presence,' he said. 'I will not share you with him or anyone. I've paid for your time and I will not be short-changed or cuckolded.' He got off the bed and picked up his track pants and roughly pulled them back up over his hips.

Her pride finally came to her rescue. She swung her legs off the bed and, with scant regard for her nakedness, stalked over to where he was standing and poked her index finger into the middle of his chest like a probe. 'How dare you tell me who I can and can't speak about in your presence?' she said. 'I don't care how much money you pay me. I will *not* be ordered about by you.'

His eyes glittered as he stared her down. 'You will do as I say or suffer the consequences.'

She curled her lip at him. 'Is that supposed to scare me? Because, if so, it doesn't.' *It did, but she wasn't going to admit that.*

His mouth was a thin line of ruthless determination. 'You want a job to go back to at the end of the summer break? Then think very carefully about your behaviour. One word from me and your career as a teacher will be well and truly over.'

Outrage made her splutter. 'You can't do that!'

His hardened look said he could and he would. 'I'll see you when I get back.'

# CHAPTER TEN

It was almost a week before Eliza saw Leo again. Apparently the project he had in Paris had developed some issues and he needed to be on site to handle the difficulties. She had no doubt his work was demanding and time consuming, but in this instance she wondered if he had deliberately taken himself out of the picture to regroup. He didn't speak to her for long each time he called—just long enough for her to give him updates on what Alessandra was doing. The conversations were stiff and formal, just like a powerful employer to a very low-ranked employee. It riled her deeply, but she was nearly always with Alessandra when he called so she had no recourse. She had considered calling him when Alessandra was in bed asleep but had always talked herself out of it out of stubborn and wilful pride.

Alessandra clearly missed her father being around, but she seemed to accept he had to go away to work from time to time. Eliza enjoyed being with the little girl, even though at times it was challenging to think of ways to help her become more independent. Some days Alessandra was more motivated than others. But it was lovely to have the one on one time with her after coming from a busy classroom where she had to juggle so many children's educational and social needs.

Tatiana, the orientation and mobility teacher, came for another session and was thrilled to see how Alessandra had improved over the week. To Eliza it had seemed such painfully slow progress, but Tatiana reassured her that Alessandra was doing far better than other vision-impaired children her age.

The one challenge that Eliza was particularly keen to attempt was taking Alessandra for a walk outside the villa or even down to one of the cafés in Positano. She had spoken to Marella about it in passing, but while the housekeeper thought it was a great idea, she had reservations over what Leo would say.

'Why don't you ask him about it when he next calls?' Marella said.

Eliza knew what he would say. *No.* She wanted to present it as a fait accompli to show him how well his little girl was coping with new experiences. She took comfort in the fact that no one would know who she was so there would be no threat of press attention.

Their first walk outside the villa grounds was slow, but Eliza took comfort in the fact that Alessandra seemed to enjoy the different smells and sounds the further they went. She couldn't help feeling incredibly sad as she looked down at the exquisite beauty of the scenery below. The bluey-green water of the ocean sparkled in the sunshine, boats, frightfully expensive-looking yachts and other pleasure craft dotted the surface, but Alessandra could see none of it. It seemed so cruel to be robbed of such pleasure in looking at the glorious array of nature. But then, if Alessandra had never seen it, would she miss it the way a sighted person would if their vision was suddenly taken away?

Their second outing was a little more adventurous. Eliza got Giuseppe to drive them down to Spiaggia

Fornillo, the less crowded of the two main beaches in Positano. It had been quite an achievement getting the little girl to walk on the pebbly shore with bare feet but she seemed to enjoy the experience.

'Have you ever been swimming?' Eliza asked Alessandra as they made their way back to the villa in the car.

'Kathleen took me once but I didn't like it.'

'I didn't like swimming at first either,' Eliza said, giving the little girl's hand a gentle squeeze. 'But after you get over the fear part and learn to float it's one of the nicest things to do, especially on a hot day.'

That very afternoon Eliza took Alessandra down to the pool in the garden for a swimming lesson. With plenty of sunscreen to protect the little girl's pale skin, she gently introduced her to the feel of the water by getting her to kick her legs while she held her, gradually working up to getting used to having water trickle over her face. Alessandra was frightened at first, but gradually became confident enough to float on her back with Eliza keeping her supported by a gentle hand beneath her shoulder blades and in the dish of her little back.

'Am I swimming yet?' Alessandra asked, almost swallowing a mouthful of water in her excitement.

'Almost, sweetie.' Eliza gave a little laugh. 'You're getting better all the time. Now let's try floating on your tummy. You'll have to hold your breath for this. Remember how I got you to blow bubbles into the water before?'

'Uh huh.' Alessandra turned on her stomach with Eliza's guiding hands and gingerly put her face in the water. She blew some bubbles but soon had to lift her head to snatch in a breath. She gave a few little splutters but didn't seem too fazed by the experience.

'Well done,' Eliza said. 'You're a right little water baby, aren't you?'

Alessandra grinned as she clung to Eliza like a little frog on a tree. 'I like swimming now. And I like you. I wish you could stay with me for ever.'

Eliza's heart contracted sharply at the unexpected love she felt for this little child. 'I like you too, darling.' *And I wish I could stay for ever too.*

A tall shadow suddenly blocked the angle of the sun and she turned and saw Leo standing there with an unreadable expression on his face. 'Oh…I didn't realise you were back…Alessandra, your father is home.'

'*Papà*, I can swim!'

'I saw you, *mia piccola*,' Leo said, leaning down to kiss her on both cheeks. 'I'm very impressed. Is there room in there for me?'

'Yes!'

Eliza didn't say a word. She wasn't sure it was wise to share the pool—even as big as it was—with that tall, intensely male, leanly muscled body. Wearing a bikini when accompanied by a blind toddler was quite different from wearing it when there was a fully sighted, full-blooded man around, especially one who had seen her in much less. She felt the scorch of his gaze as it went to the curve of her breasts, which were showing just above the line of the water she was standing in. She felt her insides clench and release with that intimate tug of need she only felt when he was around.

A silent message passed between their locked gazes.

Eliza gulped as he stood back up and tugged at his tie, pulling it through the collar of his shirt to toss it to one of the sun loungers on the sandstone terrace beside the pool.

His shirt was next, followed by his shoes and socks.

The sun caught the angles and planes of his taut chest and abdomen, making him look like a statue carved by a master of the art.

Marella came out on to the terrace at that point with a tray of iced drinks. 'I think it might be time for Alessandra to get out of the heat, *sì*?' she said with a twinkling and rather knowing smile.

Eliza felt a blush rush over her face and travel to the very roots of her hair. 'It's my job to see to her—'

'*Grazie,* Marella,' Leo said smoothly. 'I think Eliza could do with some time to relax.' He bent and scooped Alessandra out of her arms. 'I will be up later to tuck you into bed, *tesorina.* Be good for Marella.'

Once Marella and the child had gone Eliza was left feeling alarmingly defenceless. She covered her chest with her arms, shivering even though the sun was still deliciously warm on her neck and shoulders. 'What are you doing?' she asked.

His hands were pulling his belt through the lugs of his trousers. 'I'm joining you in the pool.'

'But you're not wearing bathers…are you?'

A dark brow lifted in an arc. 'I seem to remember a time when you didn't think they were necessary.'

'That was before. It was different then. This place is like Piccadilly Circus. There are staff about everywhere.'

He unzipped his trousers and she watched with bated breath as he stood there in nothing but his black underwear. He already had the beginnings of an erection, which was no surprise given how her own body was reacting. 'Have you missed me, *cara*?'

She gave her head a haughty little toss. 'No.'

He laughed and slipped into the water beside her, cupping the back of her head with one of his hands as he pressed a hot kiss to her tight mouth. It didn't stay tight for long, however. All it took was one erotic sweep of his tongue for her to open to him with a sigh of bliss. He tasted salty and male with a hint of mint. It was ambrosia to her. She responded greedily, giving back as good as he gave, her tongue tangling, duelling and seducing just as his was doing to hers. Her breasts were jammed up against his chest, the water-soaked fabric abrading her already erect nipples.

His other hand ruthlessly undid the strings of her bikini top and it floated away from her body like a four-legged octopus. He cupped her free breasts with his hands, caressing her, teasing her with his warm, wet touch. He took his mouth off hers to feast on each breast in turn. Eliza arched back in pleasure as his teeth and his tongue grazed and salved in turn. Her nerves went into a sensual riot beneath her skin. They jumped and danced and flickered with longing. That deepest, most feminine ache of all pulsed relentlessly between her legs. She could feel his hard erection pressing against the softness of her belly. It awoke everything that was female in her. She rubbed against him to get more of that wonderful friction.

He made a guttural sound in his throat as he undid the strings of her bikini bottoms at her hips. The scanty fabric fell away and his fingers went to her, delving deep.

It wasn't enough. She wanted more. She wanted *all* of him.

She pulled at his underwear to free him to her touch. She wrapped her hand around him, rubbing him, teasing him, and pleasuring him as his mouth came back to hers in a passionately hot kiss that had undercurrents of desperation.

He suddenly pulled back from her, breathing hard, his eyes glazed with desire. 'I haven't got a condom.'

'Oh…' Disappointment was like an enervating drug that made her sag as if all of her muscles were weighted by anvils.

His eyes gleamed at her as he backed her against the side of the pool. 'Why the long face, *tesoro mio*? We can be creative, *sì*?'

Her body tingled at the thought of just how creative his lovemaking could be. But then, she too could be innovative when it came to giving him pleasure. She slithered against him, from chest to thigh, ramping up his need for her with the same merciless intent he had been using on her.

He took her by the waist and lifted her up to a sitting position on the edge of the pool. It was shamelessly wanton to open her legs in full view of the villa but she was beyond caring.

The first stroke of his masterful tongue made her shudder, the second made her gasp, and the third made her cry out loud as the ripples started to roll through her. 'Don't stop, don't stop, *don't stop…*' She clung to his hair for purchase as her body shattered around her.

He gave her a sexy smile as she came back to her senses. 'Good?'

She gave a little shrug that belied everything she had just felt. 'OK, I guess.'

'Minx.' He pulled her back into the water to hold her against him. 'I should punish you for lying. What do you think would be a suitable penance?'

*Send me back to my old life.* Eliza gave herself a mental shake and forced a smile to her lips. 'I don't know…I'm sure you'll think of something.'

His brows moved together. 'What's wrong?'

'Nothing.'

He cupped her cheek, holding her gaze with his. 'Are you still angry with me?'

Eliza was starting to wonder where her anger had gone. As soon as he had appeared on the pool deck she had forgotten all about their tense little battle of wills the day he had left to go to Paris. Her feelings about him now were much more confusing…terrifying, actually. She couldn't afford to examine them too closely.

'Does it matter to you what I feel?' she asked. 'I'm just an employee. I'm not supposed to feel anything but gratitude for having a job.'

His expression became brooding as his hand dropped away from her face. 'So we're back to that, are we?'

'You're the one who engineered this,' she said, struggling to keep her emotions in check. 'You come marching back in my life and issue orders and stipulations and conditions. I don't know what you want from me. You keep changing the goalposts. I just don't know who I'm supposed to be when I'm with you.'

He looked at her for a lengthy moment. 'Why not just be yourself?'

She gave a little cough of despair. 'I don't even know who that is any more.'

His hands came down on the tops of her shoulders, a gentle but firm hold. His eyes were very dark as they meshed with hers, but not with anger this time. 'Who was that girl in the bar four years ago?'

Eliza twisted her lips in a rueful manner. 'I'm not sure. I hadn't met her before that night. She came as a bit of a surprise to me, to be perfectly honest.'

He started massaging his thumbs over the front of her shoulders, slowly and soothingly. 'She came as a bit of a surprise to me, too. A delightful one, however.'

She felt a wave of sadness wash over her. How very different things would have been if she had been free to commit to the relationship he had wanted. 'Did you really fall in love with me back then?' She was shocked she had asked it but it was too late to take the words back. They hung in the silence for a beat or two.

'I think you were right when you said I was looking for stability after my father died. Losing him so suddenly threw me. I think it's hard for an only child—no matter how young or old—to deal with the loss of a parent. There's no one to share the grief with. I panicked at the thought of ending up like him, all alone and desperately lonely.'

'I'm sorry.'

He gave her shoulders a little squeeze before he dropped his hands. 'You'd better get some clothes on. You're starting to get goose bumps.'

Eliza watched as he effortlessly hauled himself out of the pool. He was completely unselfconscious about being naked. He stepped into his trousers and zipped them up without even bothering to dry himself. He bent to pick up his shoes and, flinging his shirt and tie over one shoulder, walked into the villa without a backward glance.

When Eliza came down to the *salone* later that evening Leo was standing with his back to the room with a drink in his hand. There was something about his posture that suggested he was no longer in that mellow mood he'd been in down by the pool. He turned as she came in and gave her a brittle glare. 'Alessandra informed me you'd taken her outside the villa grounds on not one, but two occasions.'

She straightened her shoulders. 'We didn't go very far. She'd never been to the beach before.'

'That's completely beside the point.' His eyes blazed with anger. 'Do you have any idea of the risk you were taking?'

'What risk is there in allowing her to walk down the street or put her feet in the ocean, for God's sake? I was with her the whole time.'

'You went expressly against my instructions.'

Eliza frowned at him. 'But you said we'd go to London next week. I thought it would be good preparation for that.'

'I said I'd *think* about it.'

'That's not the way I heard it. You said if I thought Alessandra would cope with it then we'd make a little holiday out of it. I was preparing her to cope with it and she did very well, all things considered.'

Anger pulsed at the side of his mouth. 'Did anyone see you? Were there paparazzi about?'

'No, why should there be?' she asked. 'No one knows who I am.'

'That could change as soon as we are seen in public together.' His eyes pinned hers. 'Have you thought of how you're going to explain *that* to your fiancé?'

Eliza raised her chin defiantly. 'Yes, I have thought about it. I'll tell him the truth.'

His brow furrowed. 'That I'm paying you to sleep with me?'

She gave him an arch look. 'It's the truth, isn't it?'

He shifted his gaze and let out a gust of a breath. 'It wasn't why I asked you to come here.'

'So you keep saying, but it's pretty obvious this is what you wanted right from the start.'

He took a large swallow of his drink and put it down,

his muscles bunched and tight beneath the fine cotton of his shirt. 'You haven't forgotten you're forbidden to speak to the press, have you?'

'No.'

He faced her with a steely look. 'You're not very good at obeying rules, are you, Eliza?'

'You're very good at making them up as you go along, aren't you?' she tossed back.

His mouth started to twitch at the corners. 'I wondered when she would be back.'

She frowned again. 'What…*who* do you mean?'

'The girl in the bar—that spirited, feisty, edgy little temptress.' His eyes glinted darkly. 'I like her. She turns me on.'

She made a huffy movement with one of her shoulders, trying to ignore the wave of heat that was coursing through her at that smouldering look in his gaze. 'Yes, well, I liked the guy by the pool this afternoon much more than the one facing me now.'

'What did you like about him?'

'He was nice.'

'Nice?' He gave a laugh. 'That's not a word I would ever use to describe myself.'

'You were nice four years ago. I thought you were one of the nicest men I'd ever met.'

His dark eyes gleamed some more. 'Even though I practically ripped the clothes from your body and had wild, rough sex with you the first night we met?'

'Did I complain?'

'No.' His frown came back and the ghost of a smile that had been playing about his mouth disappeared. 'Why did you come up to my room with me that night?'

'I told you—I was tipsy and jet-lagged and feeling reckless.'

'You were taking a hell of a risk. I could have been anyone. I could have hurt you—seriously hurt you.'

'I trusted you.'

'Foolish, foolish girl.'

Eliza felt a shiver run up along her arms. She could see the desire he had for her. She could feel it pulsing like a current in the air between them. 'The way I see it, you were taking a similar risk.'

The ghost of a smile was back, wry this time as it tilted up one corner of his mouth. 'I find it hard to see what you could have possibly done to hurt me. I'm almost twice your weight.'

*But I did hurt you*, she thought. *Isn't that why I'm here now?*

'Are you going to pour me a drink or do I have to jump through hoops first?' she asked.

'No hoops.' He came to stand right in front of her. 'Just one kiss.'

She tilted her head back and held his dark brown gaze pertly as the blood all but sizzled in her veins. 'Is that an order?'

He tugged her against his rock-hard body, his eyes scorching hers. 'You bet it is.'

# CHAPTER ELEVEN

WHEN ELIZA BROUGHT Alessandra downstairs for breakfast the next morning Leo intercepted them at the door. He reached for his daughter and held her close against his broad chest. Seeing such an intensely masculine man hold a tiny child so protectively made Eliza's heart instantly melt.

Was it her imagination that he seemed a little more relaxed this morning? It wasn't as if he was particularly rested, but then, neither was she. Their lovemaking last night had been particularly passionate and edgy. She could still feel the little pull of tender muscles where he had thrust so deep and so hard inside her. It was such a heady reminder of the breathtaking mastery he had over her body. But as much as she loved the heart-stopping raciness of his lovemaking, there was a tiny part of her that secretly longed for something a little more emotional. Maybe he didn't have the capacity to feel emotion during sex. It was just a physical release for him, like any other bodily need being attended to, like hunger and thirst. But it wasn't like that for her… or at least not now…

'I thought we could have breakfast out on the water this morning,' Leo said. 'Would you like that, *mia piccola*?'

'In the pool?' Alessandra asked.

'No, on my boat.'

'You have a boat?' Eliza asked.

'It's moored down at the marina. I thought Alessandra might enjoy being out on the water. I've never taken her on it before. Marella's packing us up a picnic to take with us.'

Eliza could see he was making an effort to spend more time with his daughter. He was relaxing his tight control over where she could go. She could also see what a big step it was for him to take. A trip out on a boat might be a relatively simple and rather enjoyable adventure for a sighted child, but in Alessandra's case there were many considerations to take into account. Her experience of the outing would be different but hopefully no less enjoyable. Besides, she would be with her father and that was clearly something that made her feel loved and special.

'Breakfast on the water sounds lovely, doesn't it, sweetie?' she addressed the little girl.

Alessandra hugged her arms tightly around her father's neck and smiled. 'Can I take Rosie with me?'

'Who's Rosie?' Leo asked.

'Rosie is the toy puppy Eliza made for me,' Alessandra said. 'She has long floppy ears and a tail just like a real puppy.'

Leo met Eliza's gaze over the top of his daughter's little head. 'Eliza is a very clever young lady. She is talented at many things.'

'I want her to stay with me for ever,' Alessandra said. 'Can you make her stay with us, *Papà*? I want her to be my *mamma* now. She tucks me in and reads me stories and she cuddles me lots and lots.'

Eliza felt emotion block her throat like a scrubbing brush stuck halfway down. She blinked a couple of times and shifted her gaze from Leo's. Alessandra needed someone there *all* of the time, someone she could rely on—someone to love her unconditionally.

Hadn't *she* felt the same desperate ache for stability and love as a child? Throughout her lonely childhood she had clutched on to various caregivers in an attempt to feel loved and cherished. Whenever she had been sent to yet another foster placement, she had blamed herself for not being pretty enough, cute enough or lovable enough. The constant pressure of wondering whether she was doing the right thing to make people love her had worn her down. She had eventually stopped trying and at times had deliberately sabotaged the relationships that could have most helped her.

But Alessandra wasn't a difficult child to love. Eliza loved all children—even the most trying ones—but something about Leo's little girl had planted a tiny fishhook in her heart. She felt it tugging on her whenever she thought of the day when her time with her would come to an end. Leaving Leo would break her heart, leaving his daughter would rip it from her chest.

'I'm afraid that's not possible,' Leo said in a matter-of-fact tone. 'Now, let's go and get that picnic, shall we?'

Leo's motor launch was moored amongst similar luxury boats down at the marina. It was a beautiful vessel, sleek and powerful as it carved through the water. The sun was bright and made thousands of diamonds sparkle across the surface of the sea. It was a poignant reminder that little Alessandra couldn't see the beauty that surrounded them. But she was clearly enjoying being in the fresh air with the briny scent of the sea in the air. She lifted her face to the breeze as the boat moved across the water and giggled in delight when a spray of moisture hit her face. 'It's wetting me!'

'The ocean is blowing you kisses,' Eliza said and dropped a kiss on the top of the little girl's wind-tousled hair. She looked up and caught Leo's gaze on her. 'It's a gorgeous boat, Leo. Have you had it long?'

'I bought it just before Alessandra was born.' He brushed back his hair off his face with one of his hands, and although he was wearing reflective sunglasses she could see the crease of a frown between his brows. 'I thought it'd be a great thing to do as a family. Get out on the water, sail into the sunset, get away from the madding crowd, so to speak.' His mouth twisted ruefully. 'I only ever take it out on my own, mostly late at night when Alessandra's fast asleep in bed when Kathleen or Marella are on duty. I suppose I should think about selling it.'

Eliza looked at his wind-tousled hair and her heart gave a little leap of hope. 'Is that where you went the other night? Out here on the boat…alone?'

His expression was self-deprecating. 'Not quite what you were expecting from a worldly playboy, is it?'

Eliza was conscious of Alessandra sitting on her knee but she hoped the unfamiliar English words would not compromise her innocence. 'When was the last time you were…um…a playboy?'

'I took my marriage vows seriously, even though nothing was happening in that department, more or less since that first night. We agreed to leave things on a platonic basis. In the time since she…left us ten months ago…' he glanced at his daughter for a moment before returning his gaze to hers '…I've had other more important priorities.'

Eliza stared at him in shock. For the last four years

he had not been out with a variety of mistresses. He hadn't been with *anyone.* Like her, he had been concentrating on his responsibilities, trying to do the best he could under difficult and heart-wrenching circumstances. The night she had thought he had been having bed-wrecking sex with some casual hook-up, he had actually been out on his boat—*alone.* Probably spending the time like she did back in her life in England, tortured with guilt and desperation at how life had thrown such a devastating curve ball.

Alessandra shifted on Eliza's lap. 'I'm hungry.'

Eliza ruffled the little tot's raven-black hair. 'Then let's have breakfast.'

Leo met her gaze and gave her a smile. 'How about you set up the picnic in the dining area while I teach this young lady how to steer a motor launch?'

'Can I steer it? Can I really?' Alessandra asked with excitement. 'What if I run into something?'

He scooped her up in his arms and carried her towards the bow. 'You'll have me by your side to direct you, *mia piccola.* We'll be a team. A team works together so no one gets into trouble. We look out for each other.'

'Can Eliza be part of our team?' Alessandra asked. 'For always and always?'

Eliza blinked back a rush of tears and looked out at the ocean so Leo couldn't see how much his little girl's request had pained her. Why was life always so full of such difficult choices? If she chose to stay she would be abandoning Samantha and Ewan. If she chose to leave she would be breaking not only her own heart, but also dear little Alessandra's.

As for Leo's heart…did he still have one after what happened between them four years ago? She had a feeling he had closed off his heart since then. Yes, he loved his daughter, but he would allow no one else to get close to him.

'She's a part of our team for now,' he said in a deep and gravelly tone. 'Now, let's get your hands on the wheel. Yes, just like that. Now, here we go—full steam ahead.'

On the way back to the marina after breakfast, Leo glanced at Eliza, who was sitting with his daughter on her lap, holding one of her little hands in hers with an indulgent smile on her face. To anyone looking from the outside, she would easily pass for Alessandra's biological mother with her glossy mahogany hair and creamy toned skin.

Although he had paid an enormous sum of money to engage her services as a nanny, he suspected she would have been just as dedicated if he had paid her nothing. She seemed to genuinely care for his daughter. He had seen her numerous times when she hadn't known he was watching. Those spontaneous hugs and kisses she gave Alessandra could not be anything but genuine.

Even his housekeeper, Marella, had commented on how much happier Alessandra seemed now that Eliza was there. Truth be told, he had found it a little unnerving to see Eliza's relationship grow and blossom with his daughter. He hadn't planned on Alessandra getting so attached to her so quickly. He had felt confident Alessandra's relationship with Kathleen would override any new feelings she developed for Eliza.

And, as much as he hated to admit it, the villa did seem more of a home with the sound of laughter and footsteps going up and down the corridors. Eliza had enhanced his daughter's life in such a short time. Her swimming lessons and her trips to the beach had built his daughter's awareness of the world around her. Eliza's competence and confidence in exposing Alessandra to new things had helped give him the confidence to take this outing today. She had shown him that he could afford to be more adventurous in taking Alessandra out and about more. His little girl might not be able to see the things he so desperately wanted her to see, but she had clearly enjoyed the sunshine and the fresh air and the sound of the water and the sea birds. How much more could he help her experience?

But how could he do it without Eliza?

When they returned from the trip to London there would be less than ten days left before Kathleen returned. She had emailed him and told him she wasn't going to stay in Ireland with her family after all. A couple of weeks ago he would have been thrilled by that announcement.

But now…he wasn't sure he wanted to think about how he felt.

Eliza hadn't been wearing her engagement ring but he had noticed it swinging on a chain around her neck a couple of times. She took care never to wear it when they were in bed together but it irked him that she still clung to it. He knew she wasn't in love with the guy and yet he didn't like to fool himself that she was in love with him instead.

Their arrangement was purely a sexual one, not an emotional one. He was happy with that. Perhaps happy was not the best choice of word—content, satisfied…

OK, frustrated was probably a little closer to how he was feeling. He always felt as if she gave everything of herself physically when they were together but there was a part of her that was still off-limits.

What perverse facet of his personality craved that one elusive part of her that she refused to offer him? It wasn't as if he loved her. He had sworn he would never allow himself to be that vulnerable again. Hadn't he learnt that lesson the hard way in childhood? He had loved his mother and look how she had walked out as if he had meant nothing to her.

He flatly *refused* to let anyone do that to him again.

He had been caught off guard with Eliza four years ago. The sudden death of his father had left him reeling. He had seen something in Eliza that had spoken directly to his damaged soul. He had felt as if they were kindred spirits. He knew that it sounded like some sort of crystal ball claptrap, but it had stayed with him all the same—the sense that they had both experienced bitter disappointment in life and were searching for some way of soothing that deep ache in their psyche. Their physical connection had transcended anything he had experienced before. Even now his body was humming with the aftershocks of their lovemaking last night. No one pleasured him the way she did. He suspected no one pleasured her the way he did, either.

But she wasn't going to stay with him for ever. He wasn't going to ask her to. He would have to let her go when the time was up. He would have no need of her as a nanny now that Kathleen was coming back.

And those other needs?

Well, there were other women, weren't there? Women who wanted what he wanted: a temporary, mutually satisfying arrangement with no feelings, no attachment and no regrets once it was over.

He had lived the life of a playboy before. He could do it again.

* * *

Eliza was sitting on deck with Alessandra fast asleep against her shoulder as Leo docked the vessel when she caught sight of a photographer aiming a powerful-looking lens their way. 'Um…Leo?'

He glanced across at her. 'What's wrong?'

She jerked her head in the direction of the cameraman. 'It might be just a tourist…'

'Take Alessandra below deck,' he commanded curtly.

'I don't think—'

'Do as I say,' he clipped out.

Eliza rose stiffly to her feet and, putting a protective hand to the back of the little child's head, went back down below deck. She tucked Alessandra into one of the beds in one of the luxury sleeping suites and gently closed the door. She sat in the lounge and fumed about Leo's curt manner. She understood he wanted to protect his little daughter but the bigger the issue he made out of it the more anxious Alessandra might become. She felt it would be better to explain to Alessandra that there were journalists out and about who were interested in her Papà's life and that it was part and parcel of being a successful public figure.

And how dare he speak to *her* as if she was just a servant? They were lovers for God's sake! It might be a temporary arrangement and all that, but she refused to be spoken to as if she had no standing with him at all.

Leo came down to the lounge after a few minutes, his expression black with anger. 'When I ask you to do something I expect you to do it, not stand there arguing about it.'

Eliza got abruptly to her feet and shot him a glare. 'You didn't ask me. You *ordered* me.'

His mouth tightened until his lips all but disappeared. 'You will do as I ask or order, do you hear me?'

She glowered at him. 'I will not be spoken to like that. And what if Alessandra had been awake? What's she going to think if she hears you barking out orders as if I'm nothing to you but yet another obsequious servant you've surrounded yourself with to make your life run like stupid clockwork?'

His dark gaze took on a probing glint. 'Are you saying you want to be more to me than an employee?'

Eliza rued her reckless tongue. 'No…no, I'm not saying that.'

'Then what are you saying?'

She blew out a tense little breath. What *was* she saying? She wanted to be more to him than a temporary fling but he was never going to ask her and she wasn't free to accept if by some miracle he did. 'I'm saying you have no right to order me about like a drill sergeant. There will always be journalists lurking about. You have to prepare Alessandra for it. She's old enough to understand that people are interested in your life.'

He scraped a hand through his hair, making it even more tousled than the wind had done. 'I'm sorry. I was wrong to snap at you. It just caught me off guard seeing that guy with that camera up there.'

'Was it a journalist?'

'Probably. I'm not sure what paper or agency he works for. It doesn't seem to matter. The photos go viral within minutes.' His expression tightened. 'I can't stand the thought of my daughter being the target of intrusive paparazzi. I'm not ready to expose her to that.'

'I know this is really hard for you,' Eliza said. 'But Alessandra will feel your tension if you don't relax a bit. Other high profile parents have to deal with this stuff all the time. The more you try and resist these people, the more attractive you become as a target.'

'You're probably right…' He gave her a worn down look. 'I always swore I would never let her go through a childhood like mine. I want to protect her as much as I can. I want her to feel safe and loved.'

'What was it like during your childhood?'

He sucked in another breath and released it in a whoosh. 'It certainly wasn't all tartan picnic blankets and soft cuddly puppies. I think my mother needed to justify her decision to leave by publicly documenting a whole list of infringements my father and I had supposedly done. I was just a little kid. What had I done other than be a kid? My father…well, all he had done was love her. The press made the most of it, of course. The scandal of my mother's affair was splashed over every paper in the country but she didn't seem to care. It was as if she was proud to have got away from the shackles of domesticity. It destroyed my father. He just crumpled emotionally to think he wasn't enough for her—that she had sold out to someone who had more money than him.'

Eliza could understand now why he had such a fierce desire to keep Alessandra out of the probing eyes of the media. He had been caught in the crossfire as a child. How distressing it must have been to have all those private issues made public. She put a hand on his arm. 'You weren't to blame for your parents' problems.'

He looked down at her for a long moment, his gaze deep and dark. 'How did your mother die?'

She dropped her hand from his arm and turned away, folding her arms across her body. 'What has that got to do with anything?'

'You've never told me. I want to know. What happened to her?'

Eliza blew out a breath and faced him again. What was the point of hiding it? She was the product of despair and degradation. It couldn't be changed. She couldn't miraculously whitewash her background any more than he could his. 'Drugs and drink robbed her of her life. They robbed me of both my parents when it comes down to it. I suspect my father was the one who introduced her to drugs. He's serving time in prison for drug-related offences. The one and only time I visited him he asked me to drug run for him. It might seem strange, given that familial blood is supposed to be thicker than water, but I declined. I guess it had something to do with the fact that I was farmed out to distant relatives who weren't all that enamoured with the prospect of raising a young, bewildered and overly sensitive child. The only true family I've known is my fiancé's. So, as to tartan picnic blankets and puppies… well, I have no experience of that, either.'

He put a gentle hand on her shoulder. 'I'm sorry.'

Eliza gave him the vestige of a smile. 'Why are you apologising? It's not your fault. I was already royally screwed up when I met you.'

His eyes roved her face, lingering over her gaze as if searching for the real person hiding behind the shadows. 'Maybe, but I probably made it a whole lot worse.'

'You didn't.' She put her hand on his chest, feeling his heart beating slow and steadily underneath her palm. 'I was happy for those three weeks. It was like stepping into someone else's life. For that period of time I didn't have a care in the world. It was like a dream, a fantasy. I didn't want it to end.'

'Then why did you end it?'

Her hand slid off his chest to push through the curtain of her windswept hair. 'All good things have to come to an end, don't they? It was time to move on. Soon it will be time to move on again.'

'What about Alessandra? You've been very good for her—even Tatiana says so. And it's easy to see how attached she's become to you.'

Eliza felt that painful little fishhook tug on her heart again. 'She'll cope. She'll have Kathleen and Marella and, most importantly, she'll have you.'

'Will you miss her?'

'I'll miss her terribly. She's such a little sweetheart.' *I wish she were mine.*

'And what about me?' His eyes were suddenly unreadable. 'Will you miss me too?'

Eliza's heart gave another painful contraction at the thought of leaving him. Would their paths ever cross again? Would the only contact be seeing him from time to time in a gossip magazine with some other woman on his arm? How would she bear it? What if he *did* decide to marry again? He might go on to have another child, or even more than one. He would have the family she had longed for while she would be stuck in her bleak, lonely life back at home, trapped in an engagement with a man who could not free her from it even if he wanted to.

She forced a worldly smile to her lips. 'I'll certainly miss picnics on luxury launches and swanning about in a villa that's as big as an apartment block.'

'That wasn't what I was asking.'

'Just what exactly *are* you asking?' She gave him a pointed look. 'It's not like you want me to stay with you permanently—Kathleen is coming back. You won't need me any more.'

'We'd better get going.' His expression was a mask of stone. 'I have some work to see to before we leave for London tomorrow.'

'We're leaving *tomorrow*?'

'The bursar of your school wants to meet with me. He spoke of a project you had proposed to the board for young single mothers on parenting practices and counselling, especially for those with children with special needs. I'd like to look at it a little more closely. It sounds like a good idea.'

Eliza had trouble containing her surprise. 'I don't know what to say…'

His eyes were hard as they held hers. 'Don't go attaching anything sentimental to my interest. I have a lot of money and, like a lot of wealthy people, I want to make a difference where it counts. There are other schools and charities that are in just as much, if not more, need of funds. I have to choose the ones I think are most productive in the long run.'

'This means so much to me,' she said. 'It's been a dream of mine for so long to do something like this. I don't know how to thank you.'

'I don't want or need your thanks.' He moved to the suite where Alessandra was sleeping. 'Meet me at the car. The paparazzi guy should have left by now.'

# CHAPTER TWELVE

ELIZA DIDN'T SEE Leo until the following morning, just as they were about to leave for London. She had waited for him last night but he hadn't come to her.

She was still so deeply touched that he was considering doing more for her school. She wasn't sure what was behind his motivation, she was just grateful that he was contemplating supporting the project that was so very dear to her heart.

Had he softened in his attitude towards her? Dare she hope that he would no longer hate her for how she had rejected him all those years ago? Was this the time to tell him about Ewan? He had expressly forbidden her to speak of her fiancé, but maybe during this trip to London she could find a quiet moment to explain to him her circumstances. He came across as such a hard-nosed businessman, but she knew he had a heart. She had seen it time and time again when he was with his tiny daughter. She caught faint glimpses of it when she found his gaze on her, as if he was studying her, trying to put things together in his head. She desperately wanted him to understand her situation. As each day passed she felt more and more that he had a right to know. She could not leave him without telling him why she had made the choice she had.

'Signor Valente wants a quick word with you in the study,' Marella said as she bundled Alessandra into her arms. 'I'll get Alessandra settled in the car. Giuseppe will take the bags.'

Eliza went through to the study, where she found Leo standing behind his desk looking out at the garden. He turned as he heard her footfall and picked up a newspaper off his desk and handed it to her with an unreadable expression. 'The press have identified you as my new mistress.'

She took the paper and looked at the photo of her, standing on the deck of his boat with Alessandra asleep against her shoulder. The caption read: *New stepmother for tragic toddler heiress Alessandra Valente? London primary schoolteacher Eliza Lincoln has been identified as the mystery woman in Leo Valente's life.*

Eliza swallowed thickly. What if Samantha saw this? Would it hit the press back in Britain? What would Samantha think of her? She had told her a version of the truth rather than tell her an outright lie. She'd said she was visiting an old friend in Italy to fill in for the regular nanny who was taking a little break. She hadn't said the old friend was actually the man she had met and fallen in love with four years ago. Now it would be splashed over every newspaper in the country that she had gone off and had a clandestine affair. Samantha would be so dreadfully hurt. She would feel *so* betrayed.

'You might want to warn your fiancé in case this gets picked up by the British tabloids,' Leo said as if he had read her thoughts.

She chewed at her lower lip. 'Yes…'

'I suspect there will be quite a lot of press attention when we arrive in London,' he said. 'It will blow over after a day or two. Remember you are forbidden to comment on anything to do with your time with us here.'

Eliza straightened her shoulders as she handed him back the paper. 'I haven't forgotten.'

The flight to London went without a hitch but, as Leo had predicted, there was a cluster of photographers waiting outside for a glimpse of the young Englishwoman who had been spotted on his boat with his little girl the day before. The click, click, click of camera shutters going off sounded like a heavy round of bullets being discharged.

'Miss Lincoln, what does your fiancé Ewan Brockman think of you spending the last couple of weeks with billionaire Leo Valente in his luxury villa on the Amalfi coast in Italy?'

Eliza totally froze. How on earth did these people find out this stuff? What else did they know? For all these years Samantha had been adamant Ewan's condition should be kept out of the press. She had done everything she could to keep Ewan's dignity intact and Eliza had loved and respected her for it. Who had released his name? Someone at school? Only Georgie knew of the extent of Ewan's condition. Had a journalist pressed her for details? That was another phone call Eliza should have made. She should have warned Georgie to keep quiet if anyone approached her to comment on her private life.

'Miss Lincoln is my daughter's fill-in nanny,' Leo said before Eliza could get her mouth to work. 'She will be returning to her fiancé in a matter of days. Please give us room. My daughter is becoming upset.'

It was true—Alessandra was starting to whimper in distress, but Eliza had a feeling it had more to do with Leo's statement that she was leaving them to go back to her old life rather than the surge of the press. She cuddled the little girl close to her chest and, keeping her head down against the flashing cameras, she walked into the hotel with Leo until they were finally safe in their suite.

It didn't take long to settle Alessandra, who was tired after the journey. Marella, who had travelled with them, offered to babysit while Leo and Eliza went out for a meal.

'Are you sure this is wise?' Eliza asked as Leo closed his phone after booking a table at a restaurant.

'We need to eat, don't we?'

'Yes, but surely a meal in our suite would be perfectly fine?' She fiddled with the chain around her neck with agitated fingers. 'What's the point in deliberately entering the fray? They'll just hound us all over again.'

He gave her an ironic lift of his brow. 'You were the one who said I shouldn't hide Alessandra away.'

'We're not talking about Alessandra,' she said stiffly. 'We're talking about me, about *my* reputation. People are going to get hurt by all that stuff they're saying about me.'

'I take it you mean your fiancé?' His eyes were hard as stone as they held hers.

Eliza still hadn't had either the time or the privacy to call Samantha. Any moment now she expected her phone to ring, with Samantha asking her what the hell was going on. It was making her nervy and jumpy. A headache was pounding at her temples and a pit of nausea was corroding the lining of her stomach like flesh-eating acid. 'I don't like being called your mistress.'

'It's the truth, isn't it?'

'Not for much longer.' She scooped up her bag and

slung it over her shoulder. 'Let's get this over with. I want to get back as quickly as possible and go to bed.'

He gave her a smouldering look as he held the door open for her. 'I couldn't have put it better myself.'

They were halfway through dinner at an exclusive restaurant in Mayfair when Eliza's phone audibly vibrated from inside her bag. She had set it to silent but hadn't thought to turn off the vibration and illumination component. She tried to ignore it, hoping that Leo hadn't heard, but the glow every time it vibrated was visible through the top of her bag.

'Aren't you going to answer it?' he asked.

'Um…it can wait.' She picked up her glass of wine and took a little sip to settle her nerves.

The phone vibrated again.

'Sounds like someone really wants to talk to you,' he said.

Eliza knew it was pathetic of her to keep putting off the inevitable. It was a lifetime habit of hers to procrastinate, hoping that things would go away or be resolved on their own, but it was only prolonging the agony. Wasn't that why she was in this mess? She should have been honest right from the word go with Ewan. She shouldn't have waited for months and months without saying anything, letting him believe everything was fine when it wasn't. Hadn't she learned her lesson by now? She had to face things, not hide from them. 'Um… will you excuse me?' She rose to her feet. 'I won't be long.'

There was no one in the lipstick lounge adjacent to the restroom, so Eliza sat on a chintz-covered chair and pressed Samantha's number. 'Hi, it's me.'

'Oh, darling,' Samantha said with an audible sigh

of relief. 'I'm so glad you called back so quickly. I'm bringing Ewan up to London to see the specialist tomorrow. You know how we've been on that waiting list for months and months? Well, there's been a sudden cancellation. I know you're probably tied up with your little nanny job, but I was hoping since you're back in London for a couple of days that you could come with me. Do you think you could get an hour or two off? You know how hard I find managing him all by myself. I called the agency and asked for a respite carer to come with me but there's no one available at such short notice. I was just hoping you could come with us. I know it's a lot to ask.'

Eliza felt her insides twist into cripplingly tight knots of guilt. How could she say no? She knew it wasn't the physical support with Ewan that Samantha was after. She knew how much hope Samantha had invested in seeing this particular specialist. She also knew Samantha was going to be completely shattered when the specialist gave her the same prognosis every other specialist she had taken Ewan to had done.

How could she let her face that all by herself?

Leo would be tied up with his work most of the day as well as his meeting with the bursar so it shouldn't cause too much of a problem. Marella probably wouldn't mind giving her a couple of hours. She needn't even ask Leo's permission. He would probably say no in any case. He would probably assume she was going against his orders and sneaking in a passionate session with her fiancé.

If only he knew…

'Of course I'll come with you,' she said. 'Text me the address and the time and I'll be there.'

'You're an angel,' Samantha said. 'I honestly don't know what I'd do without you.'

Eliza took an uneven breath and slowly released it. 'I thought you were calling about the stuff in the press… I guess you've seen it by now, otherwise you wouldn't have known I was here. I should have called you first to warn you. I'm sorry. It all sounds so horribly sordid.'

'Oh, sweetie, don't worry about that,' Samantha said. 'I know what the press are like. They make up stuff all the time. You can't believe a word you read these days. It's just pure sensationalism. I know you would never leave Ewan.'

Eliza felt guilt come down on her like a tower of bricks. *But I had left him!* The words were jammed in her throat, stuck behind a wall of strangling emotion.

'See you tomorrow, darling,' Samantha said. 'Love you.'

'Love you, too.' Eliza gave a long, heavy sigh as she switched the phone off. And, taking a deep breath, she got to her feet and walked back to where Leo was waiting for her.

He stood up when she came back to the table. 'Is everything all right?'

Eliza gave him a brief forced smile as she sat down. 'Of course.' She picked up her wine glass and cradled it in both hands to keep them occupied.

'Who was it?'

'Just a friend.'

'Eliza.'

She brought up her gaze and her chin. 'Yes?'

'I don't need to remind you of the rules, do I?'

'Would you like to screen all my calls while you're at it?' She put her glass down with a little clunk. 'Or how about you scroll through my emails and texts?'

He frowned and reached for his own wine glass. 'I'm sorry. I don't want to spoil our truce.'

'Truce? Is that what you call this?' She waved a hand to encompass the romantic setting.

'Look, I don't want to spend the only time we have alone together arguing. That wasn't the point of going out to dinner this evening.'

'What *is* the point?' Was it to make her fall in love with him again and then drop her cold? Was it to make her feel even more wretched about her other life once this was over?

He took one of her tightly clenched hands and began to massage her stiff fingers until they softened and relaxed. 'The point is to get to know one another better,' he said. 'I've noticed we either have mad, passionate sex or argue like fiends when we are alone. I want to try doing something different for a change.'

Eliza looked at her hand in his, the way his olive skin was so much of a contrast to her creamy one. She felt the stirring of her body the longer he held her. Those fingers had touched every part of her body. They could make her sizzle with excitement just by looking at them. It was becoming harder and harder to keep her emotions hidden away. She wasn't supposed to be falling in love with him again. She wasn't supposed to be dreaming of a life with him.

*That was not an option for her.*

She raised her gaze back to meet his. 'What did you have in mind?'

He smiled a slow smile that made his eyes become soft and warm, and another lock on her heart loosened. 'Why don't you wait and see?'

An hour later they were on a dance floor, not in an exclusive nightclub or a hotel ballroom, but on the balcony of their hotel suite. Champagne was in an ice bucket, romantic music was playing from the sound system and the vista of the city of London was spread out below them in a glittering array of twinkling lights and famous landmarks.

Eliza was in Leo's arms, dancing like Cinderella at the ball. The clock had moved way past midnight but this was one night she didn't want to end. She had never considered herself a particularly good dancer but somehow in Leo's arms she felt as if she was floating across the balcony, their bodies at one and their footwork perfectly in tune, apart from a couple of early missteps on her part.

She leaned her head against his chest and breathed in the warm citrus and clean male scent of him. 'This is nice…'

His hand pressed against the small of her back to bring her closer. 'Where did you learn to dance?' he asked.

She looked up at him with a rueful smile. 'I know, I'm rubbish at it, aren't I? I've probably mashed your toes to a pulp.'

He gave a deep chuckle and kissed her forehead. 'Don't worry. I can still walk.'

Eliza laid her head back down against his chest as she thought of Ewan sitting in that chair, his legs and arms useless, his once brilliant brain now in scattered fragments that could no longer connect.

The line of that old nursery rhyme played inside her head, as it had done so many times over the last five and a half years: *All the King's horses and all the King's men couldn't put Humpty Dumpty together again...*

## CHAPTER THIRTEEN

THE NEXT DAY, Leo got back earlier than he'd expected from his meetings. He had particularly enjoyed the one with the community school bursar. He had made a commitment to the school and he couldn't wait to tell Eliza about it. The project she had set her heart on would go ahead, no matter how things turned out when her time with him was up.

Last night he had sensed a shift in their relationship. In the past they had had sex, last night they had made love. He had felt the difference in her kisses and caresses. He wondered if she had sensed the difference in his.

Did it mean she might reconsider her engagement? He had done a quick Internet search on her fiancé but he hadn't uncovered much at all. It surprised him for in this day and age just about everyone had a social media page or blog or website. Was the man some sort of recluse? It had niggled at him all day. After what had come out in the papers yesterday, why hadn't the guy stormed into the hotel and punched Leo's lights out? It didn't make sense. If Ewan Brockman loved Eliza, then surely he would have come forward and demanded an explanation.

It was time to have a no holds barred conversation

with her. Something wasn't quite adding up and he wasn't going to stop digging until he found out what it was—and there was no time like the present.

Leo came into the suite to find Marella sitting on the sofa with a book while Alessandra was having a nap in the next room.

'Where's Eliza?' he asked as he put his briefcase down.

'She went to do a bit of shopping,' Marella said, closing the book and putting it to one side. 'She's only been gone a couple of hours. I told her to take all the time she wanted. She should be back soon. Why don't you call her and meet her for a drink? I'll give Alessandra her bath and supper.'

'Good idea.' He gave her an appreciative smile and reached for his phone. He frowned as the call went through to message bank. He sent her a text but there was no response.

'She's probably turned her phone off,' Marella said.

'Did she say where she was intending to shop?'

Marella pursed her lips for a moment. 'I think she said something about going to Queen Square.'

He frowned as he put his phone back in his pocket. Queen Square was where the world-renowned UCL Institute of Neurology was situated. He'd driven past it a couple of times on previous trips to London. Great Ormond Street Hospital was close by. Why was Eliza going there? Sure, there were plenty of shops in the Bloomsbury district, but why had she told Marella she was going to Queen Square of all places?

Leo saw her from half a block away. She was standing talking with an older woman in her fifties outside the UCL Institute of Neurology. The older woman looked very distressed. She kept mopping at her eyes with a scrunched up tissue. Eliza was holding the hand of a gaunt young man in his late twenties who was strapped in a wheelchair, complete with breathing apparatus and a urinary catheter that was just visible under the tartan blanket that covered his thin, muscle-wasted legs.

Leo felt as if someone had thrown a ninety-pound dumb-bell straight at his chest.

*Her fiancé.*

He swallowed against a monkey wrench of guilt that was stuck sideways in his throat. Her fiancé was a quadriplegic. The poor man was totally and utterly incapacitated. He didn't even seem to be aware of where he was or whom he was with; he was staring vacantly into space. Leo watched as Eliza gently wiped some drool from the side of the young man's mouth with a tissue.

*Oh, dear God, what had he done?*

Why hadn't she told him?

*Why the hell hadn't she told him?*

He didn't know whether to be furious at her or to feel sorry for her. Why let him think the very worst of her for all this time? It all made horrible sense now that he had seen her fiancé with his very own eyes. It wasn't a normal relationship. How could it be, with that poor young man sitting drooling and slumped in his chair like that? Was that why she had taken the money he had offered her? She had done it for her fiancé.

His gut churned and roiled with remorse.

He had exploited her in the worst way imaginable.

Leo turned back the way he had come. He needed time to think about this—to get his head around it all. He didn't want to have it out with her on the street with her fiancé and his mother—he assumed it was his mother—watching on. He took a couple of deep calming breaths but they caught on the claws of his guilt that were still tearing at his throat.

Eliza had turned down his marriage proposal because she had honoured her commitment to her fiancé. It took the promise of *in sickness and in health* to a whole new level. She hadn't done it because she hadn't loved *him*. His instincts back then had been right after all. He had felt sure she had fallen in love with him. He had felt sure of it last night when she had danced in his arms on the balcony and made love with him with such exquisite tenderness.

He had felt his own feelings for her stirring beneath the concrete slab of his denial where he had buried them four years ago.

He thought back to all the little clues she had dropped about her fiancé. If only he had pushed a little harder he might have got her to trust him enough to tell him before things had gone this far. Was it too late to undo the damage? Would she forgive him?

His heart felt as if someone had slammed it with a sledgehammer.

What did it matter if she did or not? She was still tied to her fiancé. She still wore his ring, if not on her finger then around her neck.

*Close to her heart...*

Eliza got back to the hotel a little flustered at being later than she'd planned. Samantha had taken the news hard, as she had expected. There was no magical cure for Ewan. No special treatment or miraculous therapy that would make his body and mind function again. It was heartbreaking to think of Samantha's hopes being dashed all over again. What mother didn't want the best for her child? Wasn't Leo the same with Alessandra?

He would move heaven and earth to give his little girl a cure for her blindness, but it wasn't to be.

Samantha had been so upset Eliza had found herself promising to spend the rest of the summer break with her and Ewan once she got back from Italy. Even as the words had come out of her mouth she had wished she could pull them back. She felt as if she was being torn in two. Leaving Leo for the second time would be hard enough, but this time she would be leaving Alessandra as well.

Could life get any more viciously cruel?

Eliza opened the door of the suite and Leo turned to face her from where he was standing at the window overlooking the view. Her heart gave a little jolt in her chest. She had hoped to get back before he did. 'I'm sorry I'm late…' She put her handbag down and put a hand to her hair to smooth it back from where the breeze had teased it loose. 'The shops were crazily busy.'

His eyes went to her empty hands. 'Not a very successful trip, I take it?'

Her heart gave another lurch. 'No…no, it wasn't…' She tried to smile but somehow her mouth wouldn't cooperate. 'Where's Alessandra?'

'With Marella in the suite next door.'

'I hope you didn't mind me having a bit of time to myself.' She couldn't quite hold his gaze.

'I seem to remember telling you before that you are not under lock and key.' He wandered over to the bar area of the suite. 'Would you like a drink?'

'Um…yes, thank you.'

He handed her a glass of chilled white wine. 'Shopping is such thirsty work, *sì*?'

Eliza still couldn't read his inscrutable expression.

'Yes…' She took a sip of her drink. 'How did your meeting with the bursar go?'

'I've decided to bankroll your project.'

She blinked at him. 'You…you have?'

'I read your proposal in detail.' His expression remained masklike. 'There are a few loose ends that need tying up, but I think it won't take too much time to sort them out.'

Eliza forced her tense shoulders to relax. Was there some sort of subtext to this conversation or was she just imagining it? It was hard to gauge his mood. He seemed as if he was waiting for her to say something, or was she imagining that too? 'I can't thank you enough for what you're doing. I'm not sure why you're doing it.'

'You can't guess?'

She flicked over her dry lips with her tongue. 'I'm not foolish enough to think it's because you care something for me. You've made it pretty clear from the outset that you don't.' *Apart from last night, when it had seemed as if he was making love with her for the very first time.*

There was a silence that seemed to have a disturbing undercurrent to it. It stretched and stretched like a too thin wire being pulled by industrial strength strainers.

'Why didn't you tell me?' Leo asked.

'Tell you what?'

He let out a stiff curse that made her flinch. 'Let's stop playing games. I saw you today.'

Her stomach clenched. 'Saw me where?'

'With your fiancé. I assume that's who the young man in the wheelchair is?'

'Yes…'

His frown was so deep it joined his eyebrows like a bridge over his eyes. 'Is that all you can say?'

Eliza put her glass down before she dropped it. 'I was going to tell you.' She hugged her arms across her body. 'I would've told you days ago but you forbade me to even speak his name out loud.'

'That is not a good enough excuse and you know it.' He glared at her, but whether it was with anger or frustration she couldn't quite tell. 'You could've insisted I listen. You could've told me the first day I came to see you. For God's sake, you could've told me the first night we met. And you damn well *should've* told me the night I proposed to you.'

'Why?' She tossed him a glare right on back. 'What difference would it have made?'

'How can you *ask* that?' His tone was incredulous. 'I wanted to marry you. I still want to marry you.'

Eliza noticed he hadn't said he loved her. He just wanted a wife and a stepmother for his daughter. Wasn't that what the press had said? 'I'm not free to marry you.'

He came over and put his hands on her shoulders. 'Listen to me, Eliza. We can sort this out. Your fiancé will understand. You just have to tell him you want to be with someone else.'

She pulled out of his hold and put some distance between them, her arms going across her middle again. 'It's not that simple…' She took a breath that tore at her throat like talons. 'It's my fault he's in that chair.'

'What do you mean?'

She looked at him again. 'I ended our relationship. He left my flat upset—devastated, actually. He was in no fit state to drive. I should never have let him go. It was my fault. If I hadn't broken our engagement that night he would still be a healthy, active, intelligent, fully functioning man.' She choked back a sob. 'I can't even tell him I'm sorry. He doesn't have any understanding of language any more. He's little more than a body in a chair. He can't even breathe on his own. How can I tell his mother I want to be with someone else after what I've done to her son?'

'You didn't tell her you'd broken off the engagement?' Leo asked with a puzzled frown.

Eliza shook her head. 'When I got the call, she was already at the hospital. She was shattered by what the doctors had told her about his condition. He wasn't expected to make it through the night. How could I tell her then?'

'What about later?'

'I couldn't…' She took another shaky breath. 'How could I? She would think—like everyone else would—that I was trying to weasel my way out of a life of looking after him. It would be such a cruel and selfish and heartless thing to do.'

'Aren't you being a little hard on yourself? Would you have expected him to give up his life if you had been the one injured?'

Eliza had thought about it but had always come up with the same answer. 'No, because he would never have broken up with me without warning. He would have prepared me for it, like I should've done for him. We'd been together since I was sixteen. It was wrong of me to dump it on him like that. He loved me so much. And look at what that love has cost him. It's only fair that I give up my future for him. I owe him that.'

'You don't owe him your future,' Leo said. 'Come on, Eliza, you're not thinking rationally. His mother wouldn't want you to give up your life like this. Surely she's told you to move on with your life?'

Eliza gave him a despairing look. 'I'm all she has left. She lost his father when Ewan was a little boy. Now she's as good as lost him, too. How can I walk away from her now? I'm like a daughter to her and she's been like a mother to me. I can't do it. I just can't.'

'What if I talk to her? I'll make her understand how it's unfair of her to expect so much of you.'

Eliza shook her head sadly. 'You're so used to getting whatever you want, but sometimes there are things you just can't have, no matter how hard and desperately you wish for them.'

'Do you think I don't know that?' he asked. 'I have a child I would do anything on this earth to help.'

'I know you would and that's exactly what Samantha is like. She's a wonderful mother and a wonderful person. It would devastate her if I was to go away and live with you in Italy.'

'What if we moved to London? I could work from here. It would be a big adjustment but I could do it. There are good schools for the blind here. Alessandra will soon adjust.'

Eliza pulled her emotions back into line like a ball of loose yarn being wound up rapidly and tightly. 'I can't marry you, Leo. You have to accept that. Once the month is up I have to come back to my life here. I've already promised Samantha to spend the last couple of weeks of the holidays with her and Ewan.'

'You *do* have a choice. Damn it, Eliza, can't you see that? You're locking yourself away out of guilt. It's not going to help anyone, least of all your fiancé.' He sent his hand through his hair again. 'I suppose that's why you took the money. It was for him, wasn't it?'

'Yes…'

'Why didn't you ask for more?'

'I was uncomfortable enough as it was, without exploiting your offer.'

He gave an embittered laugh. 'Let's say it how it was. It wasn't an offer. I blackmailed you. I can never forgive myself for that.' He moved to the other side of the room as if he needed the distance from her to think.

'I'm sorry…' Eliza broke the silence. 'I've handled this so badly. I've made it so much worse.' She took a deep shuddering breath as she finally came to a decision. 'I'm not going to go back with you to Italy tomorrow. It wouldn't be fair to Alessandra. It will make it so much harder when the month is up.'

He swung around to glare at her. 'What…you're just going to walk away? What about the contract you signed? Are you forgetting the terms and conditions?'

'If you decide to act on them, then I'll have to face that if and when it happens.'

'I'll withdraw my offer for your project. I'll tell the bursar I've changed my mind.' His jaw was clenched tight, his eyes flashing at her furiously.

Eliza knew it was risky calling his bluff but she hoped he would come to understand this was the best way to handle things—the cleanest way. 'Will you say goodbye to Alessandra for me? I don't want to wake her now. It will only upset her more.'

His look was scathing. 'I never took you for a coward.'

'It has to be this way.'

'Why does it?' His eyes flashed at her again. 'Are you really going to stand there and deny that you love me?'

Eliza steeled herself as she held his gaze. 'I have never said I loved you.'

A muscle flicked in his cheek and his eyes hardened. 'So it was always just about the money.'

'Yes.'

His lip curled mockingly. 'And the sex.'

She gave him her best worldly look. 'That too.'

He sucked in a breath and moved to the window overlooking the leafy street below. 'I'll have Marella send your things to you when we get back.'

'Thank you.' Eliza moved past to collect her things from the suite.

'I won't say goodbye,' he said. 'I think we've both said all that needs to be said.'

*Except I love you*, Eliza thought sadly as she softly closed the door as she left.

# CHAPTER FOURTEEN

ELIZA SPENT THE first week with Samantha and Ewan in Suffolk in a state of emotional distress so acute it made her feel physically ill. She couldn't sleep and she could barely get a morsel of food past her lips. Every time she thought of Leo or Alessandra her chest would ache as if a stack of heavy books was balanced on it. But she had no choice but to keep what she was feeling to herself as Samantha was still dealing with her heartbreak over the hopelessness of Ewan's situation.

But towards the middle of the second week Samantha seemed to pick herself up. She had even been out a couple of times in the evening while Eliza sat with Ewan. She hadn't said where she was going or whom she was going with and Eliza hadn't asked. But each time Samantha returned she looked a little less strained and unhappy.

'Darling, you don't seem yourself since you came back from the nanny job,' Samantha said as she watched Eliza push the food around her plate during dinner. 'Is everything all right? Are you missing the little girl? She's rather a cute little button, isn't she?'

'Yes, she is. And yes, I do miss her.'

'What a pity she's blind.' Samantha picked up her

glass of lemonade. 'But that's not the worst thing that can happen to a person, is it?'

'No…it isn't.'

'I would've loved a daughter,' Samantha said. 'Don't get me wrong—I loved having a son. No mother could have asked for a better one than Ewan. And I've been so fortunate in having you as a surrogate daughter. I can't thank you enough for always being there for me and for Ewan.'

Eliza put her cutlery down and gripped her hands together on her lap underneath the table. It had been brewing inside her for days, this pressing need to put things straight at last. She could no longer live with this terrible guilt. She wanted to move on with her life. She could no longer deny her love for Leo. Even if he didn't love her, surely she owed him the truth of her feelings. 'Samantha…there's something you need to know about that night…I know it will be hard for you to hear and I don't blame you for thinking I'm just making it up to get out of this situation, but it's my fault Ewan had the accident that night.'

The silence was long and painful.

'I broke off our engagement,' Eliza continued. 'Ewan left my place so upset he should never have got behind the wheel of that car. I should never have let him leave like that. I'd bottled up my feelings for so long and then that night I just couldn't hold it in any longer. I told him I didn't love him any more. He was devastated.' She choked back a sob. 'I know you can't possibly forgive me. I will never forgive myself. But I want to have a life now. I want to be with Leo and his little girl. I love him. I'm sorry if that upsets you or you think it's selfish but I can't live this lie any more. I feel so wicked to have accepted the love you've given so freely and so generously when all this time I've been lying to you.'

Samantha let out a deep uneven sigh. She suddenly looked much older than her years. She seemed to sag in the chair as if her bones had got tired of staying neatly aligned. 'I suppose it's only right that you lied to me.'

'What do you mean?'

Samantha gave her a pained look. 'I've been lying to you too for the last few years.'

'I don't understand…' Eliza frowned in puzzlement. 'What do you mean? How have *you* lied to me? I'm the one who covered up what happened that night. I should have told you at the hospital. I should have told you well before this.'

Samantha took a deep breath and released it in a jagged stream. 'He told me.'

Eliza was still frowning in confusion. 'Who told you what?'

'Ewan.' Samantha met her gaze levelly. 'He told me you'd broken up with him.'

Eliza felt her heart slam against her ribcage as if it had hit a brick wall at high speed. 'When did he tell you?'

Samantha's throat moved up and down like a mouse moving under a rug. 'I called him just a minute or two after he'd left your place.' Her face crumpled. 'I'm so sorry. I should've told you before now. I've been feeling so wretchedly guilty. It was my fault. I was on the phone to him just moments before he crashed into that tree.' She gave a ragged sob and dropped her head into her hands. 'He told me you'd ended your engagement. He was upset. I told him to pull himself together. I was furious with him for being so surprised by your ending things. I'd seen it coming for months. He was livid. I'd never heard him so angry. He hung up on me. It was my fault. I caused his accident.'

'No.' Eliza rushed over to wrap her arms around Samantha. 'No, please don't blame yourself.'

'I knew you were unhappy,' Samantha sobbed into her shoulder. 'I knew it but I didn't say anything to him or to you. I wanted it to all work out. I wanted you to be the daughter I'd always longed for. I wanted us to be a family. That's all I wanted.'

Eliza closed her eyes as she held Samantha tightly in her arms. 'You're not to blame. You're not in any way to blame. I'm still that daughter. I'll always be that daughter and part of your family.'

Samantha pulled back to look at her. 'There's something else I want to confess.'

'What is it?'

'I've met someone.' She blushed like a teenager confessing to her first crush. 'He's a doctor at the clinic I take Ewan to. He's been wonderfully supportive. We've been on a few dates. That's where I've been going the last couple of nights. It's happened very quickly but we have such a lot in common. He has a daughter with cerebral palsy. I think he's going to ask me to marry him. If he does, I've decided I'll say yes.'

Eliza smiled with genuine happiness. 'But that's wonderful! You deserve to be happy."

Samantha gave her a tremulous smile. 'I've been so worried about telling you, but when I saw all that fuss in the press about you and Leo Valente, I started to wonder if it might finally be time for both of us to move on with our lives.'

Eliza blinked back tears. 'I'm not sure if I have a future with Leo, but I want to tell him I love him. I think I owe him that.'

Samantha grasped her hands in hers. 'You must tell him how you feel. You don't owe Ewan anything. He is happy, or at least as happy as he can ever be. He's not aware of anything other than his immediate physical comfort. Robert has explained all that to me. It's helped me come to terms with it all. Ewan is not the same person now. He can never be that person again. But he's happy. And you and I need to be happy for him. Will you promise me that?'

'I will be happy for you and for Ewan. I promise you.' Eliza took off the chain from around her neck and handed Samantha the engagement ring. 'I think you're going to need this.'

Samantha clutched it tightly in her hand and smiled. 'You know something? I think you might be right.'

Eliza arrived at Leo's villa at three in the afternoon. Marella answered the door and immediately swept her up in a bone-crushing hug. 'I knew you'd come back. I told Signor Valente and Alessandra you'd be back. They've been so miserable. Like a bad English summer, *sì*?'

Eliza smiled in spite of the turmoil of her emotions. 'Where is he? I should've phoned first to see if he was at home. I didn't think…I just wanted to get here and talk to him as soon as I could.'

'He's not here,' Marella said. 'But he's not far away. He's at the old villa.'

'The one he had four years ago?'

*'Sì,'* Marella nodded. 'He thinks it would be better for Alessandra. I agree with him. This place is too big for her.'

Eliza felt her heart lift. 'Is she here?'

'She is sleeping upstairs. Do you want to see her?'

'I'd love to see her, but I think I'd better talk to Leo first.'

Marella beamed. 'I think that is a very good idea.'

Eliza pushed open the squeaky old wrought iron gate of the villa that was tucked into one of the hillsides that overlooked the stunning views of the coast below. The garden was very neglected and the villa needed a coat of paint but it was like stepping back in time. The scent of lemon blossom was tangy in the air. The cobblestones underneath the thin soles of her ballet flats were warm from a full day of sun. The birds were twittering in the trees and shrubbery nearby, just as they had four years ago.

She walked up the path to the front door but before she could reach up to use the rusty old knocker the door opened. Leo looked as if he had just encountered a ghost. He stared down at her, his throat moving up and down as if he couldn't quite get his voice to work.

Eliza dropped her hand back down by her side. 'I came to offer my services as a nanny but it looks to me that what you really need is a gardener and a painter.'

'I already have a nanny.' His expression was difficult to read but she thought she saw a glint in those dark eyes.

'Do you have any other positions vacant?' Eliza asked.

'Which position did you have in mind?'

She gave a little shrug of her shoulder. 'Lover, confidante, stepmother, wife—that sort of thing. I'm pretty flexible.'

A tiny half smile tugged at the edges of his mouth. 'Do you want a temporary post or are you thinking about something a little more long-term?'

Eliza put her hands on his chest, splaying the fingers of her right hand so she could feel the steady beat of his heart. 'I'm thinking in terms of forever.'

'What makes you think I'd offer you forever?'

She searched his features for a moment. Had she got it wrong? Had she jumped to the wrong conclusion? 'You do love me, don't you? I know you haven't said it but nor have I. And I do. I love you so much. I've always loved you. From the moment I met you I felt you were the only person for me.'

He put his arms around her. 'Of course I love you. How can you doubt that?'

She tiptoed her other hand up to the stubbly growth on his jaw. 'I've put you through hell and yet you still love me.'

He cupped her face in his hands. 'Isn't that what true love is supposed to do? Conquer everything in its path and triumph over all in the end?'

'I didn't know it was possible to love someone so much.'

'A couple of weeks ago you walked out of my life and I didn't think you'd be back. It was like four years ago all over again. What's changed?'

'*I've* changed,' she said. 'I've finally realised that life dishes up what it dishes up and we all have to deal with it in our own way and in our own time. I will probably always feel sad and guilty about Ewan. I can't change that. It's just what is. But I'm not making his life any better or worse by denying myself a chance at happiness. He would want me to live his life for him. I'm going to do my very best to do that. And my new life starts now, here with you and Alessandra. You are my family, but I have to say I need to keep a special corner open for Samantha. She's the most amazing surrogate mother in the world and I don't want to lose her.'

Leo put his arms around her and hugged her tightly. 'Then you won't,' he said. 'I need a mother, too, and Alessandra desperately needs a hands-on grandmother. Do you think she would have enough love to stretch to us as well?'

Eliza smiled as she hugged him tight. 'I'm absolutely sure of it.'

* * * * *

## A sneaky peek at next month…

# MODERN™

INTERNATIONAL AFFAIRS, SEDUCTION & PASSION GUARANTEED

### My wish list for next month's titles…

In stores from 21st June 2013:

- ❑ His Most Exquisite Conquest – Emma Darcy
- ❑ His Brand of Passion – Kate Hewitt
- ❑ The Couple who Fooled the World – Maisey Yates
- ❑ Proof of Their Sin – Dani Collins
- ❑ In Petrakis's Power – Maggie Cox

In stores from 5th July 2013:

- ❑ One Night Heir – Lucy Monroe
- ❑ The Return of Her Past – Lindsay Armstrong
- ❑ Gilded Secrets – Maureen Child
- ❑ Once is Never Enough – Mira Lyn Kelly

Available at WHSmith, Tesco, Asda, Eason, Amazon and Apple

*Just can't wait?*

*Visit us Online*

You can buy our books online a month before they hit the shops! **www.millsandboon.co.uk**

0613/01

# Special Offers

Every month we put together collections and longer reads written by your favourite authors.

Here are some of next month's highlights— and don't miss our fabulous discount online!

On sale 21st June

On sale 5th July

On sale 5th July

**Save 20%**

**on all Special Releases**

Find out more at
**www.millsandboon.co.uk/specialreleases**

*Visit us Online*

0713/ST/MB422

# *Join the Mills & Boon Book Club*

Want to read more **Modern**™ books?
We're offering you **2 more** absolutely **FREE!**

We'll also treat you to these fabulous extras:

- **Exclusive offers and much more!**
- **FREE home delivery**
- **FREE books and gifts with our special rewards scheme**

***Get your free books now!***

**visit www.millsandboon.co.uk/bookclub**
**or call Customer Relations on 020 8288 2888**

**FREE BOOK OFFER TERMS & CONDITIONS**
Accepting your free books places you under no obligation to buy anything and you may cancel at any time. If we do not hear from you we will send you 4 stories a month which you may purchase or return to us—the choice is yours. Offer valid in the UK only and is not available to current Mills & Boon subscribers to this series. We reserve the right to refuse an application and applicants must be aged 18 years or over. Only one application per household. Terms and prices are subject to change without notice. As a result of this application you may receive further offers from other carefully selected companies. If you do not wish to share in this opportunity please write to the Data Manager at PO BOX 676, Richmond, TW9 1WU.

**SUBS/ONLINE/P1**

## *Mills & Boon® Online*

Discover more romance at
**www.millsandboon.co.uk**

- **FREE** online reads
- **Books** up to one month before shops
- **Browse our books** before you buy

***...and much more!***

**For exclusive competitions and instant updates:**

Like us on **facebook.com/millsandboon**

Follow us on **twitter.com/millsandboon**

Join us on **community.millsandboon.co.uk**

*Visit us Online*

Sign up for our FREE eNewsletter at
**www.millsandboon.co.uk**

WEB/M&B/RTL5

There's a Mills & Boon® series that's perfect for you. We publish ten series and, with new titles every month, you never have to wait long for your favourite to come along.

---

Blaze®

*Scorching hot, sexy reads*
4 new stories every month

By Request

*Relive the romance with the best of the best*
9 new stories every month

Cherish™

*Romance to melt the heart every time*
12 new stories every month

Desire™

*Passionate and dramatic love stories*
8 new stories every month

*Visit us Online*

Try something new with our Book Club offer
**www.millsandboon.co.uk/freebookoffer**

M&B/WORLD2

*What will you treat yourself to next?*

*Ignite your imagination, step into the past...*
6 new stories every month

INTRIGUE...

*Breathtaking romantic suspense*
Up to 8 new stories every month

*Captivating medical drama – with heart*
6 new stories every month

MODERN™

*International affairs, seduction & passion guaranteed*
9 new stories every month

nocturne™

*Deliciously wicked paranormal romance*
Up to 4 new stories every month

RIVA™

*Live life to the full – give in to temptation*
3 new stories every month available exclusively via our Book Club

You can also buy Mills & Boon eBooks at
**www.millsandboon.co.uk**

*Visit us Online*

M&B/WORLD2